TROVE

David McGukin

Thirteenth Colony Publications

Bremen, Georgia

Cover design by Gray Hamilton
Back cover photo by J David Baxter
Interior book design by Thirteenth Colony Publications

Paperback ISBN-978-0-615-69472-6

eBook ISBN-13: 978-0-615-68991-3

*To Dad and Mom for your
continual support and encouragement,
Thank You!*

For
Will, Stella, Finley, John,
and most especially, Ardoth, my loving wife who
chooses to spend her life with an insane man.

With most sincere appreciation and thanks to:
Anna, Ann, and Gray
for your tireless readings, criticisms, and
encouragements.

Ada, Janet, Ken, Sonny, and Bonnie
for your patience in reading and
urging me on.

And Cissy, without whom
I would have never started.

⊰ Prologue ⊱

Federal Judge, Moses Augustus Black, sat at his chart room desk waiting for the sun to rise on the three hundred year old plantation estate, Teachall. Keeping his keen mind attuned to his responsibilities of being Cow Bell Island's proprietor and guardian had recently begun to bear more heavily than ever before.

He took pen in hand and played docent to a short synopsis for posterity. He didn't know why this craving to divulge these tidbits of history had almost instantaneously overtaken him, but there existed a strong urge to purge his mind.

Thus he began:

Here in coastal South Georgia, sand and sea suffer the irony of existing as mortal enemies and constant allies. However, the foundations of our little island remain amazingly unscathed from nature's fierce battles. It seems coral rock forced from the depths of an ancient ocean bed created this bastion that my great ancestor, Blackbeard, named.

The pirate's keen eye admired the island's potential, so he chose it for his repository of both his treasure and his descendants. Blackbeard's genius has proven itself over the centuries since none has ever breeched his secured system.

Legend tells us that he came to the island accidentally. In 1718, a small fire aboard his flag-ship, "Queen Anne's Revenge," damaged her starboard rigging. Seeking refuge from the British Royal Navy for repairs, this odd dot of geography and its tactical advantages impressed him from the outset.

The deserted island's original inhabitants, the Guale, were long gone—decimated by introduced diseases and tribal warfare. Their mixed ethnic remnant, the Yamasee, abandoned the island and had mostly scattered farther South toward Florida.

Here, Blackbeard left his favorite of his fourteen wives, my direct ancestor, Juliana Jiminez Rosita Consuela Cordoba, Contessa de Juarez e Montalban. From deep devotion he appointed her Master-at-Arms of their shared enormous cache. After his death, she and the remnants of his crew found secure protection from man and sea in complete obscurity.

She and her compatriots, along with an entourage of Spanish architects, artisans, and craftsmen completed this expansive estate and this house, this Teachall: her Spanish-Moorish palatial mansion. Its tabby and native limestone facades have ever since stood as the island's crowning jewel. Here we have successfully reigned over their horde for three centuries.

The small hamlet of Pirate's Landing grew up around the estate and provided homes for the crew and their descendants.

Cow Bell Island's obscurity has protected our little civilization even after James Oglethorpe founded the city of Savannah almost thirty miles to the North.

Ever since Blackbeard's tragic murder, treasure hunters have sought his trove, but

He dropped his pen because of a horrid din coming from the veranda.

TROVE

1

Rude Awakening

"Luna Belle Black, open this door! I know you're in there!"
A coarse voice bellowed while slamming the heavy anchor-shaped knocker with the force of an angry bull. The yelling and banging blasted with enough noise to wake the dead, except this hour was too far past midnight and too long before dawn to roust anyone from the tomb.

Mordecai frantically tried to tie his robe with shaky fingers while he ran toward the door. He almost paused to call Sheriff Pink Tiddie to deal with this marauder's tirade, but he decided against it because whoever raised Cain outside called the mistress of the house by name. The last thing he wanted was to create a hospitality disaster.

He approached the door to release the lock and unexpectedly, Rudine Haggley bulldozed her way into the outer vestibule huffing and swearing. The woman's surge on the thick bulwark's timbers almost knocked Mordecai off his feet.

She ignored his unbalanced plight and barged her way into the great hall bellowing, "Luna Belle Black, I'm coming upstairs. You hear me? Get out of that bed!"

Mordecai staggered then forced his composure to return so he could trail the foul-mouthed woman run amok. "Miss Rudine, please allow me to schedule you an appointment. Mrs. Black deserves a chance to properly dress before receiving a guest. I'm certain she'll gladly see you once she returns from Manhattan next week."

The harridan growled from the depths of her innards while poking a finger hard against his chest. "I ain't gonna wait no matter what kind of shape she's in. Anyhow, this don't concern you none. So you better just move out of my way, or I'll plow you under."

Mordecai's breath jerked, but he bowed and gestured toward the stairs after he saw she was too drunk to pose any serious threat. Once upstairs, he would summon reinforcements if necessary.

On the first stair tread Rudine shrugged her shoulders and slinked from her ratty mink jacket. She wadded the tired fur then flung it at Mordecai. "Here, at least I know what a butler's for."

While Rudine mounted the long staircase, Luna Belle, spurred with adrenaline, jumped out of bed and ran to her closet. She snatched a pink hand-painted kimono from a shelf and slipped the beautiful robe over her emerald charmeuse pajamas.

Sleepy-eyed, Luna Belle squinted to bring the clock's face into focus. "For pity's sake, Mordecai, it's 5:30 in the morning. Shoot the bitch!"

Her feet instinctively slinked into a pair of pink stiletto mules before they carried her to her dressing table on autopilot. She grabbed a turban and leaned over to pour her black locks into the wrap while she glanced at her inverted reflection. Disgusted, with no time for makeup, she jerked a drawer open to dig for a pair of huge round pink and green tortoise shell glasses and shoved them on.

She raised an eyebrow and gave herself a delightful little smirk when she examined herself and the glasses in the mirror. "Haven't seen you tacky girls in a while … glad I kept you." Her fingertips lightly pushed the frame's temples into a comfortable position before she swabbed lipstick to complete her record setting toilette.

She quickly atomized a mist of Joy, walked through the delightful scent, inhaled deeply, then sighed and stretched as she leisurely strolled toward the upstairs hall. Opening her bedroom door, she waltzed onto the mezzanine and with a forced smile coolly sang, "Why, Rudine Haggley, how delightful. What in the world brings you out so early this chilly February morning?"

"It wouldn't be polite to yell. Let me get up these steps and I'll tell you exactly why I'm here."

Luna Belle wafted down the curving stairs to meet the rude intruder. The open kimono elegantly trailed behind her to create an effect of fanciful koi in swirling water cascading over every limestone tread. With her arms gracefully extended, she resembled a colorful butterfly whose appearance belied the haste of her composure.

Rudine had pulled herself up most of the stairs by the time Luna Belle pirouetted and laid her hand on the unwanted guest's elbow. Rudine snatched her arm away and trudged unaided with no intention of being charmed.

Rudine reeked. She brought an unbearable miasma into the house causing Luna Belle's hands instinctively to carry open fingertips straight to her cleavage. Her eyes fluttered and her head recoiled in an attempt to avoid the pungent odor of stale, cheap alcohol and cigarettes.

Rudine's upholstery of stretchy lycra slacks left little to the imagination. Cellulite pockmarks resembled a pair of pantyhose overfilled with ping pong balls or hard-boiled eggs. A sleeveless pilled knit shell covered in cigarette burns and who-knows-what came to her midriff, almost meeting the tights rolled around her waist.

Twice, Rudine's right foot slid out of its slipper whose bedraggled marabou and slicked color had long since faded to a history of overuse—their glamour forgotten.

Toilet paper and a hair net armored her lacquered do. For a smidgeon of panache, Rudine attached a long peacock tail feather to her head with an incredibly long aluminum alligator clip.

Luna Belle cooed over her shoulder. "Mordecai? Be a dear. Wake Polly and have her bring a tray. I'm *certain* she won't mind." She rolled her eyes then turned her attention back to Rudine. "Come with me to my morning room, dear. You can relax and tell me whatever it is you so urgently came to say."

Rudine leaned close to Luna Belle's ear. "Don't try and patternize me, because I come here to warn you about a big mess that's fixing to blow up in all y'all's face."

"What mess?" Luna Belle cocked her head to one side and raised a brow. A pause struck her before she could overcome the sensation of angst this vile woman conjured without even divulging her secrets.

Rudine stopped at the top of the stairs to pant and wheeze before gaining enough breath to speak. "We'll get to that. First I need to set down so's I can catch my breath. Whoo! That's one long set of steps."

Luna Belle, ambushed and without time to think, led the woman into her private suite's morning room. Rudine's mouth gaped wide while her shoulders slumped as she slowly gawked the room's simplistic beauty. Luna Belle's observant eyes narrowed as her smile imperceptibly widened, causing one eyebrow to rise. A person of Rudine's ilk seldom violated the family's private spaces.

"Welcome to my little parlor, Rudine. Sit here, and by all means—put your feet up."

Rudine could not stop looking around in a stunned stupor. The salon's carefully wrought allure had her mesmerized beyond speaking. Subtlety ruled the monochromatic decor that even the uninitiated recognized as tastefully beautiful at first glance.

Rudine walked around the room's perimeter and cautiously rubbed a hand over the laurel leaves and crossed ribbons framing the exquisitely hand executed wall panels.

"What do you call these gray picture things painted all over the walls."

"*Trompe l'oeil grisaille.*"

"I figgered it was somethin' highfalutin."

"Rudine, I'm terribly sorry, but I'm on a tight schedule this morning. I realize you have something important to say, so why don't you go ahead and unburden yourself?"

Rudine's eyes widened as her gaze ascended, totally ignoring her hostess's request. A central field around the sterling chandelier displayed a romantic sky painted in blues and pinks with billowing clouds. Dr. Mesmer himself couldn't have drawn her further away.

"I think I'll spray paint my dining room light fixture silver just like yours."

"How nice … but I thought you were the harbinger of death

this morning. Like to have scared me out of my wits. Come on—tell me what's got you so het up?" Rudine left her overwhelmed state and calmly looked Luna Belle square in the eyes. "What I come to talk about kept me up all night and I'm a little tired. I'll sit here in this straight chair to stay alert."

Rudine twisted and squeezed herself into the delicate *fauteuil*. Luna Belle winced as she watched mounds of blubber assaulting her prized antique chair.

Half awake, Polly entered the room with a large sterling tray full of tea, coffee, and hastily thrown together tidbits. "Morning Missy—Miss Rudine."

Luna Belle moved a Lalique paperweight from the tea table. "I'll pour."

Polly's incredulous eyes bulged when her gaze turned straight toward Rudine's pendulous globs squeezed under the dainty chair's arms. "Miss Rudine, let me helps you move to a more comtuble seat. You can reaches the tray better if you sits here on the divan closer to Missy."

"Good idea. This little dinky chair blocks my blood." She rose. The chair followed only to be pushed with considerable force to remove the prized furniture off her bodacious bohunkus. Rudine's struggle ended with a loud vulgar sound.

Polly turned to exit the room and left the door slightly ajar to facilitate listening. Mordecai waited in the hallway with a big shiny grin. Within moments Luna Belle's husband, Mose, joined them with an anticipation of excitement over their eavesdropping.

Rudine moved to the divan and slumped into its width. The expansiveness of the settee gave her greater room to wiggle and felt good after her confinement.

"Coffee ... tea?" Luna Belle's voice dripped venomous syrup.

"Light tea, milk, one lump. I'll get right to the point.... You have some nerve harboring that Jezebel in your own home."

Luna Belle blinked hard and almost jerked enough to upset the teapot. "I beg your pardon?"

Rudine looked out the corner of her eye and readjusted her seat. "That's right ... some nerve bringing that trollop to Cow Bell Island."

"Of whom do you speak? How dare you intrude on me like

this only to insult me in my own home." Her imposed steadiness allowed her hand to lift a sugar cube with ornate gold-plated tongs and place it in Rudine's cup. She poured steaming tea halfway then carefully added a splash of hot water before topping it with milk.

"You gonna set there and pretend you don't know who I'm talking about, ain't you? I done give you more credit than that." Rudine's snarl exposed a missing front tooth.

"Whatever are you babbling about? I assure you of one thing, this will not stand in my home. Do you understand?" Luna Belle arched her back to tower over the skulking dame.

"You may think you rule the roost around here, but you're fixing to have big trouble if you don't listen to me. I know what I've heard and it ain't good. Go on, keep that Sylvia girl here. Who is she anyway? I don't even know her last name. Do you?"

Luna Belle's scalp tingled with blood. She slowly turned her head and waited a few moments before she spoke deliberately. "Black. Her name is Sylvia Black. B-l-a-c-k."

Rudine's eyes grew wider than Luna Belle imagined possible. "The same as yours? That kind of Black?" She deflated and blanched deathly gray before blushing scarlet vermillion. Her cup and saucer rattled enough to slosh hot liquid on her lap, but she failed to flinch.

Rudine raised an eyebrow causing a huge chunk of black crusted warpaint to plunge into her tea. The flaked shard left a glaring white hole in the blackness of the heavily stenciled, pernicious arc. Rudine nervously stirred, blew, and noisily sucked tea into her pursed lips.

Her elbows drew tightly against her ribs and her voice quaked. "I ... I ... I—"

Luna Belle's blood boiled yet she calmly swished her teaspoon in little half moons with all the grace and charm of a proper Southerner. "Sylvia lives with us to research the topic of her doctoral dissertation—Spanish moss. The University of Georgia School of Horticulture also vouches for our god-daughter's fine character. It may interest you to know that her father, Mose's cousin, became Mose's fraternity brother at Yale. Now, if you'll excuse me.—I need to accomplish a million things this morning."

"Wait. I know more."

"Rudine, I find this absurd."

"It's for your own good that you listen because that girl's done been with my boy, Lars, all night. They wadn't talking nothing about no Spanish moss neither." She shoved her teacup and saucer onto the tray.

With a shaky hand she nabbed an English muffin and slathered butter and piled it high with marmalade. Without a plate or napkin Rudine dribbled all over herself and the divan's silk damask upholstery.

Luna Belle looked down and saw a huge glop of goo on the Aubusson rug that covered the marquetry floor for winter. Her lips exhaled a sigh and twisted. She leaned forward and templed her fingers. "Either get on with it or get out."

Rudine shoved almost half the muffin in her mouth, wallowed it a couple of times, then continued. "Don't matter if she's your cousin or the Queen of Zanzibar. Get rid of her."

Luna Belle rose and headed toward the door. The three faces glued to this intrigue greeted her with mimed smiles. She winked, glad they remained hidden.

In a furtive tease she called afar. "Polly? Please have Sylvia come in here."

Mose motioned for her to join them. She stepped into the hall and closed the door.

Rudine tiptoed behind to try and hear through the closed door.

Mordecai held his hands in surrender. "I tried to stop her."

Luna Belle sighed. "Not your fault, Mordecai. Is that confounded girl here or not?"

Mose said, "I don't know, but get back in there. Learn all you can. Stop trying to get rid of her 'til she spills her guts."

"I don't have time to monkey with this woman. You know good and well, I expect the Canasta Club girls early this morning."

He squinted his eyes and his rich bass voice growled, "Darling, I know these things don't interest you, but I need to know what this hag is trying to say. First things first."

When Rudine saw the door lever move, she leapt to the mantle and rubbed it in an attempt to disguise her spying.

Luna Belle walked to the fireplace. "I'm sorry your Lars went missing."

"He's not missing. My boy spent all night with that hussy. She's after something important. Like I'uz saying … run her off before she destroys y'all'n us too. She told Lars that neither one of them would ever have to work again. Her plans involve big money."

An icy finger traced Moses Augustus Black's spine. His knees almost buckled, but he managed to only sway slightly before he regained his stance. He had told Sylvia far too much over the last few weeks. Rudine's words set off every alarm his mind could call up.

Luna Belle clenched her jaws and knitted her fingers together. "You're not making a whole lot of sense."

Looking at Luna Belle's exasperated expression, Rudine sighed deeply. "I should've stayed home." She looked down at her lap and brushed crumbs onto the floor. "Lord knows, last thing I need is to get you people stirred up. Lars had a bright future ahead of him and he don't need to get involved in no scam involving that wench."

Determined to move on, Luna Belle rolled her hands in the air. "Why do you accuse Sylvia of conspiring with Lars? I understand a clandestine tryst because your boy is quite handsome, but how can you sit in my home and waste my time with this folderol? You're the mistress of your own house. If you don't like what they're doing—ask them to leave."

Rudine sucked food from the gap in her teeth then raised her nose in the air. "I know you think I'm worthless trash, but I've been around. I may not've been raised with no silver spoon but we done okay. My daddy owned the Bowl 'r Skate over at Fletch. Course, that ain't much to big shots like y'all." Her eyes glazed. "That's where I met Fuzz Haggley. Swept me away first … first time he smiled." She sighed. "He wanted off this island way back then. Told me so hisself."

Luna Belle tossed her head back and rolled her eyes as she deeply exhaled.

"I didn't know Cow Bell Island from nothing when I married Fuzz. I had'a known then what I know now I'd a'never come to this hell-hole. He called it temporary. Said I'd not have to work nor nothing. But this place'uz creepy to me right out of the loading chute.

"When he'uz killed I swore I'd get out'a here."

"Why didn't you?"

"I never could manage to scrape enough together. What with the funny-money cut off, I had to go to work. I ought to'a stole a bateau and left."

Luna Belle sighed, tensed, and twiddled her thumbs.

"You ever hear how my husband died?"

"No."

"He'uz a plumber. Whoever murdered him sent the message for me to keep my mouth shut or else." She hesitated as tears flowed. "They poured hot lead down his throat." She sobbed. "Can you imagine drowning in … in molten lead? A plumber's tortured death. Even used his own equipment … lead too."

Luna Belle shuddered. Why tell something so horrendous?

Out in the hallway Mose muttered, "Rudine my dear, I fear you've just spaded your own grave."

Rudine got a far away look in her eyes. "Got ideas about who done it. It's true, he wad'n nothing but a pile of lump but he didn't deserve that. When I found him … I'd a never known him except for the hump on his back."

"I'm sorry for all your trouble. Is this really why you barged in on me this morning?"

"That'uz over fifteen years ago. But no, that ain't why I'm here. I want to protect Lars. I need help. Hadn't we suffered enough?

"After Fuzz's murder, we'uz cut off. Had to start from scratch. You don't know what that's like. That's why I want Lars away from that harlot. She ain't no good for him."

"I don't understand what you actually want. I'm almost positive I've told you more than once this morning that Sylvia is a lady."

"Lady? Huh. She may'a fooled you but not me. I'm telling you she ain't no good. Understand?"

Luna Belle sat up and leaned forward. "No, Rudine I don't. Spit it out. No holds barred."

"I didn't want to just come out and say it but looks like I ain't got no choice. She intends to steal Blackbeard's trove."

2

An Eye for an Eye and a Tooth for a Hag

Out in the hall Mose growled, cracked his knuckles, then pushed his hair off his forehead. "Blackbeard's trove! Who does this bitch think she's dealing with? You know Mordecai, I've been getting little tidbits of information about troubles for the last couple of weeks. I need time to put two and two together."

Luna Belle kept her composure. "Rudine, you're dead wrong. Let me make myself clear. I'm going to speak slowly so you'll understand every word. You sit and listen. I won't use any *highfalutin* language, as you call it, that might fly over your head. Okay?"

"Well … I never." Rudine retrieved her tea from the tray and gulped the now cooled brew.

"I seriously doubt you have." Luna Belle interrupted with dripping sarcasm. "Like I said—listen. You barged into my home without an invitation. You made accusations against my family and my guest about some kind of fairy tale treasure. I have every right to defend myself and Sylvia."

A sudden tapping at the door stopped Luna Belle in her tracks. When the door opened, Polly stuck her face inside. "Excuse me Missy. I needs to sees you out here a minute?"

"Excuse me, Rudine. I'll be right back."

Luna Belle rushed out the door for the second time that morning. Rundine took the opportunity to roll a heavy sterling spoon into the side of her slack's waist, not even a down payment for the grief these people caused. She wanted to abscond with the butter knife as well but feared its absence might rouse suspicion.

Polly shook her head and rung her hands together. "Miss Sylvia not in her room. Don't think she been there all night, neither."

Mose whispered in a white hot rage. "We must get rid of both those women. They're nothing but trouble. Find out what she wants. She certainly didn't come here without expectation of remuneration."

Luna Belle rubbed her temples then adjusted her glasses. "What do I ask her?"

Mose crossed his arms over his chest. "You stop worrying about what to say and get back in there. You're up for round three. In my opinion you won the first two. Now get back in there and take that weasel down."

Luna Belle sighed and returned to the morning room with a big smile plastered on her face.

"I'm sorry, Rudine. It appears Sylvia has already dressed, eaten, and left. Quick as we find her I'm certain we can straighten this entire situation out. Now tell me what you want me to do."

The crone squirmed. "No, Luna Belle, I left the girl in bed with Lars. Right there in my very own turquoise single-wide mobile home. You know … the one with the happy pink shutters and plastic flamingos parading in front of my lovely orange silk ever-blooming marigolds?

"I listened to Lars and Sylvia all through the night. They tried to keep their voices down but what they'uz saying come through them paper-thin walls to beat the band. I got interested enough to turn Letterman off, and Lord knows I don't miss him unless Hell has done already froze over."

"So what did you hear them say? But—I really don't care about any sordid details."

Rudine sat back and rolled her eyes. The last time she spilled her guts to a member of the Black family came the day before Fuzz's tortured death. She told Mose her husband's entire scheme to get off the island with plenty of money. It involved going public with all Fuzz knew about the way Pirate's Landing thrived. Blackmailing pirates proved to be risky business. Especially a direct descendant of Blackbeard, who just happened to be a federal judge to boot.

At an outsider's first glance, Pirate's Landing appeared a sleepy hamlet on the nearly deserted Georgia coastal Cow Bell Island, but appearances often prove deceptive. The Contessa Juliana devised the entire scheme to horde the pirate's treasure here and keep it secreted in perpetuity by a smoldering den of buccaneers.

Mose railed, "A whole lot of people rely on the resources of this little dot of geography for their existences. The responsibility to maintain all this falls on my shoulders and I fear I've played the utmost buffoon. Mark my words. This conniving wench isn't yet through here."

Mordecai placed a hand on Mose's shoulder.

Mose looked at him and attempted to smile. "I know I'm preaching to the choir, but the Contessa's plan has been successful. We've enjoyed the booty's bounty for three hundred years. I refuse to entertain some outsider's wrecking our carefully orchestrated operation."

Rudine had entered the dragon's lair with high hopes. Even though she began to sober up, her mouth remained in overdrive with little chance of control.

She returned her head to a normal position then looked down at the floor. Her voice came softly at first. "You know good'n well she's with my Lars. She's plotting the overthrow of this entire dynasty. Thinks she has some big fish on board too, whatever that means. I never heard names but she insisted she knew more'n she's telling. Does this mean anything? 'Daddy's gonna die.' I heard her say that several times."

"I can't imagine what that means." Luna Belle scowled and crooked her mouth.

"She talked a good bit about some warehouse in Savannah. Said it'uz the undoing of the whole shooting match. Mind you, I ain't got no idea about what any of this means, but I do know it sounds real serious. Your husband has got a lot of connections all over the southeast. I expect he'd want to know somebody's got great big designs on Cow Bell Island. Reckon?"

"I realize you've been upset by all this nonsense. Why don't you go ahead and get to the bottom of the real reason you came here this morning. Something you're hiding burdens you. I want to do all I can to help you but first I have to know what you expect."

Rudine shifted her eyes to look out through the wavy antique glass of the French doors in the elegant suite. As she sat in silence she rearranged her seat and began to squirm. Her wriggling ground her messy splatters into the precious silk fibers of the divan.

"Luna Belle, you've always been nice to me, and you tip me real good over at the beauty shop. I appreciate all the kindnesses you've showed me over the years."

"Why wouldn't I treat you well? You're the best shampoo girl in the whole shop. I always appreciate a good Rudine scalp massage, but you're getting off track. I need to know more about why you came here today."

"I came as a friend to warn you."

"There's more to it than that, isn't there?"

"Maybe."

"Go ahead and say it then. Don't be bashful, now."

Rudine again looked out the windows and shuffled her feet to mush more glop into the tapestry. "I ... I need enough ... m-money to get me and Lars off Cow Bell Island."

Luna Belle thought, *At least enough to get that gaping hole in her mouth fixed. Why doesn't it whistle ... or lisp?*

Rudine relaxed her shoulders. "Just enough to start over someplace else. Don't need much. Maybe five or six hundred thousand dollars?"

Luna Belle reached over and took Rudine's tea from her hand and placed it back on the tray. After rearranging her posture and leaning forward she began her calculated reply. "Now I understand. You came here to extort money from us. I should've known. It's time for you to leave. I'll get Mordecai to show you out."

Rudine blew her chance. *If I'd only told Luna Belle about the note stapled to Fuzz's forehead.* The timely telling of the warning would have been poignant but the moment had slipped through her fingers. A blatant statement of intent firmly affixed to Fuzz Haggley's forehead indeed warranted attention:

BEWARE!
anyone
who takes lightly
the secrets of
Blackbeard.
Here lies your fate.
The note said it all. No one escaped the fury of the captain
and his crew if they broke the pirate's code. No one.

Mose whispered, "Half a million dollars, huh?" He looked
around for a weapon and shivered from having been assaulted in
his own home. The walls hung heavy with blades and guns, but
he shook his head to chase that idea away because the last thing
he needed was blood splattered everywhere in the house. Mose
was too fastidious for such nonsense except under extremely
dire circumstances. Even a pirate has standards.

The witch hexed and assured him he had every right to
eliminate her when she threatened him and his family. His eyes
glowed red. "I shot myself in the foot when I allowed myself
to be lulled into false security by Sylvia … my own kin." He
grabbed his chest and his face contorted enough to pull his head
sideways.

Mordecai saw his condition and motioned for Polly to fetch a
chair. "Are you all right?"

Mose's face returned to normal and he nodded to Mordecai.
"I'm fine." He shook his head quickly to regain his composure.
"Years ago, this woman came to me to finagle money when she
tattled on her own husband. It didn't take me but a few hours to
round up a crew to deal with that vermin. Consarned Scooter
Thadeu talked me out of killing the bitch back then. He argued
in defense of the boy, Lars. Now my mistake stares me in the
eyes.

"If I'd used my brains back then I might have seen some
kind of wild motive in Scooter's mind. Why did he care if she
died or not? It's all becoming perfectly clear. He harbored the
intention of using her against me. He thinks his time has come.
I've got other plans for the great Georgia Governor, Scooter
Thadeu."

Luna Belle rose from her seat and leaned over Rudine. "Let

me make sure I understand. You want us to give you a big pile of money and then you walk away from here and start a new life?"

"I'm sorry, Luna Belle. I ought to have stayed home. I let the Devil prod me into coming here this morning."

"Satan and money. Sounds to me like you needed to sober yourself before you made accusations against me and my family. I'm not sure an apology will be sufficient for your blatant insult. What I really want at this moment is for you to leave my home. I've certainly heard enough of your ranting for one day."

"Please forgive me. The Devil's done sent me here and now I hear him laughing at my foolishness."

"Foolishness is right. You came here imagining yourself walking away a wealthy woman, didn't you? I think you better consider what you've done to yourself and your precious Lars. I doubt you're going to find much charity here."

Rudine might have survived this confrontation sober, but she intoxicated herself with the liquor of lust and wanton desire at the cooked up smell of lucre. She wanted to throw it in the air and then roll in it, for once in her life to act like a Black.

She grossly miscalculated her adversary, and trembled because she couldn't see her next move, stumbling at every step and exposing her belly to her own sword.

Mose stuck his head in Luna Belle's morning room causing Rudine to almost come out of her frightened skin. Loud flatulence copiously followed.

Mose threw his head back and his eyes sprung wide open. "Oh, my. I didn't realize you entertained a guest this morning."

Luna Belle rose from her seat and headed toward the door to escape the odious air. "Nonsense. Please come in. You know Rudine Haggley. She's dropped by to express her concern about her son, Lars. She thinks he's having a relationship with our Sylvia."

"That's wonderful. Your Lars seems like such a fine boy. Handsome too. I'm sorry to intrude on your meeting. I know you two have much to talk about, but Luna Belle, darling, have you forgotten your previous engagement this morning? Want me to call the girls and reschedule? Your flight plan—we need to know if there's a change."

"No, no, that's not necessary. I'm sure Rudine and I have

finished our little meeting." Luna Belle approached and offered a hand to help the blob off the divan.

Mose joined his wife. "Here, allow me." He had one side and Luna Belle took the other in an effort to tag-team her. Once escape stared her in the face, Rudine seemed apprehensive.

Mose dropped her hand and started toward the door. "Allow me to get Mordecai to escort you out."

With that he left the lingering cloud and headed straight for the upstairs hall where he motioned for Mordecai to take over. The old gentleman knew how to deal with the frustrated woman.

With a genteel smile he entered the room. "Mrs. Haggley, it's been a pleasure having you in our home. Please allow me to escort you downstairs." Mordecai managed to stay with her hasty retreat all the way to the front door where he let her out and slammed the heavy slab behind her. Rudine felt an obvious message from the door's draft on her posterior.

They all breathed a sigh of relief.

Rudine rushed to her car. She fidgeted with her keys then she dropped them. After several failed attempts she shoved the right one in the ignition and turned it. The car rebelled. For an inanimate object, it appeared to have a dark comedic intuition.

She ground the ignition until it sputtered and backfired a cloud of blueish smoke. A hole in the floorboard allowed a huge gush of the asphyxiating smog into the car. Rudine followed suit by coughing and sputtering, then she stomped the accelerator. The overwhelmed engine wheezed and expired.

A grinding sound of metal against metal followed the car's death. She tried again and again but the sound of the weakening battery nauseated her.

"No. You can't fail me here." She beat on the dash of her old used-up Cadillac Eldorado, the last thing Fuzz gave her before his murder. She cherished the vehicle as a reminder of the couple's last glimpses of glorious happiness.

The tears that welled in her eyes were a mixture of sorrow and fear. Her mouth had sealed the Haggleys' fate. One last effort with the key and the car seemingly understood her terror. It cranked. This time she tried a gentler approach with the finicky jalopy. Its gold paint long ago relented to the elements and turned into an unattractive patina of rust. Shreds of a once white vinyl top tattered and fluttered in the wind while she coursed the driveway of Teachall with considerable speed, creating a billowing contrail of bluish smoke that stained the air behind her.

Luna Belle, Mose, Mordecai, and Polly watched Rudine's exit through the front gates with their own personal emotions over her visit and departure.

Polly held her hand up and pointed a finger while she flexed her wrist. "Did any y'all notice? That woman got a bignomus butt? Um-hmm."

Luna Belle burst into laughter. "We'll need to have that chair inspected. One more little indignation and it might collapse."

Mose looked at Polly with a raised eyebrow and shook his head. He started to speak but retained his composure. Polly grinned.

Mose left the group and climbed the stairs back to his chart room. He picked up the phone and called his brother-in-law, Sheriff Pink Tiddie.

"Pink. Rudine Haggley just left here. Uh ... she's tied into some kind of mess. Not sure what it's all about but I still want you to get her into protective custody soon as you can. Copy?"

The Sheriff almost swallowed his tongue as he tried to interpret Mose's words. If the crazy drunken woman had talked too much, she already shattered Mose's trust in the entire group of mutineers. The sheriff would obey without hesitation because he knew of the situation's potential danger to explode in his own face. Scooter Thadeu needed to know about this immediately. Pink called him then headed to his cruiser to chase down an old gold Eldorado.

Quandary circled Mose's head while he studied the hazard engulfing Cow Bell Island. Rudine didn't know much, but even a small amount seemed like enough to get wheels rolling that had laid quiet for three hundred years. No one on the island remained safe if she blabbed.

3

What's a Body to Do?

Mose called down the stairs for Mordecai and Luna Belle to come to his chart room occupying the top floor of the tower. Luna Belle fumed. She had no desire to waste anymore of her valuable time discussing this disastrous visit from someone of no more importance than Rudine. Her scheduled departure held no importance with Mose even though her plans benefited his relative, not hers.

When she arrived in the highest room of the palatial mansion Luna Belle saw a dull glaze over Mose's eyes. His vacuous appearance dazed her.

Mose spun in his great leather desk chair. "So … Sylvia plotted with Lars all night?"

Luna Belle cocked her head. "Sounds like it. I can see why she might fool around with the handsome rascal, but I don't believe any of that woman's tripe. Sylvia? Betray us? That's the most preposterous thing I've ever heard."

"Maybe not so preposterous. You think you know somebody. I tell you, if she's messing with that boy, serious trouble may lurk in our futures. He and his mama hold an old vicious grudge against us. She has pounded hate into the boy by teaching him that we killed his daddy. Rudine wants money. I made a serious mistake years ago when I didn't give her enough to leave here. I regretfully decided we needed to keep an eye on her. I'm not sure I made the right decision."

Luna Belle's gaze started wandering over the maps hanging

on the walls between the windows. She surveyed the space
while Mordecai and Mose talked. Their volume faded into the
distance.

Mose smiled when he saw her vacant expression. "Luna
Belle? … Honey?"

No reaction.

"Luna Belle … did you know…. I'm in … Paris?"

Mordecai grinned. He loved watching Mose catch Luna
Belle unawares.

Having been through this many times, Mose wanted
to chuckle."You want me to bring you a bottle of some rare
perfume?"

She left her far off retreat and shook fog from her head.
"Perfume? I think she chose smoke and liquor for fragrance this
morning."

"Who's that?"

"Rudine. You know exactly who I meant.—Oh Mose!" She'd
fallen for it again.

Mose chuckled with raised eyebrows. "And that my dear has
been your *modus operandi* from the first day we married."

"Why do you persist in annoying me? Didn't you schedule
going out with Pete this morning to work on a fence or
something?"

"Pete's going to Riggers Creek to clean out a sink-hole so
we can get it filled. I wanted to ride with him but I'll catch him
later." Mose squirmed in his seat. "You need to pay attention
to what's going on around here. Serious trouble is about to pop
out."

"Anything you say, dear, but right now I've got to get on the
ball. Otherwise, I'll never be ready when the girls get here. You
know I've always trusted you to take care of me. You certainly
don't need me to help with that." Luna Belle left the room
without giving Mose time to protest.

He shook his head and rose from his chair to walk the room's
perimeter, searching from the tower's observation windows over
the vast estate and the hamlet of Pirate's Landing beyond. From
this vantage point he could see almost every house and business
on the island.

His eyes stopped on Thadeu Castle, Scooter's childhood

home. The old manor house had never been as grand as Teachall, but it served well as home to most of the quartermasters since the earliest times.

Mose pointed. "Mordecai, I can feel in my bones that the events leading up to Rudine's visit hatched right down there in Thadeu Castle. Within the last two weeks Scooter and I met twice. I need to sort through this mishmash and figure out all the mutineers' identities. Rudine has stirred a cauldron of unfathomable depth, and if I don't get a handle on all these shenanigans, Cow Bell Island may erupt into an all out war."

Mordecai walked over to the window with Mose. His eyes fell on the old dilapidated mansion. "I never have understood why the governor doesn't keep that place up."

Mose glanced over at Mordecai. "I've botched things by involving Sylvia in our little secrets."

"I'm not worried. You've experienced quite an ordeal this morning. Is it so bad if Sylvia involved herself with the Haggley boy?"

"It's not him that concerns me. She came here with a raider's heart to learn the family business."

Mordecai returned to his seat and leaned forward. He rested his palms on the chair's arms and strummed his fingers on the polished wood. "I'm not bright like her, but I've been here all my life and I don't know much about how things work."

Mose turned and sat on the window ledge. "One huge difference occurs to me."

"What's that?"

"You've never wanted to know the intimate workings. Sylvia pried."

Mordecai pushed his weight further forward and threatened to rise. "Maybe so, but I know one thing for certain: Whatever magic you work appears complicated. Now, if you'll excuse me."

Mordecai rose from his seat. "I leave you to your pensive nature. Your parents, the Colonel and Miss Beulah, placed their complete trust in your judgement. I follow their instincts."

"Mind sharing an opinion before you leave?"

Mordecai leaned a hand against the door jamb. "If I have one."

Mose sat in deepest contemplation. "Never mind. Some

things I must cipher alone."

Mordecai raised his chin. "I appreciate your consideration. If I might add, I never envied your position." Mordecai again attempted to leave the chart room.

"No, wait. Before you go … don't you think it's odd that Pink didn't ask questions when I called him about Rudine?"

"Not at all like him." Mordecai rubbed his chin.

"Nick warned me the other day that Rose is involved in all this too."

Mordecai's stomach rolled as Mose's words sunk in. "You don't believe your own sister betrayed you?"

"Pink wasn't his usual bag of hot air, that's for sure. Obliged me without a fuss."

"There's more to this, isn't there?"

"Nick did rouse my suspicions."

"Nick Polk … your horse trainer? He's a total outsider. What could he know?"

"He's a smart man. I still can't make myself believe Rose involved herself, but what if she turned on us? I'll bet you one thing for sure, if my hunch is accurate, Rudine drew her last breath not long after she left here."

Mordecai nodded. "But it makes no sense for Rose to turn on you. You have given those two everything."

Mose turned to hide a tear as Mordecai slowly left the room. Mose returned to his desk chair and swiveled back and forth.

He picked up the phone and called his secret personal assistant, Pegleg. Almost whispering, he said, "Can you meet me at the folly's parapet in one hour?" He swiveled his chair. "Come up Axminster Creek and don't be seen."

Mose picked up a pencil. "Fine, see you then."

From his high position he watched a bird land in the top of a live oak as he rolled the pencil between his fingers. He wheeled his chair to a better position to observe Thadeu Castle, tapping the pencil eraser against his ear.

Looking out on the dilapidated manor, Mose scratched a quick note for Pegleg then called Luna Belle back to the chart room. While she made her way back up the stairs, he folded the small piece of paper and stuffed it in a pocket.

When Luna Belle returned Mose quietly said, "Sit down a minute."

"Mose, you need to get out of my hair this morning. The girls will arrive soon and I'm not ready." She turned to leave.

"Please, sit."

Luna Belle deferred, but she sighed.

"Please, I just wanted you to know how my chest swelled with pride this morning. You parried with that ignoramus as if you dueled to the death."

Luna Belle pinched her eyebrows together. "I never thought about it as sparring, but you're right. Thank you." She grinned as she leaned on her elbow.

"Aren't you glad I insisted we fence all these years?"

"Of course, but I'm late. You seem to continually forget that my plans concern Pinki's wedding." She sprang from her chair and disappeared in a flash.

Mose rose from his seat and retrieved two large fresh parchment sheets from a chart rack and sharpened his quill with a pen knife before he inscribed his first letter to Luna Belle.

Mose addressed his second epistle to Mordecai. In it he confessed to denying his own mortality and revealed his dread of new scoundrels. He ended with the following postscript petition:

> Friend,
>
> If something happens to me, you and Polly may remain Luna Belle's sole loyal defenders. I know I can depend on you to see her through whatever lies ahead. You understand her nature better than anyone else. See to her safety—and if possible, her happiness.
>
> You have my complete trust and devotion.
>
> Thank you, respected companion. Know I loved and appreciated you.
>
> Your devoted brother,
>
> ## Mose

Mose spilled a large pool of hot red wax onto the back of the folded parchments. He stamped both missives with the image of two dragons entwined in battle then left the letters on his dressing table downstairs.

Pegleg's silent electric skiff docked in hiding under the old rickety bridge crossing Axminster Creek, then he slipped up the bank with the surreptitious skill of a master buccaneer. Within moments he mounted the bluff and arrived at the base of Teachall's folly. It took only moments for him to climb the circular stone staircase leading to the outer terrace on top of the old Scottish castle remnants where Mose waited. This place had served as their clandestine rendezvous spot for decades.

Any part of the landscape not visible from Mose's chart room at the West end of the island came into full view through the crenelated ramparts wrapping the top of the folly on the East end. What most would consider a vanity actually served as a well camouflaged watchtower that offered an uninterrupted view all the way to the Atlantic Ocean.

"What's up? I can't believe you called me here in broad daylight. Where's Nick?"

"Nick's in Florida looking for horses. Nobody here knows you. We've got a lot to talk about and very little time." Mose handed his penciled note to Pegleg. "Put this in your pocket. I'm afraid you're going to need it sooner than I'd hoped. I'm most likely going to be counting on you to stay out of sight."

"Aye-aye, captain."

Mose cleared his throat and paused before he prodded his nerves enough to start. "Scooter Thadeu dragged Luna Belle and her Canasta Club into a mutinous plot."

"What?"

"Let me see if I can explain. About two years ago, Luna Belle took Rose—"

Pegleg dug into his pocket. "Wait ... let me write this down." He retrieved a small pad and proceeded to scrawl. "Your sister, Rose, Sheriff Pink Tiddie's wife?"

"That's right, my sister, Rose, ... Lulu Thadeu and Lolly White—"

"The Governor's wife, Lulu, and her twin sister, Lolly?"

"Correct again. You know the players. So ... Luna Belle took Rose, Lulu, and Lolly to Spain on an expedition to buy

horses. Lolly fell head over heels with a rare sherry called Palo
Cortado while they were there."

Pegleg spoke while he wrote. "Palo … Cor-ta-do …"

"Scooter pushed Lulu into getting Lolly and Irvin—"

"Lolly's husband, Irvin White, right?"

Mose nodded.

Pegleg finished Mose's thought. "—to rent Irvin's Savannah
warehouse to Marcus Gilder, an importer of Palo Cortado."

"How much do you already know?" Mose scratched his
sideburn and looked at Pegleg.

"I think I pretty much just told you all I know. Why don't
we pretend I don't know anything and let's see where this goes.
Sounds like it's more important for me to find out what you
know."

"Good idea. So don't interrupt me again … unless of course
you don't already know the answer. Is that fair?"

"Understood."

"Scooter actually only wanted to get Gilder's merchandise
into Irvin's warehouse so we could steal it."

Pegleg scratched his chin. "So does this explain all the
malarky on TV the last few days?"

"Yep."

Pegleg looked up from his writing. "You know what makes
this all the more interesting to me? It's the fact Scooter Thadeu
has never shown one ounce of interest in being a picaroon."

"You're right. He never has. That's what first roused my
suspicion, but I played along to see what he planned … well,
other than theft. From the outset of Scooter's involvement I
knew something smelled fishy. Didn't take long to figure it out.
Scooter intended ousting me and taking over as chief."

Pegleg raised one eyebrow and looked over his wire rimmed
glasses. "That idiot lacks sufficient knowledge to run the
operation."

"I know. You know. But Governor Thadeu is too ignorant to
realize his shortfalls."

"This would be funny if it weren't serious."

Mose snarled his upper lip on one side and snorted. "Tell
me about it…. At first I intended to embarrass Scooter amongst
ourselves and be done with it. Then it became obvious to me. He

wanted me dead."

"Ouch."

"That's right. Still, I played along."

"So, what can I do to help?"

"Have you heard the names Winston and Sylvia Black?"

"Virginia? Senator? Sylvia's his daughter?" Pegleg scratched the names into his pad.

"Exactly. I need for you to find out why they've gotten in bed with Scooter."

"In bed with Scooter?"

"Sylvia came here pretending to study Spanish moss."

"That's a good one."

"Yep. She manipulated me and Luna Belle like puppets. Played on our being childless. Makes my blood boil when I think about how gullible I became."

"She try to woo you?"

"Oh no. Far too clever for that. She played me like her surrogate father. That's why I think Winston involved himself in all this. She would have attempted to seduce me otherwise. Don't you think?"

Pegleg dropped his hands. "Point well taken." He swallowed hard and looked away from Mose. "I already know a little about the Virginia set of Blacks. You see, I heard that Winston lost his entire fortune several months ago."

"I find that hard to believe. How?"

"Got hung out to dry in a tobacco settlement. Way I heard it, he had a choice: Be wiped out when he paid up for the entire industry, or wear an orange jumpsuit and share a suite with a sweet."

"So my fraternity brother, my cousin, thinks he can stroll down to South Georgia and haul off all we have? I can almost see his wheels turning."

Mose tapped his index fingers together. "That part of the Black clan has been away from here too long. Damned fox hunters. We ought to have divorced ourselves from them right after the Late Great Inconvenience. He thinks of Cow Bell Island as a God-forsaken hell-hole of gnats, mosquitoes, gators, and cottonmouths."

Pegleg glared over his glasses.

Mose relented. "All right. Maybe he has a point, but it's still home sweet home. Besides, our natural pestilences keep all but the most hale and hearty frightened away."

Pegleg sat on a canted stone reinforcement behind a rampart firing slot. "Scooter Thadeu might be a slimy serpent ready to strike, but he's not much more than a hack. Winston Black sounds like a true adversary to me."

"You got that right." Mose winced and wrung his hands together and hung them off the cold stone he leaned against. "I guess when I think about it … Rudine Haggley actually saved my life. Otherwise, I might have behaved even worse."

"Rudine Haggley … saved your life? Huh?"

Mose leaned onto his elbows resting on the coping. "You ever hear about the Haggleys?"

"I didn't get involved in that, but I recollect Fuzz. Wasn't that his name? … Thought he'd leave here a wealthy man. That the one?" Mose nodded.

Mose grimaced. "That's him. Believe it or not his widow came here really early this morning. Roused everybody but me. I was already up and dressed. She beat on the front door and screamed like a banshee."

"What in the world?"

"Sylvia spent the night with her boy, Lars, last night. They also dragged him into this sinking ship. Rudine said Sylvia and Lars are plotting the theft of Blackbeard's trove. I also took her warning to mean my death is imminent. Bitch repeated Sylvia's words, 'Daddy gonna die.'"

"Well, aren't you just a June-bug on a string this morning?"

"Aren't I, though? … Scooter Thadeu…. You know, the whole purpose of having the brotherhood involved in public service has worked for a long time. Always kept the law at bay. Centuries ago, some long dead ancestor figured out having high ranking dignitaries in government provided the best way for us all to stay out of the hoosegow. To quote my venerable father, 'Ain't no crook like a politician.'"

Pegleg laughed then pushed up his glasses. "Sorry. I don't mean to laugh in the face of tragedy, but all this is rather comical when you think about it."

"I guess so. Problem arises from not knowing exactly who all involved themselves in the plotting. That's where you come in. Think you can help me patch these pieces together into a quilt?"

"I'll try, but sounds like we don't have much time. What happened with the … what was it?" Pegleg pulled his pad back up and searched. "Palo Cortado stuff?"

"Scooter thought we stole it, but that's a story for another day. Least of our worries. Right now, we need to concentrate on Winston and Sylvia."

Pegleg sat quietly for only a few moments before he spoke. "You asked me earlier about how much I knew when I came here." He flipped several pages back toward the front of his little pocket pad and offered it to Mose. "I think you may want to read this."

The more Mose read, the paler his normally dark skin became. All the vital color faded from his face. Pegleg noticed how even his hands took on a blueish cast as the strong pigments seemed to leach away by the second. After reading three pages from the pad Mose turned his back from the ocean and stared down at Pegleg. "Want to hear the worst part?"

"It can't get much worse. Can it?"

Mose turned again and looked out over the vast Atlantic lying in the East. "I've shown her the … the three books."

Now time came for Pegleg's already pale skin to bleach itself even whiter than normal. He dropped his shoulders while his pencil fell onto the cold damp stone. He gulped hard.

4

Bad News Travels Fast

Luna Belle uncharacteristically answered the doorbell herself because she expected her Canasta Club. Lulu Thadeu, first Lady of Georgia, and her twin sister, Lolly White, came promptly at ten-thirty.

"Welcome girls. Come in. If I seem disheveled it's because we've had a little commotion here this morning, and I failed at completely restoring my wits."

Lulu bristled from the morning's chilly air. "What in the world is wrong? Is there something we can do?"

"Heavens, no. It's nothing really. I thought Mose would never leave the house this morning. That's all. I'll be fine shortly. I promise. Make your way to the Ladies' Tea Room. Polly has a wonderful little brunch prepared for us. As soon as Rose arrives we'll be right in. Go ahead and start. Don't wait for us."

Rose soon shivered her way into the foyer. Her behavior should have caused concern because she never appeared affected by cold weather. "How's everything here this morning? Brrrr. It's chilly. I'm shivering. I didn't wear enough clothes for this weather."

"We'll be in South Florida soon enough. I expect it's plenty warm there." Luna Belle said as they walked toward the others. "Heard from Little Pink?"

"You'd think that rascal would at least come and help with his only child's wedding. You know he never shows his face around Cow Bell Island unless it's Christmas or his birthday.

Then he's holding his hand out expecting a big wad of cash. Where'd we go wrong?"

"Don't go blaming yourself. Little Pink will grow up one of these days. Why, he's only forty-seven. We've got enough to fuss over with Pinki's October wedding. It's already February and we've barely begun."

The adorable Pinki's mother had succumbed immediately before the child's fifteen pound birth-weight could enter the world. So, Rose and Pink took Pinki's rearing on themselves. Rose salvaged a chance to redeem herself from the total catastrophe they made with their only child.

When Rose and Luna Belle entered to enjoy Polly's pre-trip light snack, Rose preened her hair and grinned when she perused the buffet. "Key West beckons. I can't wait to soak up some warm mid-winter sun for a couple of days."

Lolly stirred her coffee. "I can't either, but I'm most excited about getting to Manhattan. I want to shop."

Lulu sat up and placed her coffee cup back in its saucer. "Me too. I'm about to pass out with excitement. I can't believe Luna Belle is finally letting us meet with her fashion guru, Emile Yvez. Woo-hoo."

Luna Belle served herself a small portion of spinach soufflé. "Y'all must realize he adores his own temperamental nature. Nothing, and I do mean nothing, can stand in our way of being in his studio Thursday at eleven. If we're late, we can forget it. Hand beading takes time and Emile refuses to compromise his schedule."

Lolly tapped her plate with her fork. "Rose, you're always the one that's late. If you don't get your act together Pinki's wedding stands a chance of being ruined."

"Y'all leave me alone. I'll be ready and waiting." Rose squinted as she pushed shrimp and grits around on her plate.

When the women finished Polly's unctuous brunch, Luna Belle rose from the table and admonished the other girls. "Get your things together. Mordecai's ready to drive us to the airstrip. Can't be late or we'll have to file a new flight-plan."

Luna Belle allowed her mind to wander back a few hours. The crazed crone interloped and turned a planned morning into chaos and disaster. Mose further annoyed her by staying under foot. Rudine had thrown the entire house into overdrive.

Luna Belle pushed herself back from the table. "Come on girls. It's time for us to go."

She marveled at their strange behavior. The women appeared overtaken by an unusual quarrelsomeness. Maybe a couple of days at the beach might cure them and rub a touch of affable into their spirits. They could then organize the wedding's most intricate details without Pinki's intrusion.

Rose giggled when she patted Pinki's thigh the first time they met at Teachall for wedding planning. "For heaven's sake, Pinki's only the bride."

Luna Belle picked up a bowl of potpourri from the pier table across from the great hall tree inside the first vestibule near the front door. She ruffed the dried rose petals, moss, and curled bark with her finger then sniffed her favorite winter fragrances, frankincense, cinnamon, and clove.

The hall tree provided a mirror for the upper torso. The pier table gave passing ladies a chance to inspect their lower garments. She returned the potpourri to the table before she stepped back to inspect her slacks and shoes.

The pier mirror reminded her of the first time she came to Teachall when she was only eight years old. She patiently sat on the floor pretending to become Alice. All sorts of creatures amazed her on her enchanted journey inside the marvelous glass. Reflections from the wallpaper covering the salon behind her turned into mystical moving pictures. Gryphons took wing and lost their ferocious faces to instantly transform themselves into angels and fairies.

These manifestations helped her pass the tedium of being the only young girl amid a gaggle of gabbing women. At the time, Luna Belle knew nothing of that visit's importance. The Black women set their intent upon inspecting Luna Belle as a suitable mate for Mose.

Nine years older, Rose considered herself too mature to play with Luna Belle, so the child found herself lost in her imaginings—a free spirit amidst connivers.

Luna Belle had lemonade while the others took tea. Served

petit fours, tea sandwiches, and cookies with homemade strawberry ice cream, Luna Belle liked Teachall. When her grandmother announced she might live there someday, Luna Belle imagined it nothing more than fantasy, similar to her pretending before the mirror.

She snapped back. Her little recollection seemed especially insignificant this morning. Too much ado loomed for sentimentalities. She reached for the potpourri for one last whiff and to admire the rare early Satsuma ware bowl's details. Mr. Kotomada, a famous kimono designer and friend, commented on the bowl's rarity. Hand thrown porcelain with atypical glazes was not something expected from ordinary Satsuma ware.

He carefully ran his hands over the glaze and squinted. "Imperial ware. Owned by an emperor. Bestowed on some valiant person as an exaggerated token of gratitude for some brave deed. Very rare indeed."

While she caressed the cherished irregularities of the bowl, her startled eyes caught a glimpse through the door's sidelight. Something terrified Luna Belle enough for her to drop the prized bowl. It shattered. She ignored the crash.

Pete Stagg's rusty pick-up truck approached and slung gravel all over creation. He careened and pitched on the loose surface not designed for speed.

Luna Belle expected him to crash into the fountain in the middle of the circle in front of the steps. A limestone Poseidon had stood sentinel there for almost three centuries. Pete now threatened the god's total destruction.

Obviously, Pete bore serious news. The custodian of that gravel surface normally protected it with his life. He would never intentionally deface the delicate surface by driving recklessly. Luna Belle stood in abject fear, daring not to guess the news, especially after the morning's debacle.

Pete's age and position as a most trusted companion kept him from such abandoned behavior. His current actions set her aflutter.

Luna Belle and he often worked side by side in the gardens of Teachall where she asked nothing of him she refused to attempt herself. He admired her willingness to get her hands dirty. Everyone at Teachall knew of Luna Belle's eagerness to help with anything except kitchen work.

Luna Belle watched Pete swerve and park, barely before he jumped from his truck and leapt up the mossy stone steps. In about three bounds he overtook the expansive veranda, but before he could knock, she opened the door. Pete's ashen countenance further upset her.

"Pete, what's the matter with you? Have you lost your mind?"

"Missy, I'm ... I ... need have a private word with you ... outside."

The hubbub roused Lolly and Lulu. After Luna Belle was outside, they crept to the front door. Lulu pushed the lever to ease the door open enough to hear.

Rose's mind ran amok as she seethed. "My Lord. Detained by a farmhand." She pulled out an emory board and started work on her fingernails. "Here we are on a tight schedule and Luna Belle fusses over some sick cow or horse. Really." Grinding away on a hangnail she continued her mumbling. "When I'm queen those mangy animals will all be banished."

Luna Belle took hold of Pete's elbow. "What happened? Where's Mose?"

"Missy, I don't know how to ... to ... Missy ... Mose left us."

"I'm afraid you don't understand. We're trying to get away for the airport. I don't have time for nonsense about some trip Mose took."

Pete shook his head. "Mose'uz shot. He's dead."

Lightening bolted through her veins. "Shot? Help me Lord." She started swaying wildly.

"Here, here, Missy. You'd better set down." Pete jumped behind her and grabbed her shoulders to guide her to a dew dampened porch rocker.

"Thank you." She shook her head. "I just about swooned."

Pete took her hand and patted the back of it. "I should'a had you set down first. It'uz my fault."

"Tell me what happened." Her numb heart throbbed.

"I'll try."

Polly noticed the twins drained expressions and faded complexions. Their pallor led her to eavesdrop for the second time that morning.

Rose became curious about the commotion and followed.

Polly poked Lolly in the back. "What's going on?"

Lulu shushed her. "Someone shot Mose."

Polly's legs went out from under her as she stumbled to the staircase and slumped.

Rose let out a sighing rumble, but went straight to Luna Belle and Pete outside.

Luna Belle looked up at Rose. "Oh, Rose? Did you hear?" Loud sobs poured from her heart. "Mose ..."

Rose slid a rocker near Luna Belle. "I heard."

"Pete, go on."

"We'uz at that big old live oak by Riggers Creek. A sink-hole formed there last summer. Me 'n Mose wanted to get it filled in before something or somebody got hurt. It'uz a good place for water moccasins to den, but it'uz cold enough early this morning to keep 'em lazy. I shore didn't want neither one of us to get snake bit."

Luna Belle fidgeted in her chair and wiped a tear from her cheek with the back of her hand.

"Last fall they'uz a flood brought in a bunch of trashy limbs and stuff. I wanted all that junk cleaned out before we filled it. Hadn't been in there long when Mose come up on his horse."

Rose crossed her ankles. "Pete, sit. You look pale."

Pete shifted his weight. "Thank you, Miss Rose, but I'm fine. Missy, sometimes he had things on his mind. Today he wanted to set and whittle.

"He'uz toting a terrible load. Said he felt sorta queer like. He just wanted to set. They's a old stump down there. Matter of fact, he helped me cut the tree last year. When that old tree fell a big split made a chair back. Last time I seen him alive he'uz setting on that stump whittling on a cedar stick."

Lolly and Lulu came on the porch with tissues.

"Tell you the truth, I don't rightly know what happened. I'uz in the hole to get a log then I got on the tractor and started out. About blowed a gasket. I heard a loud pop. Thought it was the chain that broke, but then I realized ... that pop was gunfire."

Pete rubbed fingers across his three day stubbled chin. "I didn't think no more about it. You know, it's hunting season and all. I come up out of the hole and seen Mose setting all slumped

over. When I seen he'd dropped his stick, I knew something bad
had done happened.

"I rode over on the tractor. Even that didn't stir him one bit,
so I jumped off. When I got to him, he'uz done sort of a gray
color. I jostled him but he never even grunted.

"I reached around under his arms and that's when I felt a big
hole blowed in his back. Yes ma'am, somebody shot him. Right
there by Riggers Creek. Shot him in the back, too. That's right.
Whoever killed him seems like a damned coward to me and I'll
say it to they face."

Luna Belle sat in shock and total disbelief.

Rose looked out over the vast front garden. "Is that all?"

"They's a little more. It wadn't but a few seconds after I
discovered he'd been shot when I heard another pop. Instant like
a bullet zipped right by my head. Near 'bout scared me to death.
I jumped back on the tractor and drove it around behind Mose
for cover.

"Whoever was doing the shooting hid across Riggers Creek,
but I never seen 'em. Must have been laying in the marsh grass.
I don't rightfully know where they snuck off to. When I parked
the tractor back there they wadn't no more shots.

"I called Pink. I wadn't thinking or I'd a called here because
y'all know his cell phone number, and I don't. Almost never
made that Purvis girl understand where we'uz at. Ain't real sure
she knows, yet.

"Pink called me back and knew our location right off. He led
the amblance right to us. Course, Mose was done already dead.

"I stayed 'til Pink come. Asked me a couple of questions ...
sent me here.

"Missy, I can't tell you how sorry I am. I wish he'd never
gone down there today. Mose told me something bad happened
here at the house earlier this morning. I been racking my
brain trying to figure out who all knew where we'd be at this
morning."

Rose jumped at Pete's last statement. "Who, Pete? I mean,
about y'all going to the bottoms?" Rose began fumbling with
her hair. Nervous hands kept trying to contain a little fallen curl
annoying her forehead.

Luna Belle ignored Rose then pulled herself together. "Pete, thank you for letting me know. I'm so sorry you had to see and deal with all that. I know this has been a terrible shock. Is there anything I can do for you?"

"That's right silly of you Missy. It's me needs to help you. Shore ain't the other way around."

Polly joined them on the porch, where no one knew what to do.

Luna Belle pushed herself up out of the rocker. "Look at us ninnies in this damp air. All of you, get inside where we can at least warm up." She held her composure until finally the dam broke. She sobbed into her tissue.

"I expect you need some time to get yourself together, Missy. If it's all right with you, I'll be going now." Pete turned and headed back to the creek bottoms.

Lolly tried to take Pete's hand but he refused. "Pete, come in with us. You've had a shock."

"Appreciate it but I'uz going back to see if I can learn anything else. If you need me I'll stay, but I ain't got no use for setting and moping."

"Thank you Pete. Ask Pink to come here soon as he can?" Rose said as he walked toward the steps.

"Yes'um, glad to." He hitched his britches and stooped to grab a dried leaf from the veranda floor. Crushing it in his calloused hands, his eyes welled. He walked away with his head lowered.

The weight of the world crushed Luna Belle as a rank feeling of desolation overwhelmed her. She was alone for the first time in her life. Within the span of a few hours her life had gone from excited gaiety to a joyless pit causing her to weep over the tragic irony: a sink-hole, a death, a funeral, an abysmal depression. Her best laid plans—shot in the back.

Rose guided Luna Belle into the first east parlor. "Luna Belle, what are we going to do?"

Luna Belle looked for the nearest seat as her knees weakened. "Oh, Rose, Pinki's wedding. We can't miss our appointment with Emile. We simply must collect ourselves— see if we can't create a plan. I'd call and reschedule, but he's impossible. There's simply no other way around this whole affair

… y'all must go on without me."

Mordecai broke his silence and snuffed back tears. "Missy, before you change your plans altogether, please, allow me. I've been through these things previously and—" Mordecai's voice broke with emotion and took on a hollow wail. "When … when the Colonel died—" Mordecai turned his head to hide his tears. "If you'll allow me … I have a few suggestions that I … I hope will prove beneficial to your plight."

Luna Belle rose to hug her dear friend. "Of course, thank you Mordecai. You know Mose loved you."

"I know he did, I loved him as well. He's been my little brother all his life." Mordecai cried openly then helped Luna Belle sit again.

Rose squinted and pushed her hands down her thighs to straighten her skirt.

Mordecai sat on the edge of a *bergère* near Luna Belle and gently laid his hands over hers. "I understand your trip's importance to our dear little Pinki." He smiled at Rose. "Perhaps the other ladies might go on to Florida today and leave you behind to finalize some arrangements. If so, you might meet them in Manhattan Wednesday night. Thursday's fitting can proceed unimpeded."

Luna Belle sat up straight. "I can't go off and leave Mose. It's impossible."

Rose sank.

Mordecai cocked his head to one side and smiled. "What if he were in the capitol rotunda? After all, he must lie in state somewhere. The people need a chance to say their last farewells, and he certainly deserves a fitting tribute. See?"

Rose jumped from her seat. "Mordecai, you're a genius. She reached down and hugged Luna Belle. "I don't mean to push you or insist, but Mordecai's marvelous plan will work. Who cares if you're here or there? Mose served his country as a federal judge, so he deserves the peoples' respectful farewells."

Lulu came over to also give Luna Belle a consoling hug. "Bless your heart. You know I believe they found your answer. Want me to call Scooter?"

Luna Belle sat shellshocked. She nodded in agreement without thinking.

5

Hold the Curtain

Pinki Tiddie had spent years developing elaborate ideas for her nuptials. The girl had set her heart on Teachall's grandeur for the entire affair. In her mind there was no other place for the splendor and audacious extravaganza she desired.

By nature, Pinki lived a very shy life, but she seemed to have sprouted a whole new personality specifically for her wedding. The entire Canasta Club buzzed over the amazing puzzlement of the girl's transformation from a wall-flower to an open lily. Lulu and Lolly privately discussed whether the newness would eventually wear off before the fete. If it did, Pinki would revert into her more accustomed shyness and ruin the ceremony, perhaps the entire party.

Luna Belle wanted the young maiden's plans to proceed successfully, but she foresaw an entire series of hurdles. None of them appeared pleasant. Banishing further disaster became her immediate goal for the morning, as she had held enough misery in her lap for one day.

Polly came in Luna Belle's bedroom where she had taken to a chaise with a cool moist towel draped over her eyes. Polly's aimless scurrying seemed foreign compared to her usual deliberate movements.

Luna Belle peeked from under her towel. "Mose'll rise from death's bed if I disappoint Pinki. He took his promise to her seriously. I know we've continually spoiled the girl. Why stop now?"

Polly wrung her hands. "What about them women downstairs? They ain't leaving. Course I knows Miss Pinki's wedding need to be seen about and all. Law, she sweet. Most likable child they is. Um-hmm. Good thing too 'cause she sho ain't purdy. Bless her darlin' heart…. Why didn't they ever fix that nose o' hers? I knows for a fact, Dr. Deamon offer several times to take her piggish look away for nothing."

Luna Belle again lifted a corner of her towel to cut her eyes at Polly. "Polly, that's awful. But I shan't argue. Pinki never seemed to mind the way her nose turns up into an atrocious little snoot." Luna Belle smiled and recovered her eyes.

"You'z right. Without a doubt, Pinki's got one of the most adorable personalities they is. She always smiling. Her face glow with happy, don't it? But, Law, she could root turnips."

Luna Belle left the towel in place. "That sweet personality is why she's been named Miss Sunshine for three years straight at the Pirate's Landing Beauty Pageant. The judges always seem to reward her disposition. They find it impossible to overlook her positive spirit."

"Um-hmm."

The annual gala event sponsored by Pirate's Landing's own Terrytine's Tuxedoes and Taxidermy provided a useful way to promote formal wear. Pinki even created Terrytine's catchy slogan:

We Stuff Shirts …
Hides Too!

The black tie affair occurred annually at the dank local armory. Several times, Terrytine's attempt to schedule it for Teachall's ballroom floundered because of his own stupidity.

Dolt Terrytine insisted on having his event the first Saturday night in November, far too close to the Grande Masque on Halloween's Eve. Teachall's scheduling of that major social event for over one hundred fifty years was written in stone. Luna Belle refused having her schedule stuffed by a taxidermist.

Luna Belle rubbed lotion into her elbows. "Pinki envisions herself grandly descending the front hall's sweeping staircase, so she insisted we engage the Savannah Symphony to accompany her descent. I asked Mose why Pinki wanted such extravagance and that man looked at me like I'd lost my mind. 'Girl looks like Pinki lands a man, she wants to show off. I don't blame her … do you?' 'Nough said."

Polly giggled and took the lotion back to the dressing table. "Mr. B always knowed how to lay it out plain."

A deep sigh escaped Luna Belle's lungs. "Polly, Polly, Polly, I ought to stay home and grieve like a proper Southern lady."

"You needs to do whatever fills yo' heart. That's what I says."

"I don't think I could stand it if I let those biddies outshine me at Pinki's wedding. Lord 'a mercy I'm a vain conceited shrew, but it was I who engaged Yvez. Besides, Rose will screw it all up if I don't go. Then we can sit back and watch Pinki's dreams burn into an ash heap."

"Sounds like you'z done made up yo mind."

"You know well as I do. No readymade gown exists capable of flattering Pinki. I swan, the girl needs a talented designer. Somebody with a deep understanding of the near opacity required of her veil. Can you believe I said that?"

Polly giggled then shook her head. "Sounds to me like Mr. B done rub off on *you*. Ain't no way you can stays here. You's got to go to New York. You wants me to go too?"

"I'd love for you to go, but I think you better stay here and fend off intruders. Of course, you're right. Somebody's got to pet and pamper Yvez's grand ego. He'll do what I ask with a wink and a nod. Then there's always that extra five or ten grand cash I slip him for just such considerations—that never hurts, either."

"How many things he made for you over the years?"

"Bunches. Those silly women can't make him purr. He's difficult because he's so talented. He can't help it. That's what makes him Yvez."

"How come his stuff ain't in none of the stores nowhere we goes?"

"He's far too much the couturier. Hasn't even had a runway show in ages. He depends on his reclusive clientele's happiness to generate his work, and he stays busy."

"Um-hmm, I speck he do."

"Don't forget, Mose involved Cartier in this too. He took four emeralds there in November of last year to have them set for me to wear to the wedding."

"Tells me about them stones. I knows I seen em, but I loves hearing you tells all about em. They gonna look so pretty on you." Polly sat on the opposite chaise to hear the rest of Luna Belle's story. "Besides, you done told me that since you'uz wearnin' them emruls, you'z gonna lets me wear yo grand sapphire choker." Polly laughed.

"Polly, you're as bad as I am. The emeralds: A fifty-two carat pear cut for an asymmetrical necklace, a thirty-seven carat oval for a tiara and a matched pair of twelve carat emerald cuts for ear pendants. He also demanded Cartier furnish over one hundred carats of diamonds to complete the pieces. Oh. Polly, I can't wait. Mose told them to spare no expense. That's one reason I loved him."

"And you'z gonna gets to see all that this week, ain't you?"

"Yes. The necklace arrived for Yvez to work around. He wants to see it draped on my neck—see how it wants to hang. We both know it will have a mind of its own.

"Yvez initially pitched a hissy over the constraint of a silly piece of jewelry. Then I showed him the stones. He couldn't get to his design board quick enough. Yvez even collaborated directly with Cartier's chief designer, and I really think the men enjoyed their joint efforts."

"I 'members hearing you talk on the phone about the color of your gown. Law … I thought I dies when you tells him you didn't wants to look like no tacky Christmas ornament."

"That's right. The kook wanted to put me in tomato red silk taffeta. He did omit the organdy petticoat, but I'd'a still rattled like a maraca and shined like an out of place whore in church." Luna Belle laughed and removed the towel from her eyes as she sat up. "He didn't want to give that up, either. He called me several times. I finally had enough and—"

"I 'members, you said, 'Ain't you done heard what I done said 'bout all this, I ain't gonna be no damned fool at Pinki's wedding." Both women laughed hysterically.

"Polly I can't stay home. If I do Yvez's motormouth will ruin everything. He'll spoil my jewelry surprise. I simply must take Mordecai's advice to heart and get up off this chaise, pull myself together, and get on with life. Besides, what better place to stash a stiff than the statehouse?"

"Now that's what I'z talking about. Um-hmm. Besides, Governor done called and made all the arrangements. Everything falling into place like it'uz supposed to be the way it is. Now ain't that something?"

"Yes, I may even have to rethink my private name for the Governor."

"You means … Lardass?" Polly jiggled her hips with her hands parallel to the floor.

"Yes. Although, I always say it with utmost respect." Both women sputtered their laughter all over the room.

After much cajoling, the twins finally left for Florida. Luna Belle amassed her courage and went to Mayhew and Gober Funeral Home alone. Rose stayed on Cow Bell Island to help her sister-in-law and insisted on tagging along, but Luna Belle protested and refused her company.

"Rose, dear. I don't want to hurt your feelings. I realize Mose was your brother, but I simply must decide these things for myself."

Luna Belle allowed Polly to drive her to Mayhew and Gober Funeral Home where Steve Mayhew greeted her and helped her out of her Bentley.

He started, "We expect to have His Honor's body back from the crime lab in Atlanta within the next couple of days."

"What? Why did you send him there?"

"It's standard protocol in a case like this."

Polly heard Luna Belle mutter, "Incompetents." She took her purse from off the seat. "Standard protocol, the dog's hind leg. There's not one standard bone in my husband's corpse. How dare you deface his memory with such nonsense?"

Mayhew cleared his throat and adjusted the knot of his tie. Sweat began to bead on his forehead. "I'm sorry, Mrs. Black. Sheriff Tiddie sent him there. We really had nothing to do with it. I'm sure he'd be delighted to help you with this."

"I have no intention of talking with Pink. Maybe Justice Ellmozza of the United States Supreme Court can help me. Believe me, I'm not done with this matter."

Lonny Gober came into the consultation room. "Miss Luna

Belle, I couldn't help but overhear your protests. Please accept our apologies for any inconvenience we have caused you. I assure you that we intend to do everything in our power to make you happy."

"I'm sitting here seriously considering firing the both of you before you're hired, but there's no need for me to fume, is there? I've lived here long enough to realize you're my only choice. Shut up and show me a coffin worthy of my husband's remains."

Gober found a solid bronze coffin with nautical gilt handles in Jacksonville, and he showed Luna Belle a picture from the internet.

"It's absolutely ghastly … gaudy … it's perfect." She clapped her hands together. "Polly look, it is absolutely hideous."

"I sees that."

Luna Belle pointed toward the lining. "Yes. This one will work nicely if you just change this lining to a red silk dupioni. Don't you boys think you can pass off any synthetic crap on me. You hear?"

Gober rolled his eyes. "Fine."

Luna Belle squinted. "I saw that but I'll pretend I didn't. Oh! Have an anchor embroidered with metallic gold thread in the lid. Mose'll come after me when I reach the other side if I don't get things perfect."

Grease almost dripped from Gober's lips. "As you please."

"I want a grand decorous affair, but I have neither time nor inclination to plan it. That's what I'm paying you for. Isn't it?"

"Yes ma'am." Mayhew chirped then turned his face to the wall and sneered.

After Luna Belle's visit, an entire throng of participants called the mortuary. Speakers, singers, musicians, and choirs all clamored to be placed on the important schedule. They queued for a chance to pay homage to an illustrious dignitary. The little rumor about national TV coverage brought them out of the woodwork.

Luna Belle arrived back at Teachall exhausted and ready for collapse. "Polly, please call Gloria and tell her I want the

Glorious Black Swan to be in charge of all the flowers in Atlanta. Do you think she'll mind carting flowers from here all the way up there?"

"She be honored. Besides, she know not to fuss, or I turns her over my lap and gives her what-for. She may be growed up, but she still my little girl."

Mordecai told Luna Belle of Gober's call. "The crime lab needs to detain Mose's body two additional days."

Luna Belle dusted his lapel. "At first it upset me, but my selfish side shines through. At least that gives me more time in New York."

"I've taken the liberty to rearrange your flight plans. The twins will fly back to Cow Bell Island and pick you and Missy Rose up day after tomorrow."

"Thank you, Mordecai. How does anyone plan a funeral without you? I know some people must be left on their own with no help at all. I don't see how they manage."

"Missy, most folk don't have to deal with an important dignitary like the judge. That makes a tremendous difference."

"I guess most women cancel their shopping trips when their husbands die, don't they?"

Mordecai bowed and flourished his hand. "I remain ignorant of most women's habits."

The four women journeyed to Manhattan together. They filled their flight with strange nit picking and terse words. Lolly and Lulu continued at each other about that worrisome warehouse.

The frazzled women arrived at the Plaza Hotel ready for much needed rest from their emotional and physical exhaustion. Luna Belle's compatriots had almost constantly bickered, creating tension between their exasperating temperaments. Maybe the situation of Mose's impending funeral worked against Luna Belle's nerves. Maybe the others acted no differently than usual and she had become more sensitized to their foolishness because of her emotional depletion.

That first evening in New York, Rose insisted the Canasta Club have cocktails at the Russian Tea Room while a dead judge quietly occupied a box in the Georgia State Capitol. Luna Belle sipped her sazerac then massaged her aching temples. Rose sat across and motioned for Lulu to console her.

"Why did I abandon my husband? This is ridiculous."

Rose craned her neck then snarled her lip. "Luna Belle, my brother departed this life. We need to concentrate on Pinki's wedding. Let's hear no more of all this nonsense."

Lulu shrugged her shoulders and held her hands in a questioning pose. "Yeah, who's better company, him or us?" she peered over the top of her red butterfly eyewear.

Luna Belle smiled and raised her glass. "You old rascal, you always diffuse tensions. You're right. Ching Ching." After another sip, she teared.

Lolly took a lace hanky from her purse. Reaching across the table to tuck it in Luna Belle's hand, she knocked over a wine glass. In about five seconds two of the staff dismantled the entire tableau. Within another thirty to forty seconds everything from the table cloth up reappeared.

As the two left, Rose laid her hand atop Luna Belle's. "Now that's service." Rose patted the back of Luna Belle's hand. "You'd better shape up, or we'll ship you out."

Luna Belle rolled her eyes causing them all to burst into laughter, creating a much more affable atmosphere.

Rose first expressed her excitement. "We *do* need to shape up girls. There's so much to accomplish to get ready for Pinki's wedding and I want us to be sure and get as much done as we can while we're up here. I can hardly stand myself. It's only one sleep away from getting to meet the famous reclusive designer."

Thursday morning, on schedule, the group went to the atelier of Emile Yvez. He took each lady into her own private dressing room and left her with fabric swatches for consideration before he turned his attention to the doyenne, Luna Belle.

He held a large swatch aloft and fluttered it. "Look'a at this'a beautiful green'a *peau de soie* from Milano. I think'a I swath'a you in crisp'a asymmetrical pleated'a splendor. It'a no rattle like'a the taffeta." He winked.

He helped her out of her dress then fastened the necklace on her. He held the sketches beside her to admire in the mirror's reflection. She smiled.

"You mustn't let my jewelry secret out of the bag. That would ruin everything." Luna Belle slyly slipped a hefty stack of one hundred dollar bills into the designer's greasy palm.

He turned his back to her and in a moment turned back to return a few of the bills. "I make'a the special'a favor for'a the grieving'a widow." Again he winked then tweaked his brows twice.

"I'a cancel'a the afternoon'a appointment and go with'a you ladies to the'a Bergdorf'a Goodman. There we'a select appropriate'a funeral attire. I wish'a we had'a time to design and create, but alas, it's'a not'a possible."

At Bergdorf Goodman, Luna Belle settled on the first ensemble he selected. "Oh. Yvez, this is absolute funereal perfection."

Rose insisted on creating a problem. Her inverted triangle figure proved far more difficult to fit. Her mood became unbearable and she grew down right mean.

Lolly stood before a full length mirror and glanced back and forth between her reflection and Lulu's. Her face brightened as if a novel idea had fallen on her head from Heaven itself. "Let's dress alike."

"That might be fun, we haven't done that since we left Draketown."

Luna Belle took her outfit and headed to a dressing room. "I don't think I've ever seen you two do that."

Lulu clapped her hands together and smiled. "Mother dressed us identically all throughout our humble childhood, so naturally we grew to resent it. I guess it's time for full circle."

Yvez looked them over and grandly threw his head back. "We shall'a put'a you in'a the darkest'a chocolate imaginable."

Lolly raised her hand as if to stop traffic. "Unheard of. We must wear black."

Yvez pulled iridescent copper and coffee silk taffeta suits. They relented when they saw themselves modeling the stylishly appropriate ensembles. A sumptuous pair of chocolate black-tipped mink jackets didn't hurt their feelings either.

They looked fabulous for a couple of scrawny, short, pasty white women with outdated henna-rinsed hair. Wide brimmed veiled boleros, kid gloves, and pumps further dazzled their eyes.

Yvez found Chocolate bugle bead clutches to ice the cookies' cosmopolitan outfits.

Lolly pulled her checkbook out and grimaced. "Irvin's going to kill me when he finds out I've spent sixty-seven thousand dollars on an outfit for a funeral." He constantly complained about the huge piles of money it took to keep her in the style to which her twin sister had become accustomed.

After trying everyone's patience Rose settled for a dress with a matching jacket of black wool crepe trimmed in charcoal coronation cord arabesques.

Yvez leaned into Luna Belle. "Lovely on'a the hanger … wasn't it?"

6

The Perfect Accessory

The evening's plan stared them in their faces even though they had arrived back on Cow Bell Island completely exhausted. The Black's private jet succumbed to a heavy winter fog and couldn't leave New York when they had planned. Luna Belle didn't have a lot of time to dress before the first guests arrived for the wake.

Luna Belle dug in her purse.

"Where—"

"Missy, you need some help getting ready?"

"I can't find my little gold pill box."

Polly's countenance fell. "You needs to takes one of them before the wake? You'z gonna be up late tonight. They's tomorrow too. I'uz just thinking bout the last time you take one of them 'fore a party?"

"I'm so tired. It might make me feel better."

"Will tonight. Tomorrow at the funeral, you wants to stummle around like a dope fiend? I don't thinks you does... does you?"

Luna Belle always rose early, but not after tying one on. Trying to wake a dopey, hungover Luna Belle Black was about as much fun as pulling out your own fingernails.

Polly grinned. "Missy? You know how Mr. B wasn't good at fixing things?"

Luna Belle stopped digging. She looked in her mirror and said. "Of course, Polly. He always created agony for himself, didn't he?"

"Um-hmm. He did. I'uz thinking about his thumb. Can you calls up that yarn?"

"Refresh my memory."

"A nail work itself loose in the bottom of the mailbox. Mr. B snag his thumb on it and made hisself bleed a little. Course that made him mad as a bullfrog being chased by a wadin' bird. He run to the toolshed then back to the mailbox with a hammer and a pair of pliers."

"I'm not too sure I've ever heard this story." Luna Belle poured herself a healthy shot of bourbon from the decanter on her dressing table.

Polly reached into her apron for a packet of cheese and crackers she kept for such occasions. Polly handed them over Luna Belle's shoulder then smiled in the mirror. Luna Belle gave Polly a little knowing grin.

Polly brushed Luna Belle's hair and continued her story. "He tore in and caught his thumb between the hammer and the lid. The hammer handle snap when he pulls back hard. It tore his thumb nail 'most clean off ... leave it hanging by a lil piece o' raw flesh. Um-hmm.

"He come running. I seen that bloody thang and 'bout faint, but I has t' help. If I passes out, he be without no help a'tall. So I took a deep breath and march him in de kitchen to rinch off his hand under the faucet. That's when I really seen the troubles he'uz in.

"I says, 'well you done it this time. Kerosene ain't gonna fix this. We gone has to go to the doctor.' He didn't wanna go see no doctor ... can't say's I blame him knowing the ribbing he'z gonna get from him and all. You know how old Jack Deamon is? Um-hmm."

Luna Belle smiled.

"I wraps that whole hand up good with some clean gauze. Then I twist a lil Sara Ann wrap over it t' try and keep it from bleeding more'n it already had. He yelped a time or two, but I tole him I din't want him bleeding all over the car.

"I set him in the car and crammed his hand in a plastic Piggly Wiggly grocery sack and laid a towel or two on his lap. Then I tells him to set still and behave."

Luna Belle chuckled, looked toward her bourbon but changed her mind. "This is a classic Mose tale, and can't anybody tell one like you."

Polly twisted dark locks into a low figure eight. "I drives us to town and wents around back'a the doctor's office so ain't no rednecks in de waiting room gonna gawk. Slip in the back do' and seen Miss Cherie, you know, Miss Ida Lea's granddaughter? She'uz his new nurse back then. You 'member that?"

"Of course. Isn't she the sweetest thing you ever saw?" Luna Belle relaxed.

"Um-hmm. She sweet all right. Anyhow, she clean a room close to the back do' and told me to slip him in there. Doctor come right in."

Deepening her voice Polly tried to mock Jack Deamon. "'My, my, Mose,' old Deamon say, 'What has you done this time?'"

"Mr. B look over top of his glasses, you know the way he do?"

Luna Belle nodded.

"Doc, he cut away at dat bloody gauzy passel a troubles. He look over at me and say, 'This your handy work Polly?' I tells him, 'yes t'is.' He grin big. 'That Sara Ann wrap a good idea.' I give him a big old wink. 'Um-hmm. Keeps him from slinging bloody slop all over the inside of the car. They'z enough to cleans back to the house.' Dr. Deamon sorta giggle like. When he unwraps enough to where he seen inside he laugh his fool head off."

"He's so hateful." Luna Belle said.

"I know that's right. He a good man, though. Don't mean nothing by it."

"You're right, but he can still get your goat."

"Um-hmm. Yes'um, he can. Mr. B look at him sorta stern like. 'Shut up and gets busy. I told Polly if you said something smart-ass, I'uz gonna lay into you like a house afire.'

"Dr. Deamon keep on laughing and a working at the same time. 'I'z not scared of no man with no gimp thumb. Besides, I know you ain't gonna play no golf for awhile.'

'Now I know that hurt when you done it, Mose. And bads as I hates to tell you, we's gonna has to take that nasty thang off a yo thumb.'

'I'uz afraid of that. I know that's gonna hurt worser than it did to commence with.'

'Sho ain't gon be no picnic.' Deamon keep laughing.

"Missy, the doctor give me a big wink before he tell Mr. B that if he deaden it, the shot be worser than the deed. It be quick and near painless.

"He get hisself a pair of them long tweezers what locks theyseffs onto thangs. You know the kind I'z talking about. He grab that floppy thumbnail with them tweezers and latches on to that bloody thang real good. Mr. B look at him hard and yelped in pain. 'You sure 'nough ain't gonna give me no shot?' 'Mose. I done told you the shot hurt worser than the deed.'"

Luna Belle hung on every word now. She rearranged herself on the boudoir stool and watched Polly's face.

"'I can't believe you is gonna just pulls it off.'

'I'z not. You is.' With that old Doc reach in his pocket and take out a cigarette lighter. He light it and hold it under Mr. B's thumb. Course Mr. B jek his hand away. Deamon left with the tweezers and that bloody thumb nail, laughing his fool head off.

"Mr. B come up off a that little old stool thang he'uz settin on. 'Why din' you give me that shot? You nothing but a damned jack-ass. Don't you done know what you is?'

"Doctor snicker and flips his lighter back in his pocket. 'I'uz scared I might burns you bad if I numbs yo thumb up first.'"

Both women howled so hard Polly sought a roost. On the bed she laid back and draped her wrist over her forehead.

Luna Belle supported herself with her hands folded across her abdomen. She hadn't laughed this hard in months.

Polly tried to finish her story through her laughter. "And you know Missy? Yo husband so shock, all he say were," Polly leaned down to whisper in Luna Belle's ear. "'Shit.'"

Luna Belle screamed and almost broke her ribs from doubling over in joy.

"Um-hmm. He gets hisself to the do' and walk out. We had to catch him so old Doc could wrop up his thumb. But the best part be, Dr. Deamon give him that shot fo he wrop it up."

This brought on more guffaws.

"Polly, you have to stop. I'm going to wet myself."

"Then you gets yoseff up off'a that stool. I don't wanna cleans no pee-pee out'a no petit point pillow."

Both women became hysterical.

"I means it now. You get on to the bafroom."

Luna Belle tried to regain her composure. "All the food ready and laid out?"

Polly raised her brows in disdain. "Um-hmm. Miss Lulu call and say she brings a cake and stuff. I has to get out serving pieces once I see what tis. You need any more help getting ready?"

"No. Thank you for lifting my spirits. You're always here for me."

Polly smiled and nodded.

"I best get on now ... you needs me ... call. Okay?"

Luna Belle nodded and smiled. The wake seemed easier. She picked up her bourbon, but she didn't take a drink. Instead she smiled and put it back on her dressing table.

Polly was leaving the room. "Wants me to get you some ice?"

"No. I'm not having another swallow all evening; besides, I don't need it. I might enjoy my friends and relatives better if I remain sober.

"Relatives ... I forgot about them. Maybe a few sips here and there to numb their nagging about the estate. I heard enough of that already when Lulu and Rose bantered it over, under, around, and through the whole time we were in New York. I refuse their rushing me. Their words work in reverse."

She applied her lipstick and looked at Polly who had stepped back into the room with something in her hand.

"Look what I finds on the foyer table."

Polly held Luna Belle's little gold pill box with the pearl on the lid.

"Thank you, Polly, wonder how it ended up there?"

"I don't know. Reckon you laid it there when you come in a while ago."

"How in the devil did that pillbox land on the foyer table? Maybe I need to stop this foolishness. I need to hide them away for a few days. Where? Some inconvenient spot? Ah. The wall safe. Where else?"

Polly left the room.

"Combination? Combination? Let's see. I know there are four safes in this house." Mose taught her to open them all; however, she usually depended on him and he rarely objected.

She racked her brain until it dawned on her that it was Mose's birthday divided into two integer sets from the back to the front.

For some reason Mose loved numbers. She needed to jot it down. She took an eyebrow pencil off her dressing table and wrote the date in the palm of her hand. Going to the other side of the room, she removed an old portrait of some long dead ancestor.

She had no idea of the lady's identity. It didn't matter. Luna Belle never looked at the painting with intent. It had never been anything more than a decorative object.

Her having no regard for their heritage always annoyed the entire Black clan. She'd almost listened to their history, but never really bothered. Once she learned of their pirate heritage all her interest seemingly flew out the window on the wings of a protective angel.

The painting's weight impressed when she removed it from its hanger. Its foundation was a solid wood panel which accounted for its heft. She laid it on a table nearby and inspected it in earnest. How had she overlooked so gorgeous a young lady?

She initially ignored a curious inscription on the back then rubbed her fingers into the carved wood.

It read:

Juliana Jiminez Rosita Consuela Cordoba,
Contessa de Juarez e Montalban,
Esposa de Edward Teach Drummond,
Viscount of Avery.

All these years she had lived in the room with Mose's old relative and never looked at her. Why hadn't he mentioned this gorgeous damsel with the hauntingly beautiful visage?

She stared into the Contessa's intriguingly deep, dark eyes. An elaborate carved tortoise shell comb pinned her raven-colored shimmering hair. Luna Belle never before saw one so covered in intricate carving. The comb supported a black lace mantilla of rare re-embroidered needle lace showing orange blossoms with tiny black pearl embellishments, the sort afforded by royalty. It draped her shoulders and framed her décolletage.

Luna Belle imagined wearing the tight laced bodice of heavier black lace of the same exquisite quality. The motifs appeared larger, roses and leaves studded with the same black seed pearls forming the stamen of the overly mature blossoms.

The blown-open roses must represent death. The lace fit low on her bosom and showed off a string of intriguingly large black pearls.

She continued her study of the painting until her eyes became satisfied with the piece. She laid it back on the table and for some reason turned it face down this time.

Under the carved engraving the raking light revealed a faded ink inscription. Something in Spanish. She decided to translate it later.

She had never before explored the contents of the safe. The small amount inside it amazed her:

Some old parchments rolled up for later perusal.

A tired diamond tiara she'd worn to her first masked ball at Teachall.

A flat, tatty, black velvet jewelry box that didn't interest her much; however, she removed it out of curiosity. She opened it and there laid the black pearls from the painting she admired.

She cried and held them far from her as she spun around. "These will look splendid with my outfit tomorrow." Her eyes focused intently on a stick pin adorned with a matching Tahitian pearl. It held a parchment to the lid's lining, but her curiosity over the necklace's condition urged her on.

She took the necklace from the box and tugged on it from end to end. She didn't want to risk the string's breaking. It seemed secure. She left the stick pin attached to the box lining holding the parchment since she had no desire to use it.

The quality of these large pearls told her they were natural Tahitian. Not any natural Tahitian pearls either, the most beautiful ones Luna Belle had ever feasted her eyes upon.

She saw a similar string at Sotheby's back in the fall while in New York for the opera. Oddly, Mose showed absolutely no interest in them. Later she learned the pearls went for over seven million dollars. Seeing these beauties explained things. He didn't want to buy any more, but why had he never mentioned these?

She turned the portrait back over and pieced the puzzle together in her mind. This must be the infamous Teachall Contessa in mourning attire for Blackbeard's funeral. She knew of their marriage, but failed to learn any further details.

How appropriate that she found them. "Oh. Mose. You won't believe our luck. I'm wearing these beauties tomorrow to honor you and your dear Contessa."

Returning the necklace's box she laid the pill box atop it to honor the find, closed the safe, rehung the portrait, and slipped the pearls in a pocket. She sashayed herself over to her dressing table and situated herself on the stool almost to the moment when Polly walked back into the room.

"Missy?"

"Yes?—Oh, Polly. I must show you what I—" The door bell interrupted her mid sentence.

Polly grimaced and nodded. "Now, who you reckon that'd be? They early ain't they?"

"I expect it's Lulu and Lolly. They said they'd come early … afraid they'd both fall asleep for the night if they didn't come on."

"Um-hmm."

"Polly, what did you want?"

"Nothing I'z going to tell you dat I'z going downstairs. You need anything else?"

"No, thank you Polly. See who that is. If it's the girls, send them up."

7

Stumping? Now ... Really!

As Luna Belle finished tucking in the last bits of her hair she heard Mordecai tell Lulu and Lolly to go upstairs. Polly welcomed them from the mezzanine.

"Y'all come right on up here. Missy about ready. Y'all can helps her finish while's I go on to the kitchen.—I hope y'all both feeling sassy."

"For the circumstances we're doing fine and dandy." Lulu answered for both ladies. Strange. Under normal conditions she remained quiet around Polly. She raised an eyebrow as she passed the pair.

Polly never grew a relationship with the governor's wife, Lulu. It amazed Luna Belle. Lolly always played the bigger snob, but Polly and she shared a natural affinity for each other. Maybe it was the rhyme of their names. Luna Belle didn't know. It never occurred to her that Polly despised Governor Lardass and Lulu simply suffered the fallout of Polly's disdain.

"How are y'all managing? I know you've been busy with all the cooking and getting ready for this hullaballoo." Lolly talked now, putting Polly at ease.

As the ladies passed Polly on the landing, Lolly leaned close and whispered, "I expect you and Mordecai enjoyed the house alone these last few days."

Polly almost spoke aloud. "It be okay, all 'sept'n Mordecai lost most of his spunk. Um-hmm."

They all giggled like school girls.

Before the three separated, Lolly patted Polly's shoulder. "Polly, you won't do."

"Um-hmm. That's what they tells me. Besides, what would y'all'ses do if I did?—Y'all brought stuff I needs to tend to downstairs?"

Lulu raised her nose high in the air. "I brought a few things. I gave Mordecai a coconut cake and left a couple of other things on the dining room table. I hope that's all right."

"Glad for the help."

"I have to confess." Lulu shook her head and raised her shoulders. "None of it's homemade. You know we just got back. I called Scooter and asked him to go by the Jitney Jungle, and you know how men shop in a grocery store ... no telling what's in those bags."

Polly nodded.

"I didn't even take it out of the bags. I hope you won't mind. I hate those horrible plastic containers, but I know you'll fix it up pretty for me. You always do."

Polly again nodded and smeared on a sardonic smile.

Lulu didn't stop. "I know your homemade fixings are better, but I couldn't come empty-handed."

"We'z always glad to has yo' help."

Once she turned away, Polly frowned at Scooter Thadeu's grab bag surprises. If she *accidentally* forgot, she paid when he blustered.

"Where's those Cheetos I brought, Polly ... the pretzels?"

Most folks coming to this wake attributed all the food to the Teachall kitchen. Having ghastly things on Polly's table insulted her pride. Whenever Mose pulled a shady stunt with groceries, Polly put her foot down, but the governor was not so well trained.

Several years earlier Luna Belle and Polly went all out to make a beautiful couple's shower for Margaret Thadeu and her affianced, Randall Hillier. The governor's daughter demanded the finest of their finery. Polly and the entire household staff polished silver, soaked linens, ironed, rolled the tablecloths so they wouldn't have creases, cooked, cleaned, and washed windows until the house sparkled.

Gloria Swann filled every room downstairs with unbelievable arrangements of white tulips, open tea roses, and white lilies from the Glorious Black Swan. She ordered five hundred specially grown French tulips in September, the year before. If Margaret, Luna Belle's favorite god child, wanted French tulips, tulips she would have. There could be no consideration of the trouble or expense. Gloria fretted over the off-season flowers for weeks. When they came, they glowed. Margaret's dream came true and more.

The party, scheduled in June, required Pete Stagg spend months getting the lawns and gardens manicured. He positioned trellises with sweet smelling Confederate Jasmine beside the doors opening onto the verandas. Planted in huge Italian sandstone urns, they created an arbor surrounding the doors, bathing them in fragrance.

Cape Jessamines lined the walks' boxed hedges. Their perfume filled the warm evening air before the guests became further bathed in the Jasmine's scent.

Pete planted and nurtured white hydrangeas under all the live oak trees on the expansive lawns. He bordered these with white fancy leaf caladiums.

The party, planned for a full moon, glowed from the whiteness under the Spanish moss hanging from the arms of the mighty oaks. Further illumination came from candle-lit Japanese lanterns suspended in the boughs.

Margaret wanted tea punch, one of Polly's specialities. Made of home canned grape juice, Earl Grey tea, Champagne, orange zest, and a little secret spike. The sensational beverage did Polly proud every time.

Luna Belle sat with Polly while the two discussed a menu for the event. "Polly, I know this is a shower, but the men are invited too. They'll come hungry. Let's have roast tenderloin of beef in angel biscuits. I'll leave the rest to you."

With all this preparation and finery, the governor of the Great State of Georgia, the bride's father, boomed before the entire assembly. "Polly, where are the potato chips I brought?"

Luna Belle insisted Scooter only ribbed Polly for fun. "He does that to you to watch you react. He'll stop his foolishness when you start ignoring him."

"I hears what you is saying, but why he does me like that? I'z always good to him. He know how much trouble I goes to every time he come to the house. Old Lardass. Um-hmm."

Polly puckered her lips and slapped her palm with a fist the instant she walked into the dining room and saw her previously perfectly appointed table. Several plastic grocery bags sprawled on top of her immaculate trays of garnished *hors d'œuvre* and *amuse-bouche*. The sight sent a surge of rage all over Polly.

Polly gathered wily plastic bags in a mad dash. About the time she corralled them Mordecai came to give her a hand.

"Why you ain't done already took this junk to the kitchen?" Polly snapped.

"I took a *styrofoam* cake sprinkled with coconut first. *Unfortunately*, I dropped it on the floor." He pinched Polly's posterior, grinned big, and winked at his wife.

"Thank you."

"For what?" Mordecai cocked his head.

"You knows what for. For throwing that crap in the flo. Ain't no telling if that really is cake, or when that sorry-ass piece of som'n were bake to begins with."

"You know he's only trying to get under your skin."

"We needs to get this stuff out'a here before somebody else rang that doorbell." Polly fidgeted over the junk. "Mordecai, I ought to be ashamed of myself. After all, Lulu come from moonshiners and hillbillies. Not fine, proper folk like the ones from Pirate's Landing." She giggled. "My Lord has mercy on me. I'z turned myseff into as big a snob as they is."

"Pol-ly! Lulu and Lolly were never hillbillies, their family were upstanding bootleggers." Mordecai chuckled.

Polly cackled. "I loves my life. I loves you and I 'specially loves being who I is. Living here in all this finery suit me just fine and dandy. I don't care who it belong to. I knows where I come from. I'z thankful everyday for Mr. B rescuing me. They's all scoundrels, but thank God for pirates. Um-hmm."

Mordecai beamed. "I love you so much. You light my candle."

"Get out'a here, you old goat." Polly bumped her hips against his.

Mordecai returned her smile and gave her a gentle peck on her cheek. He turned to leave the room. "Don't let the Governor get to you tonight."

"I tries."

Rose and Pink Tiddie came in with sweet little Pinki in tow. It was the first time the darling saw Luna Belle since her great-uncle died.

Pinki agreed to play the music for the service. Twice she'd gone to All Souls Church in Savannah to practice on the monster pipe organ, but Pinki hadn't played a real instrument since her days at Agnes Scott College in Decatur, Georgia.

Jason Harbree, the church's regular organist helped her orient herself. Pinki was engaged to be married; however, she tried to fabricate mental sparks between herself and her new musician friend, but Jason entertained different notions altogether about life's arrangements. Pinki was sweet but not a seer. She seldom understood people's true natures.

Luna Belle heard the voices of the Tiddie family and left her upstairs suite followed by her lackeys of the moment, the twins. Luna Belle wore a simple black A-line dress of silk moire. A scarf of flowing black gossamer silk pongee tied to each shoulder created a drapery across her upper back that fluttered while she descended with the grace of an ocelot. Her hair, held by a simple carved ivory comb, flattered her face with its plain beauty. Soft black bugle-beaded slippers for comfort completed the ensemble.

A large canary diamond ring, a long string of pearls, and simple pearl studs comprised her jewelry for the evening. Luna Belle, master of her wardrobe, knew how to dress for any occasion. Whatever she wore she remained the epitome of style, grace, and elegance. The twins followed her looking for all the world like gargoyles dressed to the nines. No one held a candle to Luna Belle.

Luna Belle lit up the instant she saw Pinki. Little Pinki—the pride and joy of the Tiddie household, beamed back.

"Now you must come with me." Luna Belle escorted Pinki into the Ladies' Tea Room and closed the door behind them.

Rose cracked the door and stuck her head in. "May I join you ladies?"

Luna Belle countered with a syrupy smile. "Not yet. I need to talk with my niece alone."

Rose closed the door and fussed into thin air. "Really! Excluding me from a meeting with my own granddaughter. Luna Belle's gotten far too big for her britches since Mose died."

Inside the private chamber Luna Belle gushed and grinned. "Oh Pinki. We had so much fun. Oh goodness ... your wedding. I can't wait to sit with you when we can discuss our plans in earnest. You're going to love it.—Won't have it any other way."

Luna Belle continued without allowing Pinki a chance to breathe or speak. "Now tell me dear ... the church? Have you had a chance to practice?"

"Yes, but I'm not good enough." Pinki dropped her chin and pouted.

"Nonsense. Get that head up. You play here at church all the time. What's the difference?"

"Here, it's a little electronic organ. That real pipe organ scares the shi-wa-doodle out of me."

"You listen to me." Luna Belle commanded with a gentle tone. "You're capable of anything you set your mind to. Don't you dare say such things in front of me. I'll not stand for it. Out of all the people involved with the service tomorrow, you're the only one I asked for by name." Luna Belle raised her brows and tucked her chin against her shoulder. She lowered her voice to an imploring tone. "There have been droves of people wanting to participate, and I know why. All because it's going to be televised nationally, and they want the exposure."

Pinki almost swallowed her tongue. "Televised? Oh Lord!"

Luna Belle coddled Pinki's chin with her fingertips. "Pinki, I'm proud of you. You're like my own child. I'd feel lost if I didn't see your cherubic face sitting at that console."

"I'll try my best but don't hold your breath. I'm sure I'll make mistakes."

"Pish-tosh. I have every confidence in the world that the service will go without a hitch. You know about your Uncle Mose's fastidious nature. He always demanded dignified and appropriate behavior, and that's exactly what we'll have."

"Yes, ma'am. Please, don't let my mistakes upset you."

"You're forgiven. There ... I've said it. I'll hear no more. Now let's go out and visit with the guests. I'm sure you want to retire early. You're staying at the house in Savannah tonight, aren't you, dear?"

"No, ma'am. I plan on coming early. I'll sleep better at home, but thank you. I love you."

"Love you too. Kissy, kiss."

Luna Belle smiled. She stood and adjusted the waist of her panty hose in preparation for her next interview. She planned a couple more pep talks before the soiree climaxed. The unbearable pressure she had placed on her niece never occurred to Luna Belle.

Lonny Gober had already agreed to Jilda Birdsong's singing before Luna Belle knew anything about it. She did leave the two undertakers in charge—but Jilda? If she weren't Moses cousin …

Polly never heard Jilda attempt to sing without saying, "That some kind of conjuration. I knows 'zakly what that is. Um-hmm."

Luna Belle almost agreed. It did sound foreign, maybe not even of human origin.

Luna Belle caught Jilda outside the Ladies' Tea Room and called her for a quick *tête-à-tête*.

"Jilda, dear, I wanted you to know. We're preparing for Mose's funeral … not a Metropolitan opera audition. I want you to behave yourself tomorrow. Okay?"

"Why, Luna Belle. When have I ever been anything but proper?"

Luna Belle dropped her chin as she smiled. "I just wanted to remind you. By the way, what are you singing?"

"My own special arrangement of Amazing Grace."

Luna Belle winced. "How delightful. Sing good, now. You hear?"

"Thank you. I'll think about you in the coming days."

"Thank you, Jilda … until tomorrow."

With that the two left the private chamber. Luna Belle made her grand entrance into the large crowded salon across from the great dining hall.

She saw Polly and followed her into the butler's pantry. "I don't want to go to Mose's funeral with huge bags under my eyes."

"Um-hmm." Polly nodded. "You wants I should keep a eye on the Governor?"

"Absolutely. Don't you dare let him get drunk."

"How's I gonna stop him?"

"I don't know or care. Hit him over the head with a skillet if you have to." They both laughed.

"What's so funny, Luna Belle? Scooter too much for Polly to handle?" Lulu chimed in.

Luna Belle turned a radish red. Polly a bright mahogany.

"Oh Lulu, why did you have to hear that?"

"Never mind, but Polly … it takes more than a skillet for that thick skull. Why don't I help? He embarrasses me too."

"Why Lulu, we love Scooter—"

"Please, if you love him, take him." Her wry laugh jiggled her tiny bosoms.

Scooter joined them with his hyena roar. He had no idea he mocked himself.

As the evening wore on a most remarkable thing happened. Scooter Thadeu stood before the fireplace in the grand salon and made an inebriated speech.

"Your attention, please. As Georgia's governor, it has been my privilege and honor to have worked with Moses Black throughout my entire political career. A finer man never drew breath. Mose proved himself a friend and confidant to many of us.

"I'm obliged to mention our ancestors. We assemble here because of them. Most of you know the great history associated with this lovely home, this town, and this island. No need for me to go into all that here tonight, though. I did want to mention that Mose left this life without an heir. This is the first time the family and residents of Cow Bell Island have been in such a conundrum.

"There's been talk and speculation about what'll happen. But let me assure you. I'm going to see to it that everything gets carried out decently and orderly.

"We have thrived in a cloistered atmosphere. It has been our secrecy that has maintained us throughout three centuries of our own private cili … cili … cilivization. I intend to see it continue for posterity through another three hundred years."

A short subdued round of applause followed the Governor's toast. His little diatribe affected various people in different ways. Rose openly fumed. She stepped into the hallway and muttered, "Why doesn't this oaf understand? I'm the heir-apparent."

Scooter's blatant insensitivity caused Luna Belle to blush. How dare the perpetual politician take an opportunity to use her home for a campaign speech. Mose tended his own affairs.

Polly leaned toward Mordecai and whispered, "Did you hear him soliloquilizing in there? Drive a body to drink. Um-hmm. It amaze me, though, how when that rascal soused, he seem to make a lot more sense."

8

Morticians' World Premiere

The undertakers brought Mose's body back to Mayhew and Gober Funeral Home the night before the funeral to make any necessary adjustments. Before the wake at Teachall had played itself out, Mayhew went over Mose's makeup with a fine tooth comb. The handsome rascal needed to look good.

The funeral home's thermostat failed by going into a heating overdrive around three o'clock that afternoon, creating stagnate swelter in the poorly ventilated structure. Mayhew huffed around and searched for a portable fan. "Call Jules and get him to come fix that blasted thermostat. I don't want Black's face to melt."

Gober went to the back of the building and started opening doors. "We don't have time to let that man fool around in here. You know he'll want to order a part. All he'll do is track up everything with his muddy boots before he scatters tools and junk all over this place without fixing a thing."

"We need to at least give him a chance because I already know that you can't do it. Of course I also realize you don't care what happens to my makeup work. You won't be the one in here at four o'clock in the morning fixing him back up."

Gober opened the front doors of the mortuary. "Stop carping. I'm airing the place out. That's as good as you're gonna get before tomorrow."

Mayhew followed Gober to the front doors and watched him fling them open. He carefully secured them with the doorstops attached at the bottom.

Mayhew fussed and fumed. "You're going to let every kind of bug and varmint in this place. You ain't got enough sense to screw in a lightbulb."

"I'm tired of your grousing. Just shut up and suck it up. Put on your big boy britches and get on with life."

"Aye-aye, captain." Mayhew needed a can opener to release more sarcasm than that. He mocked indignantly as he walked back toward the prep room. "Maybe you'll get snake-bit from all your 'airing the place out.'"

Polly, Mordecai, and Luna Belle arrived at her Savannah townhouse not long after the wake and went straight to bed. Come sun-up, they all rose. Mordecai prepared mimosas before the door bell rang, announcing the Thadeus and Lolly. Irvin had chosen to meet them at the funeral. He wanted to stay away all together because of the warehouse incident, but Luna Belle wanted him to be a pallbearer.

She jumped from her seat and arranged her dressing gown. "Thank y'all so much. We grew lonely here. Needed a little lift. Right, Polly?"

Polly nodded and picked up her frosty glass. "We expected you come by before the funeral. Um-hmm." Taking a sip, she smacked her lips and gave Mordecai a little grin.

Lulu danced over to give Luna Belle a little love pat. "Well … I talked to Rose this morning. They're coming too, and I reckon they should be here any minute. I like it when we're all together."

Luna Belle teared up. "Me too, but one of us is gone forever. You know how I felt about Mose, but I still miss him terribly."

The Tiddies arrived and shook themselves from their coats in the foyer. After greeting the others in the parlor, Scooter took Pink to the study for a quick meeting.

Pink walked over to the bar in the library and poured himself a slug of rum. "Have you found out any more about all this hogwash with the warehouse? I want some answers. If Luna Belle finds out we planned—"

"Shut up, you idiotic lubber. Not here. Mordecai?" Scooter raged a bright beet red.

It didn't matter how long Pink had been a lawman, he stayed too big a dolt to behave. If he hadn't been Rose's husband, Mose might have killed him because of his brainlessness years earlier.

Pink tugged on his tie. "Luna Belle suspect anything?"

"Didn't you hear what I just said? My Lord, Pink, you are about the biggest idiot I've ever seen." Scooter's hot skin brightened and glowed cherry-red from a fresh surge of blood.

"Can we at least talk about a heir? Mose left us in bad shape. Alls I know, our whole way of life might sink right out from under us. You want that to happen?"

Mordecai peered into the room and startled the two culprits. "You gentlemen need anything?"

Scooter and Pink almost needed clean underwear. If the suspicious old man spilled the beans, their futures looked scuttled without a life preserver.

Pink had always fancied torture for the uppity butler who thought he was superior to the other crew. With Mose out of the way, Mordecai became fair game—except for Rose.

"No, thank you Mordecai. We're about to rejoin the others in the front room. By the way, how's Luna Belle holding up? I know you've had your hands full." Scooter took a comb from his back pocket and combed both the hairs on his head. Pink's sheepish grin swept his chapped lips as he used his paw to rake thick curls off his forehead.

Mordecai grinned and watched the governor comb his sparkling scalp. "She's holding up quite well. We're all fine."

The governor's cover-up game had no effect on Mordecai, but at least Lardass's sartorial splendor entertained Mordecai: An iridescent silver sharkskin suit on a fat man—a pall bearer—why not?

Pink and Scooter rejoined the ladies. Pink sat down on the sofa across from Luna Belle's chair and spread his legs like the king of the couch. "Luna Belle, want to hear about the investigation?"

"Certainly, Pink."

Pete Stagg had stayed around Mose's body a long time

after his visit to the house that morning. Luna Belle already heard a good deal about the situation from him. Her trust in the gardener far outweighed her faith in Pink. She sat up and eagle-eyed the sheriff.

Being a lawman, Pink always hoarded details. He especially protected any information he knew about this investigation. Pete and Pink fished together often, but Pete's true allegiance remained with the Blacks.

Pink leaned forward and put his elbows on his knees. "Luna Belle, you know how much Mose meant to me. Him and his daddy started me in the sheriffin' business. I owe them for my entire professional career."

"Go on. I want to hear about your investigation."

"I got'a tell you. What I found at Riggers Creek left me hornswoggled. Weren't no ordinary shooting. They's all kinds of weird stuff going on around Mose's death.

"When I reached the creek, I discovered that Mose died before he'uz shot. That's what kept him from bleeding all over everything. According to the crime lab he'd been dead for about a hour. That's what Deamon told us before we ever left the creek-bank that morning. I guess he told you that too?"

Luna Belle sipped her mimosa and blotted her lips. "Yes, Pink, he did."

"Crime lab said Mose died of a massive heart attack. Funny thing is, I didn't know Mose had heart trouble. Did you?"

"No, I didn't. He became overly upset that morning, but I didn't sense an impending heart attack. Mose acted strong and healthy to me."

Pink tugged at his tie's knot. "I found the gun that'uz used for the shooting all the way across to the other side of Riggers Creek. Um … it'uz leaning against a tree near a old sandy road used by local hand-net shrimpers. It'uz a military issue model Remington sharpshooter rifle, a favorite amongst military snipers.

"Now, understand me. A professional ain't about to leave his weapon. I decided right off that somebody wanted to frame some innocent sharpshooter. I'uz ahead of 'em, though. Snipers are trained to clean up after theyselves. Trained military personnel know better than to leave their stuff laying around all over the crime scene. The more I studied on it, the more it disturbed me."

Pink's upper lip formed beads of sweat.

"I sent my best man over there to scour the marsh and sawgrass. Went over the area with a fine tooth comb. Found a spot where the grass had been wallowed by two people. A tidal stream behind that spot would'a been about knee deep in water at the time of the shooting. They wadn't no clues there, though.

"That's where we found shell casings. Not really all that rare, but they'uz strange enough to spark a little speculation. A .50 Beowulf bullet casing ain't something I'd expect to find out there across Riggers Creek. But they'uz two of em right there. They're 500 grain Hornady XTP FN, loaded with 28.1 grains LIL GUN powder. Slug like that travels around fourteen hundred feet per second. Tests confirm it's one of the most accurate of its class. It'uz fired from the gun I found. Whoever shot Mose knew what they'uz doing. They planned it—meant to kill him."

He wanted Luna Belle shocked and scared. The men needed her compliance. Pink's studied expression betrayed his thoughts. She yawned, covering her mouth with her fingertips, then nodded for Pink to continue.

Pink shifted his eyes. "Luna Belle, that cypress split saved him from being tore up bad. Pete Stagg ought to'a seen a exit wound right off, but they wadn't one. Way it happened, that bullet stopped short of his sternum. You know that bone in the middle of your chest." He rubbed his fingertips over his.

"I know about the sternum, Pink." Luna Belle crossed her ankles and lowered her head. She learned nothing. Wanting meat, Pink served up a huge helping of dry soup.

"I set examining that shell casing for hours before we sent it on to the lab. Wadn't no prints on it—muck and tidal currents erased them. They'uz plenty of other clues, though. Crime lab's still working on it. I'll pass it on quick as I get it."

Pink grinned and reared back into the down filled sofa. He crossed one ankle over onto the other knee to open himself up again. His sweaty arm pit shined when he sprawled his arm over the tops of the down cushions. "We found typical casing marks. They're like fingerprints—come from one gun. We still ain't sure who the shooter was—"

"Thank you, Pink," Luna Belle dismissed him by holding her hands up in surrender.

"Questions?" Pink asked.

"Not now." She winced a smile.

Scooter gave the ignoramus a big old shine-eatin grin. Their sheet appeared to have sailed without luffing.

Lulu looked at her watch. "Y'all, look at the time. We've got to get out of here and let these good folks dress for the funeral."

"I hate for y'all to run. Thank you so much for coming this morning. It's meant a lot to me to have you here with us. We'll meet up at the church in just a few." Luna Belle went to the front door and held it open.

She dressed in her bedroom. Slipping into her new outfit, she draped the Contessa's pearls around her neck, then stepped back from her dressing table to admire her costume. She painted her lips, checked her mascara, and stared blankly at herself for several seconds.

Her hands caressed the luxurious spheres while she watched them roll under her hands in the mirror's reflection. "Oh, my. Y'all are magnificent. I'll have to wear you more often."

She situated her wide brimmed hat and lowered the veil to grow accustomed to the fabric obscuring her vision. As she slinked her hands into kid gloves, Polly walked into the room. They made a stunning duet.

Mordecai drove the Rolls limo. "Those men are cogitating evil. I don't like what they're up to. I feel it in my bones that you cannot trust them."

"Don't be silly. I know they're not very bright but not trust them? That's ridiculous."

Mordecai looked in the rearview mirror. "By the way, I don't think I've ever seen a more appropriately dressed lady. In fact, you both look beautiful to me."

"Thank you Mordecai. You're too kind."

Mayhew smiled and slapped Gober on the back. "Can you believe our luck? Look at that sky. It's funeral time and we've avoided all that mucky weather from the last several days."

"I thought for sure that nor'easter was gonna linger and leave us in a foggy stew, but it blew off like it knew we had an important funeral. I guess His Honor holds a special place up there." Gober pointed toward the sky.

"Yep, the sky looks as pretty as I've ever seen it. Just enough fluffy clouds to make out of town folk sit up and take notice of South Georgia."

The unusual warmth not only consoled morticians, it roused vermin. Covetous family members seethed in their devious ploys. Years earlier Mose dubbed them spawn of mutineers. Ingrates plotted and connived against their own house, yet they remained too dimwitted to see the perils they created for themselves.

Mayhew and Gober glowed in electrified excitement. This crowd promised good advertisement for their hayseed funeral home. All these people, some foreign dignitaries, came to witness a sophisticated Georgia funeral conducted by two of the state's best morticians. Their finest hour had been rehearsed down to the smallest detail with special care taken to insure the avoidance of any unseemly incident.

At the funeral home anyone who overheard the plans expected an operatic extravaganza. In Mayhew's mind this grew from grand theater—spectacle of the highest order. Yet above all, prevailing courtliness must reign.

Gober ordered large name tags for all the employees. When he laid his slimy hands on them, he became ecstatic. The size of index cards, they were bright metallic gold emblazoned with an outstanding black script: "Mayhew & Gober Mortuary." Smaller print under the logo read, Pirate's Landing, Georgia. Lower still the employees' tiny names mattered little.

The irony of advertising escaped both men. What could possibly go wrong when a backwater pair of hacks with designs of greatness encounter a dignitary's funeral?

Inside the church the crowd talked and made quite a bit of noise. Anyone interested in carrying on a conversation with a neighbor needed to raise their volume. The melee excited the morticians and cajoled their imaginations.

Steve Mayhew paraded the aisles of the church as if on an important mission. The man swaggered in hog-heaven, high headed, sniffing the redolent scent of lilies, freesia, acacia, clove pinks, and roses that filled the front of the church. His haughty smirk failed to express condolence.

Their once in a lifetime funeral, yet they deceived themselves into thinking their stupendousness might draw other dignitaries. Who knew?—Hollywood—perhaps international fame. Mayhew had always wanted a Paris division. Anything seemed possible to the ambitious vultures when they factored in live TV coverage.

At All Soul's Church in historic Savannah, Mayhew disappeared behind a door then reappeared at another. He performed his deeds with an extreme urgency to reflect his importance. Once or twice he leaned toward the coffin. It appeared he wanted to make certain the judge hadn't left the building.

Lonny Gober acted a little more subtle. He stood at the front door of the church welcoming everyone. With great ceremony, he appropriated an employee to usher any unescorted lady whether she appreciated it or not.

The undertakers drilled their assistants on how to show off their lapel billboards with tasteful pride.

Days earlier Mayhew scratched his head. "I think we ought to pass out brochures."

Gober pursed his lips and wrinkled a brow. "That might be a good idea. We certainly need the exposure."

About that time, they passed the family room and Gober heard the coffee pot perking. "Come to think of it, that might not be the best idea. Luna Belle Black would probably have us boiled in oil." That was the last mention of brochures.

Pinki Tiddy agreed to commence playing the great pipe organ thirty minutes before the funeral.

With his wings akimbo, Gober hovered and chortled his begging. "Please, Pinki, all these people. They came so much earlier than we anticipated. We desperately need for you to help us out by getting the show started a tad early. We're counting on you."

"Okay. Okay. Now, shoo!" His rank halitosis caused instantaneous compliance. Pinki did anything to get the carrion monger away from her presence.

She didn't have an hour's worth of music prepared, but she had wormed her way out of tighter spots before. Spreading the classical music Luna Belle wanted with some of her own specials must suffice. Her nerves shattered inside her pudgy self. If only Jason played the organ. Pinki wanted to sit with the family, but she hung onto her perch.

Pinki had grown accustomed to the little Hammond console back home. This monster frightened with its complexity. She grew literally terrified of the five-rank keyboard's mysterious shark-like fangs that appeared before her eyes when she mounted the bench. If she fell into the gaping gullet ...

Jason offered Pinki many details. Her technique appeared irregular, but he warned her how to avoid a complete meltdown.

Pinki understood all grand organs came with their own quirks. That made her nervous, yet this command performance stared her in the face.

After her second practice session, Jason agreed to sit with her during the funeral and help regulate the stops, and so he arranged several presets. He was glad to oblige. His resume needed this. Besides, she might faint. He prepared himself just in case.

9

Squeeze Her In

Lulu and Lolly demanded seats behind the family's pews to be as near their dear friend as possible. Ushered in with slow, studied ceremony, Mayhew and Gober grew aggravated at the ladies' snail's pace. The pair ambled toward their goal with a determination unequaled by amateurs. This was not their first funeral, and they knew once positioned in their seats, turning to gawk would become impractical if not down right rude.

They relied on quick glances over the audience to know who came and diligently searched for acquaintances to acknowledge. Dividing the church between them, Lolly took the left, Lulu the right. They started burbling the moment their fannies hit their pew.

"Did I see Charlie Banks back there?" Lolly asked.

"Yes," hissed Lulu. "The nerve of that crook. Reckon how many head of cattle that rogue has stolen from the Blacks over the years? His being here shows how little respect he has for us all."

"Here to prove he's above the law. That's my guess."

"Slick too. Never caught him red-handed. Wonder why Mose never had him lynched?"

"Makes you wonder. Reckon how many of his women he brought?"

"I'd say none. Whoremonger! How can he show his face in public?"

"Mose said he ought'a start a national chain. You know …

franchise. I'll bet his girls are rented out for the day. Smug ain't he? I reckon he's safe here. Mose can't stop him now."

"Pink might."

"You're kidding, right? I expect Pink gets a cut."

"You are a wicked woman." Lulu chided.

Lolly patted her sisters forearm to acknowledge the compliment. "My these suits are beautiful. That Yvez fellow certainly knows what he's doing. We've never looked better at a funeral." Lolly cooed while rubbing Lulu's arm.

"Never spent more, either."

Pinki began her rendition of a Bach prelude. The girl actually played okay considering she hadn't looked at the key signature. Musicians in the audience winced quite often. Other than that, she played admirably aside for a few obtuse clunkers that even the tone-deaf in the audience couldn't ignore.

"Pinki's outdoing herself." Lulu grimaced while Pinki kept missing note after note.

"I wonder why she's attempting Bach? She's much better with homey type hymns. Rock of Ages—"

"It's a good thing Mose died. It's almost comical. Luna Belle wanted no hitches and why not? So why ask Pinki to play?"

"Lulu. It's rude to say what everybody's thinking."

Mayhew and Gober marched to the front of the church. Pinki started "God Bless America" on their cue. With rehearsed ceremony they closed the coffin. Each took two corners of the flag and with a flourish of their arms, lofted it high in the air. It floated, luffed, and nestled itself atop the bronze box.

Lulu had been to many state funerals. "These clowns are something."

"Will you hush?"

The morticians marveled at their performance while restraining prideful smiles. The flag ritual formed an enormous part of their spectacle, so a quasi-military salute snapped toward each other comically completed the scene. Then the proud bench-legged terriers pivoted and marched in tandem to the narthex.

The more they moved around, the more the undertakers grew fascinated by the cameras. Neither missed an opportunity to parade and perhaps brand their faces through the media. If things continued going this well, a few TV commercials might help spread the word of their illustrious greatness.

To their chagrin, the harder Mayhew and Gober tried, the less attention they received because the cameramen showed no interest in them whatsoever. They preferred shooting the dull crowd leaving the morticians' fabulous performance ignored and neglected. They needed air time.

After the flag act, Lolly squirmed to her left. "Who's sitting over there behind the pallbearers' seats? That's not Henry Swilley is it?"

"Surely not that Swilley swine." Lulu said. She looked hard to her left trying not to crane like an owl. Her attempt at subtlety failed miserably.

Lolly took a moment before she laid her hand on the pew's cap. "Looks like him. But tell me ... what's he here for? Mose's mortal enemy.—Really."

"You're right about that. Been hearing all sorts of awful things about the man from several people. Scooter says he's okay. I don't trust him with a penny and Mose didn't have any use a'tall for him. I'll never forget the other night—at the townhouse."

"You mean when hoodlums took over Savannah? That's the night somebody robbed our warehouse." Lolly's left eye spasmed.

"Sure is." Lulu sighed.

"You saying Henry planned it? You're trying to shift the blame from Scooter. Irvin knows Scooter masterminded that. Besides, TV says Scooter did it. Why you think Irvin didn't ride with us? He didn't even want to come, but he's a pall bearer." Lolly crossed her arms appearing to have a stomachache.

Lulu tried to pull her twin back upright. "I knew y'all held a grudge against Scooter, but didn't know it had turned that serious. How dare you accuse Scooter, again? I thought you got over all of that mess. You know good'n dern well; there's not one word of truth in any of it. Media's against Scooter, and they have been ever since that little fish ... what's it called?"

"Smelt?"

"That's it, smelt. As if Scooter caused that problem. Dam's been there at Lake Lanier for decades. Pesky fingerlings ain't worth a crap. But Lord'a mercy. Planet'll perish without 'em."

Lolly tried to look around to make sure they hadn't drawn a crowd. "Calm down. You're making an uncouth scene. Besides, you needn't campaign to me … Shug."

Lulu snuffed and snarled. "Forgive my transgressions, Saint Sister."

The twins didn't sit still long because it had never been in their nature. Their bootlegger ancestors failed miserably at teaching them to keep their mouths shut. Draketown, Georgia, became safer after they'd moved away because above all else— moonshiners need tight lips.

Lolly held her hand up over her lap and tried to get Gloria's attention. "There's Gloria. Who's that with her? She dating somebody?"

"Don't think so."

"She puts too much time in that flower shop." Lolly said.

"You're right about that. I don't know … I hope she finds herself a good man this time."

"Behave. She can't help it if she can't keep a man. She's searched ever since LaMar hauled off and left her out of the clear blue. I do wish she'd find somebody. She's so sweet." Lolly's voice dripped sugar.

"Pretty too."

"Absolutely beautiful and talented. Lawsy-loovy, look at all these flowers. Gloria designed most of them. I doubt there's ten arrangements here that came from other shops." Lolly wriggled her seat to raise her height.

"We ought to be ashamed of ourselves. We couldn't wait to get to New York … ran off and left her all by herself."

"You sure you can't tell who sits beside her? He's cute."

"Where are your glasses … stop being so vain." Lulu lurched left and leaned on her sister.

"I've got my glasses on. It's this stinkin' veil." Lolly slipped her shoes off.

"Lord'a mercy. Silly me. Forgot about the veil. I'm losing my mind." Lulu confessed.

"Won't need to pack a lunch."

"How's that?" Lulu asked.

"Don't have far to go."

Lulu pinched Lolly's arm hard enough to cause an obvious flinch. She yelped. The quieter audience made their bad behavior shine.

"Stop that, fool." Lolly snorted.

"It's a damnable sin to call your brother a fool."

"I didn't ... you're my sister."

"You're insane." Lulu almost crowed.

"Thank you. So ... is that Henry?" Lolly still refused to believe it.

Lulu squinted her eyes. "Well, you know he's married to Nick's sister, Sara. I reckon they're close to family as Luna Belle has. Bless her heart. I understand why Henry came, if only because of Sara."

Lolly nodded. "You're right ... anything for Nick. He gets whatever he wants. He's some horse trainer, yes ma'am." She crossed her ankles and sat straighter while drawing down the corners of her mouth.

"Sure does. Stop being jealous and hush."

Lolly gasped. "Well bless my soul. That's the Haggley boy over there. He's the one who shot Mose."

"No. That's not him. That's the boy who tried stripping at one of those ladies' clubs up in Atlanta for a while. What's his name?"

"Oh. I can't recall his name, but he's a real looker."

Lolly picked a little string from Lulu's shoulder.

"Stop that. You're acting like a monkey ... nitpicking, really."

Lolly nudged Lulu then pointed toward the coffin. "Huh?"

An expectant Gaye Nell Goolsby walked with her escort, Jackie Davis, the most handsome member of the mortuary staff. He allowed her to approach the coffin alone.

Gaye Nell wore a tight red vinyl Chanel-styled suit with faux-zebra trim. The shiny thing did nothing to conceal her bulging pregnant belly. The ignorant girl had sewn a black elastic pregnancy panel into the straight red mini-skirt. She almost chose red but decided the black looked more elegant with the wide silver chain she draped to separate the colors. Black fish-net stockings and red spike ankle boots with matching zebra cuffs completed her lower half.

The tight jacket gaped open and more than exposed a low-cut, V-neck, white polyester blouse. Tucked in, it almost covered her torso. Its red polka-dots made her look like half a bull's eye with measles. Her abundant cleavage coupled with the blouse's neckline formed an arrow that led the eye straight to her bounteous belly.

Lulu rolled her eyes. "Rest her soul. If Coco Chanel saw that hussy, she'd snatch her clothes off, wrap her in burlap, douse her in turpentine, and set her alight."

"Who'd blame her?" Lolly grinned big, glad she came to this funeral.

Gaye Nell left her escort's side and rested both hands atop the flag-draped coffin. She looked back at Jackie and implored, "Sorry I'm late … stuck in traffic. Open it please. I have to see him. It's important." She fluttered her heavy fake eyelashes at the young man.

Jackie Davis prepared for most anything but this. He turned three shades of red that matched Gaye Nell's ensemble. "Ma'am, if you don't mind the service is about to commence. Please let me help you to a seat instead."

"You don't understand. I have important things to say."

Steve Mayhew spotted the commotion and made his way to Jackie's rescue, impeded little by his stubby legs. Decorum? He all but ran in his haste to stop this farce.

Neither Mayhew nor Gober had witnessed her arrival. This drubbing must stop before the pallbearers and family entered the sanctuary.

This wench remained bent on destroying their minutely planned service. Rehearsals turned to dust while some televised redneck made a fool of herself and them. Mayhew winced. The cameras loved this sideshow and moved in close.

Mayhew reached Gaye Nell Goolsby's side and took a firm grip on her elbow. No longer a camera hog, the man turned into a sniveling mouse seeking refuge behind the hysterical woman. That piqued the cameramen's curiosity even further.

Mayhew implored her. She shrugged from his grasp, looked into a camera lens, fluttered her eyelids, and with a rich, smoky, sultry tone said, "You must open that coffin right now. I'm carrying his love-child."

Audible gasps spread over the congregation like wildfire.

Lolly widened her eyes. "Wow. Is she auditioning for the part of Norma Jean?"

Lulu looked at Lolly. "Who?"

"Marilyn Monroe, you twit … don't you read?"

"Yes. Now hush. I don't wanna miss anything."

Mayhew panicked, then Gober appeared out of thin air. They made very little headway because Gaye Nell grew more intent at playing to the cameras. She and they shared a tawdry love-fest that the morticians wanted to end abruptly, only there appeared no rational way out.

Pinki responded by opening the swell. Jason pulled every stop hoping to drown the hysterics. Pinki glanced back to the foyer and saw Luna Belle standing cross-armed and tapping a turned out foot. Pinki didn't miss another note from that moment on. This mayhem appeared to have considerably improved her playing.

Gaye Nell sobbed aloud, reached into her purse, and wildly fluttered a pink and blue striped polyester scarf. She blew her nose into it with enough gusto to overshadow Pinki's fortissimo.

After carefully stuffing the sullied scarf back into her purse, Gaye Nell went out like a light. Mayhew and Gober froze. Jackie stood behind her and with quick thinking, moved in to break her fall. The young man had the fallen woman under her armpits while her limp wrists dangled like dead fish on a line. With the help of Mayhew and Gober, the three finally raised her upright enough for her to pretend being wobbly.

In sibilant tone Lulu almost laughed. "You know what Daddy said? A woman who faints at a funeral always falls toward the best looking man available."

Lolly quaked with muffled laughter. This had released a gush of funny on her. With her hands under her veil she appeared to sob.

Lulu reached around Lolly pretending to console. In truth, Lulu pinched the living daylights out of Lolly's opposite arm in a vainglorious attempt to stop her laughter. Lulu wanted to join her but knew better.

The more Lulu pinched, the more her twin laughed. Tears stained with mascara began to flow from underneath her unsweetened chocolate veil. Lulu feared the cameras. That's all she and Scooter needed. Thank God for veils.

Scooter sat in enough hot water with the media from that robbery. Damned Palo Cortado. All Lolly's fault—if she hadn't wanted that shoe polish crap they'd never have even met Marcus Gilder.

Lolly kept bitching about the whole thing. She even ruined their recent trip to New York simply because she never stopped her incessant complaints. Lulu wanted it to blow over. Marcus Gilder might never speak to her again, and she had grown to like the man.

Lulu wanted now to ignore the media. Under normal circumstances she loved the attention, but Georgia's first lady didn't need this kind of publicity. If the public thought Lolly cried ... oh my ... Heaven forbid they discover she laughed. With talk of impeachment looming, it would ruin Scooter. The last thing Lulu wanted was Scooter out of politics—then he might be home all the time.

Gaye Nell threw her head back and turned into a loudmouth floor show as she raised her hands over her head. She clapped them together three times while shouting, "Oh. Mose. Speak to me just one more time."

Pinki's best effort at covering her tirade turned into nothing more than accompaniment. Gaye Nell even began working the rhythm of the music with her elevated hands. The uncontrolled woman shook her fingertips over the coffin in what appeared to be an incantation calling upon Mose to rise from his bed.

Lonny Gober insisted the coffin must remain closed. The two funeral directors forced her stiffened arms down and turned her around. A spectacular recessional began, recorded for posterity by three network cameramen barely able to maintain their own composure. She jerked away, stopped at the twins' pew, and proceeded into that already crowded space before the undertakers could say scat. Gaye Nell held her chin aloft with an attitude that advertised her undaunted shamelessness.

"Ladies please, allow Ms. Goolsby to pass." Lonny Gober's eye twitched. Then his entire face spasmed and pleached into knots.

The twins obliged to avoid becoming camera targets, propriety their middle name.

People had to scrunch together in the packed pew to accommodate the heifer.

Lulu almost whispered, "I *wish* she'd pass ... on to glory."

Gaye Nell made her way with grace for an overly pregnant middle-aged woman. Her red pillbox hat and scanty veil did little to hide her red tear-glazed eyes or her nose's snot.

Lolly didn't have to lean now. Sardines are too close for leaning. "Wants a little spending money?"

Lulu tried to hold her laughter. "She's a dummy. Everybody here but her knows that Mose's condition prevented his—"

"You're right. This keeps getting better and better."

"If Luna Belle gives her a dime—"

Pinki observed the twins' audacity and gave them a sour face.

"Abide with Me" served as the cue to seat the pallbearers. Back in the narthex, Mayhew tried to regain control. Gober arrived ready with an exhaustive apology to Luna Belle.

She knew the fault lay elsewhere, but why hadn't one of them drawn a gun on the bitch? That would have gotten her out sooner.

Luna Belle stood ready to reach for a gun herself, but thankfully, she had come unarmed. That fact alone kept her from being on national TV committing cold-blooded justifiable homicide. Whose bright idea had it been to televise this thing, anyway? Of course. Mayhew and Gober.

She flung the tail of her cape over her shoulder and prepared to enter the sanctuary, glad for the veil covering her disgusted expression.

10

Dignity and Order

A who's who of American politics comprised the list of pall bearers, preceded by Mayhew and Gober with their noses held aloft in mortuarial splendor. Unfortunately, the pair remained ignorant of their grotesque absurdity.

The pallbearers walked behind the escorting morticians in pairs. Their identities were known to most everyone in the sanctuary:

Bradley Oliver "B.O." Vines, Vice President of the United States of America. Husband of Mose's cousin, Marissa Venable Birdsong.

Aloysius Meecham "Scooter" Thadeu, Governor of the Great State of Georgia. Fraternity brother of Moses Black. Husband of Lulu Opal Sanders, one of Luna Belle Black's dearest friends.

US Senator Timony Beckler Carmichael, Virginia. Long time fox hunting friend of the Black family. Husband of Moses Black's fifth cousin, thrice removed, Armeria Steadman Black Gresham.

US Senator Garmund Edgar Waites, Georgia. Dear friend of Moses Black. Husband of Pink Tiddie's second cousin, Jemima Alberta Tiddie Corinth.

State Senator Jonas Malcom Abernathy, North Carolina. Husband of Lulu Thadeu's and Lolly White's aunt, Clarissa Amelia Hunt.

Josiah Waldrup Peterman, Governor of the great state of Tennessee, long time friend of the Tiddie family and brother of Pink Tiddie's mother's sister-in-law's first cousin, Mabel Lynne Marchman.

Irvin Tidman White, Atlanta real estate mogul. Husband of Lulu Thadeu's twin sister, Lolly Jewell Sanders, Luna Belle's dear friend.

Pinckney "Pink" Jackson Cidermaker Tiddie, Sheriff of Tetch County, Georgia. Husband of Rose Boodles Black, Mose's sister.

Mordecai and Polly escorted Luna Belle down the sanctuary's long center aisle. Passing Lulu and Lolly, the grieving widow almost lifted her veil. She appeared to wipe tears from her eyes, but she rolled them wildly with an expression indicating she had seen Gaye Nell's entire disturbingly atrocious funeral debut.

Luna Belle looked beautiful dressed in her new outfit from Bergdorf Goodman. The dress of black double silk crepe was trimmed in sheared beaver. The fitted bodice boasted a standing beaver collar. The long fitted sleeves sported rows of horizontal tucks accentuating the upper portion. Sheared beaver cuffs completed their elegance.

The tea length dress flattered a pair of Gianni Armando diamond studded black boots of shirred beaten kid leather. A matching cape was bordered in the beaver and lined in black silk velvet. It draped over her strong shoulders and added an aristocratic brandish to the otherwise severe ensemble.

Those spectacular Tahitian pearls remained obscured from public view by her black double georgette veil. She privately reveled in the obscene opulence draped around her neck.

Luna Belle brought Polly a new outfit from New York as well. Her tailored suit of black silk serge, lined with heavy ivory charmeuse, fit her beautiful torso as if it had been custom sewn. Polly's simple pill-box hat of black mink with an open mesh veil crowned her head. Her ensemble became complete with a black mink stole that accentuated her upright posture.

Mordecai dressed in his typically stylish fashion. A black bespoke suit of silk and wool gabardine with a starched white shirt and a tie of silver and black diagonal stripes gave him the dignity of a statesman. The three made a most handsome picture.

Lulu and Lolly grew saddened while their dear friend passed by their crowded seats. Gaye Nell had made Luna Belle look a fool at her own husband's funeral.

Lulu shook her head. "Poor dear. Whopped by a tasteless strumpet with absolutely no sense of decorum or concern for the living's feelings."

Lolly reached under her veil with a handkerchief. "Dear Luna Belle, bless her darling heart."

"But don't she look good." Lulu added.

Jilda Birdsong rose to render her special version of "Amazing Grace" once the family was situated.

When Mose heard her sing for the first time years earlier, his eyes crossed. "Now, there's a girl who should marry a deaf man."

Pinki was overly accustomed to Jilda's abilities. Pinki opened the swell but the singer's powerful voice held enough vibratory function to cut through six inches of solid steel. She wobbled her warble with wondrous strength that frightened the uninitiated.

Jilda cleared her throat and squeezed her nostrils, pushing her resonate, piercing shriek into a nasal cacophony able to blow any hearing aid. In a mad rush, almost-deaf folks jerked at their ears from dire desperation.

As she reached her first high note she heard her own voice's glowing vibrations and raised the pitch a full fifth. Her unabated pride and passion immediately became downright pitiable as her interminable sound lingered. Jilda surprised the assembly who had come to pay their last respects to an honored man, not to hear the wailing of a pained banshee.

"I'll bet you dollars to doughnuts that the old broad will sing at least six verses." Lolly squawked and poked a finger in her good ear in hopes it might ease the discomfort.

"I'll see that wager. Plus, she'll also have Pinki raise the pitch a half step for every verse." Lulu moaned.

Both women were right. Lulu trembled as if Jilda's vibrations overtook her entire body. "Wow. Reminds me of the old call to the mourner's bench back home. She sounds like a good way to call sinners to repentance. If sounds from the bowels of Hell don't shake folks up, what will?"

"It would be impossible for Jilda to have ever sounded worse than this caterwauling."

"And have you ever seen anybody who flat out rolls around in their own gloriousness more than her?"

It became impossible for her to let any high note go. Pinki patiently waited, wanting to move on, but Jilda refused rushing her brilliant interpretation.

Jilda jumped into her last verse with vigor. The new key allowed her *pièce de résistance,* the greatest masterpiece of her entire career. A high C followed by a trill then a sweeping coloratura flourish that went down, then up, with all the vigor of a roller-coaster. She foresaw mass swoonings from her titanic wondrousness.

She sang the words: "The Lord has promised good to me." Jilda knew she needed a full throttle of air for her next *fioriatura* feat; however, a misdirected, out of luck honey bee flew in front of the singer's gaping mouth. The hapless insect succumbed, falling victim to Jilda's mighty rushing intake. The winged creature managed to catch itself on her vocal chords before being drawn into the bottomless pit beyond. It lighted. It stung.

Without pause Jilda sputtered, gurgled, grabbed her throat then fell to anaphylaxis. Dr. Deamon rushed to her with an epinephrine injection. He was allergic himself so he always went everywhere prepared.

Mayhew and Gober ran to the front to assist in removing Jilda Birdsong. They needed a gurney but they managed to indelicately haul the rapidly swelling vocal temptress out a side door of the sanctuary.

Lolly leaned to Lulu. "One down, how many left?"

The Right Reverend Abbot of All Souls Church, Dr. Ovid Steed Richland, timidly stood and almost shook his head to remove the lingering aftermath of Jilda's aria and sudden demise. Although it didn't show outwardly, he owed a great deal to that providential bug when it stopped the chanteuse's screeching.

Dazed, he sauntered to the pulpit to read Psalm twenty-three. Forgetting that, he proceeded to ask the audience to bow their heads.

"Lord, God of all, Maker and Sustainer of life…"

As he paused, Pinki took the cue to accompany the remainder of his prayer with a simple version of "Abide with Me, 'tis Eventide."

"Grant us, Oh Lord, your benevolent presence as we have assembled to honor the memory of our dear brother, husband, friend, and companion, the Honorable Judge, Moses Augustus Black. May we find comfort in your presence during our hour of loss. Your mercy gives us hope, and that hope sustains our souls. Bless all those who have come to mourn and honor this great man. May his soul rest in Abraham's bosom. And may his life's example shine, a beacon to all who seek your glorious face. Amen."

Pinki crescendoed her music. Lulu leaned over and whispered to Lolly, "Does he know who it is lying in that coffin? Are we at the right funeral?"

"Hush. You're gonna get us thrown out of here."

"I'm all for it if they scheduled another wench to scream … just saying."

"You're terrible."

"I know."

Pinki finished her piece with a simple amen while Mozelle Abbot, the great interloper, gained the podium for the first eulogy. Mozelle was really nothing more than a wisp of smoke. She had suffered through a no fat diet so long she didn't contain enough grease to oil a wrist watch. That skin—formerly stretched to a size twenty-two, now draped like a saggy-baggy wrap of wrinkles covering an almost size one. There remained enough dry scaly crags and crevasses for a flea to envision vacationing in the Alps during an extreme drought.

Just from looking at Mozelle's dry skin Lulu shivered and scratched her arms. "How that bitch must itch."

Lolly poked her lipstick under her veil. "Bless her heart."

Mozelle still considered herself an eagle eye because she readily ignored her presbyopia. When she gazed in a mirror she still saw the cutest thing on two legs—stork legs. She prided herself in her new svelte figure.

Mozelle's actions were reminiscent of a bobble-head dash ornament. Her head swayed with an alacrity that appeared to actually relish her well earned geriatric palsy. Truthfully, she resembled Uga, the Georgia Bulldog mascot. Her white hair, heavy black eyebrows, and downturned grimace appeared almost indistinguishable from his. Her latest habit of panting while resting her tongue on her lower lip made the look complete.

"Well, I swan. Reckon she'll speak or bark?" Lolly asked.

"If you don't hush I'm gonna wet my pants."

"Dare ya."

Mozelle took a sip of water. "Friends … if I may call you so. This great honor of recalling the great life of so great a man has fallen greatly upon me leaving me greatly humbled."

Lulu shifted her weight back and forth on her hips. "This is just grr-reat. Makes me want a bowl of Frosted Flakes."

"Fallen on her—the dog's hind leg. She wormed her way up there just like Jilda. Maybe there's another bug poised to take her out."

Lolly pinched Lulu's thigh. "Where's a beekeeper when you need one?"

In her mind Mozelle remained the most eloquent living southern orator. She considered her enunciation and colorful use of vernacular unparalleled. At times her content might lack a tad of substance, but the beauty of her diction and the soothing sound of her intonation could lull a bloodhound into blissful slumber.

Major pauses fell between every word, sometimes every one of her long, drawn-out syllables. In her blissfully ignorant delusion, everyone within earshot benefited from her oratorical experience.

She adjusted her several pages of notes. "I must mention a portion of the great venerable assembly of this company. The great Vice President of these great United States; the

Governors of Georgia, Tennessee, South Carolina, Virginia and Maryland; our English and French Ambassadors; Senators, Representatives, Assemblymen, Supreme Court Justices, Mayors, Councilmen and Aldermen ... "

As she prattled on a peculiar sound came from inside the coffin. A clawing sound that grew loud enough for Mozelle to hear it between her elongated pauses. With the exception of those with destroyed hearing aids, everyone heard the creepy noise. Polly's eyes widened as she wrapped an arm around Luna Belle to comfort them both.

Mozelle didn't know what to do. She tried to signal Mayhew or Gober with her eyes. An audible hubbub festered throughout the congregation causing the funeral directors grave concern.

Pink Tiddie stood and faced the back. He didn't hesitate to interrupt Mozelle mid-sentence. She sought the bishop's chair and sat before the good sheriff spoke.

"Mr. Mayhew ... Mr. Gober, you're needed down front."

The sheriff's commanding tone told the two to hurry. Their snooty manner vanished in an instant. They looked straight ahead with gusto while trotting directly toward the sheriff.

Pink tensed his neck muscles under his chin. "You guys have a little problem.... Listen."

In a few seconds the scratching resumed with even greater intensity. The bronze box acted like a resonator increasing the sounds potential, allowing it to reverberate throughout the entire auditorium.

Any sane person knows an embalmed man doesn't scratch at a coffin lid to escape being smothered, but at that moment neither undertaker possessed sanity. With widened eyes Mayhew stared closely at Gober's lapel advertising. He could have sworn it flashed "lawsuit" in bright red neon.

Before they dared start an investigation, the bewildered undertakers looked to Luna Belle who shook her head—yes. All the while the gnawing sound intensified making both men reticent of the task staring them in the face.

"Reckon what Gaye Nell thinks now?" Lolly whispered.

The pair laid their former ceremony aside and quietly folded the flag onto the foot of the coffin to free the upper half of the lid. Their motions, shaky and tentative, as the sound grew louder with each passing second.

The instant Mayhew opened the lid, a huge possum lurched and perched himself on the coffin's rim, hissed, jumped to the floor, and headed straight for Vice President Bradley Vines. The nasty thing climbed the surprised man until the two stared each other eye to eye. The vile possum hissed and blew his sickening slobber all over the dignitary's face. Before the Vice President had a chance to react appropriately, his nose fell prey to the possum's slimy smile. Vice President Vines screamed from terror and pain as the varmint held a firm grip with its filthy fangs and started shaking his head back and forth to rip flesh, causing blood to dribble down the man's shirt.

Luna Belle Black had seen enough. She flung her double georgette veil back over the wide brim of her brushed beaver felt hat to free her face. Polly glanced over toward the furious widow in morbid terror.

Luna Belle rose from her seat and crossed the aisle with a mission. Mr. Opossum didn't stand a chance once she latched onto his neck. With her kid-gloved hand she opened the varmint's mouth and freed Bradley Vine's bleeding nose. The monster hissed and spit foamy saliva as if he had no fear of running out of the awful froth, but Luna Belle remained undaunted.

This good old South Georgia farm girl, decked out in all her finery, held him far away from her body and hauled him back to the bronze box by the scruff of his neck. With one hand, Luna Belle slung that nasty mass of ick back inside the expensive box with her late husband's carefully prepared corpse and slammed the lid shut. Then she spun toward Mayhew and Gober who seemingly had transformed themselves into rather unattractive granite statuary.

Grabbing and wiping at Gober's lapels she muttered through clenched teeth. "You'll deal with that later. Don't dare let him escape. We're going to need his head for a rabies test. That was most certainly not appropriate possum protocol."

She dusted the scruff from her gloves and proceeded to return to her seat. Polly waited with a hanky for Luna Belle to complete her wiping the gloppy possum shoo-wee off her hands.

Luna Belle regained her composure and looked at the

astonished undertakers. "Well, boys … get on with it, then."

Polly leaned toward Mordecai and trembled. "What she doing with them pearls? Don't she know they'z cursed? She crazy, that what she is."

Polly hadn't seen those pearls since the day the Colonel caught her admiring the Contessa's portrait in the bedroom belonging to the mistress of the house. He carefully explained how the bereaved widow wore them on the day of Blackbeard's funeral rite. She cursed the prized gift from her husband so that no one else ever dared wear them for any reason. Surely, Luna Belle saw the warning pinned inside the box lid. Had she no sense of the occult? Polly sat in horror.

She regained her mental composure and reared herself back. *Well, I guesses I sets back and enjoy this show. It ought to be a good 'un. Um-hmm.*

Shocked back into reality, Mayhew and Gober left the front of the sanctuary. They stood to lose everything if Luna Belle decided to take this matter to a higher level. Mayhew wanted to kill Gober for leaving the funeral home doors open the night before. That blasted furnace. Mr. Fixit strikes again. Gober didn't know it but their partnership floundered on its last leg.

While an entire flock had sat mesmerized by a marsupial, few saw that Mozelle, deathly afraid of varmints, had fainted and sprawled out in an indecent pose on the high dais of All Souls Church.

Between their knees, Lolly held up two fingers. Lulu's entire body shook from holding in her laughter.

Jason sprang from his roost beside Pinki. He jostled the organ bench enough to dislodge her and caused her to slide from her perch. She fell and belted her turned-up nose on the lower console rail with a tremendous thud. Before losing consciousness she knew her cute little angelic snoot was broken. Down, down, and down some more she slithered onto the organ pedals. Landing in a puddle, the entire lower registers of the grand instrument sounded a horrible din.

Lolly signed, three.

Jason's mind was torn. His loyalty to Pinki almost held him there with her. Instead, he rushed to Mozelle trying to arrange her legs in a less compromising position of modesty. The only thing left to the congregations' imagination appeared to be whether her bra matched her panties. If her dress had risen one more inch, even that mystery would have been solved.

The organ's mighty roar continued causing Jason to become more confused. When he left Pinki he didn't realize she lay there near death in an unconscious stupor. Certainly, Mrs. Abbot, sprawled like a spathcocked lizard ready for the spit, needed help. She took precedence over a groaning organ. Even so, seeing Mordecai head to the console greatly relieved Jason. Mordecai dragged the fallen organist from the console's pedals, summoning a hideous silence that overwhelmed the house. That vacuous quietude initially seemed far more deafening than the previous cacophony.

Both unconscious women attempted to rouse themselves at almost the same moment. Each emitted moans devoid of melody. Jason's actions on Mozelle's behalf had the effect of waking her enough to think herself compromised. Mozelle Abbot used all her strength to slap Jason's face.

The loud pop resounded in the quiet sanctuary and created a percussive accompaniment to Pinki's moans. Jason, stunned, dropped Mozelle. Her head hit the floor with a mighty thud. She sprawled back out—cold.

Mayhew and Gober arrived down front to relieve an exasperated Jason, asking him to return to the organ. He obliged.

Luna Belle had her fill of Moses Augustus Black's funeral. She didn't care about other songs, other speakers, other anything. She elbowed Mordecai. He stood and with a candid unrehearsed speech made everyone unequivocally understand. "Please accept the family's apology for this most unfortunate chain of events. Unless anyone else has something to add, we shall proceed to Teachall for the entombment."

Jason had no intention of giving anyone else an opportunity to say or do anything other than to get the hell out of his church. As his hands approached the keyboard, Gay Nell Goolsby shouted, "Help! My water just broke."

Lolly signed, four.

Jason could think of nothing more appropriate than to blast out, "Oh God. Our Help in Ages Past."

11
Nick to the Rescue

The funeral motorcade traveled from All Soul's Church in Savannah to Cow Bell Island, but its fluid string was impeded by the ferry at St. Catherine's Sound. The plan demanded meeting in Pirate's Landing and putting Mose's coffin in the horse-drawn hearse belonging to the collection from Teachall's expansive carriage house. The otherwise thoroughly modern estate held a virtual time capsule of valuable relics and treasures.

Luna Belle became more and more concerned. After the total disaster she experienced at the church, trusting horses caused her consternation and alarm. In the limousine, Polly begged Luna Belle to remove the cursed pearls, at least.

"That's the most ridiculous thing I've ever heard in my entire life. To think you believe such nonsense lies beyond my comprehension." Luna Belle argued.

Polly countered. "Well, you ever been to anything like that before? I ain't. I can tells you that. Um-hmm."

Mordecai drove on. "Missy, I don't believe in all that mumbo-jumbo either, but you'll have to admit, things did get a little out of hand back there. What if it proves true?"

"*Et tu,* Mordecai? Will you two leave me alone? I don't want to hear all this nonsense about curses and the Contessa. That woman's been dead for almost three hundred years. Do you really think she can harm me now? My Lord … we're living in the twenty-first century and ought to ignore silly superstitions."

"All I know were that Mr. B's funeral turn into a nightmare. I expect that the Contessa laughing at us all right about now." Polly mumbled under her breath.

"I can see you aren't going to drop this…. I saw something written on the portrait last night, but I couldn't read it. Why hold it over my head when I don't even fluently speak her language? It's not fair."

"But Missy, the writing translated. It wrote on a paper in blood. That make it binding on you. It pinned inside the box. Didn't you see it? Plain as the nose on your face." Polly argued.

Mordecai watched Luna Belle's displeasure growing with every word escaping Polly's lips. He caught Polly's eyes in the rearview mirror and with a look that would curdle cream demanded her to hush.

"I saw the note, but I didn't read it. I held no interest in the stick pin, so I never even unfastened it from the box's lid. I figured it nothing more than someone's name…. Reckon why Mose never told me about it?"

Polly knew exactly why and almost bit her tongue off attempting to keep her mouth shut, but even the intense pain didn't work. "Because you never showed no interest in knowing. Reckons that why? Ever thinks of that?" She regretted her words the moment they escaped her lips.

Luna Belle's mind was in no mood for Polly's mumbling outburst. She peered out the Rolls Royce's smoky window without speaking again until they arrived at the ferry. Neither Polly nor Mordecai dared speak until Luna Belle broke the silence.

"You're right, Polly. I have avoided showing any form of interest in malarky … mumbo-jumbo as you may be wont to call it. In my limited understanding you must first believe in a curse before it holds any power over you. I detest, disdain, and deny such foolishness; therefore, I'm immune. Just because things didn't go well at my dear departed husband's funeral—really— you're being silly."

Polly wanted to console. "Missy, I din't mean no harm. I guess I is silly believing in all that kind of stuff. You know I'uz raised different than y'all'ses was. When I'uz a girl I had to believe in magic 'cause that'uz all I had. The way I seen it, magic what brought Mr. B to saves me from already being dead, but you don't believes in none of that. Like I said, though, it's all I'z got."

"You're right, Polly. We see things through different eyes, and I certainly could never fault you for that. I guess I don't want to think something so silly affected my life…. Although, I will admit that I've never seen anything to equal that fiasco. Have you two wondered how Mose would'a felt about all that show back there?" Luna Belle exploded. She let out a contagious belly laugh that infected them all.

Mordecai loudly cleared his throat. "I think he would have been appalled. Yes, that's right. Appalled. By the way, lest I forget. The morticians told me that animal control will be on the ferry to incarcerate the thug."

Luna Belle smiled and inspected her gloved hands for remnants of the beast. "Good. I still think he's rabid. Back to Mose's feelings … he'd a been mortified … absolutely mortified." The double entendre of her words tickled her and Mordecai. Polly laughed nervously.

Luna Belle removed the gloves and tossed them in the floor-board. "But really, that possum … he capped the stack, didn't he? I'm pretty sure the old picaroon himself would have been rolling in the floor."

"Don't forget Miss Ozelle's drawers? That might top the possum." Polly reminded.

Again, they all guffawed. Mose always loved a good joke.

Polly had trouble speaking because of her laughing, but she finally managed to get it out. "You know, I bets you anything … if that woman … had a knowed she … she … gonna shine her fanny to the whole world on the telebision … she had her … her scrawny behind wax."

Luna Belle shook her head in disgust. She still had to finally laugh with Polly, whose laughter brought on tears of sorrow that rolled down her caramel face. Without question, Mose had died. He was not coming back. Before the funeral Polly had prayed to no avail for him to wake.

The ferry crossed the Sound with its first load of vehicles filled with mourners. Part of the motorcade was freed to head to the church at Pirate's Landing where the equine cortege waited for the final leg of the journey to Teachall's mausoleum. It took the ferry three trips for most of the procession to cross St. Catherine's Sound.

Mordecai drove the limousine into the church's little parking lot where Nick had everything ready. He and his staff presented themselves glowingly dressed in full livery. The drivers, riders, and footmen all wore black wool twill double-breasted tail coats with silver buttons, white old-fashioned jodhpurs, canary vests, white starched shirts with ivory crossed ties, black brushed beaver felt top hats and spit shined black knee boots. The entire ensemble presented a picture of studied composure. Luna Belle had never seen anything more worthy of her admiration.

The horses had feedbags tied on during the procession's arrival, but the bags came off once the steeds finished their oats. Nick wanted the horses settled and calm. They might act up if they were hungry, although chances of misbehavior to mar the afternoon lessened if they were satisfied. Nick's competence rose far above certain undertakers, whose names had become unmentionable.

Four jet black Andalusian stallions stood covered by ornate black velvet hoods to draw the hearse. Arrayed with black ostrich plumes cresting their bridles and harnesses of patent leather, these animals seemed aware of their purpose. Nick Polk, Teachall's beloved head trainer, had decked out the entire procession to match.

He had returned from Florida two days after Mose's death with an army of men and eighteen horses from the Gonzales' farm near Miami to augment Teachall's string of horses for the harnesses. He spent the last several days working with the majestic animals at Teachall to insure a dependable performance.

The Gonzales family showed their loyalty to Nick, Luna Belle, and Mose. Theirs had been a relationship of steadfastness and admiration. Years earlier they introduced the Blacks and Polks to the wonders of Iberian horses.

Luna Belle's grandfather, Cecil Brigham, and Nick's father,

Stuart Polk, met the older Mr. Gonzales accidentally. Over the course of many years their mutual love of these majestic animals drew these people and their descendants into close bonds of lasting friendship. So, when the Gonzales family learned of Mose Black's passing, they insisted on sending their best stock to help in the cortege. A small favor for such dear friends.

Nick took all these arrangements on himself while Luna Belle shopped in Manhattan. He knew she wanted this for Mose. Nick wanted it too.

Luna Belle knew horses well enough to know the havoc they might create. Another outrage might destroy her very spirit and leave nothing behind but an empty shell of embarrassment. This plan held the potential to turn into something far worse than the funeral, yet Luna Belle reassured herself because of her devoted trust in Nick. He possessed an uncanny ability to maintain control with the animals. He inspired Luna Belle's confidence.

Pink had come ahead to help Nick prepare the cortege. Nick didn't need or want the addlepated sheriff's aid, but he had it. Pink demanded his moment of glory. Directing traffic usually fell beneath him, not then.

Out of politeness Luna Belle lowered her window. "Pink? Am I crazy ... horses ... today?"

"Luna Belle, these horses ain't got a clue about what happened back in Savannah. I've seen them animals do amazing things for y'all. Don't worry one minute."

Pink Tiddie knew how to lay it on thick. Luna Belle winced at his sarcastic concern over her well-being.

Polly's motormouth overtook her intuition to remain silent. She shifted in her seat to lean forward as if to open the car door. "If I'uz to walks ... would ... would you be mad?"

Luna Belle glared at Polly Swann with a look that caused more pain than being dragged behind the coach. "Polly, darling, you started this whole thing with that Contessa's damned curse business. I'm not really interested in your deserting me now."

"No, I stay here with you. I know I upset you about them pearls. I can't get it out of my silly head, that's all."

As the other cars from the procession arrived at the parking lot, time came to get into the horse drawn vehicles. With more people than seats, the overflow walked behind.

Mordecai, Polly, and Luna Belle rode in a coach-and-four drawn by bays, Luna Belle's favorite color horse. The hearse, the family coach, and the remainder of the vehicles created a grand visual delight. Mose deserved this after the debacle at the church. It served as a fitting tribute to a man who had spent his entire life loving these special animals.

Luna Belle rode with one hand on the coach window frame and the other tightly clasping the edge of her seat. Even though all the carriages had been boarded without incident, her glimmer of hope shone rather dimly. She sat in hopes the horses didn't smell her fear.

From the Episcopal Church parking lot to Teachall's entrance was about two hundred yards; however, it still provided ample time and place for a catastrophe. Once inside the plantation gates, another half mile remained before arriving at the mausoleum.

If the Contessa had any true power to curse, the closer Luna Belle came to the dead woman's tomb, the greater her power should be. Luna Belle didn't have to believe in curses to understand and appreciate that simple fact.

The carriages parked alongside the mausoleum without incident. Nick stood beside the family coach and held his hand aloft to aid Luna Belle's descent.

Immediate family and intimates went into the mausoleum behind Mose's coffin carried by the pall bearers, with the exception of Bradley Vines who had gone to the hospital. Luna Belle followed the rector inside the building for the first time in her life. She had habitually avoided going into this place ever since she came to Cow Bell Island. There was no escape under the current circumstances.

Inside, she didn't hear a single word spoken. She delighted in the veil's obscuring powers. Instead of listening, she spent her time surveying the cavernous space. This amazing veil afforded her the candor of looking the place over surreptitiously.

The mausoleum appeared large from the outside, but once

inside it seemed capable of holding an amazing multitude of dead folks. Luna Belle didn't have a squeamish bone in her body, but this place made her crazy. She wanted out. Catching an Amen from mid-air cued her departure even though it wasn't over.

The rector of Pirate's Landing's little Episcopal chapel had prepared a final eulogy for inside the tomb. He intended to read an elegy and chant a final prayer, but Luna Belle's abrupt departure stopped him cold.

Lolly whispered to Lulu. "I figgered she offended him. She went out the door before he could say a proper adieu."

Lulu shook her head. "I don't expect he minded too much. I imagine he found generous compensation that should'a greased his wheels ... well ... add a touch of inebriation that he'll get at Teachall in a little bit. But I'll bet he's glad Luna Belle stopped the show before it came his turn to speak in Savannah."

Lolly nodded.

The power of a widow—at last Luna Belle found an advantage in her recent position. It was a good thing Rose had gone with Pinki to the hospital, otherwise she would have been infuriated by Luna Belle's behavior.

The family dutifully followed into the light of day where the entire assembly waited to greet her. A receiving line formed for the family to pass by and accept condolences. They wound their way around the back of the mausoleum to greet mourners. The folly caught Luna Belle's eyes as they passed near it. She and Mose had ridden horses to the relic many years before.

He told the story of how his great-great-grandfather wanted to build ruins emulating remains of a Scottish castle. It sounded like the most vulgar thing she ever heard. Follies should be actual ruins, or the remains of children's playhouses—not some idle nonsense.

Mose taught her differently. Follies had become the rage in earlier times. This one served as a tactical defensive watchtower on the Eastern end of the island. Luna Belle still projected this as nothing more than an extravagance of wealth—a peacock's vanity. She smiled over her own lack of vanities.

The group made their way around the mausoleum, greeting all the mourners, and arrived back at the carriages. Nick again

helped them board the coaches then delivered them to the front
of Teachall. The entire afternoon with the horses ended without
a hitch.

    Inside Teachall the company swelled into a horde. Luna
Belle wanted solitude but the guests appeared determined to
party for the rest of the evening. It was crowding dark and
winter's early sunset made the guests disperse sooner than they
might have preferred. At least most of those who walked from
the church to Teachall left. Nick waited to offer rides back to the
church with the help of his fellow equestrians. His assistance in
the matter made only a small dent in the crowd.
    Even though exhausted, Polly plowed through in the kitchen
to assuage the demand for food. This funeral had been an all
day affair, so naturally the natives grew restless with hunger.
The crowd overwhelmed the kitchen staff even though Polly had
recruited fourteen new hands from various household positions.
    The night before the wake tired them all. Today's hubbub
exacerbated their exhaustion and sapped the entire group's
steam. Polly wanted to scream, "Fire!" in hopes of clearing the
crowd.
    Luna Belle forced herself to act the gracious hostess.
Exhausted, she wanted to go outside, get in a carriage, and have
Nick drive her far away from all these shenanigans, maybe never
to return.
    Each blink of her wearied eyes brought an absurd funeral
scene to play itself out in her head, but when Nick had taken
over—there had not been a single glitch. She wanted to return
to the assurances he offered her earlier. Mayhew and Gober
certainly never offered her that kind of security.
    Luna Belle sighed while she relented to her own fears and
doubts. She rubbed and held her hand over the precious black
Tahitian pearls. Polly had marked them forever in Luna Belle's
mind. Even though she loved them, their weight grew around
her neck, and their heaviness pulled on her heart and mind.
    The value of the pearls auctioned at Sotheby's had caused
her eyes to glom onto these. She knew their worth but Polly

ruined them by laying the blame for the day's disaster on these rare orbs.

12
Will They Ever Leave?

The postmortem morphed itself into an unabashed inappropriate party of drinking, singing, and dancing. The principle players involved needed a good stiff drink or two, maybe three. Something to wash away the blues brought on by the events of the day, but this horde of unwanted rabble disgusted Luna Belle.

This rare opportunity to flood the house with people also afforded a little snooping by some of the more devious relatives. It became almost impossible to monitor their movements and motives. Mordecai stayed a step ahead of the most accomplished of those ferrets by locking and securing every room that might contain anything of value to the most malicious connivers.

Luna Belle found Mordecai. "I wanted a few friends here, but this total debauchery reminds me of a celebration, not the mourning of my husband. My stars, just listen to them while they pound on the piano and dance through every room of the house in drunken revelry."

"Missy, they mean no harm. Perhaps they are a bit uncouth, but these swabbies and knaves are only doing what comes naturally to them. This is the way of pirates, rum, and hornpipes."

"I've played hostess long enough. I can't take any more of this impertinence. I'm going to my room. Work your magic on this crowd, but leave my circle of friends. I'll change and come down after the rabble has been dispersed."

Polly rounded up the friends Luna Belle wanted to stay and directed them to the kitchen. Mordecai appeared atop the central sweeping stairs of the great hall. He commanded attention when he rang a large ship's bell from the chart room.

"Ladies and gentlemen, please excuse my rude intrusion into your affable natures. The lady of the house has fallen to exhaustion. She retired under doctor's orders for the evening and regrets asking you to vacate the house. She shall never forget the outpouring of your kindnesses, nor your deep love and devotion to the family, but unfortunately, I must ask you to kindly leave."

Huffing, snide remarks, and rude behavior ensued. Still, it took only ten minutes for the vandals to leave, even though they had only truly begun their celebration. Luna Belle Black's outrageous behavior earned her no merit among this band.

Unworthy, unfit, inhospitable, no scruples, rude, boorish, outsider … some of the words Mordecai heard while people scurried for their wraps and shuffled past him. He smiled and pretended he never heard their barbaric remarks all the time he held the door for their departures.

Polly invited the remaining guests onto the Palm Court. They relaxed there and enjoyed good food and company while they waited for the grande dame's descent.

Mordecai spoke to the assembled few. "Friends, relatives … Polly asked me to apologize for her rudeness in asking you to wait in the kitchen. We didn't know where else to stash you."

Lolly waved her fingertips. "Think nothing of it. I'm grateful for the opportunity to be of consolation to Luna Belle."

Luna Belle was upstairs changing from her funeral garb while her guests situated themselves and awaited her entrance. She spent several minutes deciding what to wear.

She chose a fitted bodice gown of heavy white charmeuse with layers of white silk chiffon flowing from its empire waist. Atop it she wore a hand painted and effect ruched tone on tone kimono in whites and palest grays. A few wisps of pinks and lavenders clouded the landscape, an absolute favorite from her extensive collection. Created by Moto Ishishi, this kimono alone cost Mose over two hundred thousand dollars. Luna Belle had never worn it and this seemed the perfect occasion.

She smiled because of Mose's admonition. "If the house ever catches fire, forget the art … save the kimono. Her majesty thinks they're the most valuable thing here."

Luna Belle rubbed her exposed chest. Reaching into a lower dressing table drawer she pulled out an enormous high necked diamond dickie that more than covered her *décolletage*. She knew it was too much with the kimono, but she smiled and admired her reflection. An opera length strand of enormous white pearls tied it all together in her mind. She draped the dubious black pearls over a jeweler's bust on her dressing table.

Luna Belle left the kimono unbelted, then she poured an apricot and blue obi over her shoulder. Embroidered plum blossoms of gold and silver threads rippled across the grand sash's surface. Being untied allowed its magnificence to flourish as it flowed and trained behind her grand gestures to charm the eye. She practiced this habit with obis for two reasons. Primarily, she liked the way they flowed behind her when she descended staircases, plus it always got Mose's goat. It seemed a fittingly private honorarium for the evening.

She smiled as she slipped her feet into soft gray kidskin ballet slippers. While the guests still wore their fitted shoes, Luna Belle's toes wiggled and basked in the freedom of unrepentant laxness.

Her guests also remained uncomfortably confined in rigid attire, but she shrugged her shoulders and luxuriated in her loose clothes, always insisting on the fashion upper hand. She rubbed her diamond bib. "See Mose, I told you I needed this gaudy thing. Look how it fixed my indecency."

She moved her chignon to the crown of her head and fastened it with a pair of carved ivory chopsticks. After a fresh coat of subtle red lipstick, she was ready to greet her guests.

Her appearance stopped conversation when she descended the grand limestone staircase that bordered three sides of the palm court. Her sophisticated beauty startled even the most jaded of the crew.

Scooter stood and raised his glass. "Ah, there's our little Madame Butterfly now. Luna Belle, you are always a vision of loveliness."

Luna Belle gave a coy smile to pay homage to the Governor's

compliment. Out of the corner of her eye she saw how this exchange infuriated Lulu. Luna Belle's small smile widened a touch. Wickedly, she loved seeing Lulu become jealous over Lardass's infatuations.

Kitchen staff brought generous food and libation in offering to Mose's memory. Luna Belle went over to the beautifully prepared buffet, took an empty old fashioned crystal, and handed it to Mordecai. Without a word between them, he mixed her an unparalleled Sazerac.

He knew the exact combination and never overdid the absinthe, always rinsing the glass with the toxic brew then discarding the excess. He also possessed the most adept hand with the Angostura bitters. Luna Belle loved Mordecai's Sazerac.

With her drink in hand she took a spoon from the buffet and dinged her glass. "If I may ... thank you for staying. It's been a long and trying day for us all. That's why I'm asking Polly and Mordecai to join us as our beloved friends. I'm sure no one here will mind. I'm also sure we can all depend on the staff to entertain us."

Rose snarled her upper lip into a grimace. She fluffed her wilted hair with one hand. With the other she rattled the ice in her glass, devoid of spirits. She almost showed her disgust with Luna Belle's waiting until Mordecai mixed her drink before the grand dismissal gesture. Pink never obliged Rose with anything, so she would have to serve herself, him too. Thank you, Luna Belle. None of the other staff could mix drinks to equal Mordecai, especially her beloved dark rum and CoCola.

All her chosen guests understood that the cataclysm, otherwise called a tribute to His Honor, Moses Augustus Black, were taboo. After all, who wanted to rehash the egg laid by Mayhew and Gober in what should have been their finest hour?

Although, some things were open for discussion— such as the undertakers' rapid departure when the mausoleum's heavy bronze door closed. Their short legs operated with uncommon haste.

Luna Belle broached the subject. "Can you believe how much gravel Mayhew and Gober slung out of our driveway with their feet? They almost ran back to the church. Good riddance."

"I doubt they'll show their faces around here anytime soon." Pink chimed in.

"Oh, I expect they will—tomorrow. I haven't paid them yet." Luna Belle said with sarcasm.

The whole room burst into laughter. They made ideal whipping boys. She needed them for that.

"At least no surprises popped up at the tomb." Scooter intoned.

Pink Tiddie scratched his nose. "You know, that's 'bout the creepiest spot around here. I'd'a done it different."

"Different? How?" Rose snapped. She didn't care for her husband's besmirching the family's careful planning, especially with her standing next in line to rule. Pink showed no promise of becoming first husband material. The royal princess's dilemma hung heavy over her head.

She maneuvered her lips into a grimacing fish-face that most people would reserve for the aftermath of smelling a rotten egg. "I mean, it's the logical way on a coastal island. Never had any floaters, have we?"

Pink turned his attention to his plate heaped with maple glazed bacon and crab puffs. "No darling we ain't, but you know what happens when that joint fills up?"

Scooter jumped up. "We consolidate."

This amused some and horrified others. Irvin and Lolly White showed strong revulsion.

"Hey. We're all family. Besides, anybody ever hear any complaints out of the occupants?" Scooter jumped from his seat and ran over to poke the Whites' ribs.

"Only at night." Luna Belle chimed in.

Her remark brought another round of boorish laughter from all but Rose who raised one eyebrow and sloshed her melting ice.

Mordecai sat carefully watching the reactions of suspects. He lost all good feelings about Scooter and Pink since having overheard them at the Savannah townhouse earlier that morning. His eyes grew reddened with the blood of his anger at their two-faced betrayal of Mose. Even Rose became suspect because of Mose's concern. She appeared to be more focused on her precious drink than the fact someone had attempted to murder her own brother.

Someone indeed shot Mose with malice aforethought. Mordecai pondered the possibility of the master-mind sitting in the palm court with the widow.

As the others continued in the humor, Luna Belle tried to recall the memory of the last time she came near the mausoleum before today. It had been over thirty years when Mose's mother, Beulah, died. Even then Luna Belle waited outside. Over the years Mose went to many services there, but she had not deigned an appearance.

The huge limestone mausoleum resembled a Grecian temple. The monstrosity sat on a mound created from the dredging materials of Hummingbird Lake during the Contessa's expansive building project.

The mausoleum's two parallel walls of panels covering chambers for the dead spooked Luna Belle. In the center of the space stood a sarcophagus of pink marble. The paramount appointment of the building was an effigy of the Contessa in death's cold stillness atop her private crypt.

Her carved hauntingly beautiful image was rendered with her face covered by a sheer veil. Any sculptor capable of creating so fine an illusion impressed Luna Belle. The gauzy drapery effect spilled off the foot of the tomb almost far enough to puddle on the floor.

A cult-like worship followed the long dead ancestor, creator of Pirate's Landing and Teachall. Her powerful influence had been the cornerstone of endurance for the island's inhabitants.

Her name decorated the upright walls of her tomb. Casting heavy dark shadows into the colored cool stone, they shone as the only incised feature of its sides.

Luna Belle was abruptly called back to the palm court's festivities by a new surge of laughter. Lulu said, "Scooter heard that Jilda Birdsong died. Anaphylactic shock. Isn't that just awful. Imagine, going out in the glory of what she loved best. Can you verify her condition, Dr. Jack?"

"We tried but I'm afraid your thesis expresses truth, Lulu." Jack slid his plate onto a palm stand as if the thought of her demise caused him to lose his appetite.

"Even if she sucked at it. That's a bit of poetic justice ain't it?" Pink blurted out as he leaned onto one hip.

"Pink, you rascal." Rose cajoled, hoping no one else had witnessed his vulgarity. After she appointed herself commander he'd be banished or trained, but even a choke chain and stout leash wouldn't contain the slob.

Luna Belle added, "Her demise hangs heavy over my head. I'll never forgive myself for letting her sing, but she horned her way in. I wanted Violetta Valéry." The sarcasm in Luna Belle's voice overpowered her affectation of sorrow.

Her present company caught on to her insincerity, although La Traviata's heroine flew right over the morons' heads, they did understand Luna Belle's true feelings toward Jilda, their relative and friend. This Valéry person must be one of Luna Belle's opera friends. Luna Belle's and Jack's eyes met over her little burlesque causing Jack to grin, then almost silently chuckle. She smiled knowingly back. Rose squinted out of one eye toward Jack.

Luna Belle had stepped out of bounds by insulting a native. Lulu and Lolly ate this with sterling forks. Neither understood the loyalty these people had for each other, even when mediocrity overtook them, Jilda being the consummate example.

Lulu saw Rose's apparent indignation and decided to poke her a little further. "Oh my, Rose, bless her darling heart. How's Pinki? She gone be okay?"

Rose turned her demeanor quickly, tearing as she answered, "Her precious little nose.... I became a mite bit angry when the plastic surgeon back in Savannah seemed confused. We showed him several photographs of her before her tragic accident. Then he had the nerve to ask us why on earth we wanted her cute little nose restored to its original splendor. Can you believe that? We hope she'll be okay. Thank you, Lulu, for asking about our little darling."

Lolly leaned to Lulu. "Little darling piggy, that is. Why would anyone on God's green earth want to restore that thing, is right."

Lulu pinched Lolly's arm. "Don't start, don't even think about it."

Bradley Vines, the Vice President, with his now nasal twang and huge bandages perked up. "By the way ... the broad with the belly?" He lifted his shoulders.

Pink put his now empty plate aside and stood to thrust his beer-gut out even further. "You mean Gaye Nell Goolsby?" He rubbed his hands over his abdomen. "The pregnant gal?"

Vines nodded. "Yeah."

Pink started blowing kisses from his fingertips into the air as if to mock a beauty queen. "Why, Mr. Vice President. She's the Rubber Queen herself. Comes from somewhere in Alabama or Mississippi. Daddy owned a prophylactic manufacturing outfit. Can you believe it? Sub-contracted for major rubber-makers."

Scooter stood beside Pink and hung his arm over the sheriff's shoulders. "And I understand they all took their business overseas. Knocked folks out'a work over in that neck of the woods. Sorta de-facto deposed their little precious queen in the process."

Vines slapped his knee. "Well shut my mouth and zip it. That explains the rubber suit."

The room again rolled with laughter.

Vines continued with his sharp nasal twang. "I reckon I imagined condoms appeared out of nowhere. Never occurred to me somebody made 'em. I'll bet working in a rubber plant is interesting."

Pink threw his arm atop Scooter's shoulders before he raised his other arm in a victory salute. "I expect it's hard work."

Laughter again overtook the palm court. A few la-di-da ladies tried to muster outrage before they too succumbed to overt hysteria.

Luna Belle looked at Bradley Vines. "Gaye Nell exposed herself as an untalented, dimwitted gold-digger. Who in their right mind would create such an escapade over the corpse of a man incapable of fathering children?"

Vines tweaked his nasal bandages and frowned. "I don't understand her connection to Mose. Oh, and does anybody have a pain pill?"

Jack pulled out a sheepish grin. "No, but I can give you a shot in the ass."

"Thanks, I'll pass. You know what strikes me so funny about that girl? You say she's the Rubber Queen, but don't seem like she knew what they were for."

Some chortled, some choked, some just plain whooped and hollered.

Scooter winced at Vines. "It's my fault. I sent her to clerk for Mose. He didn't keep her but about three days because she wreaked havoc with everything she touched. She'd been run out of every law office in Atlanta, so I figured he needed a chance to see the girl's senselessness. I never expected her to do that."

Luna Belle walked over to the governor. "Thank you Scooter. I didn't know you sent the delightful creature. I owe you. I expect she wore that outfit for dramatic effect. I can't think of any other reason."

Scooter Thadeu had plans for many more gifts ahead. He already prepared himself to be crowned grand dragon of the treasure of Blackbeard.

13

With Friends Like These

Scooter and Lulu walked to their car at the church before they drove back to Thadeu Castle. The governor's mind dwelt on his stagnated plan all evening, yet he never connected his own ineptitude to the plan's failure.

Unlike his boisterous and boorish behavior at Teachall, he sat in silent, worried contemplation while Lulu drove the short distance from the church to Thadeu Castle. She noticed his unusual quietness and wondered what cooked inside his brain, but she learned years earlier to leave him to stew in his own juices.

Scooter had two devastating meetings with the pirate chieftain. The first revealed Mose's astute observation of Scooter's malicious attempted mutiny.

Even though the drive was short Scooter found plenty of time to squirm in his seat. In his mind, the troubles he needed to worm his way out of started with a phone conversation several days prior.

Scooter had sat smugly in a meeting with the state senate finance committee when he felt three pulses under his belt. He knew immediately that this was Mose summoning him to a call on their private line. Scooter scurried to his personal washroom for ultimate security. When the Governor picked up the phone, to his surprise Mose's voice boomed. "Scooter—problem. You're coming here today."

"Can't ... full schedule. It'd take an act of congress."

"Then you'd better get congress cranked. You seen television this morning?" Mose smiled at the ace he pulled from his sleeve.

"No, why?" Scooter fidgeted with the water spigot on the lavatory to stop an insipid drip.

"They're using you for wallpaper on national news." Mose almost chuckled.

"What?"

"About a bumbled burglary. I don't think I can do much to get your behind out of this one, son."

Scooter swallowed hard, about to faint. Sweat poured. The Captain had his quartermaster cornered.

"There before dark." Scooter squirmed. "Give me a couple of hours—"

"That's enough." Mose barked. "I've already sent my plane. You're walking out the door for the strip even as we speak."

"Hangar nine?" Scooter quaked.

"Nine it is. Oh, and Scooter, don't even think about lagging behind."

The Governor hung up and went into his office to call his personal assistant, Velda Hebridge, then he yelled. "Rouse the chopper pilot. I've got to get to Charlie Brown, immediately. Cancel my schedule until further notice."

"But Governor, you have a press conference scheduled for two p.m. What'll we tell 'em?"

"Tell 'em I'm in a meeting. Tell 'em I've gone to Mars. No— wait. Tell 'em I'm in a meeting, all right. A meeting to investigate malignant crime. In fact, get on the phone and leak this:

> The Governor is appalled to have his name involved with this terrible travesty of justice. We will not rest until the culprits are apprehended and prosecuted.
>
> Such politicizing of crime will not stand. Even now, the Governor flies to south Georgia where he hopes to involve himself in the apprehension of the perpetrators."

"Brilliant."

"Mose lurks behind this can of worms on TV. All but admitted it ... turned it on me. Conniving pirate. Can you believe it?"

Velda scratched her knee. "Good grief. He was supposed to be the one to fall."

"I know but that bullet sailed right by the old rascal. Now, he's returned the volley."

"But how? We had it all sewn up."

"I don't know what he's done, but I've got to get to the island immediately. You know what he'll do to me if I don't show."

"I'll get rid of finance."

"Think you can? That's all I need right now. You know they're itching to impeach my ass ever since that endangered smelt complication at Lake Lanier."

"I can handle them ... the men ... not the fish."

Velda had worked for the governor from his earliest days in politics. She saw no need to allow all their efforts to vaporize. Especially over something this irrelevant, even with Scooter's unquestioned guilt.

Velda took a sterling flask from behind a volume entitled "Prohibition: The Machinations of Politics on a Free People." She poured an old fashioned glass half full of dark rum for the clammy Governor.

He gulped the liquor and started out the office door.

Velda chased him with a jar. "Wait. Peanuts.—Bleeding ulcer."

"Yes'um." He grabbed a handful of Carter-peas for a chaser.

"Environmental affairs waits for a presentation on the impact study ... Lake Lanier."

"Great. You deal with that too. Tell 'em how much I want to save that little stink-ass fish."

Velda rolled her eyes. "That's not why they're coming. The itinerary lists the financial impact of the Army Corps' proposal for water allotments downriver."

Scooter shook a finger. "See, I knew you'd do it. Now handle it."

Velda's husband, Bob, rushed in. His face flushed, his breaths deep and rapid. He panted. "Have ... seen ... TV? Bad, bad, bad. Saying you're ... mastermind ... Irvin's warehouse ... witnesses ... spilling guts ... television."

"Witnesses? Who? You tagged Mose to take the fall on this.

I swear, sometimes I think y'all are about the most useless bunch
of boobs left breathing." Scooter hyperventilated. "Nothing I
can do now but wag my ass to the island. Y'all tend to this end.
If I ain't there soon Mose'll cook me for supper. He's done hung
me out to dry."

Bob gulped. "Looked outside? Grounds are covered with
reporters. State Patrol can't keep 'em at bay. Water's chummed.
They're hungry."

Scooter sweated blood. His face flushed. His nose glowed
enough to guide a sleigh. He took his handkerchief and mopped.
He wanted another shot but when he reached for the empty glass
Velda warned. "Governor? You're plate's full. Reporters."

"Tarnation. What'd I do without you?"

"Appear at a presser drunk as a lord?" She chided the
imbecile as she picked a scab from her upper lip, an unhealed
remnant from excessive electrolysis.

Once on Mose's private jet, Scooter got on the phone with
his personally secreted weapon ally, Mad Dog.

"Mad Dog, my boy. How you doing?"

"Better'n you old man, better'n you." Mad Dog held back a
chuckle.

"You've seen TV?"

"Sure have."

"I think I've figured this whole thing out."

"Oh yeah?"

"Marcus Gilder leased Irvin's warehouse in Savannah."

"Go on. I'm making notes."

"These two have put their heads together. I know that's what
happened."

"Reckon?" Mad Dog sat scribbling and biting his lower lip.

"Oh, yeah. Irvin has toted a huge satchel of jealous
ever since we shared a double marriage ceremony with the
Draketown twins."

"Are you saying Lulu and Lolly are involved in this?"

"No. Listen to me. I'm saying Irvin hates my guts and will
do anything to destroy me. He's behind all this hornet's nest on

TV. I know it in the depths of my being."

"Okay. I get it." Mad Dog sighed.

"Irvin can't stand the fact that as Mose's quartermaster, I can access the vast fortunes of the family. Other words, Lulu gets anything she wants."

Scooter looked out the jet's window. "Poor bastard, Irvin has to work his fingers to the bone to keep Lolly happy. See? That's why he'll do anything in his power to hurt me. Irvin reeks with revenge. That's the only thing that makes sense to me."

Mad Dog waited a moment. "So, what do you want from me?"

"I need for you to find out if Gilder is tied up with Irvin and Mose to turn the tables on me."

"Have any ideas on how I'm supposed to do that? I mean, think about it. I've got very little connection with Mose. I can't just call him up out of the clear blue and say, 'Hey, Mose, you and Irvin working with Gilder to bring Scooter down?'"

"I see your point. I don't know how the hell you're going to do it, but get it done, one way or another."

Mad Dog snorted. "I'll do the best I can. That's all I can promise. Oh. Before we hang up, how did all this Gordian knot get started?"

"I asked Lulu if she didn't want to get a case of that sherry crap for Lolly's birthday?"

Mad Dog asked, "They're twins; don't they share a birthday?"

"Nope. Lulu popped into the world at 11:47 p.m., Lolly at 12:03 a.m., next morning."

"Interesting."

"Whatever. Anyway, Lulu jumped at the idea of getting a case of that shine for Lolly's gift. You know they come from bootleggers way over in Haralson County, Georgia, so by their very nature, getting the stuff on the sly appealed to Lulu."

"Go on." Mad Dog struggled to write fast enough.

"I told Lulu, 'Marcus Gilder imports the stuff. He rents several warehouses in Charleston. I was wondering, what if you persuaded Lolly to talk Irvin into renting that big old riverfront warehouse of his in Savannah to Gilder? That way we'd have a good chance of you getting Lolly all that shoe-polish crap she wants, maybe even for free.'"

Scooter kept going. "She liked the idea and wanted to know how she might help. I laughed and told her if she'd get Lolly to talk Irvin into renting his warehouse to Gilder, I'd throw in a ten year tax exempt plan as bait."

Mad Dog said, "And she bit?"

"Well, she fussed a little. Complained and mumbled about how I'd never helped Irvin. Said Lolly carped at her all the time about it. I told her I needed to make up for being such a jerk all these years. Said, I guessed I'uz turning into an old softy."

"Bet that worked." Mad Dog grinned.

"She melted like butter. I set up a meeting with Gilder, Lolly, and Lulu at the Piedmont Driving Club; all three of 'em swallowed the lure … shank and all."

"Brilliant."

"Wasn't it? Of course let's not forget, if Lulu found out what I've done … well … to quote her favorite threat: 'I'll scalp you, tan your bald, freckled pate and have a pair of elbow patches made for a diminutive prison guard.'"

Mad Dog howled.

The importer jumped at the notion of moving his warehouse operation from Charleston for half the rental rate. Scooter's ten year tax initiative sealed the deal. His plan had sounded foolproof to Bob and Velda.

The Governor baited Mose to rob Irvin's warehouse full of Gilder's rare wine. Gilder became the ideal pawn because none of the hoodlums had any prior connection to him. Scooter salivated while he fantasized drowning Mose and the importer underwater, yet all the while the mutineers' greed blinded them from Mose's intelligence and experience.

Mose knew the whole shebang ahead of time. Scooter wanted to use the robbery to ruin Mose; but the Captain raised the ante, refusing to fall without a fight. This wasn't his first rendezvous with cutthroats.

Mose understood Scooter didn't care what happened to Marcus Gilder because he was nothing more than a pawn.

That's what made Mose's counter-ploy so intriguing. Mose warned Gilder of the upcoming robbery and made arrangements for him to have his warehouse filled with decoys. Mose even covered all the expenses.

Before the plane landed Scooter's nerves went into overdrive. When the wheels touched the tarmac his heart almost stopped.

Mordecai waited with a limousine to take the governor to Teachall's barn. When the car entered the estate's front gates heading toward the barn, Mordecai smelled fear copiously leaking from the trembling governor. After Mordecai parked and opened his passenger's door, Scooter hesitated, but he had no choice. Entering Mose's office, Scooter Thadeu plastered a smile on his face. Mose was not amused.

"Come in and have a seat, Governor."

"Mose, I'm sure there's been a misunderstanding. I hope you don't think I'm behind any of this."

"What ... you? You're still my friend, aren't you?"

"Why ask me such a thing?" Sweat poured off Scooter's body.

"Oh, I have my reasons. They're good ones, too ... if I do say so myself." Mose reached into his desk drawer and brought out a dagger with a nine inch blade polished to a mirror shine. He twirled it in his hand while talking.

Scooter noticed how the wicked blade reflected images with clarity, whetted and stropped sharp enough to sever his head with one easy swipe. He needed to keep his intimidation hidden. Dehydrated, parched, a drink sounded good, but Mose offered nothing but questions.

"Scooter? How you reckon this began? I know how I became involved. Sounded great ... little too good to refuse. That's the pretty picture you painted."

"What deal, Mose?" Scooter raked his brow to scoop off sweat.

"Don't play coy with me." Mose mumbly-pegged the dagger into his mahogany desktop. A resonate thud followed by a springing sound traveled from the bottom of Scooter's feet to the tip of his bald scalp. Even his freckles vibrated. The idea of Mose defacing his precious antique furniture frightened Scooter more than the knife itself.

Mose pulled the dagger from the wood. "Reckon how I'd treat somebody who betrayed me? I mean, we've had a long run on this island. Plagued with a few problems, granted, but if I find out for sure what I'm hearing proves true ... well. Besides, you helped punish the last mutineer. Best I remember, you poured the lead. Begged mercy for the widow too, didn't you?"

Scooter's body miraculously found another quart of seeping fluid. He smelled urine. Correct. He had peed himself, but already soaked clothes hid it well.

Mose believed in psychological torture. He enjoyed this immensely. Scooter's reactions told the entire story as he wordlessly confessed with the quickest gut-spilling in Mose's recollection.

Thinking himself a master deceiver, Scooter had only played with amateurs before, so he never saw Mose's mastery coming. The brilliant chieftain always secreted his interrogations; subtle technique demanded no less. His father, the adept Colonel, taught Mose well. Scooter squirmed in squalor.

14

Thank You Contessa!

The official end of the funeral rites for Mose Black came
when the last of the guests left Teachall around eleven p.m. Luna
Belle sighed and gave Polly and Mordecai each a hug for their
support.

Polly held both Luna Belle's hands and looked intently into
her eyes. "Missy, is you gonna needs any help to get ready for
bed?"

"Heavens, no, Polly. We're all too beat and worn out to
fuss over anything tonight. You and Mordecai go on to bed,
too. I can't imagine how tired you two must be. Thanks for
everything."

Polly smiled and took Mordecai's arm for him to escort her
to their bedroom.

"Goodnight, Missy." Mordecai called over his shoulder.

"Goodnight to you too ... both of you." Luna Belle answered
as she climbed.

Even after all the excitement and frustrations, sleep eluded
her. The funeral replayed in her head, unfolding in embarrassing
visual displays.

Lying in bed Luna Belle's mind turned in a convoluted
matrix of desolation. She wanted to be infuriated with Polly, but
she refused to carry a grudge. Yet the heinous curse still hung

around her neck like a noose that threatened to strangle her.

She tossed and turned for at least an hour before abandoning much needed rest. Realizing the futility of her attempt to sleep, she raised herself and proceeded to something more useful. Luna Belle sat on the edge of her bed and became obsessed with the way the Contessa stared at her from the depths of the portrait. A stab in her mind inclined Luna Belle to retrieve the pearls' box and read the fabled warning. She looked at the necklace hanging on her jeweler's bust and wondered if she could face what she planned.

The Contessa's eyes beckoned. "Madame, I shall return your precious pearls to their rightful tomb. Will that satisfy you? Help me leave my pill box alone while I'm in there, okay?"

Removing the Contessa from the wall, Luna Belle shook the painting. "Well, can't you at least speak to me?" She squinted and looked intently at the features of the woman's face. "You know, I see a marked resemblance between you and Mose. Y'all both inherited the same piercing dark eyes and the same resoluteness of the mouth. Wonder why I didn't see the similarities earlier. Why don't we just agree to get along? Wouldn't that be nice?"

She used a pillow to position the painting at a raking angle face up on her bed. "There now—comfy? I want you to watch carefully while I replace your precious pearls. Perhaps then you can leave poor little old ignorant me alone. I certainly didn't mean you any harm."

She remembered the safe's combination and held that triumph as a consolation to her mental fatigue. Holding the pearls in her left hand, she used her right to count off the numbers, going back and forth with the dial. After the last setting she tried the lever and the safe opened. That little victory in and of itself relieved her. If a curse existed the safe should have rebelled.

"Ta-da. See what I'm doing?"

Of course the pill box hadn't moved. Right at her eye level, the thing mocked her intentions of avoidance, but she managed to call up enough gumption to set it aside and continue on her quest. While removing the old black velvet box, the pearls draped from her hand and cascaded out of the safe's opening.

One by one they slinked their way while each pearl clicked
its own little resonate timbre. Each sound struck a different
vertebrae.

Carrying the box to a nearby chair, she sat and opened it to
return the pearls. Particular care in arranging them in full view
of the painting made her feel secure in believing the Contessa
might now leave her in peace. The foxed parchment containing
the curse remained pinned to the lid just as she had left it the
night before. She twisted and tugged the pin to dislodge it
without damaging its message.

While she removed the stick pin she glanced over at the
Contessa. "You must have done all this because this thing
looks old enough to have floated on the ark with Noah. Who
translated it? Why did you curse the pearls in the first place?"

A crushing chill maimed Luna Belle's heart when she finally
took the thing in hand. Her heart tumbled in a turmoil of anger
and embarrassment. Cosmic energy flowed into her, creating an
immediate palsy that made unfolding the brittle note difficult.

Holding the paper to the lamp's light she read:

The treasured pearls I wear in this portrait,
Given to me on our Wedding Day
by my Dear Husband,
Edward James Durand "Teach" Drummond,
Viscount of Avery,
My Savior and true Love,
Commander, the Buccaneers
Of the Queen Anne's Revenge.
Worn by me on the terrible
Day of His
Merdure
At the hands of a vengeful
Governour,
Be cursed
Anyone
who wears these
my Beauties,
From this day forwart,
For so long as ye shall
Inhabit the halls of my home.

She cried out in amazement. "So ... long as I live here, I'm cursed? Now, how 'bout that. All right Madame, if you think I'm going to leave Teachall because of your silly curse, think again. Because I defiled your pearls? Get real."

Luna Belle fumed. She wanted to pitch a conniption fit and fling that dead woman through the antique glass of one of the French doors in her boudoir. "I refuse to play jester to you, your highness."

She turned her attention away from the portrait toward the room's vast atmosphere. "Now listen to me. I refuse to leave my home—my life. I meant no disrespect to you or any member of this household, and my motive deserves hearing and understanding." Luna Belle walked over to the portrait and sighed. "I appreciate all you did for this family, but I acted out of ignorance. Surely you can come to realize that I had no intention to insult you."

Taking in the overall beauty of the portrait caused a smile to brighten Luna Belle's face. She threw her shoulders back and lightly rubbed her upper chest with her fingertips in a pretense of feeling the pearls. "Although they did coordinate beautifully with my outfit. If you'd seen me I'm sure you would reconsider your bitterness. Well, let's say—" She continued talking to vapors. "How about we strike a little deal? Why don't you pretend I never wore them and let's just forget the entire episode?" She laughed from the depths of her soul.

The laughter turned to sobs. "Mose ... Mose ... I need for you to come and rescue me from this nothingness overtaking my soul. What future do I face without you? How could you leave me? To make things worse, I've managed in my own ignorance to call this terrible curse down on my head. Can't you talk to her over there on that side?"

Turning her attention back to the painting she shouted, "Happy now? I'm all alone. Show compassion on a poor, tormented soul. Consider my position in relation to your own when you learned of your dear husband's brutal murder. You wore the pearls for his funeral. That's all I did. Can't you appreciate the irony?"

With tears flowing down her cheeks she pinned the note back to its nest, closed the box, and returned it to the wall safe. With a slam and a quick twist of the lever the job neared completion. She turned her attention back to the Contessa propped on her bed.

As she walked her tone softened. "Please forgive me. I promise. I'll never violate them again."

She lifted the portrait from her bed and headed back to the safe. Whose brilliant idea had it been to use this particular painting to cover the vault where the pearls rested? The Contessa had dutifully watched the entire episode. Why not move her away from the pearls?

Too late now.

"Oh. Now I understand. How foolish of me. At one time this bedroom was yours, wasn't it?" Luna Belle felt goose-bumps course her entire body, leaving her hair standing on end.

As she lowered the painting into its accustomed position the thing winked at her.

"Oh, great. Now I'm hallucinating."

Luna Belle wanted to bathe away a three hundred year old dirty curse. She walked with the weight of the world pressing on her shoulders. En route to her bath she stopped by her dressing table and poured herself a good slug of bourbon.

She stopped in her dressing room separating her bedroom from her bath and threw a short black fox jacket and a China silk gown over her arm. Headed toward her bath, she hung them on a clothes tree near a mirror. She laughed. "What do I need with this silly gown? There's no one here to see me except you, is there dear Contessa? I expect you've seen me naked many times." Luna Belle couldn't contain the laughter overtaking her true need to scream from exhaustion and frustration.

She started the shower while the tub filled. In a flash she reveled in hot water, lathered, rinsed, then shampooed her long black hair. Finished showering, she then headed to the filled tub.

About to pour a handful of herbal bath salts, the cherished Lalique decanter's lid, a gift from Lolly and Lulu for her last birthday, slipped from her hand. It shattered and made the tub unsafe. Fortunately, none of the glass went onto the black and gold marble floor.

She abandoned the soak and released the water from the tub before turning her attention to her wet hair. At the vanity she took the towel wrap from her head and leaned forward to rub her raven tresses.

Her spine snapped. Nothing new, an old affliction that came and went. Experience told her to expect discomfort and not much more. Maybe she should clean the glass and soak after all. It might help with the accompanying muscle spasm.

She inspected the floor and used a towel to rake shards off the rim into the tub. When the last of the water evacuated, she leaned into the tub. The pain worsened and made the job futile. She wanted Polly's help.

"Yeah, that's right, call Polly. She might summon that most gracious Contessa. Man … this obsession clings like a tick on a dog. Everything reminds me of that wonderful winking portrait."

Luna Belle shook her head and looked in the mirror. "I need sleep." She pulled the fox jacket off the clothes tree and slid it on to ward off a chill.

She looked in the full length mirror covering her linen closet door and had to laugh at herself. The naked jay bird with unkempt falling wet tresses stood swathed in black fox and appeared ready for a winter night on the town at a nudist colony.

Closer inspection brought a sigh. "Night on the town? You look like you've already been ridden hard and put up wet." She ran her hands through her still damp hair and shrugged off the idea of drying it.

She nestled herself in bed and admired the luxury her jacket created. Luna Belle propped herself against overstuffed embroidered linen covered pillows to enjoy her first venture of repose with a fox jacket. Why had she never thought of this before? Her carved green lacquered Venetian chinoiserie bed seemed a fitting tableau for such sumptuous nightwear.

A deep healthy yawn and a cleansing stretch led her to take her favorite tome entitled, "Variations of Isotopes that Occur under Variable Atmospheric Conditions." If that didn't put her to sleep quickly, nothing would. It had taken her five years to progress to page three. In all this time, she learned nothing about the subject.

Her futile attempt at reading left her staring at the same word. She laid the book back on the night stand—maybe another slug of bourbon. Picking up her watch she saw, one forty-three. A long night awaited.

Making her way to the little media center inside a chinoiserie cupboard she picked up a recording of Fritz Wunderlich singing Schumann. She loved Wunderlich's rich tenor voice, but she and Mose never met him because he tragically died the week before they anticipated being together at Baron Grimswele's Bavarian chateau.

The recording started. Indeed his singing began to soothe her sore nerves. Although it was not live music, it still calmed the savage pangs within her breast.

She paused on her trip back to her dressing table long enough to look at herself in its mirror from a distance. "I hope to Glory I don't look like the hag I see in that glass staring back at me." Walking toward her petit point stool caused a slight grin. It had only been the night before when Polly had admonished her not to wet the upholstery.

Luna Belle sat turning her face from side to side to have different perspective views of her skin. She pulled her hair back to try a little face lift experiment. She smiled, unable to leave her vanities behind. She remained her own most trusted and loyal admirer.

She began looking at her little dressing table itself. All the things about her life she had taken for granted so long began to rack themselves in ordered rows within her mind. This table and its location in her bedroom headed the list at the moment.

The interior designer and Vice President's sister, Imelda Vines, suggested they move Luna Belle's makeup table to the dressing room. Imelda insisted it distracted from the room's overall grand elegance. Of all their years working together on the chateau, this remained their sole point of contention.

Imelda never altogether recovered and although they still often worked together, Luna Belle knew the designer carried the grudge. What a pity. Such talent, burdened by the weight of a dressing table in someone else's boudoir.

She rose from her seat and wandered her bedroom, looking at things from her new perspective. Her personal sanctuary, no one except intimates came into this chamber. What difference did it make if she had her dressing table in plain view?

Mose had surprised Luna Belle years earlier when he and Imelda decorated Luna Belle's suite while she vacationed on a six month trip to Spain. When she returned her excitement swelled his heart with pride.

Now that Mose had left her, she loved every little detail with a renewed interest. For the first time since Mose had so generously auditioned the space to her she wanted to reinspect its splendor.

She rubbed her hands over the dado of pink and white marble panels. For too long she had ignored the decoratively styled whimsical mural above the wainscot. Horses played and cavorted in fun frolic while pea fowl courted and displayed their brilliant plumage. Snowy egrets and flamingos had been rendered stalking in grass and tidal pools.

Luna Belle opened a pair of the French doors onto the upstairs veranda. The chill of February night air swept into the room, blowing the lace curtains. A few leaves were puffed in by the surges of air. The chill felt good.

She swept the oak leaves with the fireplace broom into the small firebox. Running her hands over the carved unpolished Carrara marble mantle reminded her of Mose's suede saddle seat. She spilled herself into one of the chaises longue that flanked the fireplace to revel in the luxurious silk velvet.

From her reclined vantage point she saw her little solitary chess table. Mose accommodated her love of her private sport with a diminutive carved Venetian lacquered green card table accompanied by one matching chair. A square opal-bordered Lazy Susan with an inlaid chess board of onyx and abalone held an enormous cast chess set of eighteen carat white and yellow gold.

As Luna Belle admired her room, an urge to visit her husband drew her toward his bedroom door; this being the time of night he waked her, bidding her come into his lair. She yearned to hear that great door's creak. If only he lived to invite her in.

15

Where Is Grandmother's Quilt?

With no reason for her to go there other than her own consolation, Luna Belle proceeded, knowing Mose no longer occupied the adjacent room. She longed for his presence with a passion unexperienced by her for years. Maybe if she visited his suite her pain might quiet enough to allow her to sleep the rest of the night in peace.

When she opened the door that separated their bedrooms, Mose's two giant brindled mastiffs, Samson and Hercules, lifted their heads and thumped their tails against the grizzly bear rug where they slept beside the fire. Sam rose, stretched, yawned, and went over to his mistress for a comforting pat on the head. Herc remained in his warm spot but continued his greeting by pummeling the floor.

"I see Mordecai built you boys a little fire. Y'all are savoring that old grizzly bear rug like you killed the beast yourselves." She allowed a small chuckle to escape as she watched Herc's tail pounding away on the waxed heart pine floor.

"You're almost as spoiled as I am. Mordecai will come in here early, 'bout the time the fire gets low enough to let you feel a little chill, won't he? Yes, that's right. Good boys." She scratched Sam's head behind his ears.

"I don't blame you one bit. I love this room, too." She inhaled deeply and reveled in the aromas of Mose, pipe tobacco, bay rum, and dogs—its male mystique.

She walked over to the fireplace and admired the portrait of

Mose hanging over a pair of crossed blunderbusses. "He was a man's man, wasn't he boys? I know you miss him too."

The painting correctly portrayed Mose at the height of his maturity. His hair hung straight from an almost central part and framed his face and black eyes. With a square jaw of exquisite proportions and a chiseled nose, he cut a bold swath with his spellbinding appearance. Luna Belle considered his lips his most delicious attribute. He stood as her epitome of manhood.

She looked at the portrait as she never had before. Now, more familiar with his predecessor, the Contessa, Luna Belle actually stood in awe of their uncanny resemblance. Mose had all the features of a man, but underlying his masculine features lay the delicacies of the Contessa's breeding. The more Luna Belle stared into the portrait's eyes, the more she also saw how he was a homogeneous mixture of Blackbeard's likeness softened by the Contessa's blood.

This room served as his private theatre. His stage that had served him well on her behalf. He wrapped her in his strong arms many times here. No other place in the entire mansion afforded her the felling of frailty she enjoyed in his bedroom. No matter what happened in their lives, in this room Luna Belle enjoyed confident safety. Mose always protected her from harm.

Running her fingers through her still damp hair, Luna Belle sat on a settee beside the fire and dogs, allowing tears to trace her face. "Oh, boys. Why didn't I accept his unconditional love? I've been an insolent fool all these years. Why did he tolerate me? I never treated him like anything other than a convenience." Herc rose from his repose and laid his chin on her lap.

The faithful old dog's eyes looked up at her face with a longing sadness. Her tears dripped onto her breasts that concealed her flawed heart. "I loved him because he gave me things. He loved me because he chose to. How much more unworthy can a woman be?"

As she scratched Herc's ears, she rose from her seat allowing coldness to come up from the floor and trace her naked legs. Luna Belle suppressed her desire to slip into Mose's huge teakwood, carved post and canopy bed, dressed and turned down, ready for the Master. The pillows covered in natural raw linen accentuated with drawn work beckoned her.

"No, I can't get in his bed. If I do … I'll melt. It's ironic
that Mordecai instructed his bed be turned down. Makes you
wonder why, doesn't it?" She looked down at Sam who came
to stand beside her. She patted his head. "Yes, that's right, isn't
it boy? How many times did Mose seduce me in this beautiful
bed? He granted my wishes here." Herc came over and took his
place on the other side of her. "You boys really do understand
what's going on here, don't you?"

She fingered the bed's heavy mohair draperies tied back to
the bedposts by heavy cords of port, navy, and gold. Mosquito
netting hung from the corners and puddled onto the hemp
carpet.

Her weeping intensified. She sat on a carved teak blanket
chest at the foot of the bed. After a few moments the chill in her
legs continued to cause even more discomfort. She slid onto the
floor, knelt, and opened the chest's creaking lid to plunder the
extraneous bedding for a throw to wrap her calves and feet. She
grabbed a cashmere blanket and swaddled in its softness.

Wondering if she might find the old quilt her grandmother
made for Mose when they married, she started emptying the
chest. He protected anything valuable, so she expected nothing
important because the chest remained unlocked.

The dogs returned to their grizzly pelt near the fire. "Yikes.
This thing reeks of camphor. No wonder you boys left me. The
deeper I dig the stronger it gets."

When she reached the bottom of the quilt box she exclaimed
in excitement. "Here it is! I knew he kept it. Wait! What's this
underneath Grandmother's quilt?" She pulled out an ancient
packet, a worn relic. The illegible scrawl's heavy ornamental
hand piqued her interest. "What is this thing, and why has it
never been opened?"

She pushed herself up from the floor and sat on one of two
settees covered in tapestries flanking the fireplace. A pair of
matching mahogany campaign chests, once the possession of
Lord Horatio Nelson, served as end-tables beside the love seats.
Just inside the blood porphyry fireplace surround, immense
stacked and welded cannon ball andirons stood sentinel and held
oversized burning logs. Mose insisted that the cannonballs came
from Blackbeard's own munitions.

The second largest firebox in Teachall, its impressive opening stood almost seven feet high and six feet wide. The back of the firebox supported a huge cast iron shield. According to legend, it once belonged to Hades himself.

Cerberus, Hades three headed dog with his falling brimstone and smoke trails, gave the iron plate its name: Shield of Hell. In mid winter Mose wanted the fire hot enough to make the bas-relief design glow red.

She sat on a settee near Sam and slid her cold feet under his warm belly. Sam rolled over and covered her chilly feet in a consoling gesture. Herc yawned, stretched, and again snoozed.

Luna Belle laid the envelope in her lap. Before she opened it, she reached for a qiviut throw from the settee's back. She spread it over her lap to ward off the cavernous room's chill since the fire no longer provided sufficient warmth.

She turned on the lamp and saw much better to inspect the envelope's contents. Her nimble fingers caressed the velvety genuine vellum, sealed with dripped and stamped black wax depicting a broken crown. "Odd. Reckon what this means?" Hesitant over the item's age and seal, she recovered. "Balderdash! Mine now."

Her deft hand slipped under the ancient animal skin and broke the wax to allow a portion of the folded parchment to gape. Luna Belle's excitement brimmed with the delight of discovery. This unopened document had been stored for eons. Mose hid it, but in an unlocked chest.

She was stopped in her tracks just as she was about to pop open the packet by a clawing at the window. The treacherous sound almost caused her to scream. Her body shook from the past several hours' abuses. Her nerves raced to distraction.

Everyone of Teachall's occupants slept except Luna Belle. Alone, as the noise recurred and intensified, her skin bristled with goosebumps. She turned off the lamp and threw her cover over the settee's arm.

Still naked, except for the fox jacket, she looked kooky but didn't care. She had never been one to run from anything, but now she didn't know whether to fight or flee. A night-fright seemed little reason to start running now.

With temerity she rose to investigate. The packet slipped

from her lap and landed on the bearskin between the dogs. With every breath, with every pulse of her throbbing heart, Luna Belle's anxiety grew.

Both dogs woke to full alert as if the burglar were about to gain entrance. Trained to silence, they refused to bark, but a low guttural growl escaped Herc. Luna Belle whispered a command to shush, and the dog immediately responded. Both powerful canines stalked toward the French doors where the sound originated.

She needed a weapon. Mose kept a cache of arms in every room, but his bastion remained the most well provided munition on the upper floor. Swords on the walls offered little protection against firearms. The flintlock blunderbusses over the fireplace looked old and crude, but a twelve gauge shotgun leaning against the fireplace molding caught her eye.

She wisely chose the shotgun. An excellent shot, Luna Belle prepared herself to take on the demon attempting to cut the glass. She opened a campaign chest and took out a handful of cartridges for her jacket pockets.

The scraping sound recurred. Her heart throbbed and pumped even more adrenaline. The powerful surges primed her to take on the devil himself. On tiptoe she doused the chandelier's dimmed light to allow her eyes to adjust to the darkness. Sam and Herc reached the door and poised on high alert.

Fear coursed her veins. Her shaking limbs caressed the shotgun's security even as the scratching intensified. A thief with malicious intent had decided to break into the room she occupied. The brigand surely must see her as the object of attack. Why else would a burglar come to an obviously occupied room? Shivers wriggled out the roots of her hair. She heard the shotgun rattling in her quivering hands.

The document was sprawled out on the floor in open view. She had unwittingly displayed the packet in her attempt to prepare for attack. If this was the chosen object, she had offered it like a sacrifice on an altar to the malicious intruder.

Her eyes began accepting the glowing full moon light spilling through the casement curtains. She saw no one. Their invisibility unnerved her even more.

The hidden thief still attempted cutting the glass. The scratching sound continued. A hand appeared from the bottom of the door. Someone definitely lay on the veranda to work their mischief. Now, at least she knew where the assailant waited.

The dogs sensed the situation's urgency and wanted outside to tear the offender limb from limb. Neither paid attention to Luna Belle's movements because their singular intent remained focused on the veranda.

She commandingly flipped both door levers and released the cremone bolts fast hold. The doors had barely flung open before the dogs pounced outside in a flash of muscular exertion.

Luna Belle saw no one lying on the veranda's floor. Confused, her head reeled. She saw no one anywhere, but the dogs pursued something.

Then her eyes landed on the dastardly possum causing the disturbance. He headed in an all out gallop toward the veranda's edge. Herc caught the frightened varmint and dispatched it with one bite and shake of his head. He turned in triumph to his mistress and offered her the repulsive limp body. When she refused his gift he turned and tossed it over the railing, ending his interest in the mangled quarry.

Luna Belle roared with indignation. She needed to congratulate the dogs but her heart wanted vengeance. One of these vile varmints had offended her for the second time in twenty-four hours.

Once her breath settled she laughed at her fortune. Pillaged by a pernicious possum. Relieved, she called Sam and Herc inside and turned her attention to the packet on the floor, but she remained disturbed enough to leave the veranda doors wide open.

Her ire spun more toward Polly than the opossum. It occurred to her to take the shotgun and blast a hole through the Contessa's wary smile. With her destruction, peace might once again fill Luna Belle's breast.

Before she stopped herself, she called out to the room's atmosphere. "I dub you Possum Queen. How you like that old girl? ... Possum Queen?"

That helped relieve her tensions. Luna Belle returned to the settee and once again turned on the lamp beside her to illuminate the retrieved packet. Her pang to open it weakened. She had lived in Teachall for over four decades and always avoided the mansion's mysteries. Why this new anxiety over an antique packet of worthless papers?

Although less curious, she still had enough interest to warrant further investigation. Battling herself, the exercise stood a chance of helping her forget her recent misfortunes.

As the parchment gave way to her prying she saw inside an incredible inner wrapper of tooled Spanish kidskin also sealed with wax. The huge boss covered at least half the back of the pouch. Bright scarlet wax stamped with the image of two dragons facing each other as if ready for fierce battle sent an unexpected shiver up her scalp. Its appearance spoke of certain antiquity. On the face she saw an inscription but the ornate lettering refused becoming legible in the night. Maybe by daylight the image would appear sharper.

Luna Belle hesitated. Should she continue to open this? Secreted for many years, perhaps even centuries, putting it away until morning made more sense. The sun drove away nighttime spooks and haints, but something compelled her to strangely cotton to the tensions created by her find—her treasure.

She threw caution to the wind and broke the seal, while her heart throbbed as if she had spilled some sacred sacrificial blood. Almost hesitating, she had gone this far, why stop?

As she unfolded the back flaps of the wrought leather she saw a smaller flat parchment covered in ornate cursive script. This bore the marks of a high-ordered legal document of noble European origin.

She sat and tried to translate the Latin, but after a few lines her heart throbbed in shock. Her eyes remained fixed on a bill of sale for none other than the Contessa herself.

16
Sleeping With a Fox

Going back to her own bedroom tired and dazed, Luna Belle found little solace in her newly acquired knowledge from the antique document. She shuffled through a stack of LP's before she saw an old recording of the little prayer of Hansel and Gretel by Humperdinck. In the sweet duet, fourteen angels are invoked to watch over two innocent children lost in the deep wood. Luna Belle put the record on the spindle and fell to her knees for spiritual oversight in her torment.

She rose from her petition and walked over toward the wall safe and started talking to the Contessa's portrait again. "Why did I have to go snooping around and find that cursed bill of sale? It's like hearing fingernails on a blackboard. Your plight is going to stay in my head, isn't it? No wonder you cursed those fabulous pearls. Somebody carrying around so much bitterness would be bound to curse something precious."

She turned her attention to the phonograph disk whose worn illegible label offered no clues to the singers' identities. She usually insisted on knowing singers' names. Not tonight. Maybe those fourteen angels could help banish the Contessa's curse.

Finally, Luna Belle drifted into an unusually fitful sleep. She dreamed horrid nightmares about possums, rabid possums, possums doing all sorts of disgusting things, coming in droves, unrelenting, hideous, wrapping themselves in balls and trying to suffocate her.

Somnambulating, she removed the Contessa's portrait from

the wall, turned it backwards, rested it on the floor, and leaned it against her linen press. Returning to her bed's anxiety, she remained unaware of her hands' deed with her adversary.

Early morning, Polly knocked on Luna Belle's door. An habitual early riser, Luna Belle never wanted to miss mornings. Polly heard no response from the bedroom so she tentatively entered Luna Belle's room.

Disheveled linens indicated an anxious turmoil. Polly had never seen such a twisted mess. Luna Belle hunkered uncovered on her knees in fetal position with her black fox jacket wrapped and twirled around her head. Her bare posterior poised itself brazenly in mid-air.

"Um-hmm, bless her heart." Polly shook her head and perused Luna Belle's bed, then the room.

Luna Belle hadn't slept well. That was immediately obvious to anyone who saw her condition. Polly brought a tray of coffee, juice, ambrosia, buttery toasted English muffins with cream cheese, lox, and tart cherry preserves. She placed it on a table beside the bed.

She lofted the top sheet in the air and watched it gently nestle itself to cover Luna Belle's nakedness. Polly wanted to avoid Luna Belle's waking in that state of rank exposure. "She wakes up ill as a old wet setting hen. Um-hmm."

Polly's action caused Luna Belle to thrash in bed. She twisted onto her back with matted hair and fox fur covering her face. The normally refined lady so closely resembled Cousin It that Polly almost laughed aloud.

Polly's eyes widened when they fell on the gaping void where the Contessa's image usually hung. She quickly discovered the portrait and almost rehung it, but she changed her mind. If Polly had realized Luna Belle's unconscious state when she had taken it down, Polly would have probably rehung it and never said a word.

Instead, while Luna Belle continued to squirm in bed, Polly gathered the clothes strewn about the entire room, closet, and bath. She discovered and cleaned the broken glass from the tub, then filled it with hot steamy water. All the while, she tried piecing the night's events together. Luna Belle had been busily seeking something to occupy her energies in her loneliness.

A gentle knock on Luna Belle's bedroom door called Polly away before she awakened Luna Belle.

Mordecai beckoned Polly into the hallway. "Missy all right?" He sweated. His quick breaths scared Polly.

"She a mess but she okay. Why, what wrong with you? Something ain't right. You look like you'z done seen a ghost."

"I went to see about the dogs. I found the doors to the veranda unlocked and standing wide open with a bloody mess dried outside. A loaded shotgun leaned against one of the settees. Chunks of red and black wax were scattered over the floor. Someone opened something that looks important. I tried to figure it out but it's in Latin. Wish I had paid more attention when we studied it as children. I never read foreign tongues well."

"Reckon what all that mean? Don't sound good, do it?" Polly trembled. "Law. Somebody done tries to break into the house. I can sees in your eyes. That what you thank, ain't it?"

Mordecai shook his head. "I wish I knew exactly what I think."

"You's scaring me. You thanks they'z somebody still in here, don't you?"

"I'm totally uncertain, Polly."

"Better uses caution. Das' what I says."

Mordecai handed her a small pocket pistol. "Maybe you can find out if Missy knows what happened."

"Reckon you oughts to call the law?" Polly's voice quivered.

"Not yet. We don't need Pink Tiddie running around asking all kinds of questions. He'll snoop all over this house, and you know he will, too. I want to ascertain more information for myself before we call that nincompoop. If Missy's okay, we know whoever tried to break in here last night meant her no harm … at least for the time being."

Mordecai turned and headed back to Mose's bedroom, upset with himself for becoming so agitated. He rubbed the Glock stashed in his slacks' waistband with his still trembling hand. With his other, he rattled a stash of extra clips in his jacket pocket.

Polly went back into Luna Belle's bedroom to awaken the addled damsel from her disturbed slumber. Polly and Mordecai wanted answers in a hurry but she had enough sense not to frighten Luna Belle right away.

Luna Belle waked in a groggy stupor to a throbbing headache. She looked around confused, dazed, disoriented, sputtering fur from her lips. "Where am I ... the Okefenokee Swamp?"

"Morning Missy. Gets any rest last night?" Polly asked through her sweaty upper lip.

Luna Belle fought against the fur's restraint. "Oh. Polly, I'm about to die. My head throbs so bad I can't stand it."

Polly trembled. Someone must have clobbered Luna Belle's head in the night, causing her to spend the night squirming. After all yesterday's excitement the Contessa's curse still seemed to hold onto her with an intensified vengeance.

"You had a little excitement in the night? Somebody try and hurts you?"

"Only myself."

"Say what? Now, how you tries and hurts yoseff?" Polly hadn't yet seen any evidence of blood. She had seen an eyeful— but no bleeding. She didn't press the matter. Luna Belle's mood didn't appear to accommodate interrogation.

Polly climbed onto the side of Luna Belle's bed and rubbed hair from her face then massaged her temples. Polly's nimble fingers searched in a desperate effort to inspect for injuries and relieve some of Missy's headache at the same time.

Luna Belle relaxed from the tender loving care. Polly fretted long enough to discern Luna Belle's condition showed no sign of coming from a bandit's malevolence.

"Missy, I drawed you a good hot bath. It ready right now. Why don't you go soaks in the tub? It'll makes you feels so much better. Might even helps that headache of yorn."

Luna Belle's mind cleared some, not much. She groaned, "There's glass in the tub, Polly."

"I done cleans it out. Go on whiles it's good 'n hot."

Luna Belle slid out of bed half dazed. A hot bath sounded

marvelous. Even more so than it had in the night. Her back remained a touch sore, maybe a good soak and her little muscle spasm might banish itself beyond memory. She staggered toward the bathroom. When she passed her dressing table she caught a glimpse of herself in the mirror.

"Well no wonder I dreamed possums crawled all over me. This horrid coat tried its best to smother me." Luna Belle muttered under her breath. "Bed jacket ... ha!"

She looked to see the mirror reveal the Contessa's picture missing. Its absence brought a wry, wicked smile making Luna Belle believe Polly wanted to confound her mind. But she couldn't imagine how that served a purpose. She concocted other torments emanating from the hovering spirit.

She tested the water's temperature. "Polly ... why did you take the painting down?"

"Why I what?"

"The Contessa's portrait ... you know what I meant." Her squinted eyes cut a frowned gaze to Polly. Luna Belle hated for Polly to play innocent. Luna Belle was in no mood for cat and mouse this morning.

"I ain't touch no picture, Missy." She pretended to act surprised as she looked at the blank space. "Look at that. It gone, ain't it?"

"I'm aware of that, now where did you hide it?"

"I ain't touches it. No ma'am. Nuh-uh!" Polly played the game. She chose to volley.

Luna Belle didn't care to argue. Polly crossed the room and almost laughed. She called out loudly. "Here tis." The rest of her speech she muttered, "Few minutes ago I found you with your bohunkus stuck up in the air for the whole world to see. Least the Contessa's rear-end be covered by the board she painted on. Um-hmm."

Walking into the bathroom in mock triumph Polly held the painting up. "Here it is, Missy, pretty as you please. Right there on de flo lent up against the bureau."

"Oh. Wonder how it got there?" Almost under her breath she counted on her fingers. "I know I rehung the portrait after I returned the pearls last night. Focus, girl, focus. Yes, I did rehang it ... the damned thing winked at me."

The fox piled itself into a beautiful heap on the cold black
and gold marble floor when she slinked it off her shoulders. She
looked at it in disgust. "Polly, if you want this coat, it's yours. If
not, give it to somebody else or throw it out. I don't ever want to
wear it again. The thing almost suffocated me in the night."

She slipped into the hot water's relaxing comfort and scooted
herself far enough into the expansive tub to float. Her hair
wafted as she allowed her head to soak up the scrumptious heat.

"Wants me to turns on the jets?" Polly asked.

"Please." Luna Belle braced herself for the powerful surge
about to come from the hot burst of bubbles and swirls.

While Luna Belle soaked, Polly went to find Mordecai. He
tried to recreate order while he went on his detective mission in
Mose's bedroom. Mordecai first and foremost needed to know
Luna Belle's condition.

As Luna Belle relaxed in the powerful water, a wild dream
came to mind. "Oh, yeah. I threw that cursed picture into the
bowels of Hell last night. The thing went up in flames." She
loosed the handholds on the side of the tub and rubbed her
temples. "I hope I never have another night like that. Polly must
think I've lost what little sense I had left."

With Mordecai, Polly asked, "You thinks it's a good idea to
poke around into all this stuff? Somebody sure have been in
here, ain't they?"

"Yes, Polly, someone has been in here. I'm not sure, but I
think I may be onto the answers to our questions. Did Missy
know anything about all this?"

"Well, I didn't ax much. She a little woo-woo in the head....
What if you's ruining some kind a impotant clues?"

"I'm pretty sure I know what it all means. Look. See this?"
He revealed the old parchment. "I've sat here and deciphered
enough to understand that it's the original contract where the
Contessa's father sold her to the Governor of Santa Domingo
de Flores. See, it says right here, his name was Raolo Jimenez
Jesus Petrososi Ortega." Polly rolled her eyes. Mordecai
continued, "Missy is the one who opened this. It rested in the
bottom of the blanket chest there." He pointed to the teak chest.

"She may be adding two and two together. You see, Polly ...

the Colonel bought Missy."

"What?"

"That's right ... he purchased her for Mose." Mordecai had never breathed this news to another soul.

"She know?"

"I doubt it. Although curiosity may be rising in her mind. I'm almost certain it was she who found this document last night."

"Why you so sure 'bout that? Hmm?"

"Well ... whoever removed it replaced the blankets back in the box. Not like any prowler I've ever heard about, see?"

"Um-umm. I has to agree with you on that. Most folk what steals ain't too neat, is they?" Polly agreed.

"Come out here with me." Mordecai motioned for Polly to follow onto the veranda.

"Look down there."

Polly saw the mangled body of a dead possum.

"That's where all this blood came from ... dogs' work there."

"How they gets out?"

"I told you that the doors were open this morning. I expect Missy released them originally. If I gambled, I'd wager on it. The guns ... the blood ... the dogs ... the possum. See? After yesterday Missy has every right to count any living possum her mortal enemy." Mordecai's eyes glowed over his astute detective work.

"Why don't you go back in there and see if she's presentable? If she is, I want to ask her a few questions." Mordecai instructed Polly.

Polly trotted back to Luna Belle's room. "Missy, you done with your bath?"

"I'm still soaking, why?"

"Mordecai say he likes to ax you a few question, that's all."

"Questions? About what?" While the words left her mouth, Luna Belle knew what he wanted. "Tell Mordecai everything's fine. I know he thinks something terrible happened in Mose's room last night. Assure him, it's ok. I want to soak a little longer." Luna Belle sloshed water over her face. "I'm starved. I want us all to sit at the kitchen table and have some bacon and eggs. We can talk there."

"Ready time you can get yourself downstairs. You wants a

little cheese in your eggs?"

"Sounds wonderful. Oh ... Polly, please overlook my atrocious behavior the last few days. I'm sorry. I've been a royal bitch."

"Don't you worry yourself a bit about something so silly. You knows I loves you." Polly smiled.

"Polly, you're a dear friend. Might I ask one little favor?"

"Ye knows I does it if I can."

"Call down to the barn and see if Nick wants to join us for breakfast?"

"I calls him right now." Polly jumped at the request. She wanted to dance and shout for joy. Exactly what Luna Belle needed in her life ... a good man, and the sooner the better. She wanted to tell Mordecai.

Luna Belle still reveled in her hot bath. She heard Polly tittering on the phone. In a moment Polly called out, "Say he come to the house if you goes for a ride with him after we eats."

Luna Belle's mood didn't accommodate a horseback ride but she heard Polly say, "Say she loves to go ... wonderful ... good for her to gets out of the house."

No escape now, Polly had committed her to go with Nick on a foray over the plantation that would most likely take the entire morning. Maybe Polly was right. Luna Belle hadn't sat a saddle in over a week. It dawned on her—she missed it. A good canter might restart her heart and restore her mind.

Ready, revived, it was time for Luna Belle to get out of the tub and on with her day. She started humming. A little time away from the house with Nick sounded good.

17

Dear Honey

Dressing seemed to be all she lacked before heading downstairs to face the day. Going straight to her closet of equestrienne attire, she slipped into a pair of camel stretch jodhpurs with a suede seat and a crisp white cotton high neck shirt with a neat little cream silk ascot.

A tattersall vest and maroon Spanish-cut melton double breasted jacket with suede elbows coordinated with the breeches. The jacket's detailing of gold bullion scrollwork looked regal and combined the best of her love for their Iberian horses and her own English riding heritage. Black boots with camel sueded cuffs completed her ensemble.

The chill from being outside in the night reminded her to don chaps to keep her legs warm. Mose had given her new ones for Christmas and they would remind her how much she missed him.

Knowing she wanted to ride Fazio, a light bay, her ensemble blended well with his coat. Even when she planned nothing more than hacking around, her overall appearance remained paramount in her mind.

She grabbed a dark green flat felt sombrero and headed for her dressing table to apply eye makeup and lipstick. Luna Belle enjoyed riding without her full complement of warpaint, but she went nowhere without lipstick.

Placing the hat on the wig stand to her left she rolled her hair into a low chignon. Putting a net over the ball of hair drew a slight grimace because it reminded her of Rudine's disastrous intrusion into her life.

When she reached for a hairpin, an odd, folded paper caught her eye. Because she knew it hadn't been there earlier, its mysterious appearance startled her.

She picked it up and read the inscription:

> For Luna Belle
> My loving wife.

Mose's handwriting covered the face. She rubbed a finger over a bulky raised wax boss on the back and turned it over. The fighting dragons stamped in blood red wax surprised her. Luna Belle threw the paper on the floor in revulsion. This sick joke failed to amuse her.

She regained her wits and picked it up from its position with the wax seal staring at her. Turning it over, the handwriting unquestioningly belonged to Mose. Why had she never seen this mysterious wax stamp? Why had it appeared twice in the last few hours? This was the hidden image from inside the first layer of the document pouch that held the bill of sale for the Contessa.

The design covered at least four inches—large enough to represent a ridiculous royal decree. It must be indicative of some important symbolism; otherwise, why did Mose go to the trouble of melting this much wax?

Luna Belle wanted to compare the two seals side by side, but she had defaced the first one badly enough to make that impossible. If someone recently forged the older of the two for her benefit, why stow it in a blanket box where the chances of her finding it were remote?

This mystery added to her emotional instability. Rushing to Mose's bedroom she immediately saw Mordecai's handiwork. He left not a single piece of wax anywhere near where she'd sat to open the document, leaving her no chance for comparison.

She scrambled around, frantic, angry with herself for leaving it exposed. Distracted by a bedeviled possum. Luna Belle wanted to scream.

Her mind raced in overdrive. Knowing Mordecai always protected Mose at all costs, did he destroy the ancient

document? She rushed over to the bell pull and gave it a good
hard yank to call Mordecai. He might have lost the rank of
spring chicken, but he still appeared out of thin air when
summoned. While waiting she peered into Mose's brass waste
paper receptacle. It was clean as a whistle, scrubbed and
polished inside and out.

She sat on the same settee and held tightly onto the letter in
her hand. If a forger wrought this, she wanted to burn it. But the
death of cats over curiosity hung in her mind as well.

Inspecting its details she trembled. "Should I open it? If it's
from Mose, I need to read it."

She heard Mordecai and stuffed the letter behind her back.
Not sure why, it seemed a good idea at the moment.

"Missy, did you call me?"

"Yes, I did."

"I came with haste. I feared trouble."

"No, no. Nothing wrong. Well … yes…. Where is it?"

"The parchment?" Mordecai asked without hesitation.

"Exactly … the parchment. I'd like to have it back. Mean
anything to you?"

"I don't know how to explain all this. Mind if I sit?"

"Of course not. Be my guest."

"I came in here this morning and found a disheveled
situation. At first, I assumed someone had broken into the house
with ambitions of burgling. I feared for your safety."

"Thank you."

"I found the papers right where you left them. You did leave
them there … where you're sitting … right?"

"Yes, of course. A possum tried to break in, but please don't
tell Polly. She's already hounding me enough." Luna Belle saw
his grin. "Already knows, huh?"

In a most informal reply, Mordecai said, "Yep." His lips
uncharacteristically popped. "Already knows."

"Well that's just great … more ammunition. She'll mention
it again, you just wait and see." Luna Belle giggled. Infuriated,
where did she see humor in this?

I need a shrink.

Mordecai said, "I expect Polly has learned her lesson. You
don't have a more loyal friend on the face of the earth."

"Thank you Mordecai. I appreciate both of you. Now, please, back to the document. I need answers."

"Did you read it?"

"To the best of my ability in the dark, but it's in Latin."

"I understand. I had daylight, but I fear I failed being a good student of languages. I did manage to decipher the thing's intent."

Luna Belle almost exploded. "Is it real? I mean … it remained unopened? Did you destroy it?"

Mordecai rose from his seat and headed straight to the blanket chest. He opened the lid and there it lay, right on top. He handed it back to Luna Belle before he resumed his seat.

"In all honesty, I neither know if it's real nor why it existed intact. The one person who probably knew for sure recently departed our presence. Rose might know but before you ask her, I'd advise you wait a few days … see what happens. By the way Missy, did you read the letter in your room?"

Luna Belle raised an eyebrow and looked directly at Mordecai. "How you know about that?"

"Little birdie told me?"

"Little bird my toenail. Did Polly tell you?"

"Polly knows nothing of this. She knows a ruckus occurred here last night. I assure you, that's all she knows.

"Why don't you read the letter? It'll explain more than I can. It contains your husband's last words to you. I saw him writing but I haven't a clue what it says. Now, if you don't mind I'm going back downstairs and help Polly get breakfast together. Why don't you sit right there in that most appropriate place and read? You do have it with you? If not, I'll fetch it."

"I have it. Before you go…. What about the wax seals?"

"That will take some time. Trust me, for right now it's more important for you to read the letter than to concern yourself with the seal. I'll gladly fill you in later. Maybe after your horseback ride we can talk."

"I'll look forward to it."

"So will I." Mordecai rose to leave the room.

Before he made his way across the floor, he turned. "When you came here, I knew my dear friend, Mose, found happiness. You complemented one another. I watched him grow up from

infancy. In fact, as you well know, I helped raise him. We ate
and played games together. We even sat at the same tutor's feet.
Reminds me of a certain gentleman from your own childhood.
Aren't you going riding with him this morning?"

Luna Belle had seldom heard Mordecai call her husband
Mose. It struck her heart as a sign they considered themselves
brothers in a convenient way. Mose always insisted she trust
faithful Mordecai.

Mordecai left the room knowing she needed more than a
few minutes to read and reflect. He hadn't a clue what Mose's
correspondence said, but he knew Luna Belle stood a good
chance of being stunned.

Staring intently at the letter addressed to her, the trembling
returned and her eyes welled. Luna Belle almost wanted to set
the paper alight. She faltered in her will to destroy the thing but
managed to slip a wary finger under the flap and pop the seal.
The cold crisp wax broke off in chunks. Some sailed through the
air in a familiar way.

Weary and shaken she unfolded the page and held it in a
position to read. Its beauty impressed and dazzled her eyes.
Mose scrawled in an old, ornate, practiced penmanship all but
lost to posterity.

> My dearest darling Luna Belle,
> I write this in my own hand
> on the morning of
> Rudine Haggley's visit.

If you are reading this, I am gone. Those who wish
to end our dynasty cannot succeed while I live. I wish I
could tell you who they are. I have ascertained that their
forces are powerful, their knowledge overwhelming, and
their purpose, selfish gain. I fear they may prevail.

I instructed Mordecai for you to receive this soon
after my death. I have written on one folded sheet, wax
sealed, for your eyes alone. For safety, I urge you, burn
this after reading.

I want you to know how much I loved you. From

that first day at Ashwood while still children, my heart
has belonged only to you. You have been a beacon of
hope in an otherwise desolate world.

How many times have I slipped into your room at
night and watched you sleep? How many times have
I wanted to hold you, calming an upset spirit? Those
times are the reason I write. Above all, I want you
happy, taken care of, and well. Maybe what I have been
unable to accomplish while living, in death I can achieve
through your own efforts.

Dark clouds gather over Teachall. You will have a
difficult time knowing the trustworthy from your mortal
enemy. I don't mean to scare you, but I fear I must. Even
the most trusted must fall under suspicion. I learned that
for myself all too late. I shall not attempt to distinguish
between the two. You must decide for yourself, based on
your perception and intuition. Never forget: Offer your
loyalties with great care and concern. Ignore old ties,
familial or friend.

I know this because my old friend, Winston Black
and his Sylvia have become our mortal enemies. I learned
of them this morning through the hag. I'm sure many
others lurk. Beware.

I have begun to lose control over everything
entrusted to me. My laxness has led to attempted theft of
all we own. It may be delayed justice. It may be time. It
still isn't easy to accept the fact that after three hundred
years of careful guardianship, the treasury of my
heritage comes under siege. Triumph depends on you.

Some may say a pirate's treasure belongs to others.
The circumstances creating the bulk of this estate beg a
rational person to differ.

In my last will and testament, you alone are heir

to everything. I advise you to wait before reading the
instrument to the family. In a state of limbo, no one will
know you control the entire horde.

No one except me knows the true value of the estate.
I will not divulge it here. I've told you. No one knows the
true value of the estate. That information may become
essential to you.

You are not one of us Cow Bell natives, a curse you
have borne well. Now, that fact stands to become a great
blessing. A few others here share this gift. They may
prove strong allies for your quest, but beware, they too
may prove dangerous and have liaisons with the wrong
people.

If you have no patience to fight what lies ahead,
leave. Take whatever you want and get out. Alas, all
things must end at some time. If, on the other hand
you decide to take a stand, you have my most profound
blessing and encouragement.

Look under the Contessa's tomb. The lock, her
name—the key, her comb. I dare tell you no more. I
found no time to show you. Let no one see you.
Hard work lies ahead.

Never forget, I loved you with all my heart.
Your adoring husband,

Mose

Luna Belle sat back in disbelief. She needed to read this
several times. Memorize it. Moses Black had always expressed
his love for her but never so intently. She had for the last forty-
two years ignored many of her husband's deeds on her behalf.
She found herself cast adrift at sea without chart or compass.

What had she read? What did it mean? She wanted someone
to help her understand the depths of the letter's enigma. Mose
warned her to burn it after she read it—but not yet. Maybe after
she had time to memorize its contents—but not now.

Rose popped into her mind, but she had gotten more peculiar since the trip to New York. Something changed her. Rose acted too unusual, rousing Luna Belle's suspicions, especially after reading Mose's warnings.

Maybe Mordecai. No. Mose refused allowing him to read it before. Besides, Mose warned her to avoid everybody until she found out if she trusted them.

She screamed. "Thanks Mose. Thanks for nothing."

Her mind raced to Nick. He might be nothing more than the horse trainer at Teachall, but she had known him all his life. Best friends from childhood, Luna Belle always preferred Nick over his younger sister, Sara. The two older children saw her more as an inconvenience. Sara often argued the horns off a billy goat, then argued with him for being butt-headed.

Mose warned her of Nick without calling his name. He shared the curse of being an outsider. Her bombarded mind wanted rest, but Mose insisted she possessed little time. Winston and Sylvia had turned to betrayal. Her head spun in disgust over her confusion.

Nick must hold her answers, but Sara, married to Henry Swilley, might also fall into the enemy camp. Figuring out trustworthy friends became more complicated than Luna Belle imagined.

Even if Nick convinced Luna Belle of his steadfastness, what if he let something slip to Sara? She'd go straight to Henry and Sara always had been an obsequious blabbermouth.

Even though confused, she needed to get downstairs—she certainly didn't want Nick asking Mordecai and Polly questions. Luna Belle folded the paper and stuffed it into her bra. She wanted time to think and having it close to her heart reminded her of Mose.

18

Is it Hot in Here?

Luna Belle's ravenous appetite spurred her to beat Nick to the kitchen. She anticipated a simple country style breakfast, something light before her ride with Nick, but Polly had prepared a feast.

The folds of Mose's letter reminded her of its being tucked in her bosom. Having it prodding her seemed a good thing. For some reason Luna Belle feared she might forget herself.

She pulled a chair from the old work table where she and Mose so often ate breakfast with Polly and Mordecai. Once a pantry, this little anteroom had been neglected, but Polly understood the view from its window was too important to waste on storage. She left a few shelves around the perimeter for convenience, but she gutted the room to make way for her own ideas.

The lone window overlooked the herb and kitchen gardens where Polly found peace away from the kitchen staff. Whether planning menus, peeling potatoes or onions, she loved sitting here.

Some of her most delicious flavor combinations came from thinking at this old table. She studied the plants outside, imagining various combinations, utilizing one of her greatest gifts. Without question the woman possessed a refined pallet. Her keen senses of smell and taste discerned the slightest nuances of ingredients. With an unparalleled mind for blending flavors she knew before hand how things would taste once mixed.

Years earlier Mose named this intimate space in Polly's kitchen the Sunday Night Supper Room. The appropriate name stuck because of a memorable evening spent there with Luna Belle, Mordecai, Polly, and their two children while a terrible storm raged outside. Because of the Swann's daughters, the adults restrained their emotions and acted as if nothing important occurred around them.

Ever since, Mose often asked Polly, "When are we having Stormy Weather Soup again? That remains your best tomato bisque, ever."

"Next time they a bad storm. I guess that's when." She always giggled while holding her palms up in surrender.

"Aw, come on Polly at least share the recipe."

"That be between me and the Lord. Go on now, get out'a here and leave me be."

Polly had long since forgotten how she concocted the delicious soup that night. Unlike her, frightened out of her wits, all she knew was it contained tomatoes.

That wasn't the case this morning. Once she heard Nick agree to come to her table, she concocted some of his favorites along with some of her newest creations. After Mose, Polly loved to feed Nick best because he savored her instinctive culinary powers. Polly loved watching grown men gorge on her food. Nick loved giving her the great pleasure of seeing it happen.

He always said, "If you weren't married…."

She smiled. "You a sight, Nick Polk, that's what you is."

"I'm serious. I'm glad I don't eat here three times a day. Otherwise, I might weigh so much the horses would run in terror."

She loved to stimulate the palette. In her mind boredom killed the senses and caused the mind to turn. She wanted no part of that.

Luna Belle went back to the kitchen proper to pour herself a cup of coffee. While she added about three drops of cream, Nick bounded in and startled her.

"Halloo," he called.

"Gets yourself in this house. So good to sees you." Polly purred through a broad smile.

Nick immediately went to Luna Belle. This was his first chance since Mose's death to approach her without a swarm of people lingering nearby.

He took the cup from her hands, grabbed her shoulder, spun her around, and wrapped her in a tight embrace. His hold began to melt both of them.

She lost resistance then wilted in his strong hold. She sighed. Her breath rushed from her lungs over his virile shoulder. Luna Belle had never experienced this from Nick before. His vice-like arms cajoled the pain from her heart.

All their lives the regal gazelle had treated Nick like a brother, but Luna Belle recognized this as more than the consolation of a sibling. Polly saw it too and smiled. The power of his hug crushed Mose's letter into Luna Belle's breast. It reminded her of his recent passing. Panicking, she pushed her way free from the strength of the man's arms.

Luna Belle had avoided looking at Nick, at least since children together at Ashwood. In her mind he still thrived as a sandy haired boy, skinny, perhaps even snaggletoothed. When had he become this Adonis with the embrace of a love god's charm.

Picking up her coffee she backed away. She wanted escape and a better look at the man who assaulted her emotions. She needed to understand the cause of her heart's lying somewhere in her chest, a molten pool.

As Nick poured himself a cup of Polly's coffee, Luna Belle looked him over from head to toe. There the chiseled Raphael model stood. His rakish blond curls, his beautiful posture, the way his riding clothes accentuated his manly physique. She had avoided seeing any of this before.

Stirring her coffee she thought, *Am I oblivious or what?*

He turned and spoke. Instead of listening to his warm voice, she took the opportunity to examine his face.

"Luna Belle, I'm so sorry for all you've been through."

She wanted to touch his shaved cheek and feel the way the light danced off his shiny skin covering a strong chin that almost sported a dimple. Luna Belle's mind swam in the blueness of his piercing Caribbean eyes. She wanted to have and hold all these new discoveries forever.

Almost quivering she replied in sultry tones that embarrassed her while they escaped her lips. "Thank you Nick. You've already done more than I ever dreamed."

"Stop going on, now." His voice matched her husky tone.

She snapped back to reality. "The horses performed so well that I enjoyed coming here and feeling confident. Mose deserved it. From the depths of my soul, thank you."

"Thank you, Luna Belle, but hordes of vital people became involved. The Gonzales team ... wow ... we owe them."

Polly's mind danced. Dared she hope? She wholeheartedly believed in the Contessa's curse, although Nick appeared to evade the malediction's powerful clutches. His work hinted at absolution that created Polly's powerful ideas for further debate.

Luna Belle remained ignorant of anything around her except the physical specimen standing before her. She wanted to revel in the handsome man.

Nick had always seen Luna Belle's beauty. Her long flowing black hair. He loved it when her tresses overcame their confinement and cascaded over her shoulders because it never seemed to bother her. He admired little things like that about her.

Her eyes compelled him in with their deep pools of intense sky blue. Her flawless ivory skin that he wanted to caress was covered in her well fitting habit.

Nick almost tweaked her dainty chiseled nose, but feared it might keep him from later kissing her round full lips. As he looked at her petite ears, exposed by her tied back hair, he marveled at their intricacies.

A long graceful neck and gorgeous figure had driven the man to distraction for most of his life. All these things he kept catalogued in the furtherest depths of his mind. Nick loved Luna Belle and often avoided her presence because he couldn't trust himself.

He ofttimes saw her thrown from horses, get up and dust herself off, ready to retry. He'd witnessed first hand her willingness to work. If someone fell ill at the barn, Luna Belle filled in and worked admirably. She never complained.

He loved the way she sat a horse. The way she held a fork, whether for eating or mucking stalls. The way she smiled whenever something around her went amiss. Luna Belle had always stood as his perfect, ideal woman.

Mose had consistently treated Nick well. He never questioned that. Conversely, Nick's loyalty remained true while the two nurtured a great and fast friendship. Now with Mose gone, Nick looked at Luna Belle with freshened eyes. When children, Nick reconciled himself to living without her as a lover and wife. It was not of his or her doing, her grandfather saw to it so that Nick never stood a chance.

Luna Belle remained oblivious to Nick's true passion, feelings he kindled after his return to Ashwood from South Florida where he apprenticed at Nuevo Jerez for two years. He left Ashwood Luna Belle's surrogate brother, then returned an accomplished equestrian with the eyes and longings of a fully fledged man.

Now, Nick found newborn freedom, unencumbered by any personal commitment between Luna Belle and Mose. Secreting his heart for all these years, he never dishonored himself or his friend. He loved Luna Belle too much to have ever defaced her existence with a tawdry affair. truly preferring life without dishonor.

Nick clung to his father's own heart. Stuart Polk taught his son to live life with great nobility and Nick still depended on his patriarch's example to guide him. He attributed all his successes in life to his upbringing.

Polly broke their spell even though she hated to disturb them. "It's on the table. Y'all come on now. Um-hmm."

Luna Belle was called back from Nick's spell. She became ashamed of herself, her husband not cold in the ground. She reached for her breast—her heart—her consolation—the letter Mose had written with his own hand. Her true loyalty must remain with him.

Nick and Luna Belle salivated at the feast spread before them. Even Mordecai fell victim to the unbelievable repast, the likes of which Polly hadn't taken upon herself to spread for breakfast in a long time.

Luna Belle's appetite had been whetted even stronger since

coming to the kitchen and inhaling the aromas. Polly had
outdone herself.

Luna Belle put her palms together and held her hands
extended in front of her in a diving position. "Get out'a my way.
I'm gonna eat."

Nick bowed and flourished his hand. "The lady has spoken."

Nothing pleased Polly more. She knew Luna Belle's appetite
matched Nick's bite for bite. Polly's excitement mounted as she
contemplated watching them gorge themselves.

Polly's menu started with Ruby Red Grapefruit supremes
accompanied by the same fruit's juice with a splash of
Champagne. She served the meal family style with everything
placed on the table for the four of them to devour.

She had:

Paper thin sliced country ham poached in bourbon, maple
syrup, and orange juice; sprinkled with fresh chopped mint,
rolled around huge fresh sweet strawberries from the early
garden. Grown under a cloche, the first offerings of late winter
South Georgia fare.

Chicken breast medallions poached in white wine and cream
with a mushroom, chive, parsley, and pimento garnish, rested on
a bed of fresh creamed spinach.

Individual ramekins of oysters covered by soft shirred eggs
under a cream and Gruyere topping with home cured bacon,
crisped under the hot salamander.

Morning Power: grilled skewered shrimp with a spicy dry
rub, sauced with a sweet vinegar, cayenne, and lemon paste. A
signature creation.

Hot buttered biscuits with both onion and orange
marmalades, blueberry jam, blackberry preserves, and a cheese
tray of extra sharp white cheddar, *Parmigiano Reggiano, Délice de
Bourgogne,* and Maytag Blue.

Earl Grey or English Breakfast teas—offered with either
milk or lemon.

After gorging themselves, Polly tried shooing them out of her kitchen. The pair had stuffed themselves and they needed strength enough to ride. She began to fret over her heavy menu perhaps having been a mistake.

Mordecai sensed her anxiety and rose from the table. Back in the kitchen he called, "Pol-ly."

She came into the kitchen perplexed, wringing her hands. "What you wants?"

"I need a little help over here, that's all." He said from across the room.

She approached and grumbled, "What?"

"Leave them be. They need time. In my wildest imagination, I never knew. I saw ... his eyes." Mordecai professed.

"I seen something you din't, too. She have feelings for him, but she either don't knows it yet, or she running from it. She nearly turns into a puddle in the flo. That's what I seen. Um-hmm." Polly whispered.

"Either way, leave them alone. Let them work it out."

Polly wanted to help nature along but Mordecai made sense. She needed to back off. These two had known each other all their lives and neither Polly nor Mordecai possessed the ability to control this situation between mature loving friends.

Leaving the room, he turned. "By the way, you outdid yourself with breakfast. Thank you."

Polly nodded her approval and blew him a kiss. The longer she lived, the more she loved Mordecai Swann. She married him with mixed emotions but those had vanished years ago.

She heard them in the adjacent room talking, laughing, cajoling, enjoying innocent fun. The spell he cast over this jaded woman seemed miraculous.

Polly heard chairs being pushed away from the table just before the couple appeared in the kitchen. Each took the opportunity to hug the chef in appreciation for her marvelous meal.

"You're my dear, wonderful friend." Luna Belle gushed. She had forgotten curses and poppycock.

When Nick hugged to thank her, Mordecai walked into the kitchen. "You two better watch out, I'm seeing things I'm not sure about." He followed with a hearty belly laugh.

"I've warned you for years, old Man. Any woman who can cook … well … you're in jeopardy of losing her. If not to me, Lord knows who." Nick beamed.

Luna Belle wanted to feign jealousy, but her instincts refused the show of emotion. She didn't know how to bear Nick's already seeming to think of her as his own possession. She had no desire to spur him on.

Polly handed Nick a saddle bag packed with a Thermos of Irish coffee, a couple of juicy ripe pears, and a little of the white cheddar.

"Just in case y'all needs a little something later." She insisted.

Nick argued, "I can't eat again for a week."

"Speak for yourself. Don't you dare think you're gonna starve me. I'm ready to conquer the world. I'll want a full tummy for that, right Polly?"

"Um-hmm." Polly smiled after Nick took the bag and slung it over his rugged shoulder.

The two left the kitchen headed toward the barn while Polly watched out one of the windows with a hand over her fluttering heart. "I wants Missy to has a little happiness, Mordecai. She been running from her true feelings all her life, ain't she?"

"I expect you're right."

"She been making herseff happy with thangs, but the best part of happy come from inside. Thangs ain't got the power to takes the place of love. That's all I knows about it."

Mordecai kissed Polly's cheek. "My dear, in many ways, your wisdom far outshines Missy's."

19
Foundling

Nick and Luna Belle walked to the barn with an uncomfortable electricity flowing between them. Wanting to reduce the obvious tensions, Nick said, "Want to hear a little story of the slip of a girl without a mother that Mose found on the sidewalk in Savannah?"

"Mose told that one so often. Sometimes I wanted to scream."

"But you've never heard my version, have you?"

Luna Belle looked off toward the horizon and braced herself as Nick started his diatribe.

Mose had only been sworn in as a lawyer for six weeks when he encountered his first deposition with a murder witness. A drug-crazed man stood accused of murdering three women on Tybee Island and Mose ended up with the responsibility to interview the only eyewitness.

The brutal initial inquisition in Judge Meecham's chambers in Savannah lasted three grueling hours. Mose left with his head bowed, shuffling latent fallen leaves with his feet while his steps slid along the rough brick walkway leading to his car. He stopped to peer into several shop windows while he meandered and contemplated the wisdom of his decision to practice law.

He arrived at his car only to find a young woman sprawled unconscious on the sidewalk. Her right eye obviously bruised, cut, and severely swollen shut. Mose crouched near her face to see if she lived. Once low enough, he saw blood drying in a puddle under her cheek. Her knees bled from being dragged on a rough surface. Flies lit on her abrasions and cuts before they could adequately scab over. With his ear close to her mouth, Mose heard shallow breaths.

He ran into a nearby bookstore and called out for help. "Call an ambulance, please."

"Who's that?"

"I don't know. I found her unconscious. Please, get some help."

The clerk dialed the operator. "An ambulance, please.— Habersham Books on Lafayette Square, and hurry." Hanging up, she ran out the shop door to see the commotion. "Why, she's a negra. Why'd you have me call an ambulance?"

"Madame, she is a human being. Why think her skin color relevant to her situation?"

Nick recalled how furious Mose became every time he told this story. He held no sanction for racial bigotry. Nick agreed.

"Say what you will, Mister, but the fact remains, she's nothing but a piece of black trash. Look at her. She needs hauling away to a county work detail."

"Madame, you're a bigot and a discredit to our species."

"Well, aren't you the uppity, arrogant, snot-nosed son of a bitch?" She huffed back into the bookshop and slammed the door.

He talked in an attempt to rouse the stranger while he admired her innate beauty. Mose couldn't believe anyone would treat another human in such an atrocious manner.

Within minutes an ambulance arrived and two attendants hopped out. When they saw the situation, they turned to leave but Mose confronted them with a malicious sneer.

"Gentlemen. As a junior district attorney I assure you of one thing. If you leave, I will have you indicted for dereliction of duty."

The driver sauntered up to Mose and got in his face. "Look. It's not that I don't want to help but we'd get fired. No need for you to sue me then. Can't get blood out of a turnip."

Mose advanced even closer to the arrogant man. They stood almost nose to nose. "I'm not talking about suing you. I'm talking jail, you imbecile. Are you paying attention?"

The man's head jerked back slightly and he began slowly stepping back. "Uh …yes sir, but I can't take her in this ambulance. I'm telling you we'd get fired. We both got wives and kids. Give us a break."

Mose took another unrelenting step toward the man. "Then at least help me get her in my car."

"Sure. That we'll do. Fred … help me get this gal in his car. Bring a couple of sheets and a blanket too. She's bleeding. What happened anyway? She sass you or som'um?"

"I found her this way." Mose's dark fiery eyes stared indignantly into the ambulance driver's face. The two strangers gently placed the young woman into Mose's car and covered her with a cotton blanket.

The drive to Pirate's Landing took too long causing Mose to grow concerned about her incessant blood loss that seeped through the sheets and pooled on the leather seats. After hearing horrors openly discussed during his first deposition, Mose grew even further disgusted by this young nubile creature's condition. He tried imagining the debased coward who inflicted this damage.

Dr. Deamon came to the car and called for help. Two nurses brought a gurney and managed to get the young woman onto it without injuring her further.

They rolled her into the hospital. Then cut off her bloody, raggedy, tattered, filthy clothes and assessed her injuries.

"Somebody's beaten her with a crowbar. Look at this." Dr. Deamon yelled in white hot anger.

"She's trying to wake." A nurse said.

The helpless creature tried to open her eyes. In terror she attempted escape.

Thrashing and screaming, "Whu' is I?"

"Calm down. We're here to help. My name is Dr. Deamon and these are my nurses. Mr. Black over there found you in Savannah."

The doctor's patient screamed in terror at the sound of his name. "Lemme out'a heah. Now."

One nurse approached the battered girl and covered her with a sheet while another took a warm wet wash cloth and positioned it on her brow.

"Who did this to you?"

"He kilz me if'n I telz."

Mose stepped to this beauty's side and asked.

"What's your name?"

"My name be Polly. P-o-l-l-y. Polly."

"Okay, Polly. I found you on the sidewalk. I brought you here to my hometown for help."

"Whu' is I?"

"Pirate's Landing."

Polly trembled at the sound of the word pirate. Her blood almost curdled. A demon—a pirate—had she died and gone to Hell?

Deamon stood alongside her and looked patiently at her quivering body. "Allow me to give you a shot to ease the pain of cleaning your wounds?"

She tried to raise her head in search of his gun.

"Don' shooz me." She wailed, "I'z too young t' dies."

"It's not a gun. Let me show you." Dr. Deamon showed Polly the syringe.

"Nu-uh. Don' shooz me wif no pin neither."

Dr. Deamon took the syringe and held her arm, injecting the drug cocktail. Within an instant Polly drifted into peace.

When she regained consciousness she discovered herself cleaned and bandaged with her left foot elevated in a sling. Mose had dutifully stayed by her side during the entire ordeal. He observed her waking and approached the bedside.

"Polly. You don't ever have to go back. If you like, we'll all help you adjust here. I only ask that you realize a choice exists."

Polly lulled herself off into a place she had never been. A place of peace and comfort where her former fears seemed momentarily stowed away. This time when she drifted off, it was into a peaceful slumber of heaven.

Dr. Deamon kept her in his little office hospital for several days. All this strange concern over her overwhelmed her feeble spirit.

Everyday Mose faithfully came to console. Dr. Deamon told him that if her wounds continued to remain infection free, she might soon go home. Mose's head concocted a strategy to salvage the young girl's life.

"Jack, go along with me on this, okay?"

"What?"

"Tell her she needs a few more days of convalescence. Let me take her to Teachall. She might like it and stay. I poked around Savannah and learned that the trash she claims as her father inflicted her wounds. The girl has never had an opportunity in her life and I want to give her one."

"What if she's dangerous?"

"Jack, look at her. I don't think she's any more dangerous than a Jenny wren. Haven't you seen enough to realize she deserves a chance to escape the torment of her bane existence."

"You're playing with fire, but I know there's no need to argue. You're as bullheaded as—"

"As you?" Mose interrupted.

"Okay. As I."

Mose spent the next two days at Teachall trying to persuade his folks to accept his plan to give Polly a life. His mother, Beulah, took to the idea. His father, the Colonel, initially resisted. Mose finally convinced them of Polly's deserving a chance to find happiness.

"But you must remove her from this place if she gives the slightest offense. We can't afford to have a renegade living in our home. She's a wild creature," the Colonel said.

Mose promised, "I understand your concern. I promise you on my word as a gentleman that if she creates a problem, she's gone."

Early the next morning Mose brought Mordecai with him to take Polly to Teachall. For the last few days he regaled Mordecai with fascinating tales about her. Mordecai already anticipated having to assume responsibility for her when Mose tired of her.

Mose tried to get Mordecai interested. "You haven't even seen her. I'm almost certain you'll agree with me once you have a chance to stay around her for a little while. Mordecai, she's a beautiful, scared rabbit. If she goes back, I'm afraid next time her excuse of an old man may kill her. Help me, please."

When Mordecai saw Polly, still with bandages on her knees and forearms, his heart almost melted at the sight of her beautiful face. He was the first black person she had seen since leaving Savannah. His warm smile shined, a welcome sight to her. She timidly returned the favor.

"Polly, meet Mordecai, a dear and trusted friend."

"Good morning, Polly. I hope you are feeling much better."

Polly eyes widened. Taken aback by his eloquence, she had never heard such polished language coming from any black man. It intimidated her, but she saw he continued in graciousness. Even his eyes smiled.

She vowed to remain silent around him. If the handsome man heard her, he would run for certain.

Mose cocked his head gently to the side and in a soft voice said, "Polly, aren't you going to even speak to Mordecai."

Betrayed, forced to speak, she muttered, "Hey."

Mordecai looked into her eyes and said, "Hey, to you too."

Mose continued, "Polly, I know you haven't eaten this morning because I asked them to withhold your breakfast. I wanted to let you enjoy one of Mordecai's mother's incredible feasts. I hope you're hungry."

"Yes suh." Polly's voice cracked. They proved their intention to make her talk.

When they arrived at Teachall Polly's eyes bulged; she never expected a palace. Surrounded by a subtropical paradise with all sorts of blooming plants and green on every side, this was utopia.

They confused her by driving to the front entrance. She knew better than that. Being ignorant didn't mean she was thickheaded. Surely they knew she should enter such a place around back. Maybe the white man exited here, but she and the black man ought to go to the rear of the mansion.

When Mose opened her car door and beckoned her out,

Polly became even more confused and anxious.

"Well, come on, get out."

Mose leaned over and looked into the car with imploringly arched brows. Even his white Panama hat didn't conceal them. His teeth gleamed behind his warm smile while Mordecai joined Mose. Both men held their hands out offering assistance.

She painfully attempted to stand upright while she watched the front door of the house open. The Colonel, Beulah, and Berta Mae came onto the veranda. Polly realized the intent to climb the mount where three gods awaited in judgement—Olympus. Their sight frightened Polly enough for her stomach to turn.

Both men helped her hesitantly mount the steps. They paused on each tread. It never dawned on Mose, fear caused her apprehension and delayed climb.

About the time they made the veranda's landing Mose's two giant mastiffs, Thor and Thunder, bounded outside. Polly feared being eaten for the beasts' breakfast. She leaned over and allowed the men to support her arms. She retched.

"Colonel. Get those beasts off this porch. How insensitive of us. Berta Mae get a cold cloth. To the front salon and recline her in a chaise. Get her feet up." Beulah barked these orders in a split second.

No questions followed. All jumped. As they made their way inside, Polly regained her composure enough to look around at the overwhelming interiors.

Beulah looked at Mose in total disgust because Polly wore only a scant hospital gown. "Mose, how dare you embarrass this elegant person? No proper clothes. Really."

"Sorry. I didn't think. Jack destroyed her clothes when he cut them off to treat her."

"I'm ashamed of you." Beulah rubbed her hands down the sides of her torso to straighten her dress.

Berta Mae came back in a flash with a basin of cool water and several wash cloths. She went straight to Polly and knelt beside the chaise. "There, there, dear. Allow me to lay this cool cloth on your pretty forehead." She took another and wrung it out in the basin. "And this one we'll place right there on your throat. Doesn't that feel better?"

Beulah disappeared and headed straightway to Rose's

summer chifforobe. She found a white cotton dress with short
sleeves of insertion lace, beading, intertwined with little blue
silk ribbons, and all joined with entredeux. It had a small yoke
of the same rows of lace. Tied around the waist with a blue satin
sash, it was a simple, elegant little summer dress.

When Beulah returned downstairs she found Polly sitting
up.

"My poor dear, I hope you're settled. I know we
overwhelmed you. Please forgive us. We meant nothing more
than to welcome you."

"Than-kee, ma'am." Polly smiled.

"Berta Mae, she needs to change. If you think your tummy
can take it, we'll have a little light breakfast."

The women led Polly into another parlor where a large
Coromandel screen stood in a corner. Beulah instructed her to
go behind the folded screen and toss out her gown. This privacy
relieved Polly.

Polly stepped out from behind the screen and Beulah said,
"Turn around, dear. Let us button your dress and tie your sash."

Polly obliged. She felt like a princess in her new dainty
French style dress. Polly had never worn anything but hand-me-
down calico and homespun. This simplistic elegance made her
heart sing and brought a wide smile to her lips.

"Feeling a little better now?" Berta Mae asked.

Polly shook her head. She saw a large mirror hung high in
the room, tilted at an angle so she saw herself from above. Polly
loved the dress, but fussed with her tangled hair.

Beulah's instincts again took over. "Polly, we want you
comfortable. Berta Mae will you help her brush her hair before
we eat?"

Polly and Berta Mae agreed.

As she followed Berta Mae, Polly asked, "Whu you and da
man learns' to talk like white folk?"

"Polly, we both learned here. All the children in this house
are educated by accomplished tutors. The Blacks insist on
everyone's learning to read and write. Polly's smile vanished and
her head bowed.

Berta Mae brushed and tried to arrange Polly's hair. "Polly,
once we have eaten, we need to wash your hair. There's still

some dried blood in it. I know you're starved. After breakfast,
I'll fix you a steamy hot bath."

Polly closed her eyes and thanked God for the dream
she experienced. She prayed they never fully understood her
ignorance.

"Polly?"

"Um-hmm."

"How'd you get in this mess? What happened to you?"

Polly hesitated before she said, "My pappy done dis to me.
Bout de worser he done ever beats me. Dis time he tries an kills
me."

"Why?"

"Cause I ain't gonna be no ho. Das why. He want de money
for his moonshine likker."

Berta Mae laid her hands on Polly's shoulders.

"If you stay here you will learn many things over time. Trust
me now. God has delivered you."

"What about dem dog? Dey is dogs, ain't dey?"

"They're dogs all right, but think of them as friendly kittens.
Now, if a body tried and hurt a member of this family, they'd
tear them limb from limb."

Polly marked that in her mind. She wanted never to hurt
anyone here. The dogs terrified her.

20

She Wants to What?

So, just as Mose had hoped, it happened. When Mordecai saw Polly he fell hopelessly in love.

Polly needed time to adjust to all the unaccustomed kindnesses she found all around her. Everything at Teachall revolved around magical flavors that floated in the air. Their auras beckoned her to explore the intrigue created by all the flowers and gardens.

She had arrived during rose and lily season's unfolding. Such unimagined perfumes overwhelmed her mind's pleasure senses. The heady aromas saturated the landscape and every room with overwhelming fragrance.

Especially fond of the kitchen garden, Polly loved breaking off tidbits, smelling, then tasting. Such a wide gamut of new flavors tickled her tongue and excited her pallet as much as the flower gardens had stimulated her nose. Taking different combinations of vegetables and herbs, she mushed and chewed them together, reveling in creation.

She knew of pinto beans, corn pone, and onions when she came to Teachall. Even potatoes were more prized than most children rate candy. All these new fangled tastes and smells brought ecstatic joy.

Polly's citron eyes gleamed like rare Columbian gemstones.

Naturally refined posture highlighted her elegant stance. Soft ebony curls accentuated her striking face. Rich bronzy caramel skin completed her physical perfection. One small hairline scar annoyed her mostly because it came to her as her father's parting gift.

Her good fortune led the sot to beat her senseless, causing Mose to rescue her from certain death. She loved him for it.

Saved, she wanted Mose; however, he remained tied to a preexisting commitment Polly didn't understand. She managed to stoically accept what she perceived as rejection.

She saw Mordecai as grand and handsome, but it was Mose who had captured her heart. Over time Mordecai made himself more appealing, although she remained most curious about Mose. Polly took to wandering without purpose whenever he was not at Teachall.

She slowly began accepting Mordecai's company more and more. He took her for early morning walks where quietude allowed them to pass unvoiced feelings between themselves. Polly often ran ahead of Mordecai to explore some new discovery. He patiently watched her show him different ways of seeing his own world.

Polly would run ahead to the barn to be near the horses. Back in Savannah, spare money went to moonshine, never to animals. They rarely found money for food much less a pet. Here, all kinds of animals infatuated her.

Everyone and everything at Teachall made life interesting. She determined to further improve her already bettered life and grew overly insatiable in regard to being educated. Beulah observed and remarked about Polly's inquisitive spirit. Beulah's astute judgement became more evident as Polly transformed herself into a refreshing zephyr that swept boredom from Teachall with her curiosity.

She began admiring Mordecai's appearance and the way he looked at her. His skin glowed slightly darker than hers. His eyes blazed the same golden brown she observed on the painting of a tiger in Teachall's expansive gallery. She wanted to drape Mordecai in tiger skin.

Another painting also reminded her of Mordecai. That dashing figure with mocha skin was mounted on a fiery red horse.

Colonel Black caught her admiring it. "Ah. Polly, you possess a good eye for art. I see you have zeroed in on a noble sheik mounted on a glorious Arabian mare."

He gestured toward the background. "Notice the landscape. It's foreign to our eyes because it is the Arabian peninsula. Come, look at the globe with me." He carefully pointed out their position then showed Polly how far removed that environment was from Teachall. "Polly, the man is mounted on a mare. The oriental peoples preferred them for their war mounts."

"Mr. Colonel, how does you know all that kind of stuff? Looks to me like your head might splode." She looked at him hard. "Sometime I think I'z too dumb to live here, but I does loves to learn all I can. That man there, he dress up so fancy. If I could gets my hand on all that stuff, I dress up Mordecai just like that. I likes t'see that, wouldn't you?"

"Yes you're right. That's a marvelous idea. I'm certain, Mordecai might oblige you for the Grande Masque we have here Halloween eve."

"Whu' uh gran mast?"

"Oh. Polly, you'll love it. It's a most wondrously marvelous party. Everybody dresses up fancy. I think you and Mordecai should come as an oriental potentate and his consort."

"Do what?"

"Come with me and I'll show you."

The Colonel took her into his private library. There, over a green tufted leather Chesterfield sofa hung another painting.

"I ain't never done been in this room yet, Mr. Colonel."

"Well, then welcome to my little personal retreat, Polly. Look at this painting. It is perhaps my favorite in the entire house, that's why I had it moved into my own office."

"Now ain't that something? Fancy, sho nuff."

Colonel Black stood back and compared Polly's face with the eastern beauty reclined on silk pillows that created the focal point of the large image. The two women's similarities amazed the Colonel. If Polly twisted her hair back and had a gossamer drape over her head, she looked like this alluring princess.

"She got on a purdy dress though, ain't she?"

"Yes, she does."

"Yes-sir, she do."

"And Polly, look at her simple gold ribbon crown."

"Um-hmm. That look like a big old bug right there on her forehead."

The Colonel chuckled. "It is a bug, Polly, but it's not real. It's called a scarab and its carved from jade."

"Why anybody want a bug tied on they head?"

"I'm not sure, but I think it's for good luck."

"Um-hmm. So them folks believe in a little ju-ju hoo-hoo, too?"

"Most likely." The Colonel had to break to chuckle. "See the light shining in from that upper window. That's called a crepuscular ray and it lights her up pretty, doesn't it?"

"She do glow, all right."

"Now turn your eyes over toward the man standing in the shadows. He's beckoning her to rise and join him. Do you see his resemblance to Mordecai? His white turban is crowned with a huge diamond, and an ostrich plume."

"He a looker rascal, that's right. He standing over there without no shirt, all muscle and man, ain't he? Why you reckon they both be bare foot?"

The Colonel exhaled as he smiled then said, "I think it indicates a prelude to a romantic episode."

"Um-hmm."

Colonel Black added, "I'd love to see you and Mordecai dressed like them."

"Yes-sir, but I wants me some shoes and I spect Mordecai want him a shirt too."

The Colonel chuckled and said, "Then shoes you shall have."

Polly envisioned Mordecai, dressed in dashing robes and pantaloons, swooping her onto the back of a noble charger and whisking her away to some far off palace.

Berta Mae was not amused when, out of thin air, Polly expressed an interest in cooking. Having been in charge of Teachall's kitchen for decades, Mordecai's mother, Berta Mae Swann, proudly wore her sterling reputation and had no desire to see it tarnished.

"She doesn't know a tomato from a chicken leg. When she came here, she hadn't even tasted bacon. Not worth a toot in a skillet." Berta Mae humphed.

"Mama, please, let her help you. She's going to stay here, I can feel it in my bones. I want her in the house with you and me. If you teach her to cook—"

"Mordecai? Are you telling me you're falling in love with that trash? She can't even speak English. That gibberish she utters, what is it supposed to be, anyway? What kind of life can you hope to have with her? You know well as I do, Mose found her in the gutter. If that don't tell you she's trash—"

"Mama, how long have our people been here?"

"You know same as I do. Since the earliest days with the Contessa. That's a silly question?"

"Have you forgotten the original family occupation? True, our education happened in this house, but how can it elevate us above Polly? If we have grown so high-and-mighty important, perhaps this place fails to serve me in a manner befitting my outlook on life. Maybe I shall find my place out on my own."

Mordecai glared at his mother with a piercing stare.

"You're talking foolish now … talking with your heart, not your head. Don't look at me like that. I'll slap the shine off your face, boy. You hear me?"

Berta Mae grimaced over her spectacles. Mordecai sat dejected, but he knew his mama well enough to know she needed to stew a while.

She lifted the blue and white tea towel protecting her bread bowl and began mixing biscuits. Mordecai had seen it thousands of times. She worked a mound of lard into the flour then poured in buttermilk. While white paste squished through her practiced fingers, her mind relaxed.

"Well, I guess she can come in a little. Maybe I can teach her to peel onions, or churn. I don't know if she possesses enough brainpower to do much else. I promise to try, but you listen to me. If she ruins things just one time she leaves my kitchen for good. You hear me?"

Berta Mae started forming her biscuits and placing them on a baking sheet. "Why in the world did I let you talk me into this? That heifer won't last a week in this heat. No-sir, maybe not even a day."

It didn't take a week for Polly to turn herself into an indispensable cook's assistant. She took to the kitchen like a cat to cream and never breathed one word of complaint. She pranced and hummed around like a natural born chef. Polly had found her home.

In no time her true gift shined. At first Berta Mae appeared jealous; however, Polly soon became a consummate stateswoman. She always credited Berta Mae with any new discovery. If Polly added a little rosemary to the pork roast—Berta Mae's idea. A little grape juice in the iced tea, guess who thought of that?

Berta Mae became embarrassed by Polly's continual fibbing. Finally, Berta Mae's dam broke.

In the middle of a marvelous meal Berta Mae started, "Miss Beulah, I reckon I need to 'fess up."

"Fess up? About what?"

"Nothing, that's what."

"How can you confess to nothing? I'm confused."

"Polly, come in here." Berta Mae commanded.

Polly's widened eyes peered around the door. Berta Mae's voice frightened. Maybe the mentor had seen her when she took a swig of apricot brandy just to see what it tasted like. Maybe she had peppered the gravy with a far too heavy hand, but she smiled when she tasted it. She twitched in anticipation of being expelled from her newly beloved home.

Beulah said, "Polly, come on in. Berta Mae, what's wrong?"

Polly entered and trembled.

"I'm glad to get this off my chest. It's kept me awake at night long enough.

"Polly minced onions and soaked them in vinegar before she added them to the mashed potatoes.

"Polly chopped chives and sprinkled them on the shrimp bisque.

"Polly broke milk chocolate and added it to the homemade ice cream.

"Polly added a little cream to the vegetable soup.

"You see where I'm going?"

Polly quaked. She had trampled Berta Mae's sacred recipes and stood with no excuse in the world.

"Yes, Berta Mae, I understand. Colonel, your opinion?" Beulah templed her hands, resting her elbows on the table's edge.

He took his napkin from his lap and wiped his lips, annoyed at being called from his sumptuous repast. "You two have never disappointed me before."

Polly sweated and trembled.

Mose saw her condition. "Have y'all no shame? Polly quakes in abject terror. Look at her. She appears ready to faint."

Polly did approach passing out. She had fallen in love with Teachall, the Blacks, Berta Mae, and Mordecai. She saw her imagined diaphanous gown fly out a window—no grande masque for her. She still didn't know what one was, but she wanted to go.

Beulah jumped to her feet and pulled a chair away from the wall. "Polly, sit down. We had no intention of frightening you, did we Berta Mae?"

"No ma'am. The furtherest thing from my mind." Berta Mae wickedly smiled, raised her brows and peered out a window.

"Polly, I believe what Berta Mae tried to say ... she thinks it's time for her to retire. Right, Berta Mae?"

Berta Mae nudged Polly's chin up to look into her eyes. "Exactly. Polly, you possess a gift, child. No other way to say it. You're a better cook than me. Besides, it'd take weight off my shoulders."

"I's no more ready to take over that kitchen than I'z ready to run for prezeedent."

"Careful what you say, Polly. You might serve better than the one we have now." The Colonel chuckled.

Beulah admonished, "Don't mock Polly."

"I mocked not. Furthermore, I resent the implication."

Beulah continued, "Berta Mae, you're willing to stay and help, right?"

"Naturally."

"So you see, Polly, It's your decision. But if I might suggest, why don't you try being in charge for a few days ... see how you take to it. That way if you don't like it, Berta Mae can return."

Berta Mae chimed in, "Wonderful." She knew in her heart, Polly's conquering ambition guaranteed her own freedom.

Polly nodded reluctant approval.

Within a month Polly turned herself into master of the kitchen. For the first time in her adult life, Berta Mae experienced freedom without the responsibility of feeding a multitude. Whenever she missed something sacred in her life she gave Polly a break. The arrangement suited both women to a tee. Berta Mae even returned to singing around the house. Out of the clear blue, meeting Mordecai in the hall one day, she grabbed her son's cheeks and gave him a big kiss on his forehead, smiled at him and waltzed off humming toward the palm court.

Mordecai announced, "Polly, I want to teach you to read."

"I can't reads, it nice of you to offer, but I'z too stupid to learns to read."

"Utter rubbish, you are not stupid. Don't ever let me hear you speak such nonsense about yourself again. We'll work as slowly as you like, although you shall read in no time. I promise."

Mordecai's astute assessment of her capabilities proved true. Soon she read anything. "You says I ain't stupid, but why can't I learns to talk right?"

"Your childhood afforded you so little opportunity. Old habits sometimes reside too deeply to remove. Besides, everyone here understands you. Stop fretting over silly nonsense."

"I tries best I can to talk right but don't seems to works. I wants to, but I knows one thing in my heart for sure: I don't never wants to conjure no more verbs."

Mordecai smiled. "Then my dear, you never shall."

Polly's resistance melted, her heart won by Mordecai's kindness and persistence.

As all these things unfolded before Berta Mae's eyes, her uplifted heart thought, *Now I can die.*

Mordecai persuaded his mother to cook for a month because he and Polly wanted time for a honeymoon. Polly wanted the Colonel to perform their simple ceremony. He obliged with great pride.

Beulah took Polly into Savannah and commissioned a lovely gown of Egyptian lawn. It featured an empire waist and sported criss-cross blue silk ribbons like the lady in the painting. Polly looked positively radiant.

The Colonel said, "Polly, you're Josephine at her coronation. I don't think I've ever seen a more beautiful bride."

Polly had no idea about Josephine but she knew he liked what he saw. Mordecai whisked her away—not on a flaming charger, instead it was in a brand new gleaming silver Panther De Ville roadster with a black tooled leather and walnut burl interior, a small wedding gift from the Blacks.

21

Coming to Teachall

Luna Belle and Nick prepared to mount the horses for their morning ride.

Nick said, "Reckon these horses can carry us after all that food?"

"I'm not sure … bet I gained ten pounds."

Amused, she still thought of the past as she looked over the saddle and saw Nick. He had been at Teachall so long she took him for granted, yet it hadn't always been that way.

"Nick, I was just thinking about when Mose moved you up here."

"Yeah. After you left, Ashwood fell apart."

"I've tried to block all that out of my mind. I'm sorry for the way things turned out back in Brunswick. I never intended for you or your dad to be burdened by my family."

"No need to worry over that. Wouldn't 'a had it any other way. We loved y'all like our own kin—besides, y'all gave Daddy a home when his folks were killed. How could we abandon y'all when you needed us?"

Luna Belle smiled while she adjusted her chaps.

"Tell you the truth, when Mose asked me and Daddy to come here, I really got excited."

"Yeah, I know but you delayed coming because you were too stubborn to leave Granddaddy."

"We weren't about to go off and leave him or your mama. Since we're talking about this, I don't mean to gripe, but that was one of the worst times of my life. Within one month, I lost your granddaddy, your mama, then Daddy died."

"If anybody ever went the extra mile, it was the two of you. Y'all did too much, and I didn't even know about it until it was too late. I feel so guilty about how much I failed to help."

"Luna Belle, you were a newly-wed. We didn't want to burden you with all that depressing trouble. What could you have done about it, anyway?"

"I could have done something! It still aggravates me to think you did all that without asking for help."

"Last thing I wanted for you was to hear your granddaddy begging to be taken home. Hell, he was at the place he'd been born and raised. Couldn't get any more home than that."

"You've never told me all the excruciating details."

"Sorry, I should learn when to keep my mouth shut."

"Don't be ridiculous. I want to know."

Nick nodded and chuckled. "Sometimes, after Mr. Brigham's mind went, Daddy would take him out in a bass boat to try and fish. Sometimes your granddaddy would just flail the water with his fishing pole. Daddy never seemed to mind, at least the old man was more peaceful out on the water."

"They both loved to fish but it sounds like your dad was just coddling an old demented soul. I'll bet that was a sight."

"It brings a smile to my face now … didn't then."

"Your daddy was so patient with all of us. He remains one of the greatest blessings in my life."

Nick nodded.

"I remember coming back to Brunswick for the funerals and settling the estate."

"Yeah, Mose took the bull by the horns and got everything done without even thinking about it. He was good to you."

"I took him for granted, too."

"That's none of my business."

"Well, it's the truth, but we've gone off on a wild goose chase. I wanted to talk about more pleasant memories, like when you came here."

"What about it?"

"Mose was as excited as I was that you were coming here."

"Oh, yeah?"

"Sure, he knew you had great connections with the Gonzales and could help him acquire new stock. Of course, I reminded him of my philosophy: A woman can never have too many kimono, jewels, furs, or Andalusian horses." Luna Belle laughed.

Nick shook his head. "Never made any bones about it, did you?"

"Nope."

"I would tell you to never change, but I'm not sure that's very good advice."

"Back at you, mister."

Luna Belle walked into the tack room and returned with a mild pair of blunt spurs. "If Fazio's as frisky as he seems, these will be plenty."

"I'd say you're right."

She giggled.

"You sound like a kid over there, what's so funny?"

"Talking about burying folks reminded me of what I told Mose the last time he threatened to tell the story of you two trying to bury me."

"Oh yeah." Nick exhaled and smiled. "What'd you tell him?"

"That I'd pinch his nostrils shut and use an oyster fork to tediously remove his tongue. It sounded excruciatingly exciting at the time."

"You can really be a cold witch sometimes. Besides, we had fun that day. I haven't thought of 'kick the can' in ages."

She grinned with one eyebrow raised enough to send chilling goosebumps over his hide. Her mind raced back to long forgotten memories. Mose's first day at Ashwood, she, Nick, and Sara decided to take Mose on a tour of the farm to get better acquainted.

They took turns swinging over the creek, plunging into the warm water, and wading near the sandy bank looking for crawfish and tadpoles. They tired of the water, then laid in the sun to dry their clothes. It didn't take long in the summer's heat.

Nick and Sara argued and fussed most of the time, but they warmed up to Mose and backed off their usual routine. His influence seemed to help calm them. Luna Belle loved his stabilizing effect, even if the respite was temporary.

As the four children rolled in the sweet grassy pasture that

adjoined the creek, Nick suggested they play Kick the Can.
None of the other children knew the game.

Sara scrunched up her nose and shook her head. "You're
making that up. Ain't no such game."

"Is too. It's a old game."

"Oh yeah. Where've you played it? Mr. Smarty-pants." Sara
chided.

"I've played it lots of times."

"So how's it go, Nick?" Mose asked.

His demeanor and obvious curiosity in the game had the
effect of a snake charmer on a cobra. The girls instantly liked
the idea once Mose had expressed an interest.

"It's simple. We divide into two teams. How 'bout boys
against girls?"

"Fine with me." Mose said.

"Tell us the rest of the rules before we say it's okay. I bet
there's a catch in there somewhere. Don't you, Luna Belle?" Sara
fussed with her fists firmly planted on her waist.

"Ain't no catch. If you'll just shut up long enough to listen."
Nick's quip angered Sara, but she did settle down enough to pay
attention.

"We all hide. Teams together. Teams take turns. One
member of the team leaves their hiding place and kicks a can
in the middle. A rock in the can rattles when it's moved. When
the other team hears the noise from the can they both chase the
kicker. If you get caught before tagging base, that team loses a
point. If you get to base safe you score a point."

"Sounds like fun to me." Mose said.

"Me too." Luna Belle added.

"But not boys against girls. The boys'll cheat." Sara cut her
eyes toward Luna Belle.

"No, Sara, I'd just as soon hide with you than some dumb
old boy." Luna Belle hoped this might persuade Sara. Luna
Belle had no desire to see Sara partnered with Mose and Luna
Belle knew that would happen as sure as rain wets the ground.

"Okay." Sara agreed out of frustration.

So the boys were pitted against girls and they all decided the
barn plaza made a perfect playing field. The space was created
by the horse barn, dairy barn, mule barn, smoke house, and

chicken house. They shared the common rectangular ground Brigham had named the plaza.

Nick commanded the rules. "We'll mark our scores on the side of the smokehouse with a piece of coal."

"How 'bout we mark in the sand. 'Member the last time we marked on the smokehouse?" Luna Belle inserted.

"Oh yeah ... sure do. Fine, but nobody can go near the scoreboard unless we're all together." Nick shook his finger just like he had seen his own mother do so many times.

"Fine," came three responses.

Mose asked Nick, "So we take turns kicking the can then we're chased?"

"That's right." Nick replied.

"I like it. What happens after each round?" Mose winked at Luna Belle. Her heart fluttered.

"We hide again. After your team mate kicks the can you can come out and watch the other team try to catch your partner."

Mose asked Nick, "So it's good strategy to hide close to the center?"

"Yep. That means you have a better chance to catch the girls."

"What I thought."

"Yep. You're smart, Mose."

"Thanks. I like games. Especially when you get to chase girls." They laughed.

The four met in the center of the playing field after the boys found an old paint can in an out-building. They dropped a rock in it and sealed the lid closed and shook it to test its rattle. They all agreed it made a swell noise.

"How you hide without the other team watching where we go?" Mose wanted to know.

"Honor system. We keep our backs to each other when we leave the plaza to hide."

"Good enough. Where's base?" Mose asked Nick.

"Old hay rake by the tool shed, either wheel." Nick pointed.

They all agreed. Nick took a nickel from his pocket and flipped it into the air. Sara yelled, "heads."

"You win, Sara, want to kick first?" Nick asked.

The two girls looked at each other then Luna Belle said,

"We'll kick first."

"Fine."

Nick commanded. "Let's hide."

Luna Belle and Sara headed toward the mule barn. "Stupid Nick. This game sounds dumb to me."

"Might be fun. Let's play a little before we quit, okay?" Luna Belle wanted to play with Mose. That little wink had made her tingle.

"Might turn out okay." Sara agreed.

"Let's hide in the loft. No animals there to give us away." Luna Belle whispered.

"Great idea. There's a little hay pile right under the loft door. You can jump out 'n land in the hay. That way if the boys cheat you can get to the can faster and have a better chance." Sara said with an excited voice.

Sara climbed into the loft first. "Come on. You go first."

Luna Belle slowly climbed then looked out the barn window. "I don't know. I'm not sure about this idea."

"Oh come on scaredy cat. Frettin' ain't gonna get you nowhere."

Luna Belle positioned herself in the doorway and tentatively looked down at the tiny pile of hay. Her eyes widened.

"Go on, jump."

"I don't want to. It's a long way. What if I miss?"

"You won't miss. Go ahead … jump. Don't be such a suck-ninny. Want me to fix you a sugar-tit?"

Not even Sara's chiding moved Luna Belle's feet. Transfixed, she did not want to jump.

Sara shoved Luna Belle.

The fall seemed to take hours. She still lacked time to orient herself but managed to twist herself enough to land flat on her back, unfortunately missing the hay by a country mile.

Sara looked down in abject fear and yelled for help. She jumped and landed on her feet running toward Luna Belle.

Luna Belle lay dead. By time the boys arrived Sara's face had been lined by tears and dust.

"She's dead. She's dead. They're gonna kill us all." Sara cried.

Nick looked around for adult spies. "First thing, shut up.

Your bellering ain't doing none of us no good. All your yelping is gonna do is bring grownups out of the woodwork. They'll fall on us like a plague in Egypt. We gonna have to drag her around back and bury her. Ain't no way around it. She's gotta be buried, quick too."

Sara gasped for a breath. "And what are we going to tell everybody? Huh? Mr. Smarty-Pants."

"We'll pretend we don't know what happened to her."

"They'll know we know, you fool. We can't just bury her. Ain't had no funeral." Sara wailed.

"We ain't got no choice. We gotta act quick before they see us."

Mose, a stranger, a kid, felt sick. He wanted to enjoy some fun and play an innocent game, not bury a dead girl.

"Mose, grab a hand to help me drag her out back." Nick commanded.

"Sara, you go get some shovels and a pick. You know where they are. Meet us behind the mule barn. Nobody ever goes back there. Maybe weeds'll grow over her grave 'fore anybody finds it."

Sara left crying. "This must be the most moronic thing you've ever thought up … idiot."

"Oh yeah? Got a better idea? And you go on now, quick like. Don't let no moss grow on you, you dumb old girl."

Nick and Mose each grabbed a wrist and pulled Luna Belle's limp body behind the barn. Her head dangled like a watermelon in a sack. Sara soon came back with shovels and other digging equipment. She and Nick started digging.

"We need a deep hole. I reckon she'll stink 'fore long. If we bury her too shallow some varmint'll come along and dig her up. I don't even want to try and imagine that yuck."

Mose knelt over her to admire her tanned skin from a closer perspective. He pushed her short bangs off her forehead and laid his hand on her face as if to check for a fever. He tried to free her long black braids but they were caught under her back enough to make them difficult to remove.

He hadn't paid very close attention to her before her death. Her closed red lips hid those big funny teeth he saw back at the creek.

For some strange reason, he now recognized her true beauty. Her face caused him to have a strange quiver where he'd never felt one before. Mose used his hands and slicked his own hair back. He'd never cared about his hair before.

"Mose, quit messing around and help us dig."

This called Mose back. As he pulled his knees under himself to get up, Luna Belle fluttered her eyes.

"She ain't dead, y'all." Mose yelled in a triumphant tone.

Nick and Sara rushed to Luna Belle.

Luna Belle revived as quickly as she had passed out. All three accomplices hovered over her. Nick shook her face. Sara patted her hand then pulled her jaw open to inspect her tongue. "Yep. She's alive all right."

Luna Belle opened her eyes and saw Mose. Her pale blue eyes appeared paltry compared to his, so filled with mystery. She had never seen such beautiful eyes before. His straight black pendulous locks hanging around his face made his eyes even more powerful. Luna Belle fell hopelessly in love while she lay there on the dry dirt.

The three children still worried. "You sure you're all right?" Sara's voice trembled.

"I'm fine ... I think." She stood and dusted herself off. Sara helped her.

"I'm fine. Why are we back here?"

Sara didn't want to tell her what she'd done. Nick patted her shoulder. "You must'a jumped out of the loft and landed wrong ... knocked the breath out of you."

Sara's shove came flooding back into Luna Belle's dazed mind. She left Mose's gaze long enough to look at Sara's tracked face.

"Luna Belle, I'm sorry. I shouldn't—"

"That's all right, Sara. I'd do the same to you, but I ain't never gonna hide in no loft again. Specially with you."

That ended Kick the Can.

"Ready to ride?" Nick shocked her mind back to Teachall's stable.

"Yeah. I'm glad we're going. I've got some things I need to ask you." Hidden from Nick's sight by the horses, Luna Belle reassured herself by pressing Mose's letter into her breast.

"Nick?"

"Hmm?"

"How often you talk with Sara?"

"Least once a month. Why?"

"Just wondering ... really, I miss her terribly. Being with you today has made me yearn to see her again. I remember how she met Henry all those years ago in Brunswick."

22

City Slicker Meets Farm Girl

"Morning—may I help you?" Henry Swilley welcomed Sara Polk into Judge Manier's outer office.

"I'm here to drop off a brief from Cecil Brigham. His honor expects it."

"Yes, I heard him say you were coming." Henry scanned Sara Polk from head to toe. "I'm Henry Swilley. Judge Manier's clerk, and you are?"

"Late, that's what I am. You from out of town, Mr. Swilley? We've never met."

"I'm from Jacksonville. Judge Manier grew up with my father. He's been kind enough to offer me this position to help me get a start."

"How nice. I'm sure you'll do well with so distinguished and honorable a mentor." Sara smirked then her attention flew out the office window overlooking the yacht basin to keep from giggling.

She had never seen anyone who looked like a flamingo wrapped in a toga. His threadbare, used-to-be white linen suit slouched over his wiry shoulders and hung like loose plumage. A long neck goonked out of his too big shirt collar and his pink tie was too much. Sara pictured his sneezing through that great hooked nose and almost laughed in his face. His blushed skin, white hair, and pale beady eyes completed the avian picture.

His ogling eyes took in her every detail and made her skin crawl.

Sara clenched her teeth. "I received instruction to place these in the judge's hand."

"He left not ten minutes ago. Should return in about an hour. I'll see he gets them first thing when he returns."

"That's all right. I'll come back."

Sara walked to a nearby diner. Her dawdling had caused her to miss the judge, but she laid all the blame on the pink bird shrouded in old oily linen. Her personality never took to punctuality. Brigham should have known better than to trust important papers to her.

After seeing the scrawny young man she wondered why Mr. Brigham asked her to deliver these papers. The thought left her feeling like a sacrificial virgin.

Walter Manier, an old friend of the Brighams, often visited the farm and rode with Brigham and Stuart. Sara smelled a rat. She grew even less amused by Manier's ploy when she thought about the boor who had disgustingly surveyed her body.

The setup started a few days earlier when Stuart and Manier met for coffee at a local drugstore. Stuart poured sugar into his hot brew. "You know this boy real good?"

Manier added a splash of cream to his. "Pretty good. He's clerked for me for about six months. I knew his father like a brother. He was as fine a fellow as I've ever known, my best friend from childhood. Lost contact when I left for school. Died right after the boy's nativity. Raised dirt poor. Young man's raised himself up by his own bootstraps. That means a lot to me. You too—see'n as how you did that for yourself."

"Yes sir. You're right 'bout that. Man with enough gumption to make something out'a hisself gets my vote."

"Good, good, I hoped you'd agree. Mind if I bring him along for a ride?"

"Sounds good to me. He ride?"

"We'll find out won't we?" Manier laughed.

"Let me know when you're coming and I'll have Sara ready. See what she thinks."

"Excellent. How about Saturday morning? Around nine?"

"Wonderful. I'll have four horses ready."

Sara balked at the plans. "I met him. He's a jackass."

"Watch your mouth, young lady. You're at least going Saturday morning. I promised the judge. That's that."

There appeared no need to argue. If he showed himself a dud with horses, her dad might back off.

Judge Manier and Henry Swilley arrived at Ashwood's barn ready to ride. Sara immediately became amazed at how he had changed since she first saw him. He was out of his bird-suit and now wore a starched and pressed plaid shirt. His unblemished jodhpurs fit him well enough and he even sported a silk ascot. Sara recognized all his horsey finery as the judge's handiwork.

What impressed her at first, turned revolting. She straightened her dad's collar and mumbled. "Look at that. Judge shined him up good, didn't he? Turned him into a brand new lacquered bass lure. He's a dandy, ain't he Dad?"

"You behave yourself. You hear me? I reckon he's a fine enough young man. Stop with the snob routine."

Sara sneered behind her father's back because she expected him to take her side. Any of the several boys she had brought around, he turned away. Now her own father tried to offload her onto the first spit-polished fop that came along.

She would go riding but nothing else. If none of the suitors she paraded through the house seemed good enough, why oblige this?

"Miss Sara, may I present Henry Swilley. He's from Jacksonville and clerks in my office. I believe you two met there a few days back?"

"Yes sir, we did. Morning, Mr. Swilley." Sara walked over to her horse and adjusted his cavesson. "Mr. Swilley—"

Sara stopped dead in her tracks when Nick walked into the barn wearing a broad smile. She dropped her shoulders and her expression the moment she saw her brother.

"Please, call me Henry. Mr. Swilley sounds far too formal for riding. Don't you think, Sara? Mind if I call you Sara?"

Nick intruded with his hand extended to Henry. "Hello …

Swilley, right? I'm Nick Polk, Sara's brother. Pleasure to meet you, and allow me to answer that. No. She doesn't mind if you call her Sara. She's excited about your ride."

Sara wanted to kill Nick who devilishly grinned. Nothing new, this time she meant it.

"Mind if I ride along?" Nick inquired.

"Of course not." Manier answered.

Sara clenched her teeth.

Manier jostled himself with one foot in a stirrup and the other on the ground. In a moment Nick approached the almost helpless jurist and gave him a boost.

Manier settled himself in the saddle. "Henry my boy, you're about to ride with one of the finest equestrians in the world. Sara, Stuart, and Nick aren't too bad either."

The Polks and the judge all laughed. They'd ridden with Walter Manier enough to know that he almost achieved competency. Henry looked confused.

"Don't worry, Henry. It's an inside joke." Manier prodded the boy's rib with his crop.

"He's a dolt with no sense of humor." Sara whispered to Nick.

"Looks okay to me. Give him a chance. I don't want'a be stuck with you the rest of my life. Besides, daddy seems to like him." Nick replied.

"Kiss my foot ... three joints up."

"Ha ha. That's original."

"Shut up."

"You first."

Stuart interrupted. "You two. Am I gonna have to separate you? You're acting worse than three year olds."

"He started it." Sara argued.

"Yeah right—"

"I'm not kidding. I'm 'bout to take a buggy whip to both of you." Stuart flushed crimson.

Henry admired their sparring. Maybe he had found his soul mate after all.

It soon became evident, young Henry had never been within a hundred yards of anything larger than a small dog, although he exuded enough moxie to get himself hurt. Trying to mount

Silver, the most gentle horse in the barn, the young clerk looked the saddle over from cantle to pommel. "Where's the horn?" Henry mumbled.

Manier laughed. "Henry, my boy, you're looking at an English saddle. It's … it's not supposed to have a horn. We're going for a short hack, not herding cattle or a rodeo."

Nick took pity on the gangly young man. "Grab a chunk of mane and swing yourself up and over."

When Henry plopped himself down, Nick winced. He and Sara both knew their new friend injured himself. Henry almost fell off the horse, his eyes crossed in pain.

"Ouch. Points for that. Especially if he manages to stay onboard." Nick whispered to Sara.

"Never have children, will he?" Sara whispered back.

The five rode off at a walk. Henry's discomfort seemed to be growing. Nick watched as each step the horse took further insulted Henry's privacy.

"I've had enough for a minute. How do I get off this thing?" He queried.

"Reverse of getting on. Throw your right leg over his back and step down." Stuart said.

Nick guided his horse alongside Henry's and held Silver's bridle.

"That's it." Nick instructed. "Now step to the ground."

"Thank you. A few minutes to … to well … rest and I can continue."

Henry walked bandy legged over to a log and sat with considerable caution. He put his elbows on his knees and doubled over with his abdomen spasming. The fire in his groin showed no sign of going away any time soon. Nick pitied Henry's condition and dismounted and walked over to sit beside the young man.

"Nobody told you about sitting on a horse, did they?"

"No, but I know what I did wrong."

"For future reference—" Nick couldn't continue with a straight face. He turned his head away and almost laughed aloud. "Why don't we just sit here for a few minutes and we'll catch the others in a while?" With that, Nick couldn't hold in his chuckle any longer and rose to fetch both horses.

Henry looked at him through squinted eyes. "You don't have to be a smart alec about it." They both laughed.

Nick took both horses' reins and walking back to the log again sat beside Henry, whose improved condition allowed him to become more sociable.

Sara wanted to head to the barn but her dad and the judge persuaded her to continue.

Manier adjusted his horse's reins. "Give him a chance."

Sara found herself hooked, at least for the day.

The three rode ahead at a slow pace for about thirty minutes. When Nick and Henry caught up, the two young men had bonded. Nick had taught Henry to post a slow trot, and as a bonus, the young clerk appeared no longer to suffer agony. Although he proved himself short on aptitude, he did ride; however, Nick remained unsure about Silver's approval of the greenhorn.

Nick cantered ahead to Sara. "He's an okay guy, Sara. Give him a chance."

Henry caught up. "I may seem like a dolt but I'm trying."

"You heard?" Sara asked.

"I heard."

Not long after that morning's ride Sara asked Luna Belle to stand with her when she wed Henry. It delighted Luna Belle. Sara and Henry asked Judge Manier to officiate in his Brunswick office. Instead, Luna Belle insisted on reserving the romantic Christ Church, Frederica. She also provided flowers from the gardens at Teachall.

Sara had yearned from childhood for a fairy tale wedding. Luna Belle heard Sara's fantasies far too often to agree to anything less. Fulfilling her lifelong friend's dreams became an obsession.

Luna Belle commissioned Roberta Rivers for a gown. The two young ladies selected a Swiss batiste for the outer layer. Roberta suggested a straight dress of lace and beading. Sara fell in love with the sketch's simple charm.

The sleeves boasted accents of vertical stripes of beading

and lace. Pintucks terminated into cuffs that closed with a row of mother of pearl buttons. Set on the back of her wrist, they luminesced to create a subtle spark on the gown.

The mitered lace provided a beautiful frame for Sara's lovely face. Pintucks went from the bottom of the square neck opening almost all the way down the front of the gown. They terminated in a scalloped pattern giving a flounced effect near the hem that billowed with the undulations of the tucking accentuated by more shirred lace.

Luna Belle found a beautiful piece of white silk gauze for the veil. Roberta made a halo of silk stephanotis that crowned and created an upper frame to make her face the focal point of the ensemble.

After the sweet, intimate ceremony, a reception followed at the Cloister Hotel on Sea Island. There, Henry's mother came to Luna Belle in tears of appreciation for the Blacks' generosity. Mose overheard and it greatly pleased him and caused him to love his new bride even more. Luna Belle learned that day, there's nothing like a wedding to spark old romances.

Mose arranged an extravagant honeymoon for his old friend Sara and Henry. The next morning Mordecai drove the couple to the Atlanta airport in the Black's silver Rolls Royce Gurney Nutting Saloon limousine. When they arrived in Atlanta Mordecai slid an envelope in Henry's inside jacket pocket. "A little gift for your trip."

Henry opened the envelope once they were inside the terminal and away from Mordecai. His eyes bulged. He expected tickets. Along with those he found fifty thousand dollars wrapped in a note. "You'll need a little spending money. Love, Mose and Luna Belle."

Their flight took them to New York where they boarded a luxury liner bound for Europe.

Mose hadn't given them the trip or the money expecting anything in return, yet the more he thought of his investment in the young attorney the more he saw Henry's potential as an accomplice. Originally, his generosity had been one of the few times in his life he had given of himself for no reason other than his remembrance of a special day when he, Nick, Sara, and Luna Belle played and enjoyed being children.

After mulling it over in his mind, why shouldn't he have a little payback? That thought process was what had ensured the fortunes of Blackbeard's descendants for three centuries.

While Mose contemplated, Henry and Sara spent three dazzling months moving from city to city all over Europe. Henry saw this as their single opportunity to travel in such grandiose style.

They "bumped" into Mose and Luna Belle in Venice. Of course, Mose had planned on finding them there, and Luna Belle loved the whole idea, since it gave her an opportunity to show Sara around her favorite European city. Mose had his own purpose.

The girls shopped and explored while Mose took some time to get to know Henry better after he had talked with Judge Manier at length about the young man. Manier impressed Mose with meritorious adulations about Henry. Mose appreciated the way the man had bettered himself, a hungry fellow with a strong initiative.

Mose guessed that Henry willed success at any cost, so there in Venice, Mose offered Henry a position in the family enterprise. Moses Augustus Black never acclimated himself to losing at anything. He had the looks, charm, and training to create his own destiny, plus his father, the Colonel, gave the boy what he needed to wield his power. Mose had honed his pirating skills to a razor's edge.

Henry appreciated Mose's suave and manly nature, but he saw through the folly, not fooled for one minute by his intrigue. Henry worked too hard to throw his life away into some dust bin of history. A life of piracy and underhanded business dealings held no allure to him. With many reasons to command his own destiny, there in Venice Henry refused Moses Black.

These remembrances did little to comfort Luna Belle. Mose remained dead; she continued alone. Trying to determine where Henry stood in all the conundrum caused more confusion as time passed. She needed Nick's advice on the topic. Henry's cleverness might prove useful, if only she could trust him.

Mose's letter kept reminding her of a strong need to comprehend the status of her allies. If only she had paid more attention while her husband lived. Her heart wanted to trust Nick, Sara, and Henry, but her mind wandered—befuddled by a sword of Damocles.

23
Hacking Around

As they prepared to ride out of the barn, both Nick and Luna Belle grew preoccupied. Polly and Mordecai wanted them together, but at that moment Nick searched for one thing, Luna Belle another.

Nick felt a stirring in his loins when he embraced Luna Belle earlier that morning before breakfast. Luna Belle felt it too but refused romantic thoughts concerning Nick. It lived somewhere beyond taboo in her mind. Even though ardent energy flowed through her, she denied it.

Nick looked at her eyes and sensed something. "What?"

"Oh, nothing. The horses reminded me of something else about the first time Mose came to Ashwood. Remember?" She grinned.

"I'm sure not the same way you do. He wasn't my husband, was he?"

Luna Belle laughed as she braided Fazio's forelock. "Not far as I know."

Nick joined her laughter. "If I'd been a woman, I'd'a grabbed him in a heartbeat and stole him right out from under yo' nose. I mean, where else you gonna find a fella with enough money to buy the kind of horse-flesh I like?"

"My exact sentiments." Luna Belle adjusted her chaps straps one last time before mounting.

"Turned out pretty good for us both, didn't it?"

"Yeah, it did." She turned her head and looked out the barn

hall toward the landscape beyond. "Nick, I don't know what I'm gonna do. I mean, there's so much I took for granted. It's scary."

Nick adjusted his horse's bridle and threw the reins across his neck. "I've known you all my life. I'm sure of one thing. You ain't afraid of one cock-eyed thing. No need for you to start now."

Luna Belle fell silent as she once again pressed the letter against her heart. Before she read that confounded thing, except for a pagan curse, her world appeared to revolve steadily without incident. Not only had he died, Mose managed to rock her entire being with devastation through a folded piece of paper sealed with red wax. She desperately needed to trust someone.

"What has you so preoccupied?" Nick wrinkled his brows as he led Gallant III toward the outside.

"My mind … Mose … I'd just turned eleven that day we played kick the can. You know, I'd been to Teachall three years earlier, but that first day when he came to Ashwood seems to be stuck in my mind. Do you remember how we decided not to like him before he even got there?"

"Sure do."

"That didn't last long, did it?"

"How could it? I'll never forget the way he walked right up to those two stallions. Sara and I figured he'd run away like a chicken with his head cut off."

"Yeah, but the boys took right to him. Amazing."

"Those two horses understood what happened around them. I recollect one of them pushing you into Mose's arms."

"I'd forgotten that. Sometimes these horses act like uncanny psychics."

Luna Belle's mind called up an image of Mose from that day. His smile that showed his beautiful teeth lighting his face like a chandelier in a dark room; his tanned skin made them appear even more luminescent. Tall for his age, he stood head and shoulders above Luna Belle.

Luna Belle squinted. "You and Sara refused to get dressed for tea that afternoon. Left me to fend for myself. At first I didn't like Mose one bit. He acted far and away too rehearsed with the tea. Why, you'd'a thought we'd gone to Japan for some ritual offering. He doted on me like I was some kind of old invalid.

Mama loved it. I saw it in her eyes. I got my creeped out self out of there quick as I could."

"Your mama also let you know to behave. Said if you didn't mind your manners, she'd take away your barn privileges for the rest of that summer. Sara'n I thought if you didn't cooperate we'd commit … I was gonna say suicide, but I guess *seppuku* would fit in your little Japanese theme more appropriately." Nick tried to imitate an oriental bow.

Luna Belle slowly shook her head and rolled her eyes. "She could come up with some doozie punishments. That one remains the worst to this day."

"Yeah. I distinctly remember how Sara and I begged you to control yourself. I've never told you this, but the reason we didn't come to your little tea party was because Daddy forbade us. Said you needed all your mental powers to concentrate, and we might sabotage your best effort. Truth is, I'm almost certain he wanted you to not lose your barn privileges either."

"Your daddy wore his wisdom well. He was a true gentleman."

"Yeah, I miss him."

"Me too. The more we talk about it, the more I realize how much he did to raise me than any of my family."

"That's nice of you to say."

"It's true."

That fateful day at Ashwood Luna Belle fell in love with Mose. She finished her tea, excused herself, and went upstairs to change from her white lacy linen dress. She preferred a pair of dungarees or twill slacks and a flimsy cotton blouse tied at the waist.

She braided her hair in two pigtails, then grabbed her barn boots and sneaked down the back stairs while no one occupied the kitchen. Not until she slipped outside did she don her noisy boots.

Freed from the intrusion of strangers in her life, she ran straight to the stables knowing that Nick and Sara waited. They'd want to hear everything.

"What's he like?" Sara asked when Luna Belle turned the corner, entering the barn.

"He's a creepy little—"

"I'm a creepy little what?" Mose interrupted as he came in the other end of the barn hall.

Luna Belle blushed a fair shade of ruby.

Nick rescued Luna Belle. "Shucks, Luna Belle. He don't look so creepy to me."

Sara twisted back and forth at the waist. "We watched him earlier from the loft. Acted normal."

Mose stuck his hand out to Nick. "Mose Black ... and you are?"

"I'm Nick Polk. This here is my sister, Sara. We live right over there—our Daddy trains these horses. He's out back riding right now. Wanna see?" Mose's firm grip impressed Nick. His father had taught him that a good, firm handshake revealed more than a sheepskin hanging on the wall.

"I'm sorry, Mose. I didn't know you followed me." Luna Belle said out of embarrassment.

"I understand. I have to admit that I didn't like you right off too much either. Which one of these horses belongs to you?"

"These two big boys are Luna Belle's, Mose." Sara walked toward the Andalusian stallions' stalls. "Why don't you go over there and meet Cletus and Rufus? That is if you ain't afraid of 'em." She taunted, expecting Mose to get his comeuppance when the two mighty steeds scared his liver out his *derrière*.

"Cletus and Rufus?" Mose laughed in a deriding chuckle.

"Yes, that's what I named them." Luna Belle lowered her chin and looked directly toward Mose much like a mad bull ready to paw the ground.

"Well, how about that? Two of the finest horses I've ever seen and their names are Cletus and Rufus... that's just swell." Mose said through his laughter. Nick and Sara smiled all the while Luna Belle's face grew red. Mose noticed her expression."No, really. I mean it. I like their names."

"Mose, you're a swell kinda' guy." Nick grabbed Mose's shoulder and gave it a gentle shake.

"Why, thank you, Nick. You're okay too."

Mose saw the two beautiful stallions earlier when he and

his parents first came to the barn. He witnessed the amazement
on his parents' faces while they tried to retain their composure.
From their expressions Mose knew the deal had been made.

Luna Belle adjusted her stirrups. "We all thought him
an arrogant little brat. He strutted around like a little banty
rooster."

"I think maybe that was your assessment, not ours, but at
least your husband had a good eye for horses. He acted fearless
… or out to lunch."

"Yeah, he did … good eye I mean. Never lost it either. Smart
enough to rely on you." She watched for a reaction.

Nick dusted Gallant III's rump before he mounted. "Mose
paid no attention to us that day. We tried to warn him, but he
went right ahead like he'd known those two stallions all his life."

"And they offered to nuzzle him. That impressed me about
him. I knew the horses judged character without fail. I relied on
their instincts."

"Yep, they sure as shootin took to him. That's the only way
to say it."

"Mose grew up in a saddle like we did. That's why we all
hit it off that day. He yapped on and on about fox hunting in
Virginia. It never turned me on, but I know you enjoy it." Luna
Belle wanted to proceed past fond recollections, but her entire
body had relaxed itself.

Nick thought about another little conversation from that
childhood day. It became relevant to his present life.

Mose skipped a rock on the creek. He smiled after the stone
jumped four times across the water. "Hey Nick? Ever want to
run away?"

"Why?"

"Oh I don't know … wondering… that's all."

"What a loser." Sara shook her head.

"Why, Sara?" Luna Belle asked.

Sara turned her palms up and gestured over the Ashwood
estate. "Oh I don't know, why leave a good home and run off

into the wide open world without a roof over your head?"

Mose looked around and scratched his head. "Well, if I did decide to run away, I just might find a place to live where there ain't nobody trying to take over my whole life."

"Who's trying to plan your life?" Nick asked without thinking. He knew full well why Mose came to Ashwood.

Luna Belle picked up a smooth flat stone and skipped it, besting Mose by two. "Just like today. They gotta mess us up. Don't they?"

Mose put all his effort into his next attempt. His sailed across the water for a seven. He smiled at Luna Belle then gave her a little sly wink. "Well, they might not mess us up. That is if we like each other. Why don't we see how we feel about all this after we've had a chance to get better acquainted."

Nick watched Luna Belle's eyes. They never seemed to leave Mose.

Luna Belle mounted Fazio briefly then stepped off to again adjust the length of her stirrups.

Nick walked over and adjusted the off side for her. "What hole are you buckling into?"

"Three."

Nick slid the buckle into position. "The studs liked him a lot. Took to him like they did you."

"They sure did, better'n they liked you and Sara. I never figured that out. I mean you possess a special gift with horses. Why didn't they like you?"

"Because I didn't like them. I knew a lot more about your granddaddy's plans than you did. Plus, when I saw them I wanted to keep them. I was so jealous of the Blacks when they went down there and hauled 'em off. I never gave the horses much of a chance. Didn't treat them too good. Not mean, just not nice."

"Nick, I find that hard to believe. You of all people. I've never seen you mistreat a living thing … well …" she chuckled, "with the exception of Sara."

Luna Belle avoided thinking of Sara. In New York, while

Mose lay dead in Atlanta, Rose told her how evil Henry had
become. According to her, the demon had made a good bit of
headway in his efforts to turn Mose's own people against him.

Mose had conditioned Luna Belle to estrangement from
Sara. Rose demanded Luna Belle's attention about Henry. Rose
had become increasingly adamant in her appraisal of the man.
According to her, he was not some little pesky biting gnat. He
threatened to become a full fledged monster waiting to grab
and devour. Rose also made it clear that Luna Belle's adversary
wanted to consume the entire Black family's fortune.

"Nick?"

"Hmm?"

"What you know about Henry?"

"Let's mount up. We'll talk about that while we ride."

The two led their horses out of the tack area and tried to
mount. Fazio, energized by crisp morning freshness, pawed
the ground. She had ridden him several times before. Now he
seemed overly anxious to run.

Lil' Roost came and held Fazio's bridle, allowing Luna Belle
to climb aboard without further incident. Nick mounted Gallant
III.

As they rode out of the barn Luna Belle became quiet for a
while. "Nick?"

"Hmm?"

"I don't know how to run this place. I mean, I've been more
of a parasite than a host. Mose did everything around here."

"Well ... not everything."

"Oh, that's not what I mean and you know it."

"I knew what you meant ... go on."

"Well, I pretty well said it. I don't know how to go on. Who's
gonna take over here? I don't know if I can. I'm willing to try,
but he did so much. It's overwhelming me."

"Luna Belle, don't you have enough to worry about right
now? Let some things slide off you. Why are you bothered with
loading guns when you need to plan battles? Quit worrying
about the little things. Concentrate on the big picture."

Luna Belle tried to consider what he told her, but she didn't
know how. She wanted his help to get through all this, but she
avoided putting ideas in his head. He smelled her vulnerabilities

enough without her fertilizing the crop.

Even though they remained inside the barn's hall, Luna Belle squirmed in her saddle. "Okay, we're riding. Tell me about your brother-in-law."

"I reckon Henry's an all right sorta fellow. He has his faults. Who doesn't? All in all though, Sara found a man who puts up with her, and as you well know, she's a rascal." Nick sat deep in the saddle signaling Gallant III to stop. He quickly dismounted to snug the girth before he remounted.

"Sara's a doll. You're her brother—she's supposed to get under your skin. Rose detests Henry. Do you know why?"

"Luna Belle, that's some story. Besides, I'm not too sure I'd put a whole lot of stock in anything Rose has to say."

"Nick, I need to know what you're talking about. Why are you trying to turn me against Rose? Everything we take for granted around here hangs in the balance."

"Not turned against, I just think you need to keep your eyes and ears open. Who has gotten you so stirred up, anyway?"

Luna Belle stopped short of pulling out the letter from her bosom and unfolding it before Nick's face. If only she knew about his true loyalty.

It had not been long since she read Mose's letter. If she took time to ruminate over its message maybe her perspective's focus would clear. Time ran short and she clung to a hope that might vaporize before her eyes at any moment.

As her mind raced through all her friends, she thought of none more trustworthy than Nick. He held no internal associations with this whole sham.

"Nick, how did I manage to fall into so depraved and isolated a society? Why didn't I seek outside acquaintences?"

Nick smiled and looked directly at her. "Can't answer that first question because I fell into the same pit. As to your second question … I expect you didn't go looking outside this place for friends because you had me right here all the time." He gave Gallant III a light brush with his spurs and cantered away laughing heartily.

24
I'll Do the Shootin'

Outside the barn Nick raised his brows. "Wanna ride to the creek?"

"You think Fazio will settle enough?"

"Sure, he's a little frisky, that's all. A good brisk canter will calm him down. May buck a couple o' times, but nothing serious will happen. I promise. You can do it."

Luna Belle set her blunt spurs lightly against Fazio's ribs and as Nick promised, Fazio's hind feet flew up. After a couple of running bucks and passing a few bursts of hot air, Fazio grounded himself. He was definitely ready for a good brisk canter.

"See, I told you. All he wanted was to toot his horn. Ain't a suede crotch the grandest thing since garden tomatoes? Let's go." Nick laughed.

Fazio collected himself. On a loose rein, he caught Nick and Gallant III then Fazio instinctively slowed for them to work in perfect tandem.

They made their way toward the creek. With every rocking motion a corner of Mose's letter stung Luna Belle's left breast. She kept trying to adjust it to avoid its jabbing. No matter how many times she moved it, the thing found its way back to a position to grieve her while she rode with Nick.

"Nick, I miss Mose. It's funny. When he was alive, I didn't care where he was. He came and went at leisure and I never really even noticed. Now that it's too late, I want him with me all the time."

"I guess you're going to have to reconcile yourself to being stuck with me. I realize you're confused and lonely. You're also bound to be overly enervated. Luna Belle, do you reckon you're suffering from years of denying your true emotions about your husband?"

"I don't know why I thought it would be a good idea to come out and ride with you this morning."

"At least you knew I'd speak my peace. I've never tried to be dishonest with you before, have I?"

Luna Belle stopped Fazio and dismounted. She walked in little tight circles, shook her head, and mumbled.

"Go ahead, have a little conniption fit … run … scream … purge your mind. You need the release. You really are wondering why you wanted to be with me this morning. Maybe you realized I wouldn't cut you any slack. Eh?"

"Polly's doings. I asked her to invite you to breakfast so I could thank you for all you did at the funeral. She took it upon herself to get me involved in this little jaunt. I actually had no desire to come riding."

"Oh really? Yet I see you dressed for the occasion." Nick nodded and looked down his nose at her standing on the ground. He stayed on his horse and watched her pace.

Luna Belle climbed back onto Fazio and reined him toward the barn. "I'm finished with this charade." She leaned forward to urge Fazio into a trot. "This is the most futile thing I've encountered since last night's possum hunt."

"Possum hunt? Last night?"

Luna Belle's face flushed. "In a dream."

"I see." He crossed his wrists over the saddle and relaxed his shoulders to watch her little tirade.

Her fuming caused her to miss the first beat of posting. The letter jabbed into her flesh when she slammed hard into the saddle. Mose reminded her once again of his presence. He was going to demand her attention as long as that thing poked her breast. She turned around and headed back toward Nick out of a desperation for answers even though she feared asking him the right questions.

"You know, Luna Belle. We have a way of communicating that transcends words. I expect that comes from our having known each other so long. Don't you imagine?"

"Sure, but—"

"I can see by your expression that you're troubled about something other than what you've said. It's true, Mose quizzed me about Henry. I had nothing to hide. I never lied about my brother-in-law to Mose. Why would I?"

They rode along at a slow trot and he gained courage. Using his seat Nick asked his horse to walk. Luna Belle followed suit. Both horses dropped their heads and ambled.

Nick fiddled with a shock of his horse's mane. "For a long time, in fact, since they returned from their honeymoon, Henry has been trying to infect my mind with malicious ideas about Teachall. I never knew what happened while they traveled all over Europe. When they left, Henry thought y'all hung the moon."

Luna Belle leaned forward to adjust Fazio's curb chain. "We ran into them in Venice. I don't know what Mose did to Henry while we were there but something changed. Mose insisted on the accidental rendezvous. That's about all I know."

"You're certainly right about something changing. When they returned, first thing … well … Henry ordered me to get away from this nest of pirates. I laughed at him. I knew my situation better than he."

"He did? Ordered you to leave here?" Luna Belle turned her attention directly to Nick's face.

"Sure did. It didn't bother me. I mean—I wasn't a pirate. My ambition revolved exclusively around working horses. Mose's occupation remained his own personal affair. Same with you, right? You found yourself here. Were we supposed to leave because my brother-in-law had wild notions about our safety?"

"Go on."

"Really? Tell the truth. Why'd you have Polly call me this morning?"

"I don't know. Freudian slip? Glad I did though, aren't you?"

"I'm always happy with you around … I was gonna change the subject, but I gotta say what's on my mind. I wonder if Henry may have been one of Mose's worst enemies."

"How long have you thought that?"

Nick looked off toward the eastern horizon and the vast Atlantic beyond. It took him a few moments to answer. "Not long.

I've batted junk back and forth for years. You see, the governor came to see me several days back. Wanted me to help him get Mose. Said he'd give me lots o' money and a free ticket out'a here."

"Scooter … came here … to see you?"

"Oh yeah. It had something to do with a warehouse in Savannah."

"How were you supposed to be involved with that?"

"I don't know. I walked away. Wish I'd stayed and heard him out. I thought he'd always been such a close friend of Mose's but something smelled rotten from the first things he said to me."

Luna Belle's blood ran cold. "I've heard a little bit about that warehouse business. Lulu and Lolly bitched and snitted about it the whole time we were in New York. I didn't pay them much attention. I had other things on my mind. Imagine that."

Nick stopped Gallant III. "Oh yeah?"

"I asked Rose what they were fussing about and she uncharacteristically clammed up tight as a drum. I thought my mind was vacating reason. I attributed it to Mose's death and my overall emotional state. You know my head was reeling. Even though he died prior to being shot, someone had intentionally tried to murder him. That alone seemed like enough to jostle me into thinking the real problem was all in my head."

Luna Belle stopped Fazio and turned in the saddle to see Nick sitting several yards behind. "Nick?" She turned Fazio and walked back to be closer.

"Hmmm?"

"Does the name Marcus Gilder mean anything to you? Who else has talked to you about all this?"

"Marcus Gilder? Not right off the top of my head. Luna Belle, why are you doing this to me? I don't want to hurt you. You've been my best friend forever. I'd never want to bring you harm."

"I know that but I needed to hear it from your lips. Thank you. You know you're special to me. If things had been different, who knows—" Luna Belle stopped.

Nick knew Luna Belle well enough to finish the sentence in his mind. "I love being here and want things to continue but to tell you the truth, I don't really see too much hope for success. Too many jackals skulk at your door for you to remain safe here. Plus

… the fellow who kept you safe has gone."

Nick spent a few minutes in deep thought before he spoke. "Pink mentioned a couple of things to me. I don't know which side of the fence he's on."

"That doesn't surprise me. He gives me the creeps. He's a snake dressed up in a uniform. You know, years ago Pink busted a still down on Rigger's creek. Guess why."

Nick grinned and rubbed his chin. "Kill competition?" Using his hand he raked hair off his forehead.

"How'd you know that?"

"I've been here long enough to see lots of shenanigans. The barn served Mose well. He often conducted business there. I've never been an eavesdropper, but some things became impossible to miss."

This time Luna Belle reached inside her blouse for Mose's letter but stopped short. Mose's warning of fidelity still hung over her head. Mose told her enough to piece together part of a list of conspirators. Luna Belle smelled more. She needed full confidence in Nick. Perhaps he held the keys to piecing this together. Thank you, Mose.

She looked into Nick's eyes. "Grandmother made Mose a quilt when we married."

"I know. She made me one too. Keep it on my top shelf so I see it everyday. It reminds me of good times and the happiness of being innocent children. It's one of my favorite possessions."

"Mose kept his in the bottom of a blanket chest in his bedroom. He never saw it."

"He lacked those memories, didn't he? I'm not a complicated man. What you see's what you get."

"Yes. You are the simpleton, aren't you?" Luna Belle raised her eyebrows and rolled her eyes. "You, uncomplicated? Ha. That's a good one."

Nick looked toward the sky. "So what about the quilt?"

"Forget about the quilt. A wax sealed document lay hidden under it. I shouldn't have but I opened it."

"And?"

"It's in Latin. I managed to decipher enough to recognize it as a bill of sale for the Contessa."

"Bill of sale?"

"Nick, her father sold her into marriage. Unbelievable isn't it?"

Nick turned his head away from her gaze. "People do strange things to their loved-ones."

"The thing looks original. Two wax seals sure made it look authentic. I've never seen anything like them before.

The one on the outer protective wrapper was black wax. Then when I opened it, on the inside there was one with red wax—"

"Fighting dragons?"

"How'd you know that?"

"I'll show you one. It's in the barn office."

"What?"

"I told you. You think I live in a little insulated box? What's it gonna take to convince you? I'm on your side. I don't belong here any more than you do. We're both captives. You had no choice. I—"

"Go on."

"I'm gonna say it. I bound myself to you. Now are you satisfied?"

"Why Nick Polk. I never once asked you to come here. I never made any kind of insinuation. You have some nerve to insult me like that. I suppose you intend that to send me over the edge?"

Nick smiled while she fumed.

Luna Belle threw her hat to the ground. "You are the most arrogant, selfish, awful man. I can't believe you have the nerve to say that to me."

"Nerve to what … love you?"

"Don't think for one minute you're gonna lure me into your little trap. I know what you're trying to do. You want me to … wait … I see. You want it all for yourself. Wow. That plan sounds stupendous. It sure does. You sidewinding jerk. Did you think I'd fall for a lowlife like you? Did you shoot Mose?"

Luna Belle spun Fazio on his heels and headed to the barn at a full gallop. "All I want to do right now is bite your hateful head off."

The farther she rode the more she lost her resolute spirit. She had known Nick all her life. He never owned a conniving bone in his entire body.

She had stabbed her true friend's heart with a jagged dagger of

rage. They could argue all day long and never raise his dander, but
to call him a gold digger—a gigolo?

She wanted to rein Fazio back to rejoin him. When she looked
over her shoulder she saw it was unnecessary. Nick followed right
on her tail. He appeared more red-faced than she had ever seen
him. He had every right to his anger and she expected vengeance.
His fury deserved reconciliation. That might even help assuage
her guilt.

As they neared the barn he turned and headed for his cottage.
Both steamed horses needed cooling and relief from their winded
condition, but at that moment neither Luna Belle nor Nick cared.

Luna Belle swung and managed to get to Nick's house about
the time he did. He ignored her and jumped off Gallant III to rush
toward the porch, glad she followed.

Opening the door to his little bungalow he strode into the
space and slammed the door. Nick grew even more livid.

Luna Belle heard his tirade through the walls. "How dare I?
You no good self-righteous bitch. How dare you ask me such a
question."

He stood at the window, looked at her. "I'll tell you how I
dare. I've always loved you. I wanted to spare your being hurt
more. I never told you all I knew because I didn't want you to
ever know that your sorry-ass grandpa *sold* you. Yeah, that's right.
Just like your blasted Contessa friend back at the house. You
became unavailable at a young age. Now you have the nerve to
ask me how I dare love you? Well, sister, you've opened my eyes
for the first time in my life."

The door opened and Nick stood there in tears. Luna Belle had
never seen the strong resilient man in such a state. Not even when
his parents died. Nick almost came apart at the seams. She saw
a Colt revolver in his hand. An intense quiver rushed her entire
body.

She didn't care if he shot her because she deserved killing.
She'd been horrible, despicable, hurting the one innocent thing
that had ever graced her life.

She had behaved worse than any evil fairy-tale queen. Bitter
tears poured down her anguished face. They burned her, branded
her heart and her flesh, inside and out.

As she sobbed she called out, "Go ahead—shoot me. It'll save me the trouble. I'm a miserable excuse of nothing. I don't deserve to live. There's no way I can calm your spirit. I can't ask you to forgive me … not after what I've done. Go ahead shoot."

Nick calmed himself enough to stop shaking. "Why act in haste? After all we've been through, why did you call me trash?"

Nick raised the pistol in her direction and took aim. Luna Belle didn't stand down. She straightened her posture, thrust out her chest, and stood ready to take what ever Nick Polk offered.

"Luna Belle, step out of the way. The gun's for the snake."

"What snake?" She almost screamed.

"The one you're about to step on." He pointed behind her with the pistol.

She turned. After she managed to draw herself back into her skin she saw it coiled farther from her than he thought. How she missed the enormous monster in striking position about eight feet away, she couldn't discern. The menacing reptile poised agitated—ready.

"Didn't hear him did you? Ain't got no rattles."

The diamond back shook its tail but remained silent. Luna Belle had heard of them before but had never seen one.

"Well, are you going to shoot him, or what?"

"Ain't decided yet. You talked trash about dying, why don't you go over and get friendly—pet him?"

"Give me that gun. You think you're so cute." She reached and took it from his hand, aimed, and blasted the snake.

"I know I am … cute that is." Nick grinned.

"Yeah, right."

"I'm glad you admit it."

25
Oh You!

The gunshot brought Lil' Roost out of the barn. Using his hand to shade his eyes he saw the two lathered horses and called for help.

When Nick realized two men headed toward his house he stopped worrying about the animals. About halfway to Nick's bungalow Lil' Roost whistled. Fazio sprang toward him. Gallant III didn't budge before looking back at Nick who said, "Well. Go on then." At that the horse trotted off.

Luna Belle grinned—Nick, the master horseman. She was lucky to have him at Teachall—luckier still to have so devoted a friend near her.

With her life in chaos, here stood a man who commanded everything around him with the ease of a king, yet he possessed a meek spirit. No wonder the horses and the stablehands loved him.

"Grab yourself a rocker and have a seat." Nick offered.

"Thank you, I believe I will. My emotions are frazzled."

"But even so, you're still a crack shot."

"Your daddy was a great teacher and a wonderful man, wasn't he? I'll never forget all the things he taught us, shooting, riding, honesty, integrity … took the place of my own daddy."

"Did, didn't he? Be right back."

While she rocked, Nick went inside and poured them a shot of bourbon and finished filling the tumblers with milk. He used cinnamon raisin bread and created two hearty sandwiches with almond butter, Polly's preserved figs, banana, and raw cashew nuts.

Walking back outside Nick said, "Here." Without ceremony he shoved the sandwich into her hand and set the glass on the arm of her chair.

"What, I don't even get to wash my hands?"

"Luna Belle … I didn't wash mine before I made them. You ain't gonna die now any more'n you did when we ate dirt back in the day."

"I've changed, Nick."

"Pity."

Luna Belle ignored her revulsion and took a bite of the sandwich.

"Mmm. Pretty good for filth."

"Just creating a few antibodies. Nothing but a little horsey, that's all. I didn't know you'd gotten so munk-di-munk. Just shut up 'n drink your moo-juice. It'll wash the snooty right out of you."

Luna Belle took a sip of the milk and grinned. "Why Nick, are you trying to take advantage of me?"

"You sure tote a high opinion of Luna Belle, don't you?" He rested his hand on his hip to mock her feminine ways.

The two sat eating and drinking in silence while chilled air moved in. Luna Belle buttoned her jacket. Nick loved every minute of February's effect. To him the cooled air was better than the unusually warm afternoon, but he actually remained uncertain whether the heat came from the company or the weather.

"I don't guess you'll ever forgive me, will you?" Luna Belle asked.

"If you'll stop the baby talk. Whining's worth about a nickel in a whorehouse to me."

"Sorry. Nick, I feel vulnerable."

"You are vulnerable. That's enough to make you nervous and upset. I understand, but there's somebody who loves you. Know who that is?"

"Why don't you tell me?"

"No. You tell me.

"I'm not here to play games. If that's what you think you

can—"

"Luna Belle, we're never gonna get anywhere if you keep spinning into a tizzy.

Keep in mind:

Who you are …

Where you came from …

Who I am …

What we've been through …

All of that …

Then, tell me why I said I love you."

"Nick, why torture me? Don't I have enough to deal with? I need to feel a sense of accomplishment, not be treated like a schoolgirl with a twenty-question test staring her in the face."

"I hoped you'd take my shoulder. Silly, huh? After all these years, you're still the gal for me."

"I'm nobody's gal."

"Then you lose."

Nick stood, turned, and headed for the door. "You can leave your glass on the rocker. I'll get it later." He went back inside. Luna Belle heard the lock turn.

This was the second time she deserved abandonment. He had no intention of entertaining her wiles. He wasn't Mose and he refused to play the part.

That's the reason he'd gotten away from Sylvia Black. The pesky girl underestimated Nick. She thought a couple of dates and he'd spill all he knew.

She lured him to her room in Teachall with no one else there. All the mansion's other occupants had gone to the Black's house in Savannah. She wooed him with her nubile body in the empty mansion.

Sylvia stalked Nick from her first day on Cow Bell Island. She drafted him to be her companion on "Spanish moss excursions." The girl proved herself an accomplished equestrienne, and Nick enjoyed her company.

It took him about two seconds to realize how little she cared for the epiphytic relative of pineapples. It equaled his interest in toilet brushes. She paid little attention to the elegant ghostly drapery while they rode. Even though he lived around it all his life, he still found it far more fascinating than Sylvia. Quizzing her, his knowledge of the plants far surpassed hers. For him to be advanced on the topic of her doctoral dissertation opened his eyes.

Luna Belle wanted to knock on Nick's door but didn't. She finished her milk and ate the last bites of the simply wondrous sandwich. The aroma of Nick's manly hands permeated the bread. Several times while eating she inhaled his redolent scent deep into her lungs. Horses, leather, and man intoxicated her enough to override the bourbon and milk.

She never wanted Mose's company the way she did Nick's that afternoon. Neither had she ever been so infuriated with Mose. Their life together fell into a humdrum of complacence on her part. On the other hand, Mose's letter reminded her of his deep affection. Why had Luna Belle avoided his truest devotion?

Her perceptions strode in mists. Mose may have loved her, but not enough to get out of the pirating business, yet her own culpability stared her in the face. She encouraged his craft by loving the extravagances he provided.

Her imposed ignorance of their existence clouded her judgement. Had she paid attention she might have seen how impossible it became for her husband to leave and live because too many people depended on him.

Many off shore accounts existed where monies had been scattered all over the globe. Brokerage firms and foreign agents connected to the operations of Teachall abounded. Even with all those burdens Mose remained devoted to her happiness. Many lesser beings might not have managed to continue being so considerate, especially in the face of her lack of attentive caring.

Nick professed his love. Why? She sat there in that old creaky porch rocker and determined to never become the straw for Nick's camel. If she did decide to trust him, she'd help him— not burden him.

Several questions needed answering. Soon. She didn't have the advantage of time on her hands. Various people had purposefully tried to destroy her life, and they had no intention of allowing her to rest until they accomplished their deeds.

Luna Belle cast herself adrift. Reefs lay ahead although she had no watchman. Mose tried to protect her with the letter still affixed to her flesh.

She tugged at it. A sharp sting bit as she coaxed it from the grip it acquired in her tender flesh. Unfolding it with care she winced as a small brown cross became obvious to her. It was a blood stain from a folded corner that had pierced her skin earlier.

Luna Belle remained perplexed at Mose's reticence to name her enemies or allies. She was left to decide the nature of each person in her life.

Nick walked over to the front window and saw Luna Belle with the letter. Curious, he wanted to read it but admonished himself. He was no Peeping Tom.

Instead, he turned and headed toward the back of the house. He impatiently started again toward the door. This time he surprised them both and opened it. She seized in shock. He had caught her red handed with the most private letter she ever received.

Almost ready to fuss at him for disturbing her privacy, her resolutions from moments prior resurfaced and made her unexpectedly blush. What privacy did she expect on *his* porch? If she wanted to play pirate she must become more sophisticated in her own subterfuge.

Nick again sat in the other rocker. Luna Belle refolded the paper and held it. If Nick skulked as an enemy, why had he not asked what she was reading? It didn't make sense to her.

Nick spoke first, "Luna Belle, I'm still hoping we can reconcile our feelings for each other."

"Nick, it's so soon after Mose's death. Don't you think I need a little time?"

"I know I'm being an ass. It's unfair to you, but you're so vulnerable. The villains trying to get you ain't gonna give you any breaks. They're crooks and they mean business."

"You know more than you've already told me. Don't you?"

"I'm afraid if I tell you, you'll never speak to me again."

"I promise you, if you don't tell me—"

"You'll what?"

"I'll ... I'll ... well ... I don't know what I'll do. But you won't like it."

Nick laughed. Luna Belle joined him.

"I need to know."

"You don't need to know. You must know. It's imperative."

"Are you gonna talk or are we gonna keep playing dodge-ball? If you don't want to talk now—"

"Hush—listen. Where do I begin?"

"This comes from a hodgepodge of memories. There've been various attempts by several folks to drown me in this quagmire. I don't know why they thought I'd cooperate. I've never given most of them the time of day. I mean, Scooter Thadeu. His honesty compares with that rattle-less snake. No, wait ... snake wins.

"He came to involve me in a scheme. I didn't know it at the time but it had to do with killing Mose. I still don't have the details. He wanted to get your friends, the Whites, to rent a warehouse to some guy—"

Luna Belle interrupted, "Marcus Gilder. I know a little about that, but not much."

"Maybe. You asked me about him a while ago, didn't you? Anyway, whoever it was had filled a warehouse with liquor. Mose was supposed to clean the joint out. Scooter hired a private eye to get proof by catching Mose in the act. He told me it was some dude named Mad Dog. Their plan failed. It's been all over TV. Didn't you see it?"

"Nick, you know I don't ever watch TV."

"I heard the robbery occurred before any chance for a snapshot. There was a new moon and it was cloudy to boot. Some kind of shindig went on in the historic district and there was way too much commotion, nobody had so much as a clue."

"Nick?"

"Hmm?"

"Give me a minute."

"Anything for you." He smiled.

"That must have been the night Mose and I had a party for Scooter at the town house. I never understood any of it. I didn't care. I've never cared much for the lush, Lardass. I love Lulu ... but him? Besides, party, party. The whole thing turned into one gigantic Pandora's box—involved almost the entire historic district. Most humiliating thing in my entire life ... well, except maybe Mose's funeral."

"Yeah, I've heard that stands with the best of the doozies."

"You better believe it. We should have video taped it."

"Oh! I expect it was recorded for posterity. After all, it was televised."

"My stars and garters. That never even crossed my mind. Anyhow, some hooligans tried to break into our house during the party. A shootout followed. Shots wounded seven people on the sidewalk and back alley right outside our house."

Nick interrupted, "Some of Scooter's men, reckon?"

"I don't know. Be something if someone verified it. It grew into an almost full fledged riot. I've never been so horrified. On top of it all, Mose disappeared. Wait. Oh, and Mordecai left too."

"Diversion?"

"Police swarmed the area. Their cars clogged the streets. Ambulances came and went. It turned into absolute pandemonium. It went on into the wee hours of the morning. Even after the initial melee, we heard occasional gunshots all over the historic district. I was far beyond embarrassed. Imagine, a federal judge hosting a private party for the governor of the state and all that trash and mishmash going on outside."

"When did Mose reappear?"

"I'm not sure. I gave up and went to bed; however, I do know he stayed out late. I figured he liked being out on the streets talking with the policemen. You know what else tickles me about that night?"

"What?"

"Lardass left about the time it all cranked up good and he didn't take Lulu with him, either. She stayed there with Polly and me. He left faster than a sore tail donkey."

"Ain't he a democrat?" Nick cajoled.

Luna Belle laughed. "Yep ... never did figure that one out. Scooter Thadeu? Shouldn't a pirate be a republican?" They both laughed.

"Politics and bedfellows." Nick reminded.

"Who'd a thunk it?" Luna Belle answered.

"Luna Belle, the other Blacks—they attend the party?"

"Other Blacks?"

"Sylvia's folks?"

"Oh, them. Matter of fact, yes. Why?"

"I didn't want to tell you this part. I'm afraid you'll get mad."

"You mean about your and Sylvia's little romance?"

"Now how did you know that? I mean, I sweated bullets and you already knew."

"Not born yesterday. But thanks for offering to tell me. Anything else I need to know about your mysterious past?"

"Not that I can think of."

"What about Mose's past? You know anything else about that?"

"Luna Belle, I thought the world of Mose. He never treated me any way but good. When all those hooligans tried to get me to help them I wanted to tell them to drop dead. Why'd I want to bite the hand that fed me? It dawned on me that it didn't matter if I helped them or not. That's when I decided to go to Mose about it."

"You told Mose? When?"

"About two days before he died. It's all a little blurry. So much happened. I went to Florida to look at some horses, but before I left."

"What did you tell him?"

"Well ... before I answer that, let me tell you a little more. Then you'll see why he didn't pay a whole lot of attention to me."

"Go on."

"Luna Belle, how close are you and Rose?"

"You know she's one of my best friends on the face of the earth, but now I'm left to wonder if I can trust anybody."

"Well, that's for you to decide, but I don't trust her, period. Mostly because she's married to Pink Tiddie."

"Nick I can't believe—"

"Keep your eyes and ears open. That's all I'm asking."

She listened to Nick's words then handed him Mose's letter. "Read this and help me decide whether to burn it or not."

Nick read it. "I'll get the match."

26
Finding the Bride Price

After Luna Belle left, Nick went inside and grabbed a rough Shetland wool cardigan then headed back to the barn. On his way, he dropped the dead snake's carcass in a gunnysack to show the men.

The short walk from his bungalow to the barn allowed time to rehash things. He, an honorable man, had been at Teachall for almost forty years and hadn't made any advancements in his relationship with Luna Belle.

Nick stopped in his tracks. He looked the barn over from stem to stern. How often he walked past it and never even glanced in the huge building's direction. Smiling, he admired the windows, the design, then the whole thing.

"Hey Nick. Took care of them horses for you." Lil' Roost greeted Nick as he walked in the barn.

"Thanks. You're a good man. I can always depend on you."

"Wadn't nothing. What's in the poke?"

"Have a gander." Nick held the burlap bag open. Lil' Roost peered in and jumped back.

"Now, that's a big-un there."

"That's why I shot him. I hate it, but one this big is too dangerous ... quiet too ... no rattles. Something like this ought'a have a warning."

"Daddy used to say that a snake what ain't got no rattle is the Devil's pilot."

Nick nodded agreement and tossed the sack into a corner.

"Lil' Roost? When's the last time you looked at the barn. I mean looked at it like you'd never seen it before?"

"I don't know. I guesses I don't pay too much attention. Why? Something wrong?"

"No, nothing's wrong. I just take the place for granted. We've been here about the same amount of time. Your mama had you a couple of months after I moved here."

"You been like a second daddy to me. Why, you'z the one taught me to play poker 'fore I'uz six years old."

"I did, didn't I? Thanks for the complement man, but you had a good daddy yourself. Rooster shined as a friend, a fine horseman, too. I still miss him."

"Me too. He been gone a while now but he still live on right here." Lil' Roost pointed to his heart.

"He holds a spot in mine too—sure does." Nick smiled, "Come in my office with me. I want to talk with somebody. Seems like you're the unlucky winner."

"Glad to. Ain't no misfortune about it."

"Have a seat. We really do take this place for granted, don't we?"

"I 'spect we do. Yes-sir."

"Look at all these photos of horses that have lived in these stalls. I knew a whole lot of them personally. You know how the Blacks' came to own their first Andalusians?"

"Don't reckon I do. I member Daddy telling about how two studs come up here from Brunswick. He'uz proud of them rascals. Always said they'uz as fine a animals as he ever seen."

"Yep. Put your feet up and rest a minute. Let me tell you a little story."

"Loves to hear it."

"You know, these horses brought Missy and me to Teachall. Lil' Roost, you grew up around them, but not everybody lives with such fortune. These horses are one of the oldest breeds on earth. Because they've been around people for centuries, they've been bred with care to be docile. I reckon most all the bad's been bred out of them."

"I reckon—they easy horses. I know that."

Nick unplugged his answering machine and wrapped the cord around it before he dropped it in his bottom file cabinet drawer. He wanted Luna Belle to hear Scooter's messages.

"We used to set around the fire at night in the winter, pop corn, snuggle together under warm quilts. Lots of nights, Luna Belle spent the night with Sara. Daddy would tell us tales about horses. I always loved hearing how they came upon these horses.

"You know my daddy trained horses for Missy's granddaddy, Cecil Brigham. They were good friends and liked to fish together. One time they went down to Lake Okeechobee, Florida to fish. You ever been there?"

"One time. Went with daddy and Pete Stagg. I ain't never been much of no fisherman myself, but that's one big pond, ain't it? Whoo-wee."

"Yea. It is. Daddy told about one trip when they met Raoul Gonzales. He'd gotten sick and drifted out on that big old lake, out of fuel, all alone on the water. They rescued him and towed his small bass boat back to the dock.

"Gonzales not only looked rough, he stunk to high heavens. Daddy always said they didn't think they could stay in the boat with him because he smelled so bad. He looked like a penniless vagabond, but they allowed him to join them in their boat to say thanks. They tried to ignore his deplorable condition. He looked so bad that Mr. Brigham really thought Gonzales stole his boat."

"I understands that." Lil' Roost rearranged his feet to get comfortable.

Nick propped his feet on the edge of his desk and locked his fingers behind his head and leaned back. "Gonzales apologized for the shape he was in, but didn't explain why he'uz in such a sorry condition until much later. Said while they'uz headed back to shore, Gonzales learned daddy trained horses, and he perked right up because he had horses too. Course they tried to act polite when they asked Gonzales about his.

Gonzales said he had the horses of kings and emperors. Daddy thought he sounded crazy. I reckon Mr. Brigham did too. Gonzales told them his family had been in Florida for generations and still had some of the original horses brought over by the Conquistadors."

"Now that's something, ain't it?"

"That's what I'm saying."

"Well, how 'bout that?"

"Yeah, how 'bout that, sure enough. I reckon they assumed the old man had lost his mind out there on that big lake all by himself. Daddy said the next morning Gonzales appeared like a different man, spit polished and in a brand new Packard roadster. Their mouths fell open when they saw him."

"I'll bet that's the truth. Sounds like he clean up good though, don't it?"

Nick smiled, "Yeah."

A groom knocked on the door and came into Nick's office. "Lil' Roost, you want us to finish up in the feed room?"

Lil' Roost got up. "Nick, you mind if I leaves?"

"Of course. Thanks for listening to me go on about back in the day."

"Don't think nothing of it. I'z ready to hear the rest of that tale sometime when you can spare the time."

After Lil' Roost left the office Nick closed his eyes to daydream the rest of the story. It connected him to Teachall and Luna Belle through its convoluted path.

"Mr. Cecil, we'z here. You need to wake up'n see this. Looks like the white house or something. You ever seen such?"

Brigham woke and rubbed his eyes in disbelief.

"No Stuart, I don't think I have."

"And this is the horse farm?"

The huge entrance, built of weathered cochina stone, possessed a grand majesty with its vibrant magenta bougainvillea covering the walls and sweeping in an arch over the drive. Inside the gates, large cassia trees' pendulous yellow chains of flowers cast an exotic air over the area. Behind them purple royal crepe myrtles created an enormous backdrop of regal color. All of this had been underplanted with crotons of reds, yellows, and oranges.

Flamingos waded in a shallow pool alongside the drive, but the birds showed no signs of disturbance and continued feeding. Off in the distance cattle egrets punctuated the landscape while they scoured the pastures for insects.

Polk and Brigham sat speechless. It had only been hours earlier they doubted Gonzales' ability to feed his family. This riot of colorful birds, blossoms, and leaves brought Shangri-La to mind and spoke to them of an unexpected grandeur.

They followed the Packard down an avenue lined with king palms before turning onto a narrow drive toward a cottage where they stopped. Gonzales parked his roadster and walked toward Brigham's car. "You gentlemen mind if I ride with you? My larger vehicle seems missing at the moment. I apologize for the inconvenience."

"No inconvenience. Hop in."

Gonzales hopped in the back seat.

The men hadn't driven much farther when Gonzales instructed. "Turn left ahead."

When Stuart made the turn they advanced through lush pasture, followed by a thicket of scrub. Once past it, the vista reopened and the barn became visible in the distance.

"Your barn?"

"Yes sir." Gonzales beamed.

"Beautiful." Brigham said, humbled.

Polk regretted their children's absence, but they might receive an invitation for a later visit. Broaching the subject he said, "I wish the kids had come with us."

"You have children? Are they horse lovers too?"

"Yes sir. As a matter of fact they are."

"Perhaps at some later time you can return with them. We'd love to have them come."

"Thank you, Mr. Gonzales. That's kind of you." Brigham said in delight.

A band of brood mares gathered near the barn. Gonzales beamed. "My pride and joy."

The men left the car and soon were surrounded by a group of curious mares with babies. A little stud colt picked Stuart out and approached him.

"He likes you, Mr. Polk. That's a real compliment since he's usually a little bashful. He's one of the finest in my entire herd."

Stuart scratched between the colt's ears.

"I can tell you have a way with horses, Mr. Polk."

After a while it became obvious that the colt refused to leave Stuart's side. The young horse's mother joined them. The mare also bonded with Stuart from the moment she walked up to him.

Gonzales offered Stuart a cigar. "Here, Mr. Polk, my friend.

You've won the day's prize. The finest Cuban tobacco hand rolled for me. I hope you will like it. You gentlemen care to come inside to see the stallions?"

"Absolutely." Brigham replied.

The barn was stuccoed an off white and sported a red tile roof. In the shape of a cross, the barn sprawled out over what appeared to be several acres. It stood proudly adorned by a large crowning cupola in the center where the four wings met. This diadem stood high above the structure and displayed louvers and stained glass windows, hinting at luxurious accommodations for the stallions.

Each horse's box stall was graced with a stained glass window high enough to remain out of reach from inquiring noses. The translucent blue and green colors of the glazing made the stalls glow with a cool light. A fan located in the cupola blew the heat of the day out the louvers Brigham had observed from outside. This caused a pleasing draft in the hallways and kept the temperature moderated.

As the three men walked down the long corridor the horses grew excited to see their owner. Polk understood the horses' greetings to Gonzales. He saw how much the man involved himself with them. Not a cavalier owner, he insisted on being part of these animals' lives.

"All these horses stallions?" Polk asked.

"Yes. The mares' barn lies over the pastures about a mile away."

"Impressive." Brigham added.

Under the cupola stood a waist high solid walnut ring. Topped by a round polished brass rail, the bright finishes reflected the subtle light from the stained glass above.

A groom led a young energetic horse ready for freedom.

"El Dobar XIV, gentlemen. He is five years and sixteen hands." Gonzales beamed. The groom unsnapped the lead, raised his hands, and swung the rope above his head. This simple gesture set the horse off in a display of pride.

"Look at that neck." Brigham exclaimed.

"Not just neck, look at that whole picture." Polk whistled. "I ain't never seen nothing like that."

"Neither have I, Stuart. Neither have I."

Both men's eyes fixed on the animal. Neither blinked for fear of missing a portion of this majestic stud's display. The intrigued men watched in amazement at the mighty stallion's powerful show of beauty and innate majesty.

Gonzales delighted in their reactions. He signaled for another groom to bring in what looked like El Dobar's twin. "This is Cordoba XX, El Dobar's half brother. Their mothers are full sisters. He too reached five years and stands one inch above sixteen hands. Let's see them together."

The two men expected a nasty confrontation. Instead, the two noble beasts met, shared breath, then romped, and bucked together in colt-like play.

"Old friends you see. Born three days apart."

Both stallions coats glistened a beautiful light gray with searing black points. They separated, trotted, then cantered off from each other. One called, the other answered, rousing the pair to meet again center ring where the entire choreography replayed. Then they trotted side by side in sync around the perimeter, nipping at the air. Their calls roused others to join in, creating a din from all four corners of the barn.

Stuart rested a hand on the polished rail. "You own some happy horses here, Mr. Gonzales. That's a fact."

Gonzales signaled for yet another horse. The grooms knew what he expected and had already prepared to accommodate his wishes.

After a few minutes El Dobar and Cordoba XX came over to the men for close admiration. Gonzales allowed them to nuzzle his chest while he scratched under their chins.

They revealed fire in their eyes only moments earlier. Now the flames dissipated into a kind of enjoyable stupor. The two young stallions stood almost mulish while their owner comforted them with his deft hands.

"Well I'll be. I can't believe they're so relaxed. It's like they're out'a steam, but I know better'n that." Polk said.

From the moment of their arrival at the farm Brigham had been trying to figure out how to acquire horses from Gonzales. He realized from the outset that these wondrous animals possibly held the key to Luna Belle's future and save his hide to boot.

"Ever sell any of your stock?" Brigham asked.

"Only in the most dire economic circumstances. We occasionally give them to people who have performed a valiant service for our family."

While the men admired the stallions, a stable hand brought another behind them.

Gonzales turned. "Coraje, gentlemen. He sired these two magnificent young specimens. He's fourteen years old. His name represents his great valor when still a yearling."

They turned to see an even more outstanding specimen. The bright-eyed Coraje was tacked with a simple snaffle and quilted pad held by a surcingle with rings for short reins. His ebony mane draped almost to his knees; his braided forelock hung far below his nose.

"Paolo, mount him and go inside with the others." Gonzales ordered. "Gentlemen, these two know what to expect. Observe their anxious nature." Gonzales held his chin high.

Paolo guided Coraje to the center of the arena where the other two joined him, one on each side. When the rider commanded, the three obeyed. From a standing position they all trotted together. They maneuvered in tandem figures inside the arena while the rider guided the trio without observable effort.

Taking them back to the center they stopped together, awaiting Paolo's next command.

As the young horses fidgeted, Paolo ordered. "Stand … stand. That's it, my good boys."

Paolo raised his hands and waved a small crop over his head. The two young studs bristled and separated. Each approached opposite sides of the arena, then turned.

Paolo ordered and both cantered the ring's circumference. Their collected slow deliberate gait was unlike anything either man had ever seen.

After a moment Paolo again commanded and both horses came to a complete standstill. They backed slightly then leapt into the air, reminding Brigham of Pegasus.

Paolo whistled, both stopped. He bade them come. They obliged by coming back alongside him.

"That amazed me. How about you, Stuart?" Brigham said.

"Yes-sir. About the most sum'n-sum'n I ever seen."

Nick's cell phone's ringing startled him back. With reluctance, he left his dream, glanced at caller ID and saw Teachall's main number.

"Nick here."

"Hey to you too, dis be Polly. Missy wanna know if you come to de house for supper?"

"Tonight?"

"Um-hmm."

"What time?"

"'Bout seven. We eats about eight. That good? We eats in the kitchen, don't go dresses up."

"Polly, you know I'd never miss one of your meals."

Nick hung up and retrieved the answering machine. Walking out into the barn hall he saw Lil' Roost finishing up with the other stable hands.

"Lil' Roost, gotta go. Missy calls."

"I hears that. Oh … Nick. Thanks, and don't forget about finishing up that story sometime."

27
Gamblin Man

"Polly, I could skin you alive for inviting Nick back to the house on the same day. He's going to think I'm chasing after him. Is that what you have in mind?"

"Why, Missy. What you means accusing me of making you look like you ain't got no more sense than that? You knows how much I cares about you. I just thought it'd be nice for him to joins us for supper. See'n as how y'all done already been together most of the day anyhow. Um-hmm."

"I wish you would ask me in the future. That's all I'm saying. Okay?"

Nick again enjoyed Polly's incredible cooking skills. Her dinner was simple compared to the enormous breakfast she had spread earlier, but it was still a delicious combination of a fresh salad and grilled shrimp with remoulade. She followed this delightful opener with a grouper ceviche then pigeon peas and rice.

After dinner and a dessert of lemon mousse, Polly and Mordecai left the pair in the Sunday Night Supper room to talk. Polly wanted the space branded in their minds. She understood how matters of the heart worked. She wanted them to have every opportunity to flourish in the feelings she had witnessed before breakfast.

Luna Belle's expression grew distant and her eyes seemed to haze over with a reluctant sadness. "I hope I dreamed this, but

I have to know. Earlier today … did … did I hear you say … Granddaddy … sold me?" A sigh followed and a tear formed in the corner of one of her eyes.

Nick leaned toward her and placed one of his hands over hers. He remained speechless but looked deeply into her soul's windows.

She had to break their staring by looking down. "I hope I imagined it. It's been preying on me continually since I came back to the house. I've never heard a word about anything so preposterous."

Nick's voice dropped to an almost muttering rumble. "Yeah. It's been on my mind too." He inhaled deeply and sighed. "Those two stallions Daddy and Mr. Brigham found in Florida years ago. You know, the ones that ended up here."

"Of course, Grandpa sold them to the Colonel."

"That's right he did. You fell in love with them. When they unloaded them off the horse trailer, for some reason they went straight to you. I stood there like a jealous slug."

"You, jealous of me? I find that hard to believe. You kept Gallant and I lost both of mine."

"We didn't know all that until later. In fact, Gallant belonged to Daddy. He gave the colt to me because he followed me around like a puppy all the time."

"You never gave Gallant any other choice. I've never seen you so smitten with a horse. You spent every waking moment with him but I guess you've forgotten that. Your dad didn't have much choice. You two grew inseparable, almost like Siamese twins."

Nick grinned, "Oh, yeah. We did, didn't we?"

"Without question. Sometimes Sara and I hoped you'd forget about Gallant. We wanted you to play with us."

"I never stopped playing with y'all."

"You might not have stopped but you cut back."

Luna Belle was forced to miss the best part of those two horses lives. When they came to Ashwood as five year olds she loved feeding them apples and carrots. Whenever she entered the stable they nickered and waved their noble heads as she stood between them to give them treats.

By the time she married Mose and was reunited with the

stallions, they were older horses whose greatest vigor had
passed. Even though they immediately recognized Luna Belle,
she saw that their ardor for her had waned like jilted lovers.

"Made me furious when the Colonel liked them. I wanted
him to go away and leave them and us alone. I never understood
why I couldn't keep them."

"You ever wondered about what it took to make your
granddaddy give them up? You know how much he liked them
too."

"What do you mean?"

"None of us believed how those two took up with you. From
the instant they came out of the trailer, you mesmerized them
like a Svengali. They called to you like psychics every time you
left the house. Daddy said they could smell you. Must 'a been
right, too."

"They liked me all right, but that's ridiculous."

Nick scraped the remainder of his mousse from the ramekin.
"Luna Belle, we grew up so happy. Even though life had its ups
and downs we still had a good childhood, didn't we?"

"Yes, thank you Nick, we did."

Nick licked his spoon. "Know how much he was paid?"

"No, of course not."

"Daddy told Sara and me that if we ever told you about any
of this, he'd skin us alive. We knew he meant it."

"So, you know?"

"Sure do." Nick reached over and took Luna Belle's chin
gently in his fingertips and turned her face toward his. "Two
million dollars ... for you and two horses."

Luna Belle's scalp flexed tight as she jerked her head back
away from his eyes. "Sold? Two million dollars? That makes me
feel dirty. Nick, if that's true I'm nothing but property. Even at
two million bucks I'm mere merchandise. Counting for inflation,
that's oh ... I don't know ... a huge pile of money."

"Yep. Preposterous, isn't it?"

"So you lie?"

"Nope. May make a mistake or two but that's the way
Daddy told it."

"Your daddy? He told this? Why?"

"Because Brigham made him furious, that's why. You know

the story of how they discovered the horses, don't you?" Nick overcame all reservations.

"I'm sorry … what?"

"I never intended to betray your granddaddy but you need to know this. Daddy stayed at Ashwood because Mr. Brigham treated him with great respect."

"Of course. Your dad was a wonderful man, Nick. Why wouldn't Granddaddy treat him well?"

"Thanks, but don't get me off track. Daddy and your granddaddy scoured the known countryside for fine horses. That was no small task since Mose and the Colonel both liked fine equines. Of course at the time, Daddy didn't understand all the details. That came later."

"I've heard part of this story but refresh my memory."

"You've heard it several times. Then again … listening ain't ever been your strong suit. Plus, you never heard the whole story, just the parts your granddaddy wanted you to hear. You're bound to know about the fishing trip when Daddy and Mr. Brigham found Gonzales out on Lake Okeechobee?"

"Yes, but since I never heard the whole thing, go ahead. Enlighten me."

"Turns out Gonzales had drifted solo for three days and nights without food or water. He almost faced the grim reaper. Daddy said mosquito bites covered his whole sunburned dehydrated body."

"Go on."

"Gonzales gave Mr. Brigham and Daddy the three horses because they saved his life. Daddy said at first they turned him down, flat. All they did was give him a tow and some sustenance. It certainly wasn't anything worth three Andalusian horses but Gonzales insisted. Been an insult not to accept his gift since they held his life in their hands and had shown kindness to a rank stranger."

"Oh, yeah?"

"All the way home Mr. Brigham kept going on and on about how he had what he needed to protect your future and pay off his debt to Albert Durrey. What could Daddy say? He'uz just hired help."

"This part I've never heard. Our next door neighbor? That

Albert Durrey? How's he involved in this?" Luna Belle's brows tensed.

"Six months earlier Mr. Brigham lost big when he gambled with the old coot. Time came to pay up. Came down to money or Ashwood. That's pretty much it."

Luna Belle pushed her coffee aside. "Gambled? Grandpa never gambled."

"I don't expect he did after that. He sweated bullets big time. Daddy even looked for a new place to work. He had no intention of working for Durrey when he took over at Ashwood. Daddy didn't know anything but horses, and around Brunswick, that made for uncertain job opportunities. He stayed wiry and cross most of the time while all this was cooking. Mama said for us to leave him alone. Sara and I heard them talk at night. That's how I know most of this."

"Go on."

"Durrey gave Mr. Brigham a year to produce the money. Daddy said Durrey never wanted the money. He wanted Ashwood."

"I never cared for Mr. Durrey. Now I know why."

"He was a weird cuss, that's for sure. Daddy avoided him. Said he'd as soon find himself cornered by a rabid wolf."

"What'd they bet on?"

"Horse race ... million dollars or Ashwood."

"That's hard to believe."

"Cross my heart, why lie now? It's all water under the bridge."

Luna Belle's eyes glazed with a transparent veil of water. She used the back of her hand and tried to stop the flow.

"Nick, have you considered what being sold makes me?"

Nick looked out the window into night's blackness. In a few moments he looked back inside toward her. "Victim?"

Startled, a new wave washed over Luna Belle. Before his simple word, her perspective had become clouded to the point of making her ashamed and valueless. Nick gave her opportunity to see through different eyes. Yes, victim. Auctioned on an invisible block.

"Thank you. I went another direction. Victim. That's a powerful concept for me at the moment." She inhaled her tears and almost broached a smile.

"I'm not telling all this for you to wallow in pity. I ought to have kept my mouth shut but I couldn't take it anymore. This crap's been bottled up inside me far and away too long."

"Maybe, but this defines who I am. If I'm going to move forward I need to sweep away all the garbage out of my life. This sure sounds trashy to me. I've kept my nose in the air, thinking I'm somebody, but I'm nothing more than a slave."

"Oh, for pity's sake Luna Belle, you may be a whole lot of things but you ain't a slave."

"You keep going and I'll decide."

"Mr. Brigham found himself left with nothing but appearances. He hung onto life like an empty cicada shell caught on a piece of dead bark. Don't you know whenever Mr. Brigham looked in a mirror, he had to see his mistakes glaring back at him? Sold the most precious thing he possessed to cover his drunken foolishness."

Luna Belle's eyes again started pouring tears. Only now she let them wash in an unabashed flood.

"Mr. Brigham found himself over a barrel. Witnesses to the wager was all that saved him. Like I said, Durrey wanted Ashwood, not money. Had all that he wanted. Daddy said Durrey didn't know how cunning an old South Georgia lawyer became when caught with his hand in the fire. Durrey got the shock of his life. Brigham cooked his plan, not wanting to burn the stew. He'd had a bait of scorched rot."

Luna Belle took her napkin and tried to stem the flow of her outrage.

"Mr. Brigham told Daddy something his own Grandpa told him when he was growing up. 'When ye get yo' hand caught in the mouth of a lion, get it out with as much hide as possible.'

A slight laugh escaped her mouth. "That aphorism hadn't crossed my mind in years. I never really understood the poignancy of it until this moment."

"Yeah. It is a powerful quote. So consider your Grandpa intended to overcome this obstacle—hide and all." Nick slowed his speech and softened his voice. "Even if it meant selling you."

Luna Belle's voice trembled. "I realize you're telling the truth. I just don't like what I'm hearing."

"I know." He adjusted his seat. "When we found out. It made us all sick to our stomachs. I don't think I ever felt the same way about Mr. Brigham after that. Even when Daddy and me tended the old man, it hung heavy over my head."

"I never realized how much I owe you and your dad."

"Forget all that. Daddy told us back then to get over the whole shooting match because it was none of our business."

She knew deep in her heart that after the horses went away, her Grandpa never recovered. She imagined it was because he missed the stallions. Now, she recognized his condition as nothing more than guilty remorse.

Luna Belle contemplated for a few moments. "Our destinies are tied into strange bundles. I mean, I wonder if all that about what happened with Granddaddy's mind had anything to do with me?"

"All I know is that once you were away, things went downhill fast with him and your mama. All these years, I couldn't bear what they'd done to you."

"Why did you come here?"

Any shyness Nick may have felt to this point vanished in a flash. "To be near you." He paused a moment for that to sink in. "I worked two years at Nuevo Jerez learning to train."

Luna Belle eyes narrowed and her voice shook. "You left Ashwood a child and returned a strapping, handsome man. My heart fluttered the first time I saw you, but my arranged engagement stopped me from looking deeper. I tried to erase that memory from my mind long ago." A sudden fear overtook her face.

Nick observed the reaction and smiled. "While I worked in Florida it occurred to me. You and I shared no blood. I missed you more than anybody else. My heart ached because of your absence from my life. I wanted nothing more than to make something of myself. Something you'd be proud of. I threw my whole heart into learning. Became pretty good at it too."

"Not good, Nick. You're the best and you know it."

Nick bowed his head. "I did it all for you."

"How did I fall into this trap?"

"Maybe it's time for you to call up your old demons and demand they vacate your mind."

"Go on."

"Luna Belle, it's not my place to say a lot of this."

"You're my friend, aren't you? I want it all with no holds barred."

Nick bit his lower lip and forged his face into a look of authority. "Do you know how your father died?"

"In an automobile accident."

"Not really. At least that's not the way I overheard Mama and Daddy telling it late one night."

"Do I want to hear this?"

"I honestly don't know. If you want me to stop just say so at any point and I'll get my raggedy ass up and leave."

"Deal."

"Your dad refused to marry the young lady your grandparents arranged for him. He ran off and found himself the love of his life."

"But they weren't happy." Luna Belle had heard so many times from her grandfather how miserable her father had been.

"That's what they wanted *you* to believe but according to the best I know, they weren't just happy, they were blissful."

"So what happened to make them separate?"

"They never separated. Your granddaddy kept at your dad all the time—"

Luna Belle touched Nick's trembling hand. "Call him Geoff. That's what I always called him. You do know his name, don't you?"

"Okay. Geoff then." Nick cleared his throat. "Mr. Brigham finally got to Geoff so bad that he ran away one hot August afternoon. He didn't go far. Wound up at a honky-tonk down close to Fernandina Beach where he got himself plastered. The sheriff called Mr. Brigham the next morning. He had found Geoff in the gravel parking lot of that dive with his head bashed in. Daddy said he bet the thief didn't get more'n twenty dollars out of Geoff's wallet. Seems like Mr. Brigham sold you and your daddy." Nick's voice began to break from sorrow.

"Is there more?"

Nick had to inhale deeply and sigh before he could keep the frog in his throat at bay. "After Geoff's funeral the Brighams learned of your mama's pregnancy. Hadn't been for that she'd been thrown out with nothing. I got a good idea that's why she was always so distant with you. Luna Belle. I'm sorry I've told you all this, but you've got so much to figure out. I really want to be part of your life. I've carried this load of garbage around far too long. I'm glad to be shed of it. If I'm to be any help to you, it's got to leave me forever."

"Wow. I never heard any of this. Seems like you know more about my life than I do." Luna Belle sat back and looked far toward the horizon.

"I never thought about it, but I guess I do know more about the crap that happened to you in secret than you could have ever heard."

"Nick? I want to hear the rest of this, but not right now."

"Whenever you think you can take it. We're worn to a frazzle for one day. We need rest."

28

If He Walks Like a Duck

Luna Belle couldn't stand the thought of facing Nick again. In fact many days had passed and Luna Belle still refused to be in Nick's presence. He attempted to contact her but she never agreed to his requests.

Polly talked with Luna Belle over a cup of cocoa late one evening. "Missy, let me calls Nick back up for breakfast again in the morning. You needs to see him, don't you?"

"I can't Polly. He told me things that I haven't been able to overcome."

"You'z mad at him?"

"Oh, no. Never. I'm more upset with myself. I want to trust him so badly my whole body aches but I can't drag him down to my level."

"You'z talking nonsense, Missy. That's all they is to it. I don't wants to hear it no more."

"Polly. I was nothing more than a possession to Mose."

"I done told you to hushes that foolishness with me. I ain't never gonna believes Mr. B didn't loves you. No ma'am, I ain't. I seen the way he looks at you all the time. You was more to him than a sparkly doo-dad."

Luna Belle blew on her chocolate to cool it. "I'm so tired and sleepy but I can't get rid of this insomnia. It's driving me to utter distraction."

"Um-hmm. I know you is roaming the house at night. You's bound to be wore slam out."

"Polly, I've been such a fool. I have learned one thing, that—"

"I knows. That ignorotic curse hanging over yo' head. Ain't it? But you know what I'z worried about?"

"What?"

"I'z worried that Nick gonna turn his head to other things. That's what bothering me. Um-hmm."

"I really can't say as I would blame him either."

In truth, Nick had turned to his own devices for dealing with getting away from Teachall. In order to survive he needed to remove Luna Belle and himself from her own mind's haunting. He craved one last effort at happiness with his love. Making a place for them, if she rejected him after that, he'd abandon her forever.

Nick's plan utilized the animals since Luna Belle had lost all her interest in them, Nick knew once she found peace her affection for them would spring back, but not at Teachall. So he carted off horses and cattle with a purpose in his heart.

Without Mose the entire plantation began to crumble. Nick realized the futility of staying at this God forsaken place any longer than necessary.

The Contessa's continual hauntings left Luna Belle terrified even though things at Ashwood convinced her as a child never to fear a spirit. Her mother's hard bearing taught her to prevail under most any circumstance.

Luna Belle always dismissed ghost or demon. How silly, to live scared of something lacking solid form. Purely psychological, but then night would fall and the terrors unrelentingly sought her.

The Contessa called, "Luna Belle … Luna Belle … Luna Belle. Why mock me in my torment? Why despise my memory? Why can you not accept the love I lost at my dear Edward's murderous execution? You defiled my memory. Leave my home."

"This has turned into ridiculous nonsense. You're nothing more than a figment of my imagination. Why don't you leave me alone?"

After time the apparition also came by day. Maybe she had been too irresponsible with the pearls.

"I want no further part of your curse, Possum Queen. Ha. I bet you love the name, Possum Queen. Can't you muster something more daunting than a mangy possum or two? I want to appease you but don't know how to persuade a phantasm. What if I built you a new home, or better yet, why don't you move into the mausoleum?"

Luna Belle walked the upstairs halls carrying her lighted kerosene lamp. "Curses. Ignoramuses believe in superstitions. People with nothing better than to occupy their existences with frivolous worries. Anyone with the tiniest bit of sanity scoffs at such tripe." Luna Belle fussed at the spirit.

"Even as a child I disdained all forms of hoodoo. Old warnings and sayings about cracks in sidewalks and any other silliness ... black cats ... whatever. My dear grandmother ascribed to those notions, but not I."

She began sitting alone in her morning room where she managed to sleep a little in her chair. For some reason, even when the spirits left her in peace, she fretted, yet she lacked a clue of what concerned her. While she refused belief in the Contessa's curse, in truth Luna Belle allowed the spook to overcome her soul. Whether of her own mind's tricks or whether of reality, the Contessa and Mose came to her.

She disdained her bed. Her sunken eyes transformed from their beauty into dark circles with hanging baggy lower lids. Her skin turned pallid and clammy.

Her sole relief came from sitting in an old high backed bishop's chair while burnishing its arms' acanthus leaves with her fingertips. She eroded the finish by tracing veins and ridges. The Belgian tapestry affixed with large antiqued brass headed tacks showed the effects of incessant writhing. Where her calves and shoulders rubbed the tacks they lost their rich patina, becoming polished. She feared stillness. She might doze, yet a strong passion for sleep never left.

No one outside Teachall knew of her true desperate unrelenting condition because Mordecai and Polly guarded her from public scrutiny. Some islanders grew suspicious over Luna Belle's sudden cloistering of herself from society, a rare event for the otherwise gregarious woman. After weeks of this downhill spiral Mordecai called Dr. Deamon who came with haste.

Polly cracked the door. "Missy, Dr. Deamon come to see you. Wadn't that nice of him?"

Polly led him into Luna Belle's room otherwise unannounced. Mordecai and Polly wanted the good doctor to see her current state. The old phonograph turntable spun since the last track had completed its music making hours earlier. The needle traced the inner circle over and over, creaking and popping.

Jack Deamon lifted the stylus and returned it to its cradle. He removed the record and examined the label. "Maria Callas Sings Great Tragic Arias," emblazoned below the manufacture's logo. He scanned the list.

He thought, *Just what she needs … suicide and desolation.*

"Didn't we hear Callas sing Gioconda at the Met?" Jack asked.

Luna Belle never acknowledged his presence. She continued staring out into a nebulous nothing. "You're mistaken. That was the winter we spent at the New York townhouse. We saw her sing three times. Perhaps Tosca, Norma, and … Lucia? Yes, Lucia for certain. I was so jealous of her. I've always wanted to play Lucia. Murder and insanity seem like exquisite bedfellows. Don't they Jack?"

"You're making me very uncomfortable."

"Nonsense." Luna Belle laughed then snapped her head toward her old friend. "Lighten up, Jack. We get one chance at this merry-go-round."

"That's why you're frightening me."

Luna Belle laughed then again grew distant. "I lived in misery that winter in New York … well, except for the parties and the opera. I hate that city when it's cold unless I'm shopping or otherwise occupied. I'm happier here or at our little hacienda near Almería where it's warmer most of the time. But Mose loved the bustle and cold."

"You're still in love with Spain, aren't you?"

"How could I not be? You've been several times, didn't you love it?"

"Not like you. How about you explain this macabre music and your current condition."

"Jack, how can you ask me? You know how much I loved

watching and hearing Callas. She was the most beautiful and elegant creature. Some may argue that there have been better voices but I dare you to find one with the looks to match."

"You may be right. She sang like a bird. Her beauty and elegance remain unquestioned. Is it crass to call her untouchable?"

"Maybe to a Hindu?" Luna Belle chuckled. "Such a charming person. Did you know Mose arranged her meeting with Elsa Maxwell who then introduced Maria to Onassis in Venice? I think my memory serves well enough to assert that as fact."

"Can't prove it by me. I missed a great deal of the season. I went to the opera with you several times, but Mose flew me back and forth."

"Oh yeah. That's right … you and your patients."

"I try to maintain competence, Luna Belle."

"So that's why you came?"

"That's cheap and tacky."

"Can you believe it Jack? I need help."

"I'm concerned for your welfare. Polly and Mordecai both tell me you've become a reclusive hermit."

"Ah, maybe. Mose left me in a bind. Don't know who to trust. All my old friends are behaving in strange ways. What's their ulterior motive? It's driving me crazy."

"I expect their motives are based on your demise, but that's pure speculation. There's talk in the village. The natives act restless."

"That's nonsense. Utter rubbish … restless, indeed." Luna Belle furrowed her brows and turned toward his waiting gaze. "Are they really, Jack?"

He nodded slightly. "Oh, yeah. They are." Jack waited a moment for Luna Belle to reply, but she sat in silence and turned her head back to the expansive plantation. "So … then, Luna Belle? The bottom line for me is, how are you feeling? Getting any rest?"

"You need to go and peddle your sensitivities where they're appreciated." Her intonation turned sarcastic, changing in an instantaneous flash.

"Ouch. Hope you think more of me than that."

"That's how I'm doing. I told Lonny Gober several years ago when he asked me the same question. I looked him square in the eyes and said, 'Lonny Gober, I don't appreciate the local mortician asking me how I am while you wring your scaly hands in anticipation. You shameless buzzard.'

"I walked away, giving him my most charming smile. Similar to the one I'm giving you at the moment. I find it so much more genteel than a vulgar hand gesture."

Dr. Deamon laughed, "Luna Belle, your dry humor. I wish I could bottle'n sell you. I'd be rich."

"You and how many others?"

Luna Belle revived and straightened her slumping posture. The Contessa whispered in her ear. "Not so fast my love. You still haven't answered my questions. I'll not leave your side until you have paid back what you owe."

"Please, Contessa, how can I finish with you? Will you leave me be?" She blurted, embarrassing herself.

"Luna Belle? Am I interrupting something?"

Luna Belle blushed. She had tipped her hand. Her mind reeled desiring recovery from her faux pas.

"Jack?"

"Yes?"

Luna Belle hesitated. "Have any advice for someone visited by a spirit?"

"As in ghost?"

"I mean, I don't believe in specters, yet one keeps calling and asking all sorts of questions."

"Tell me what you're seeing and hearing."

Even his most conciliatory tone did nothing to budge her stubbornness while she became a sullen mule, as her countenance once again fell. Polly looked at the doctor and raised her brows. He returned her gesture to imply he didn't know.

Luna Belle wanted to console her anguish and darkness but much more turmoil bubbled underneath. Always immaculate in her appearance, she had turned into an unkempt, dirty, and uncaring tracing of her former self. Even Jack's coming here in her current condition upset her little. He saw her embarrassment as nothing more than pretension.

He wanted another take. He held up the phonograph record to examine it.

"Beautiful music."

"Suits me."

"Why listen to this now?"

"I guess it helps. I mean … I wonder. Maybe I'm trying to go back in time. Mose and I lived so happily before we drifted apart while floating on the same raft. You know how we doted on each other. You saw it.

"We both loved the opera so much. Surely, you can call up some dusty old memories about opera week in Atlanta when the Met came to town? I miss that. Remarkable, entertaining all those fascinating singers. So much wonderful fun. I know you came to the house when that tenor … what was his name? He sang such a phenomenal Rodolfo."

"Björling?" Jack asked.

"Björling, yes. He sang in the conservatory at our house in Buckhead. Polly was there, weren't you? Mordecai opened a bottle of champagne and the cork escaped him. It popped Björling right in the kisser." Luna Belle laughed hard.

Polly delighted in seeing Luna Belle responding. "Um-hmm, I 'member that. Sho does. That man sweet about it though even though his mouth blow up like a hog bladder."

"Ah. Yes, Luna Belle. Happy times. After Lola died you became my surrogate family. I still miss my darling bride. Having your friendship meant more than I can tell. That's why I'm worried about your melancholy. Luna Belle, are you aware of the burdens Mose carried? Every person in this community depended on him."

"I know that. It's one of the things making me so despondent now." Luna Belle inhaled, smiled, and retraced the acanthus leaves. "Jack, you know Mose didn't leave an heir. You tell me all these people want to destroy me. I'm worried for my sanity but more for my safety. I don't know who to trust. My Lord. That sounded selfish and silly. Something so trivial … no. This isn't trivial. My life. He cast it aside … our love."

"Luna Belle, Mose never cast you aside. I know. Mose loved you with all his heart. Everyone has an Achilles heel. His might have been loving someone who didn't return the favor with equal ardor."

Luna Belle rubbed the acanthus leaves while her gaze went far afield and her face grimaced.

"You'll never convince me you fell into second place. He lived in perpetual exhaustion. We talked about it several times. I wanted him to have an examination but he continually refused. The crime lab determined that he suffered a massive heart attack about an hour before being shot."

"Sure, I know all that."

"Luna Belle, granted there's too much at stake here. I just hope you don't let yourself get swallowed by a bunch of thieves. Take care of yourself. After Lola, you and Mose have always been the most important people to me on this island. The two of you are the reason I stayed here after I lost her."

Jack rubbed his eye to mask a tear. "Married six months when she died from an aneurism. Lord help me, I still love her. She was the Cow Bell native, not me. Ring any bells? Why stay here? Mose left, assassin or not."

She reached over to a small table and took a handkerchief from the top drawer, offering it to him.

He took it and wiped his eyes "Luna Belle, Mose quit golfing with me. Several times we'd take a cart out and ride the course. We'd stop and sit. Sometimes we watched birds or other golfers. Sound familiar?"

For the first time in days, Luna Belle sobbed. Tears of exhaustion and deep despair flooded. Jack made sense but Luna Belle didn't appreciate his words.

Jack held the phonograph disk. He called attention to it once again.

"Little dark, isn't it? I mean the words are disturbing."

"You have something to say, Jack? Why are you here?"

Her sour face and poignant stare once again chilled him. She went from warm to freezing in a split second. Her worn guise exposed her anger.

"How dare you come into the suite of a lady unannounced." Looking down, her attire shocked her.

Jack feared for her safety. He wanted no part of causing any disaster yet her depression demanded attention. "I'm sorry Luna Belle. Polly, Mordecai, and I share concern for your well being. Mordecai called me and asked me to stop by. I didn't mean to disturb your privacy. We were only pleasantly visiting as friends."

"Some people need to learn when to mind their own business." She peered at Polly.

Dr. Deamon talked in a most quiet and consoling way. He had experience with grief, but this outweighed common grief. He saw deep and troubled introspection.

"Polly, get Mordecai in here right now."

"He gone to the store. I sends him here when he gets back." Polly started toward the morning room door.

Truthfully, Mordecai held Scooter Thadeu at bay in the barn. The Governor seemed intent on overtaking the entire plantation. He demanded Mordecai allow him to search the premises for Mose's will.

Without a probated will everyone in Pirate's Landing suffered. The longer she avoided the issue the higher the local temperature climbed.

"Polly." Luna Belle screeched. "You wait a minute. You're not going anywhere. I want to know why you called this quack out here."

"Now wait a minute." Jack protested.

"You shut up. I'll deal with you later."

"We din't mean no harm, Missy. You knows we concerned about you 'cause you's falling off so bad. Doctor, we can't gets her to eat. She nibble a little but she don't eat good."

Polly wanted to switch back to a different channel—the one with the kinder attitude.

"Both of you listen to me. There is nothing wrong with me. Things happen here at night. I've seen them. Apparitions move about at their leisure after darkness falls. I need someone to protect my home. Protect us. I don't need or want some incompetent doctor coming in here and disturbing my privacy. Do I make myself clear?"

Jack decided to come back later.

29
Ladies, Please

Polly started to walk Dr. Deamon to his car. She wanted him aware of the Contessa and the way Luna Belle succumbed to the ghost. Polly knew Jack had seen the situation's urgency, and she felt the need to reinforce his involvement.

Before they made it into the hallway Luna Belle screeched. "Polly, I'm not through with you."

Polly cracked the door just enough to speak. "I comes back soon as I shows de gentleman out."

"He can see himself out. You get in here right now."

Polly closed the door and proceeded downstairs with Jack. Their calmness stopped when Luna Belle flung the door open and ran to the mezzanine railing, leaning over, shouting for Polly to return at once. Polly ignored her.

"You see, Doctor? What I tells you. She crazy ... losing her mind ... go on and on about that curse. Say she don't believes in it but won't stop talking about it. I thanks she turning herself into one of them obsessive repulsive. We's got to help her somehow."

Jack smiled. "We can't give her much other than patience until she collapses or agrees to treatment. I'll come back in the morning. If she doesn't cooperate tomorrow, I may have to cart her off kicking and screaming."

"She seeing things and scaring the shoo-wee out'a us."

Dr. Deamon and Polly proceeded to his car where he sat with the door open. Within an instant the mansion's front door opened with such force the side lights popped from their lead tracery.

"I'm not going to stand for this. You will not talk about me behind my back. I'm going after a gun. Jack, if you're not off my property by time I return, well… let's say there'll be some slow driving and sad singing."

Jack left. He had no intention of abandoning Luna Belle but he needed help, or a straight jacket.

Polly didn't know what to do. She ran to the library and pressed the alarm behind Blackbeard's portrait three times to call help from the barn.

After Luna Belle armed herself she found Polly. "Why are you in here?" Luna Belle demanded, pointing a double barrel shotgun.

"Why nothing Missy, nothing a'tall."

Polly forgot to push the portrait back to its normal position. Luna Belle saw it. "So you think somebody's gonna come and rescue you? You arrogant—"

"Missy, please, calm down. I wants what's best for you. I ain't never wanted nothing else."

"Don't you try to tell me anything, you traitor."

Polly's fear grew by the moment. She hoped for help soon, but the distance from the barn offered little immediate hope.

"I ought to blow your brains out right there under that painting you've always admired so much."

Luna Belle looked at the lady reclined on the pillows and back at Polly. She softened. "The first time I met you, Polly, it was yours and my first masked ball here at Teachall just before I married Mose. He and I were so much in love. You and Mordecai dressed up like that pair in that painting right there, didn't you?"

Luna Belle gestured. "The Colonel brought me in here that night. He was so proud of the two of you … the way you both looked like the models who posed for that painting. I'll have to admit. You both really did look like that couple."

"We was all happy back then. I'z glad to 'member all that."

"The Colonel insisted I understand something else that night."

"What were that, Missy?"

"That you and Mordecai were beloved family members, not servants. Polly, I've missed several important parts of who I am. My life is riddled with holes. The time when I could have been kind and generous to the people who have waited on me hand and foot has long passed."

"Missy, that's condiculous. You'z gettin yoseff all het up over nonsense."

Luna Belle grew quiet while she looked intently at the painting then back toward Polly. "I've turned myself into a sunken vessel waiting for worms and maggots to feed on my being." Luna Belle's knees felt weak and a tremor overtook them, making her feel unstable. "I noticed how you looked at Mose back then."

For the first time in her life, jealousy gnawed at Luna Belle. It infested her psyche with malicious intent. Her white hot rage flared and consumed her ability to reason. Instead of redeeming herself, her tired, worn spirit succumbed to hatred. "You pompous, dim-witted ... did he love you?"

"Who dat, Missy? What you means?"

"You know damned well what I mean. Don't toy with me. I'm considering blowing you to kingdom come this moment, but first I want to know.... Did he love you?"

"Missy, you's talking crazy. Mordecai love me. You know he do."

Polly understood what Luna Belle meant but she forbade herself to say it. She knew she loved Mose, yet she cast her forbidden love for him to a hidden corner of her heart long ago. She never allowed herself the delight of her affection for him.

Mose never told her he loved her. Even so, thinking of it brought a smile to her heart. Polly's torn troubled spirit fell in surrender. She didn't care if she went to her grave because of the deep love she held for her deliverer.

Not love Mose? If she needed to die now to honor his memory, so be it. She knew he held the key to her whole life as an adult.

Luna Belle saw Polly's countenance change. "So that's just what I thought. You did love my husband."

Polly witnessed the fire in those glaring blue eyes that burned holes in her spirit. She calmed herself and aimed to console her heart for the first time since Luna Belle came to Teachall.

There always existed a strong yet resilient tension between the two powerful women. Both held domineering attitudes toward the other. Years earlier Polly acquiesced and relented her power because of Mose, the Colonel, and Beulah.

"Missy you know over the years I has come to love you just as much as I ever loves anybody else. You knows that. How can you ax me these questions? I come here without a pot nor nothing else. Didn't even have no clothes on my back. You come deck out in finery. Ain't no sense in you being jealous of me."

Luna Belle did arrive a spoiled, elegant ingenue. Teachall never really meant that much to her. She existed in blissful ignorance of her bondage. Luna Belle was the unknowing bondservant, Polly the free spirit.

"Far as I know, Missy, yo' husband never love nobody but you. Minute ago you ax me if'n I love him. Yes ma'am, I did. I ain't ashamed of it no more. I did love Moses Black with all my heart."

Luna Belle lowered the gun. For some reason hearing Polly's words shuttered her heart. She no longer feared Polly's admitting her love for Mose. Luna Belle discovered a brief peace in her mind.

"Polly, I'm sorry I doubted your loyalty. I don't know how to fix it."

"Nothing to fix, Missy. I know you been under a lot of strain. We wants what best for you. That's all."

Mordecai burst into the room, frightened. The house had been a den of troubles and he worried the fuse sparkled alight. Scooter had further set Mordecai's nerves on edge when the governor demanded the will be read.

Mordecai panicked when he saw Luna Belle standing between Polly and escape with a shotgun slung against her hip. His breath didn't slow because he feared for his loving wife.

"Get out'a here, Mordecai. Polly and I have unfinished business."

"Missy. Please let me have that gun." Mordecai begged.

He had chosen the worst possible moment to enter. Luna Belle's mind wavered on a slope too volatile for reason. She raised the gun back toward Polly. "Mordecai, if you want to see her alive much longer, you'd better get out now."

He saw no recourse other than to leave. Getting a gun and dispatching the crazy woman himself came to mind, but that played right into the enemies' hands. There had to exist a more tenable avenue of escape.

He thought of calling Nick. Over the course of the last few weeks they had become good friends. Mordecai had great expectations for Luna Belle's improvement. On the other hand, Nick had developed other, foreign ideas.

As Mordecai walked to the kitchen he determined to give Nick a chance to help rescue Polly from Luna Belle. Nick being the other person on the farm who loved both women.

With Mordecai out of the room Luna Belle continued, "Polly, Polly, Polly. I've heard your pitiful tale about coming here so many times. I'm sick of it. You did love my husband. You admitted it."

Polly straightened her posture and raised her chin. "Missy, you knows I'z been devoted to you. I'z bent over backwards. What you wants from me? If you thinks killing me help ease yo' troubled mind, go on. I don't wants to stands in your way. You ought'a knows a few things before you kills me, though."

"Oh, really? What?"

"Missy, you needs to know that years ago I did come here a sorry sight. I didn't have nothing. Your husband brought me here on his own. To this day I don't know why. I reckon it'uz because he saw me 'bout dead and took pity."

Luna Belle softened slightly.

"I'z bound to loves the man that save my life. My excuse of a daddy tried to puts me out to walk the streets and ho around. Not me, no ma'am. Not me. I'd a let him kills me first and he nearly did."

Luna Belle's eyes closed.

"You thinks you scares me with that gun but my life been blessed with all these years what didn't belong to me. See, if your husband hadn't took me in, I'd been dead long time ago. That's the truth. If you shoots me you still can't take away what he give me all them years ago. Can't nobody. Cause it's in the past. I done had more'n I'uz supposed to.

"Now you ax me, did he loves me? I don't know what to say other than if he didn't, why he take me in? But did he love me like a wife? No ma'am. I might a let him then 'cause I didn't know no better. Now I does."

"Polly? How can you abide living in your skin? I think carrying around all that love ought to weigh you down."

"Missy, love ain't no burden. No ma'am, ain't no burden to it at all. In fact, they ain't nothing 'bout it drags you down, but it lift you up—way up high. That's what it do. It more like you floating on a cloud. Ain't you still got a little twinge of that feeling you had from away back when you loved?"

Luna Belle sobbed and her whole body jerked in convulsions. "Polly, you've reconciled yourself to your existence. I haven't. The Contessa's haunting has grown in my heart as a manifestation of my guilt, hasn't it?"

Nick arrived from the barn and joined Mordecai in the hall.

"Missy, I don't know about you and her relationship. I'z sorry I ever mentionsez her to you. Yes ma'am I sho is."

"Your wisdom has matured and I've remained a foolish child. You're the one who should need to be nurtured, but long ago you emerged a dignified and upright soul. I've turned my preoccupation toward things and now my vanities circle me like vultures."

"Missy, you'z being far and away too hard on yoseff. Um-hmm."

"I'm not so sure. All my love's ambitions faded into trinkets and gewgaws, but the jewels Mose gave me didn't matter because they hung on a hollow corpse. Until I fill my body with a living worthwhile person, my life holds no chance of improving. I had a good run. I whooped it up with hedonistic parties and gulped the flowing Champagne but the piper's bill has come due. The Contessa stands to collect an account in arrears. Polly, will you help me?"

"Missy, that's all I've ever wants."

"If these spirits are nothing but figments of my imagination, why won't they vanish? If I understood a purpose to all this, I might become a better person. Will you help me rid myself of the Contessa's curse, or at least understand it?"

"I didn't thinks you believes in no curse."

"I don't. Polly … I don't know. Sometimes at night I hear her voice whispering in my ear. I have no idea how to send her away. I want peace. When Mose lived I ran around without a care in the world. I fabricated cares but I was just being silly."

"You's just having growing pains. That's all. When a body been ignoring everything around them they finds theyseff in a mess. Seem like to me that be where you living right now."

Polly laid a gentle hand on Luna Belle's shoulder. "About the Contessa? If she tormenting you, I don't know what to tells you. Maybe if you's to go someplace else … one of your other houses. She might not come after you. You been here way too long. Body like you used to moving around. You needs to get out and get some fresh air and sunshine. Feel the wind blow that pretty hair."

Polly pushed Luna Belle's hair away from her face and smiled at her. "I know it ain't easy. You've lost the life you had. Who can blame you? It were fun. I'uz loving it just as much as you was, but Missy, all things end sometime. I guess your big ride end a little before you'uz ready. That's all. Your life ain't over, though."

Nick and Mordecai listened in the hall with tears coursing their cheeks. Nick whispered, "I want to rescue Luna Belle from herself so bad I can taste it. I hope my plan is going to work."

Mordecai quietly answered, "I have tremendous faith in you. I've watched her former strengths vanish while she transformed herself into a frail, delicate creature."

Nick quietly responded, "She's eating herself alive. I've got to get her away from this place."

Luna Belle reached up and took one of Polly's comforting hands in her own. "Polly, I need you now more than I ever have in my entire life."

"I'z right here."

"What's your opinion of Nick? I want to trust him. He's been a faithful friend all these years. He told me he loves me, but I don't know whether to believe him or not. Mose wrote me a letter the morning he died. He warned me not to trust people until they prove themselves."

"Nick ever do anything to make you think he not your friend, Missy?"

"Oh, Polly. I don't know. No. I can't think of a single reason to lose my confidence in Nick. You and Mordecai are my true friends. So many people want what Mose left. Sometimes I want to run screaming."

"You knows Nick all your life. Ain't that right?"

"Yes, all my life."

"What you so concern about, then? You know what kind'a heart the man got. You ever think about what he gained by staying here all these years? I know he had a job but what else?"

"He told me he stayed here because he loved me."

"Well, I don't reckon I can does no better than that. Can you?"

Nick almost rushed to Luna Belle, but Mordecai grabbed his arm. "Not just yet young man. She needs time to sort her wits back into order. Plus, she is badly in need of rest and sleep."

"Polly, there's one more thing I'm going to ask of you. I already know it doesn't make a whole lot of sense."

"Yes ma'am, you know I does whatever you ax me to do."

"I want you to leave here. I don't think we can stay together and me learn to stand on my own two feet. It's becoming more obvious to me all the time. I've depended on you too much."

Polly's soul fell into a pit.

"Yes ma'am." Polly's body failed her for the first time in her life. She passed out on the sofa. Mordecai came into the room and looked hard at Luna Belle but he dared not speak.

30

Hope Springs Eternal

Jack returned the next morning prepared to haul a tormented soul away. When he left the evening before Luna Belle appeared unfit to remain isolated within the confines of her emotions. She needed freedom. When he heard about the events of the previous hours a glimmer of hope for her recovery coursed his mind.

Upon Jack's returning to her room a different Luna Belle sat cleaned, dressed, and apparently greatly improved. She appeared rested and much less agitated.

Jack smiled. "Good morning."

"Jack."

"I trust you slept."

"Some. Amazing what a little sleep will do."

"You said it."

"Jack, where did time go? Years ago we saw no end to ourselves or time for that matter. Now, I'm alone. Mose left me. No assassin's bullet took him. If he had been murdered—"

"Luna Belle, you're nothing more than a masquerading child. You've spent your entire life running from yourself. Aren't you tired? It's time you light and rest your wearied wings."

"What else can I do? It's all I know, but you're right. I have spent my life chasing my tail. Poor dogs. Now I know how they feel. I've sought everything outside myself. No wonder my husband ran from me. Why not? I chased him away like I have all good things."

Jack walked over to the phonograph. "Ah. Brahms first Symphony, much more uplifting."

"I'm afraid I've injured Polly beyond repair. I've lived here in these confining walls for the greater part of my life. I thought I was free, but I was the captive. Funny isn't it? You think you know what's happening. You laugh and scoff at poor souls you see, thinking yourself their superior. Time stops and you are given a chance to look into a new mirror. Oh, you've looked in mirrors before. Me? I gazed. That's all I did. I avoided my eyes as if they revealed death itself."

"Having a little cathartic discovery, are we?"

Luna Belle locked her fingers together. "This should make me even more depressed, yet it's not. Somehow, I wish it did. I'd love to enjoy my own misery ... but wait a minute ... that's what I've been doing these last several weeks, isn't it? Abandoned myself for no good reason." A deep belly laugh overtook her spirit. "Anyway, what good is depression if you can't find at least a small amount of pleasure?"

Luna Belle sighed and fell silent. Jack sighed with her and shook his head, allowing her a few moments.

"I expect the gossip vines have already announced what I did to Polly?"

"I've heard. You appear gullible and vulnerable to your enemies. With Polly gone from Teachall the mutineers feel one step closer to their coup. They smell the lust of blinding gold. I understand Rose and Scooter are particularly jubilant."

Jack sat down beside Luna Belle to look out the salon's wavy antique glass French doors with her. He saw Nick riding a beautiful bay stallion on the lawn. Jack smiled and looked toward Luna Belle. "Have you ever ridden that horse?"

"What horse?"

"The one Nick is riding out in the east garden. Don't sit there and tell me you can't see him."

Luna Belle's eyes forsook staring into a nebula of infinity long enough to focus, but she sat silent.

"I think he's the most beautiful I've ever seen."

"Whatever." Luna Belle returned to her staring into space.

"This is a beautiful plantation." Jack watched carefully for any sign of interest. His companion slumped and turned her stare to the floor.

Luna Belle sat up before she broke their silence. "Why did I accuse her? I'm sure Mose loved her ... more than me."

"Are you talking about Polly?"

"Who else? Jack, you're going to have to keep up if we continue."

Jack twisted his mouth and raised an eyebrow. "Luna Belle, uh ... Mose had tremendous responsibilities. He made his choices, but you were his only real love. You're overreacting to this fetish you've developed about Polly and Mose."

Luna Belle rolled her eyes.

Jack leaned forward to have a better view of her face. "I told you earlier that Mose and I often rode the golf course, not playing. You did listen, didn't you?"

"So."

"Mose never abandoned his love for you. He may have let other things take precedence in his life, but I assure you that it made him feel terrible pangs of guilt. His responsibilities took over his life leaving you to feel alone."

"How would you know?"

"He told me. He worried about you. He wanted things right between the two of you. He even took you to Venice to try and patch things up, didn't he?"

"Yes Jack. Then he received a call from Pink. We left Venice early. 'Family business' he said. That's all he ever said. I thought I was his family, but apparently he thought otherwise."

"Luna Belle? Have you ever stopped just for one moment to contemplate exactly what Mose did?"

"I'm not sure. He tried to explain it but I never wanted to listen. All I ever wanted—" Luna Belle wailed.

"Come with me. You need to see a few things."

Jack helped her into his MG. The little two seater with the top down allowed Luna Belle a different perspective. Driving all over Cow Bell Island, he showed her things she'd seen many times, but he pointed them out differently. The wind blew her hair while she relaxed from the confines of her Bentley.

"Luna Belle, every one of these homes, businesses, all of it depends on the treasury of the Black family estate. I don't know how to explain it because I don't know how it worked. It exists because of Mose, the Colonel, and whoever came before them. All these people depend on the system."

As they approached the ferry landing at St. Catherine's Sound, Jack turned his little car around.

"Luna Belle, even this ferry belongs to the inhabitants of the island … to you. Look at the enormous thing. You'd think the government owned it, right?"

"I never thought about any of this."

"It's a land unto itself. Mose pointed these things out to me years ago. One of the key factors in its survival has been high ranking officials. Judges, governors, vice presidents … get the picture? Irony of ironies, the politicians are how they managed to keep the government out'a here for three hundred years."

"Do you know that Hinkley woman?"

"Old money bags? The woman who runs the bank?"

"That's her. She contacted me two days ago to tell me the general account is almost overdrawn. Do you know what that means?"

"I imagine it means the cow is going dry, but Luna Belle, I don't even know what the general account is. Do you?"

"Not really. I was too embarrassed to just flat out ask her. You know? Funny thing is, since Mose's death I haven't spent any money. So how is the general account almost overdrawn?"

"Is that all she said?"

"That's all I remember, but it's just another thing for me to worry about. It's not like my mind is clear. I don't know what I'm doing or what to do for that matter."

"Luna Belle, this whole bailiwick came to a screeching halt when Mose died. See why some people here want your hide? I don't want to add another log to your fire—but think. This isn't a game and you're not playing with school children. Your adversaries mean business. For three hundred years this dynasty has operated in some strange shrouded mystery but the fabric's threads are unraveling."

"You're scaring me."

"As you well know, the Black family always had someone waiting in the wings ready to take over as the captain. I'm hearing through the grapevine how several of these goons think they deserve to run the show and have joined forces to take you down."

"Down from what?"

"I don't know. Your high horse, I reckon." Jack chuckled.

"What high horse?" Luna Belle looked at him with a scowl.

"The one they think you're riding. From what I hear they think because you refuse to read the will publicly you know something. Plus, you've almost let them run out of money, but I'm only filling a reporter's shoes at the moment. My assumptions are possibly not all that accurate."

"Oh. I'm almost positive you're hitting the bullseye. I thought you had my best interest at heart. Seems like you're intent on frightening the whoopee out of me."

"Maybe. You've worried about spirits and goblins. What's coming after you is neither spirit nor goblin. They're blood thirsty furious folks plotting their vengeance against you even as we speak. Luna Belle, they've sharpened their pitch forks and axes. They want—"

"Money. They want money. Jack, you are about to make me scream."

"Good."

She glared at him. "How can I survive?"

"I reckon you must decide between the lesser of two evils. Stay and fight or tuck tail and run."

"Don't I deserve a more creative plan?"

"Hey, this doctor lacks the acumen of a politician. You married the fellow with the brains for this sort of thing. He was taught to manage it at that. Maybe the light to awaken you shines in your own eyes. Look at this island. What would life be like without it? I thought of leaving this hell-hole myself. Why stay here?"

"So you suggest I pack my bags and leave? Mose mentioned that option as well in a letter he wrote me the morning he died but Nick burned it. I wish I could re-read it."

"Luna Belle, I'd be a traitor if I failed to point out current events. Mose tended the machinations while you flitted around without worrying yourself over any of it. Your turn at the helm has arrived. Steer or sink."

"If only we'd had a son."

"Get over it. It's not your fault. You know Mose couldn't sire offspring. His plight came from generations of inbreeding. You know when that pregnant girl—"

"Gaye Nell Goolsby?"

"Yes. Her. Made a fool of herself. I almost wet myself laughing."

"Years ago when you told me about his problem, I found it hard to believe. Everything worked fine, but I remained childless."

"Your body functioned perfectly. You were never the problem."

Jack sat silently for a few moments. "They wanted new blood. That's why they sought you out, although they waited about a century too long because the damage had become irreparable."

"Yeah, so you say. Did you know they bought me? Paid two million dollars for me. It's actually more insulting than that—for me and two horses."

Jack chuckled. "Two million, eh? Think they got their money's worth? I mean … I knew they bought you to freshen the blood of pirates who'd inbred for centuries. Now the remnants of the crew want to kill you because you stand in the way of their own lust."

"Jack, you … wait a minute. How'd you know about my being sold?"

"The Colonel told me after you didn't conceive. They wanted to blame your childless condition on you, but I set them straight. You know what's funny?"

"What?"

"He never told me you were so expensive, or was it the horses?" Jack roared with his head thrown back, hair flagging in the wind.

"Never mind." Luna Belle squinted as she turned her gaze out the corner of her eyes toward Jack.

Jack saw the comedy. "No wonder the Colonel and Beulah snatched you with grappling hooks. Two million dollars. You know when I first heard they bought you I considered it to be more like a dowry or something. I never envisioned it as an actual purchase. Examined you like horse-flesh, didn't they? I don't know what's more insulting … being sold or being part of a package deal. These are some more kinda folks."

She nodded. Grabbing a handful of hair in each hand she yanked as she screamed. "I can't decide which frustrates more, being chattel or the dealing with that ornery Contessa."

"Luna Belle, I assure you. Chattel you ain't."

"Yeah, Nick says the same thing."

"Smart man. You ought to listen to your oldest living friend." Silence fell.

"Jack, consider how I frustrated Mose."

"You did that all right, but it wasn't just you. Trust me, he worried more about not having an heir than about your flippant lifestyle."

"But I showed no interest in how he made things work. You know, right before he died, I think he had a premonition. He wanted to shake some sense into me, but I flitted off on another one of my irresponsible tangents. Maybe I'm already avenged. They paid two million for a dud. Well, they did get two fine horses." Luna Belle howled in laughter.

Jack joined her.

"So who's against me with these pitchforks and axes?"

"Not sure, but I think Scooter's a ring leader."

"Seriously? Lardass?"

"Lardass ... been a while since I heard that. Fits, though. Whoever tagged him hit it spot on."

"Thank you. T'was I." She held her hands in a voila pose. Jack sputtered, almost popping a gut.

The fresh air helped wake her from her stupor. Jack headed his convertible back toward Teachall with Luna Belle's eyes opened in a way she never expected. Jack practiced a peculiar type of medicine by wanting to cure the vacant woman's spirit with a big dose of reality. Luna Belle almost gave him a big hug and kiss, but her upbringing never allowed such an expression of affection, especially toward a servant.

She thought, *There I go again. I do ride a high horse.*

When Jack stopped his car Luna Belle began fidgeting. Teachall appeared nothing more than a clammy, dank dungeon. Her spirit again thrashed in anguish against slave shackles.

Jack watched her transformation. "Luna Belle, why are you

letting an old house squeeze the life out of you? I don't care how grand it is."

"I don't know, Jack. At first I fought to hold onto everything. Teachall is supposedly the greatest tabby mansion ever built, you knew that, right?"

"Yes. Matter of fact, have to admire the strength of an oyster shell."

"For centuries the indigenous people built colossal piles of shells while they ate oysters from the creeks. Middens … I think they're called middens."

"Yes. They furnished a large part of the materials."

"I suppose so, yes. If you walk barefoot around here you're liable to cut your foot on one of those shells. They're everywhere. I guess I live in an oyster shell…. Pearls come from oysters."

"Luna Belle, you're not back to that stinking curse again?"

"Why not?"

"Can't you see, your thinking is counterproductive."

"Have I ever told you what the curse said?"

"No."

"Come with me."

The two made their way to Luna Belle's bedroom where the Contessa's portrait hung. Luna Belle opened the safe then took the box and laid it on her bed. Taking the portrait and turning it over beside the box, she asked him to examine the script on the back.

He tried to read it but it was written in archaic Spanish dialect. Luna Belle opened the box and removed the stained parchment.

"Polly swears blood served as the ink."

"I'd say she's right."

"Read it."

> The treasured pearls I wear in this portrait,
> Given to me on our Wedding Day
> by my Dear Husband,
> Edward James Durand "Teach" Drummond,
> Viscount of Avery,
> My Savior and true Love,

Commander, the Buccaneers
Of the Queen Anne's Revenge.
Worn by me on the terrible
Day of His
Merdure
At the hands of a vengeful
Governour,
Be cursed
Anyone
who wears these,
my Beauties,
From this day forwart,
For so long as ye shall
Inhabit the halls of my home.

"I didn't know Blackbeard was a peer." Jack said.

"Forget that nonsense, Jack. Read the last line."

"Yeah, so? For so long as you inhabit the halls of my home? What ridiculous nonsense."

"Jack, I've been fighting this thing for a while. I blamed Polly for my own faults. Don't you see? I missed the oyster shell prison part. I maimed myself. Polly planted the seeds of doubt. No question about that. You attended Mose's funeral. Have you ever seen anything like that in your life?"

Jack laughed. "No, Luna Belle. I haven't. I have it on DVD. Poor Jilda Birdsong, she didn't live long after that sting. I left with her and went to the hospital where I watched her expire. I missed the rest of the show."

"I can't believe you find it amusing." Luna Belle laughed. "Some day I want to see the movie."

"Oh, I promise, you shall."

"Back to this curse. I doubt the Contessa had any idea she wrote about pearls in oysters. I find it interesting, that's all. I've been confined inside a big old oyster. Can you believe it? I want out. I think I deserve another chance at life. Thank you Jack.

"Now, if you'll excuse me I have accounts to settle and fences to mend."

31

Conniving Wench

Rose stood to become captain until Mose was born. Her initial training as a master pirate chieftain made her happy. Then out of the clear blue Mose came along and everything in her life went topsy-turvy. She became a pariah to her own destiny once she was removed from the position she coveted. Rose never understood why her father cast her adrift.

After choosing Mose, the Colonel grew distant to Rose. She realized Luna Belle felt the same pitiful detachment to Mose once the Colonel died. Why would two people choose to live together like that? Rose befriended Luna Belle to support her feelings of abandonment after Mose took over the family business. The similarity of Rose's life with Pink eluded her.

When Luna Belle first came to Teachall she and Rose bonded like fingers on the same hand. Rose saw how Mose and Luna Belle looked at each other in abject bliss. He remained her devoted lover until the Colonel died. He changed almost overnight by becoming insolent and removed. Rose knew Mose loved Luna Belle, but his life no longer revolved exclusively around her. Thus worked the Black family power on its possessor.

They all sacrificed their personal lives on the altar of possessions. Rose almost realized what they missed but she had tasted enough power to understand its importance. In Rose's mind no one else knew how deliciously the nectar dripped from the crown.

Rose's parents respected each other and managed to stay together, persisting in a facade of love. No one had gone to the trouble to arrange Rose's marriage. They talked of finding her a suitable mate when she was still a small child in training, but once Mose took her position, her destiny in marriage also was dropped completely.

Left to her own devices Rose succumbed to Pink Tiddie's irresistible wiles, yet over time he turned himself into living proof of the efficacy of an arranged marriage. Rose had plans for Pink as her majesty's admiral in the upcoming battle; however, once she was installed as reigning monarch of Cow Bell Island she was finished with his incompetence. When the right time came she would dispose of Pink and never look back.

Pink lived a life outside their marriage. His mistress was the same as her father's and brother's, a hoard of gold and money. This inner circle of men who guarded and grew the treasure appeared to function in the world, but their real purpose in life stayed underground in a heap. They curled atop the mound like ancient dragons guarding their lairs. Pink spent his life serving and coddling Mose, the dragon.

Rose intended to rule the roost with an iron fist. Her confederates served as nothing more than a tool to that end. After the coup could be accomplished, Rose presumed she held enough dedicated allegiance to gain and maintain control of the entire enterprise.

Several days passed since Polly left Teachall. Rose was coming to a realization of how she might turn Polly into a marionette of mayhem. Rose schemed in a devious quest to annihilate Luna Belle. Even after all these years Rose assumed Polly's loyalty meant compliance. Polly might appear faithful to Luna Belle, but in Rose's mind Polly belonged to her.

With Polly playing against Luna Belle, all looked optimistic to Rose. She wanted no part of further victimization. She wanted vindication and the time was ripe. So, Rose scurried her flat hiney to Gloria's to draft Polly as pawn.

"Polly, I don't know how you tolerate the way you've been

treated. I don't blame you one bit for leaving Teachall. Should've left years ago. Luna Belle has been my friend for years. Now she's acting like a bitch. I can't stand it."

"Missy ain't no bitch. Missy confused. That's all. She returns to normal when she figures out what going on."

Rose didn't like the sound of that. She saw no purpose in allowing Luna Belle's recovery. Polly almost told Rose about the Contessa's curse, but for some reason she decided against it.

"Well, I'm glad you're away from there. You needed some rest from all that misery." Rose watched Polly carefully.

"This here ain't no real story book life. You knows that better'n me. All this broodin' ain't doing nobody no good. No ma'am, it ain't."

"But Polly … I'm an incurable romantic, you know that."

"You ain't no more romantic than me, and you knows that, too."

"You're right. I haven't forgotten my dear sweet Polly. When you came to us you appeared as a fragile thin crystal goblet, scared and abused. I can still see you. My heart ached when I heard you crying in the night. You didn't know I knew that, did you?"

"Um-hmm. I know. I never forgets how you come in my room. That's when I still living upstairs with y'all, before me and Mordecai get ourselves hitched. You set on the edge o' my bed and rub my forehead. I didn't tells you den 'cause I din't wanna hurts yo' feelings but it bout kill me when you rubs over dat place on my head where my old man clobbered me." They both giggled.

"You may also be interested to know that I watched you. I saw how deeply you loved Mose."

Polly's expression turned molten. Her face dropped as she once again was reminded of the pit in her heart—that secret place where she had buried her love for the man she called savior. Being reminded made her upset. Especially after her recent bout with Luna Belle.

Rose saw her turned expression but didn't stop. "I knew then that you would have given yourself to him with all your heart." She looked out the corner of her eye to make sure her arrow hit its mark. "I felt so sorry for both of you. He would

have loved you too. He did love you. You know that, but he had
to marry Luna Belle. He couldn't break the code of honor."

"I knows all that. That's water under the bridge now, ain't it?
Um-hmm."

"Polly?"

"Yeah."

"I've never told you all this but I think you should know."
Rose paused. Her intentions required calling demons to
abuse an old friend, but the risk meant Polly possibly became
compliant with Rose's plan.

"What laying heavy on your chest, Missy?"

"I don't know if I should tell you this. It's about your life
before you came to us."

"I don't expect you know much about that." Polly squirmed
in her seat. Even her horrible scene with Luna Belle hadn't
bothered her like this.

"Well I know more than you do. I mean … of course I don't
know all that happened to you, but I know who you are."

Polly sprang upright. "How's that? Who is I, then? Wait jus
a minute. What you means you knows who I is? That don't make
no sense."

"Well, I should've told you all this a long time ago but I
always figured it was more than you wanted to hear. Now, I see
it as a big mistake on my part." Rose glowed.

"I's thinking right now that you better tells me what you
knows. I spent my whole life not knowing who I is and where I
comes from. I knows in my immortal soul I'z not what I appears
to be."

"Well … you are from Savannah."

"Um-hmm. I knows that. What else?"

"Uh …" Rose stalled.

"Go on."

"Your father … not really your father. There I said it. That's
right, I said it. Whew. He wasn't your father." Rose cut her eyes
to see the effect of that punch.

"How you know about my daddy?"

"Oh Polly, please don't hate me. You know not long after you
came to Teachall, Pink became sheriff. He remodeled the old
Tiddie home-place. Daddy arranged for him to get his job. Just

exactly how did I get him to fall in love with me?"

"I bakes de bait, that's how. It took several of my special pecan pies. Um-hmm."

"Well, before Daddy gave him the job, he gave Pink a mission."

"Mission, what kind'a mission? Wait. I don't like where this going. No ma'am, I don't."

"I know you've never held Pink in very high regard and you most likely don't want him to know all this. But I'm sorry, he does know and there's no way to fix that."

"I ain't never stuck my nose in nothing about your business with Pink. What y'all'zes does together ain't none of my concern, but I won't kids you none. I don't appreciate him poking his nose in my business. No ma'am."

"I know, Polly. Pink loves you. He just doesn't know how to show you." Rose picked at a hangnail.

Polly's voice was filled with sarcasm. "Investigates me? Well, now how 'bout that. I reckon I wants to hear what he learnt."

Rose sheepishly continued, "That's right. Daddy sent Pink to Savannah. Polly, don't allow this to upset you. We lived in fear for your safety. Daddy needed to know all this, or we couldn't protect you if that horrid man looked for you … and he did."

"How's that? He come after me? That old buzzard. What'd he do? How he knows where to come?"

"This all goes way back to the time when Mose found you in Savannah. You'll never allow that to leave your mind, will you?"

"Not planning on it no time soon."

"Mose told you about the bookstore clerk. I'm sure he must have."

"Yes. I heard all about that bigot real good."

"She poked around and found out where we lived. She'd seen you around. You lived close to there, didn't you?"

"Um-hmm."

"She wanted a little pay-back to Mose, so she sicced that horrid man on us. She didn't appreciate the way Mose talked to her. The biddy said Mose acted like he was too big for his britches. Imagine that?"

"Trash. That old cow. Um-hmm."

"The old sot appeared at the gates of Teachall, three sheets to the wind. He demanded you go back with him." Rose rubbed her nose as she peered out the corners of her eyes.

"What happen?"

"My dear brother told the old coot we all knew about him. Mose gave him five minutes to leave … said, next time he'd turn the dogs on him … blow his guts out, and if he ever even so much as mentioned you, he'd soon become gator bait with not even a scrap left."

Polly sat back, sighed, and twisted a curl between her elegant fingers. "You know what tweaking my goat 'bout now?"

"What?"

"I din't get to sees and hears all that." She threw her head back and laughed from the depths of her essence.

"Yeah, that would've been fun to watch, wouldn't it?"

"How—"

"Please, hush and listen to me. Let me get this all out while I have the nerve … I need rum."

"You don needs no rum. Keeps on talking."

"Polly, your mother worked for the family of your real father."

"Wait a minute. Is you telling me my daddy be white?"

"That's what I'm telling you. Now will you please hush long enough for me to finish?"

"Yes Ma'am. I hushes up, all right." Polly sassed.

"Polly, don't pout."

"I hush, I hush … but first jus lets me say, you'z answered something been bothering me all these years. Now I knows why I can't sang."

Rose rolled her eyes, shook her head and they both almost fell onto the floor.

Recovering slowly, Rose continued her story. "Son of a wealthy cotton broker. Your mother served as a maid in their home. Pink found out they treated her badly. When they learned of her pregnancy they threw her out on the street with nowhere to go. They didn't even give her enough to live the next day. Tossed out like a piece of trash."

"I don't know if I wants to hear this or not."

"Then I won't say another word."

"Is you kidding me? I has to know, go on."

"The man you recognized as your father found her and took her in. Good to her at first and helped her give birth to you. Your mama thought she had found a place to live and thrive with you. After you were about six weeks old he forced her to walk the streets."

"Dat old SOB. Das what he spect out of me."

"I know. You told him to go to hell. That's when he almost killed you. A mother's strong instincts causes her to act in strange ways. She felt responsible for you and saw no prospects of finding a job in Savannah, no money to leave, nothing. Some people's capabilities allow them to survive on the street, but within a couple of years an assassin's blade slit her throat. Pink never found out who did it, but he assumed the old man himself killed her."

"You means my daddy?"

"Yep, exactly. That trashy piece of something took in another woman to raise you. He had every intention of using you ... well you know the rest of the story."

"Not quite."

"Huh?"

"That family what throwed my mama out. What they name?"

"Oh yes. Berble. Your real father's name was Alexi Berble, son of Hezekiah who married a woman named Henrietta. Pink and Mose learned later, Henrietta turned your mother out. Alexi wanted to marry her but they refused. From what Pink discovered your mama may have been half white herself."

"Did they find out her name? My Mother?"

"Her name was Polly."

"So I name after my own mammy. Well how 'bout dat?' Um-hmm. How 'bout dat? What come of them Berbles?"

"Old man started drinking ... turned into a pure'n tee sot ... bankrupted. Alexi ran away from home. Old man died right after that. Stroke. Wife committed suicide. Pink said she drank a whole lot of Red Devil Lye. He talked with a doctor who saw to her afterward and said she died a horrible, painful death."

"What happen to my real daddy?"

"Pink and Mose looked for him all over. They never found him. I expect he moved and tried to take up a new life. Pink wanted to find him and beat the stuffing out of him. He never got the chance."

"I'z glad he didn't. I wants to think in my heart dat he a good boy. Jus' din't know how to stand up to his mama and daddy. I can lives with that."

"Polly, I'm so glad you're not upset by any of this."

"Well, I din' say I'z happy, did I? But naw, I ain't mad. I guesses I needs to let this simmer for a good long while. You know, kind'a like stew ... sees how I thinks about it then. Um-hmm. Mordecai know any of this?"

"Not far as I know."

Rose grinned in her triumph. She had turned Polly's head. What remained behind for Rose to accomplish seemed so much easier with Polly's will softened.

Luna Belle turned her out, but Rose had just showed her how much she cared.

32
Work, Work, Work

Early one muggy afternoon Luna Belle cleaned herself up and commanded herself to leave Teachall long enough for a mission. Knowing there existed no faster way to disseminate information on Cow Bell Island, she headed straight for the Glorious Black Swan.

There she announced, "I'm getting rid of all the horses and cattle. I can't keep up that place the way Mose did. It's too much. Y'all know of anyone interested in the stock?"

Lulu smiled, "Why, I don't blame you one little bit. Your plate is full, what with all that's been going on. It's time for you to simplify. I'm proud of you."

"Thank you, dear. What about you, Rose? I thought you might object to my decision."

"Ridiculous, you know what I think of all that vermin. Never tried to hide it one smidgeon."

"I don't think you realize how valuable the animals are. Prized Andalusian and Lusitano horses, Santa Gertrudis, and Texas longhorn cattle. Rose, they are extremely rare." Luna Belle preened a cactus.

Rose sat fumbling with a bow. "I know how much all that crap is worth. Get rid of it. I don't care if you haul the whole nasty herd to a slaughter house. The family's already wasted far too much money to suit me."

Lulu smiled. "Rose, I do declare. You're a peach."

Polly was in the back of the florist working on plants. She was unaware Luna Belle had arrived until she came into the workroom to pick up a sympathy card. The two women looked coyly at each other, then Luna Belle followed her back to the potting shed.

"Hey, Polly. I miss you."

"I misses you too, but I'z glad to sees you'z doing better."

"Polly, I want you to come home. I am better. Can you ever forgive me?"

"Missy, they ain't nothing to forgive, but they'z thangs going on around here that I'z in a lot better place to watch than if I'z at the house with you and Mordecai. I thank it better for me to stays where I is for the time being. I'z keeping in touch with Mordecai. You don't fret 'bout me none now, you hear?"

After Luna Belle's cavalier announcement about the stock, she sank further into remorse. How she managed to allow Nick to talk her into the stock's liquidation escaped her. It all began to make her sick, but she realized she lacked the drive to continue the farcical facade of being mistress of the plantation. So, she convinced herself that new homes served the animals better than staying at Teachall.

For the next few days Luna Belle diverted her mind from the stock. She busied herself trying to unlock the Contessa's tomb, but her despondence deepened after her announcement.

Nick watched Luna Belle's health become more fragile while she continued to draw herself into the blackness of her mind. Even though better, she still rode a wild roller-coaster and she refused Nick all but short visits.

He pleaded, "Let me take you away from here. Don't you realize it's this God forsaken house that's flogging your spirit into oblivion. Please, go away with me."

She refused to answer and dismissed him with small gestures then devolved into psychotic numbness. She barely slept when the demons left her by day, while at night she still roamed the mansion with her kerosene lamp, searching for relief from her delusions. Strangely, with the lights off in the darkened house she moved freely. Worn with wandering she continued to move or the spirits found her.

Like her unrelenting umbral tormentors, mutineers hounded Luna Belle in the physical realm. Rose and her cohorts wanted the will probated. Mose's letter warned her to delay; otherwise, she might face an assassin's cold-blooded revenge. Suspicions of mutiny ran rampant.

Before dying, Mose realized the situation, but his heart started to fail while Rudine spewed her poison. With little time he wrote his infamous letter to his beloved Luna Belle, and then called his long time friend, US Supreme Court Justice Elmozza. The two men decided that things must remain under wraps for the duration.

Justice Elmozza helped protect Luna Belle from afar but she remained ignorant of his beneficence. After the ignominious farce of the warehouse escapade Mose asked his long time fox hunting companion to rewrite his last will and testament a week before he left the earth.

With things around him crumbling, Mose realized his faults. He had taken far too many people and situations for granted.

Summer's sultry swelter hit hard. Nick knew so much lay ahead, yet he possessed little time. Mordecai had used the tunnels all his life and thought he knew them well. He hurried back and forth with ease, yet even he had no knowledge of the passage to the tomb. It hid itself from even the most experienced spelunker.

Nick had found it quite by accident. Years earlier, his inquisitive nature piqued, Nick followed Mose and saw him use the opening device. Mose never realized Nick's subterfuge. Nick understood the seriousness of his surreptitious action after Mose died and he explored the passage for himself.

An old wooden bridge marked the half way point of the trek. This bridge, about eight feet long, held the key to opening the passage to the tomb. The third plank from the Teachall side remained loose at one end. When lifted about an inch then dropped three times, the wall beside the bridge opened back into another passage.

When securely closed the swinging door became invisible, disguised into vertical crevasses. These features had been designed by Teachall's original architect and daunted all but those who knew their secrets. No one set out to discover them without predetermined knowledge.

The first time Nick entered the treasure chamber his mind could not believe his eyes. A cavernous space filled with unbelievable riches engulfed his disbelief. A circular staircase in the center of the room led to a trap door. Nick figured out, it lay directly below the Contessa's tomb.

Night after night while Luna Belle suffered in her misery, Mordecai and Nick moved gold. They often questioned their wisdom but treasure lust drove them on. Nick figured there remained several more nights of hard work.

Mordecai and he had already labored on their project for almost three months. Heavy exertion demanded moving through stifling tunnels in the middle of the night. During the daytime they occupied themselves with their normal routines; otherwise, someone might become suspicious of their absence. This all increased their perpetual exhaustion; plus, it doesn't take much gold to weigh a man down.

The tunnel from the barn to the house ran in a straight shot, not so from barn to tomb. That convoluted route made it impossible to use a wheelbarrow or anything other than a couple of pails.

Even with the use of make-shift yokes, arm and shoulder tendons and muscles began to tear and yearn for freedom from the abuse. At first the men gained tremendous strength from their labor. Eventually, they weakened from constant strains and lack of adequate rest, almost becoming quarrelsome.

Mordecai said, "Nick, we need help. I'm unable to continue at this pace. My body suffers and I'm wracked with pain."

"I know what you mean. Mordecai, I've been thinking … Lil' Roost. He's young and has a good strong back and I trust him."

"I never developed a relationship with the young man but I knew his father well. He held my complete trust. If you think we can depend on the lad, I say let's engage his services."

"I'll go wake him. We need help."

More than faithful trusted employees, Rooster and Lil' Roost loved the horses. Rooster worked around other breeds enough to realize the special nature of the Andalusians. He trained his son well.

Since Rooster's untimely death Lil' Roost grew strong. Out of his father's shadow, the man blossomed into an accomplished trainer. He served Nick as much more than a groom. Lil' Roost received offers to move away from Teachall, yet he stayed and remained Nick's loyal associate.

When Nick returned with Lil' Roost Mordecai warned, "Nick, Lil' Roost, you can never conjure what horrors Scooter may work on us if he discovers our actions."

Nick said, "Go on … you know far more about these folks than we do."

"Scaring you seems counterproductive but you must understand that these people possess the capability to perform unspeakable acts of torture and death on any who oppose them. It's unfair, Lil' Roost, to continue this work without your understanding the risks."

"So you's telling me that if they find out what we's doing then we all get killed?"

Mordecai pointed with an index finger. "Yes. You understand the full implications of my warning."

"Reckons we better keeps the lid on it then." Lil' Roost chuckled.

Mordecai grabbed Lil' Roost's shoulders. "Just so you understand, young man. No middle ground exists. Whole hog or none, our lives hang by a thread. We need and appreciate your help, but we all risk our lives by these actions."

"I'z okay with that. Let's get to work." Lil' Roost smiled.

Nick said, "That's what I say."

"Oh, they'z one more thing…. Missy know what we'z up to?"

Nick answered, "No, Lil' Roost. It breaks my heart but now's not the time. Her mind can't handle it."

"I been worried about her. Don't never sees her around the barn no more. She okay?"

"She's been better.—We're doing this for her."

"That's cool. Let's get busy." Lil' Roost grabbed two buckets and followed Nick.

"Lil' Roost, I want you to understand one thing. I don't like deceiving Luna Belle one bit. She rejected me time after time, but I still love her. This treasure has blocked her heart. I know it did. That's why we're hauling it off. Catch my drift?"

"No, not sure I does, but I'll help."

As the men worked through the nights the temperature rose with each passing hour. Nick wanted this finished, soon. His ideas became muddled with fears of discovery.

"What if Rose tells Pink about the tunnels?" Nick asked Mordecai.

"I doubt Rose has ever been more than a few inches into any of the secret chambers. She's terrified of spiders—always has been. I assure you, she has no working knowledge of the tunnels, and perceives them as mere passages from one room to another in the house. That's all. If she doesn't know, neither do the others."

If the tunnels actually owned anything, it had to be the creepy crawling critters that lurked and spun their webs everywhere. No matter how many times the men destroyed the spiders' traps from one end of the tunnels to the other, within a few minutes more webs filled the voids. Since they had no means of swatting them with their hands loaded, the men grew accustomed to the annoyance and tried to ignore them.

Customarily, Mordecai traveled with a broom to sweep the air, but laden with buckets his occupied hands never found a way to make it work. Spiders often crawled on the men while they walked. Lil' Roost detested them but he managed to acclimate his psyche to the constant intrusion. At least, so far, none of them bit with a deadly venom.

Several trips a night reduced the men to serious fatigue that created tension and seemed bound to lead them to make mistakes. Since Lil' Roost joined them, the job had gone faster, not easier. The tedious and hard work grew in scope.

Maneuvering through the tunnels meant twisting and turning and keeping the load balanced. In some spots enough water seeped onto the floor of the tunnel to cause slippery slop. The men grew accustomed to sliding down and grew proficient at falling. They learned from experience that when slipping to give in and collapse. Fighting led to injury. The muddy floor cushioned their falls.

The only real rest came by day when Nick's ingenious plan to transfer the gold worked its magic. They removed the floor mats from the huge eighteen wheel horse trailer then laid a layer of bullion to cover the floor. When covered by the mats, the gold became invisible. With a few horses loaded, the driving time provided a little respite from labor. So far it worked without a hitch.

One night Mordecai sat his two buckets down and wiped his brow. "You know what amazes me most about all this?"

"What?" Nick asked.

"The Contessa devised this marvelous concealment. Since we realize how desperate Scooter and Rose are to discover the treasure, it seems absurd that Rose's mind hasn't dissected the inner workings of her female ancestor's mental acuity."

Lil Roost scratched his head. "Huh?"

Nick grabbed his shoulder. "I think what Mordecai tried to say is, why can't Rose figure out any of this?"

"That's pretty much what I implied. Yes, I was an ardent supporter of Rose, but she has tried several times to use Polly as an agitator against Missy. She opened my eyes.

"On the other hand, Polly thrives with Gloria. She enjoys the time they spend together. Perhaps Polly created her own problems when she revealed the curse, but Luna Belle mentally embellished and grew the monster of her own demise. She has come to believe it, and has created her own personal hauntings."

"You think they'll ever recover? I miss Polly's cooking." Nick chuckled.

"Actually, at present, their misadventure is being used as a ruse of discovery, but keep that under your hat."

"By your leave." Nick bowed.

Mordecai patted his shoulder.

Rose and Scooter became more and more desperate. Finding the trove became imperative.

If Luna Belle refused to cooperate through the will then

the inevitable must prevail. None of the adversaries had any intention of allowing the treasure to escape their clutches, if they ever found it.

One night Mordecai came to the tunnels much later than normal. Naturally, Nick became concerned with his safety. About the time he decided to find out if trouble brewed, Mordecai appeared, huffing.

"Scooter came back to see Missy. He's pushing hard for her to read the will. I also heard him demand to know the whereabouts of the treasury. He didn't see me. He never realized I heard him. I fear our time grows shorter by the moment."

Nick asked, "What do you think we should do?"

"You know our adversaries have no intention of losing one ounce of this treasure."

"They have a surprise in store don't they, friend?" Nick roared with laughter.

33

Election Time

Early one torrid Thursday evening the chief conspirators met for the pirates' right of parley. The group's boldness allowed them to think nothing of meeting at the Georgia Governor's Mansion on Pace's Ferry Road, right in the swank heart of Buckhead. Scooter and Lulu entertained the rabble on the patio where they served barbecued ribs, Brunswick stew, and plenty of rum punch to inebriate and lubricate.

After sunset Scooter left Lulu with the bulk of the assemblage before he called the mutineers' nucleus together in his conference room. The conniving, devious band of rogues plotted even before Scooter banged his gavel to call the meeting to order. "Luna Belle's takedown must come soon."

"Here, here." Rose blurted.

Scooter puffed out his chest from her encouragement. "She's served her purpose and her time has run out. We intend to install a new Teachall captain here tonight. With Mose out of the way there's no reason to wait."

Pink interrupted. "Some of you may be aware, like me and Rose is, that the general account is being bled dry. I've got good reason to believe it's Luna Belle that's stealing the money."

Winston muttered under his breath. "Idiots."

Scooter shook his head and banged the gavel. "Yeah. I called the bank the other day to transfer some money to Atlanta and Hinkley told me there wasn't enough to cover what I needed."

Rose slid her glasses up on her nose. "It's complicated. We

don't have the time to delve into all that this evening. Let's move on."

"Who keeps money in the bank?" Sylvia asked.

Rose sneered at her. "Why, the new captain.Who else?"

Pink said, "We've heard enough of all this bank business. Let's get on with why we're really here."

Winston quipped, "Sounds to me like the bank business is part of why we're here."

Scooter retook the floor by standing and leaning heavily on the conference table. "Luna Belle continues to show little interest in reading her dear departed husband's will. I've been out there to see her several times, but that damned raggedy-ass uppity butler won't let me anywhere near her."

Sylvia interrupted, "You're afraid of Mordecai? Get real. Let me go. I'll put an end to this whole shooting match once and for all."

Scooter cleared his throat and looked down his nose at Sylvia. "As a respectable bunch of buccaneers, the only recourse I see for us is her death."

Sylvia hissed, "Yesss."

Scooter peered at the girl. "That's the most logical approach to finding the key to our problem. It's a sure-fire way to stop her foolishness. Finished, kaput."

Rose demanded, "Sit down Scooter and for once in your confounded life, listen. Y'all are getting way too far ahead of yourselves. Who among us knows the treasure's location? If you think for only a moment, the whole scheme becomes apparent. I alone hold the key to our success because I own Polly Swann. We need her back in that house, and she'll get Luna Belle to point us toward the treasure. That removes our biggest complications. I hope I make myself clear."

Sylvia answered, "We may not know about the gold, jewels, and silver, but I've seen the three books. That's all I need. Have you thought about the folly of putting your trust in that negress? What if she took off with the whole stash? Are you forgetting, I lived in that house. I doubt Polly would ever betray Luna Belle. They're like sisters."

Rose interrupted, "Sylvia, You're a fool, darling. Those books are worthless. Do you have the decoders in your possession?"

"What decoders?"

"Exactly." Rose's smug smile scorched Sylvia's eyes. "As to your questions about Polly's loyalty, don't think for one minute I would ever lose control of her. She belongs to me. You may think Luna Belle and she are close but you don't understand Polly's true fidelity. She came to Teachall destitute. Luna Belle didn't save her. The Black family did. Polly owes me big time and she knows it."

While the two women argued, Winston sat mulling the facts over in his mind. As a male Black, he deserved to become head of the clan. He had experience with large amounts of money, even if he had been fool enough to lose his to even more devious thieves.

Scooter leaned forward from his chair's position at the head of the table. He picked up a gavel and banged hard. "We need to decide on a leader." He thrust his chin in the air, reminding Rose of *Il Duce*, but she perceived Mussolini as a much cuter man than flabby Scooter.

Everyone else turned away from his demands and proceeded with their own greedy daydreams.

"I've had a great deal of experience." Winston inserted.

"Your family's been gone from Cow Bell Island way too long." Pink argued.

Rose thought, *How asinine, some jerk from Virginia comes waltzing in here trying to steal what's mine by divine right.*

Winston thought, *Once I'm captain, these other connivers deserve elimination. I want a clean slate. These numbskull fox are begging for the hounds.*

Scooter stood. One hand clutched a lapel. "As governor, I feel I deserve due consideration. My experience makes me the obvious choice. It was I who initiated Mose's involvement in the warehouse ordeal and plotted his death." His other hand swept widely toward his chest as he cleared his throat. "Besides, I love this family with all my heart."

The rest rolled their eyes, accustomed to his campaign schlock. He noticed their disdain but remained the obvious choice. It galled him that he needed Mose's backing even now.

Rose couldn't hold her tongue. "It was also you who bungled the warehouse deal and brought the entire national media to

our front doorstep. I do hope you consider that, dear Governor."
She discretely picked her nose and peered over her bright blue
framed rhinestone encrusted butterfly glasses.

Pink leaned back and poked his chest out before he
leaned forward, placing both elbows firmly on the edge of the
conference table. "I've been closer to Mose and the treasure than
any of you. Ain't nobody here more qualified than me. Besides,
I'm already in charge of most of the crew. How many of you
think you can control that bunch of cutthroats?"

"So, Pink? Are you telling us you know the treasure's actual
location?" Winston squawked from the side of his snarled lips.

"I'm working on it even as we speak. I think I'm getting real
close."

Scooter, Winston, and Sylvia almost came out of their
skin in excitement. Each in their own way created scenes of
eliminating the sheriff once he completed his treasure mission.

Rose sat biding her time. She smelled a lit fuse and wanted
to keep the explosion at bay long enough to establish her reign.
After all, the legitimate queen should rule. No one had any right
to dethrone her from her pinnacle.

Scooter pounded the gavel again. "I'm telling you all. I had
this thing sewn up from the beginning. You meddlesome fools
ought to have stayed out of it."

Rose protested, "Yeah right ... Lardass."

"I beg your pardon ... Lardass?" The Governor cocked his
head toward Rose in disdain.

"Yes, Lardass. Don't tell me you never heard your pet name."

"Well, I most certainly never heard it before in my entire life.
I never. Who started that hideous moniker?"

"Believe it or not, 'twas Luna Belle." Rose said in the most
mocking tone she could muster. The entire room, except for the
governor, erupted in laughter.

"Oh the irony." Sylvia shouted while she crossed her arms
over her abdomen, wailing.

Scooter stood again, cleared his throat and said, "If you'll
stop with the insults, dear Rose, *'twas* you who suggested we
assassinate Mose. And by the way Sylvia, honey. It was you and
that trash, Lars Haggley, who pulled the trigger."

Sylvia snarled her lips. "You're right Governor sugar, but

he was dead before we shot him. We have never even been charged."

Pink interrupted, "Listen, *Mossy*. Don't think just because I ain't done nothing about it don't mean I can't."

"Oh yeah?" Sylvia mocked as she clicked her fingernails together causing polish to flake off onto the table.

"Yeah." Pink turned red-faced.

Winston stood and laced his fingers, turned his palms out and cracked his knuckles. "All of you shut up and listen to me. We have serious business to decide here and all this yammering isn't getting us anywhere. Do I make myself clear?"

Rose wrinkled her nose and pushed on her hair then twirled her finger in the air. "Who-hoo. Y'all, listen to the Injun Chief. Ride 'em cowboy."

Scooter started banging the gavel against the sound block with enough force to break the handle. All the others laughed at his incompetence, but they did manage to quieten themselves.

He took the opportunity to speak alone, "Everyone, listen. If we accomplish nothing other than arguing with each other, I'm afraid we'll scuttle our ship right out from under us. Then we'll all drown. We have to reach some kind of working arrangement. Let's have a secret ballot. Every one writes his choice for commander on a slip of paper and the tally tells all."

Winston said, "Finally, some logic." He cocked his head and looked around the table with the confidence of a pole-cat amidst coyotes.

They had finally struck an agreement. Scooter handed each of the five a sheet of paper. They wrote their choice and folded the ballot. Rose tallied the votes. Opening the pages one by one, each person at the table received one vote.

Scooter said, "Oh, great. Now what? Why don't we allot ourselves five minutes each for speeches? I'll even allow you all to go before me."

"Oh no. Not so fast, Governor. You, the professional politician, you go first." Winston argued.

The entire bunch again erupted into a palavering pestilence that grew more adamant with each passing incident.

Scooter again started banging the gavel without the benefit of a handle. Several months earlier he slid around like a walrus on an iceberg, bragging to everyone in his clique about his imperious plans. While sauntering his way through his erstwhile job the governor waited for his opportunity to take over as pirate captain. He bragged about seeing no conflict on his horizon. If all went as planned, within two months he would stand at the helm and deal handily with all his competition.

Those two months passed and then some. He still slithered in a conundrum of what happened to his carefully planned insurrection. This current meeting showed him and the other cutthroats how sadly their actions usurped their ambitions.

His cohorts refused his control and turned this meeting into an uncanny disaster. Scooter wanted an inauguration but all he got was anarchy. He saw if he gained control of this rowdy bunch it would have to come through one-on-one assaults. This was turning into a job for Mad Dog, fast.

This whole situation smelled like a bucket of rotten Lake Lanier smelt. The only thing it might attract would be sharks or other carrion eaters. Looking around the room that's exactly what Scooter saw.

As delusional Supreme Potentate, his governorship would become about as valuable as a codpiece on a tuxedo. If he managed to get himself impeached, which looked more probable by the hour, who cared? It furthered his ability to hide in obscurity. No one expected a disgraced governor to live in the spotlight. That made him the most logical choice.

Even after contemplating one of his last meetings with Mose, he still didn't understand his vast unprepared condition to run the empire.

He recalled Mose telephoning someone and saying, "Hey. Pegleg, deliver it." Scooter didn't even know who Pegleg was, but the governor had his Mad Dog. Why couldn't Mose have his Pegleg?

Even while Mose spoke, the stolen worthless water masquerading as Palo Cortado sherry appeared at an Atlanta warehouse rented to Governor Aloysius Meecham "Scooter" Thadeu. Reporters soon discovered the fact and crawled into unwashed places the governor didn't know he owned. All he could do was sit and grin like a dolphin on a diet of electric eels.

To further the insult that day, Mose opened another drawer

and slowly removed an envelope, sliding it across the desktop to Scooter.

Mose said, "Go ahead, open it."

An impressive stack of photos showed Scooter helping load cases from Irvin's warehouse onto the barges in Savannah. Careful timing had been vital to the operation's success. With no detail left to chance, both men participated in the heist. Mose's brilliant plan kept them separate.

How little Scooter understood the position he wanted to destroy. He couldn't have been more ignorant about how to run the enterprise. Surely his skills as a politician were enough to take him sailing through the toughest parts of what Mose did. If he did suffer any shortfalls, Mad Dog would fill in the gaps.

So, the mutineers wrote their history in blood. They shot Moses Augustus Black in the back; however, the shot didn't kill him. For some odd reason Scooter, Pink, Rose, Sylvia, and Winston never understood—nobody cared about the shooting after the fact. A covert master manipulator appeared to lurk behind the scenes to run the entire show. Scooter began to wonder if it might be that Pegleg fellow he had just reconciled in his mind. Finding out suddenly seemed imperative to the conspirators survival.

Scooter tried trusting his allies but even they all proved nothing more than a big bunch of buffoons. He seemed to have created his own team of grave diggers. The Governor's plan outlined killing Mose, the master stroke to set him in high cotton.

The paradox of his ignorance eluded him. Without Mose, he stood no chance of being elected manure scooper in an elephant compound. Except for Mad Dog, the people he expected to fall at his feet had just turned against him.

He tried to stay optimistic. He saw his own genius as he pulled his flaming career out of the incinerator when he sacrificed his long time aides, Velda and Bob Hebridge. He saw no need for their clattering and clamoring around his dignified feet once he was installed in Blackbeard's seat. There were far too many other vassals waiting to fawn over his magnificence when the time and need arose.

Having thrown them onto the flames of political fervor to save himself was the height of Scooter's genius. Framing Velda and Bob stemmed the flood long enough for him to feel scot-free and ready for the next battle.

Roast scape-goat satisfied a weasel.

34

Enigma

The pilfering of Blackbeard's treasury neared completion.
The three men plundered enough gold for generations to live in
sumptuous lavishness.

While loading a bucket Mordecai held up a small bronze
chest. "Look what I found. I've never seen anything like this
before, have you?"

"Nope." Nick looked over toward the box and gave it a
quizzical once-over.

"Me neither." Lil' Roost shook his head.

"It's locked. I wonder if the key you found a night or two ago
will open it," Mordecai said.

Nick reached into his pocket and fumbled around. "I don't
know but I have it in my pocket. Let's try it."

He pulled the diminutive key and fob from his pocket. The
men usually placed such trinkets in a file drawer in the barn
office, but Nick thought this key might reveal some secret later
on. He had pocketed it when he found it, just in case.

"I doubt it fits. Why hide the key and the lock in the same
place?" Nick protested, handing the key to Mordecai.

Lil' Roost watched then said, "Y'all plays with that box all
you wants. I'm taking another load out."

Nick replied, "Take a breather if you like."

"Naw, that's okay. Just as soon gets done."

Mordecai inspected the key and fob, a miniature Spanish
lady's *peineta*—the comb worn with a mantilla. The key didn't

share any relationship with the lock. He dropped his hands about ready to abandon the quest.

Nick reached for the box and key. "Let me see that thing."

"Be my guest."

"Look. See this?" Nick squinted in the dim light to discern the shape.

Mordecai inspected it then said. "I'm uncertain."

Nick suggested, "Let's try the comb."

Nick held the comb's teeth near the lock. They fit into the orifice. He jiggled a tad, but with a few tries the lock popped open.

Mordecai said, "Clever. Who'd ever think to try the little do-hickey?"

Nick grinned. "Do-hickey? Really, old man, you're eloquence slips."

"My apologies for your annoyance."

"Annoyance? Shoot man. I'm glad to hear you're human." Nick laughed. Mordecai joined him.

Nick asked, "I haven't told you about the letter Mose wrote to Luna Belle, have I?"

"No, you haven't, but I already know of its existence. Did you read it?"

"Yep, Luna Belle let me read it that afternoon we went for a ride. You read it too?"

"I never became privy to its contents."

"The letter said, the lock is the Contessa's name, the key her comb."

Nick opened the box and withdrew three leather bound books.

"My primitive thought processes pique my curiosity, but I don't see her name anywhere near this lock." Mordecai asserted.

"My friend, there's one thing I know for certain. Your thought processes aren't primitive."

Mordecai allowed a slight smile to overtake his lips. "So the answer to the riddle remains hidden?"

Nick said, "Something else stands in our way."

Three leather bound books locked inside created new mystery. Enough space existed for one more volume. The small books fit into the palm of a man's hand.

Mordecai had seen these books before on Mose's desk. Always closed with the hasp secured, he never knew how to use them. Nick took one and examined the plain brown vegetable tanned leather cover.

Darkened with age and the oil of hands, the leather had become patinated even though sealed away. The books themselves had been secured with locked straps.

The leather's simplicity surprised Nick. Mose liked ornate leatherwork. He always wanted tooled Spanish leather goods for the horses and himself. Even many of his shoes and boots bore worked designs.

He held his breath while he took the comb and fitted the decorative end into the hasp style lock. Amazed, he saw the mechanism yield. Once opened, he leafed the pages of the volume in his hand with care. Columns of numbers, that's all he saw.

Mordecai said, "There are no clues to the annotations are there? Just those columns of figures. Flip all the way to the back, perhaps there's a legend."

Nick thumbed every page. "Nothing, just numbers. Curious."

"Very much so."

"Let me see that other book. It may contain the legend."

No such luck, another book filled with more columns of numeric entries. Nick had no intention of giving up. He noticed one difference.

"Hold them side by side, Mordecai. Do you see what I do?"

"Why yes. This one contains sets of six, that one, fives. That seems very significant."

Nick asked for the third book. With trembling hands, he unlocked it and peered into its pages.

Thinking he had unearthed Midas's horde, Nick exclaimed, "Voila. No numbers."

This book consisted of columns of letters. Leafing through it backwards, out popped page one with its graphic design in dark brown ink.

When Mordecai's eyes saw the design he stepped back in disbelief. He was looking at the original design of the Contessa's fighting dragons. He'd seen this symbol many times but never hand-drawn in blood.

"Nick, I'd almost bet the Contessa herself drew that."

"Wow, that's the stamp design Mose used, isn't it?"

"Sure is."

"These must be code books." Nick asserted.

"Yes, but codes to what?" Mordecai asked with an excited voice.

"I don't know, but this seems important because you look like you've seen a ghost."

"Sorry, but like I said, that is the Contessa's mark and it's drawn in blood. I suspect it's her own."

"Whatever."

Mordecai didn't respond.

"Mordecai, look at these and tell me if you think it's in Mose's hand?"

"No. It isn't."

"Look harder. Every few pages the writing changes."

"I agree. These are old."

After a succession of different handwritings, Mordecai said, "Look, the Colonel's handwriting. I recognize it without reservation."

In a moment he said, "Ah. Mose's own hand."

Mordecai handed the book back to Nick. The other book revealed the same secret.

Mordecai said, "I've seen these before on his office desk."

"When?"

"Several times. He never left them out. If I entered his office with them exposed, he'd hide them away in a drawer or his pocket. I always assumed they were his personal diaries."

"Are you sure these are the same books?"

"They look the same to me."

Nick said, "Something troubles your mind, Mordecai."

Mordecai rubbed his chin as he cocked his head to one side and furrowed his forehead. "Why bring these here when a safe in his office conveniently awaits?"

Nick's face lit up. "Can you open that safe?"

"No, but Missy can. We might trick her into opening it." He grinned at Nick.

"You devil. I didn't know you had it in you."

"What? We've been in this God forsaken pit for how many

weeks? Stealing all this gold and you ask me how I'm cunning enough to trick her into opening a safe? I've misjudged you, Nick Polk."

"*Touché*. So how will you trick her?"

"You leave that to me."

This new little find left the two men exhilarated. Their bodies grew nearer total exhaustion but their minds raced.

"Mordecai … how much gold is left here? Guess."

"I'd say probably three to five percent? At first, the stacks came up to my shoulders. Now they're below my ankles."

"Listen, I don't know why but I think we need to leave the rest. It might come in handy."

"I'm all for it. Tell you the truth. We've already hauled out enough for Croesus' ransom. I don't know what you have in mind, but I say let's quit."

About that moment Lil' Roost came back into the chamber covered in sweat and near hysteria.

"Somebody in the tunnel." He whispered.

"Where?" Nick demanded.

"Not sure, I heard talking back toward the barn. I'uz at the bridge. I don' think they saw me but I'm not sure."

Nick said, "I'm going back to jimmy the door."

He left with Mordecai and Lil' Roost right on his tail. Nick would have preferred going alone. Still, they might come in handy.

The convoluted tunnel's design didn't allow much room for commotion. Traveling in single file, they made it to the bridge where the chamber opened enough to accommodate them and the mechanism.

Nick saw no obvious way to barricade the door. Lil' Roost, being taller, saw a handle above the door. He flipped the latch and accidentally broke it off.

Two bolts fell, jamming the door shut. Their hearts sank with no clue how to escape. They heard three voices outside the door. Nick knew one of them was Pink Tiddie.

"This bridge connects to a side tunnel. Look at the mud tracked from the other side. We found something."

Another replied, "Let's get through with this. A bad storm is stirring itself up out in the Atlantic. Saw on the news this morning. I don't want to drown underground when it hits."

Pink said, "Quit borrowing trouble. Ain't been no hurricane hit this part of Georgia in years. Don't ever get hit hard. Stay focused."

Lil' Roost panted and whispered in excitement. "They's a hurricane coming? Let's get out'a here, quick."

Nick knew this news meant their time had run out for certain. They had to open the Contessa's tomb or stay buried alive. Outside the door he heard all sorts of clamoring.

"We need a crow bar." Pink demanded.

"Got one in the truck. I'll go get it." Another voice said.

"Wait a minute, might need some'n else." Pink ordered.

Lil' Roost whispered, "That'uz Lars Haggley. I'd know his voice anywhere. He used to go with me out cattin' around."

Mordecai said, "Didn't they claimed he shot Mose."

"Quiet. You want them to know we're here?" Nick said.

"Nothing but a solid wall here Sheriff." Lars said.

"Ridiculous, boy. Look at them footprints."

The sheriff's men pushed against the cave wall trying to move the door. Jammed, it refused to budge.

The lug-head surprised Nick. Tiddie had solved a clue.

"Reckon where it goes?" The unknown voice said.

"Search me? I've had this place staked out for the last three nights. I never trusted that uppity-ass butler or Nick Polk either. That Rooster kid's involved too. Deputies been seeing them working around the horse trailer then disappearing. They pop back up out of nowhere. That's when I started quizzing Rose about these damned tunnels, but she don't know nothing about them."

Had Mordecai not been trembling in anticipation of being discovered, he might have laughed at Rose's ignorance. His fear kept him quiet.

Pink continued, "Scooter's beating me over the head to get his greasy hands on the treasure. Told me to kill these arrogant farts if I have to."

Lil Roost whispered, "That nut come near me, he dead."

Nick held a finger over his lips.

Pink ranted on. "Anybody hiding a screwdriver in their pocket? As for Scooter Thadeu, he's 'bout to get his ass impeached. Serves him right. Dumbass tried to frame Mose. Stupid ignoramus. Really sorta funny, ain't it? Mose bites our butts from the grave." Pink answered.

The stranger asked, "How, Pink? I mean—from the grave?"

"Rented a warehouse in Atlanta in Scooter's name and had all that liquor delivered there. Then somebody called all the TV stations. Scooter's time's about out. He's postponed all that crap about long as they gonna let him. He thinks he's riding high after he threw the Hebridges to the wolves but I got a real good idea that dam ain't gonna hold water long."

"The sooner the better." The strange basso voice answered.

Mordecai whispered, "That's Winston Black."

Pink yelled, "Where's that crowbar?"

"Lars Haggley answered, "You said to wait."

"While we're all still here, let's give it one last heave. All together on three." Tiddie demanded.

The sheriff counted one, two, three. They pushed against it with all their might.

About that moment a loud crashing sound roared on the other side of the jammed door. The bridge had collapsed. Cursing and screams of anguish followed.

"He's hurt. Go get the doctor. Can you climb out'a this trap?" Pink yelped in obvious pain.

Lars answered, "No, it's too slippery, but look, another tunnel. I'll follow it. Back in no time." Pink didn't know it at the time, but he would never see Lars Haggley again. The young man wandered down the drainage tunnel toward Rigger's Creek where Stump, a fourteen foot gator, laid in wait for the unsuspecting young man. The disastrous meeting left little indication of Lars Haggley's ever having existed. Stump belched and grinned.

"Hurry up. Bring equipment to get us out." Pink Tiddie called after him.

"Birdbrained Rose ... now we're, trapped."

Nick, Mordecai, and Lil' Roost headed back to the vault. Nick hoped to find the key to opening the door at the top of the stairs.

Mordecai suggested, "I know the tunnels better than you. Permit me."

Lil' Roost said, "While y'all trying that, I'm going back and listens. See if they gets out'a that hole."

Mordecai excitedly looked down at Nick. "I've found the mechanism to open the tomb."

"Go ahead and open it," Nick muttered.

Mordecai said, "We need to take our shoes off. Pink saw mud on the bridge. I don't want any mud on the floor."

"I'll go get Lil' Roost."

Lil' Roost panted when he reentered the chamber with Nick. "Mordecai, Lil Roost says he thinks things are worse for Pink. He thinks he heard a cave-in."

Lil' Roost's placed a hand on Mordecai's shoulder. "I thinks they's buried alive."

"Let's get out of here." Nick ordered.

Nick grabbed the bronze box and its contents. Mordecai pushed the lever. It took a few seconds but the men watched in amazement as the Contessa's entire tomb pivoted open. The spiral stairs continued to the floor above and landed on the mausoleum floor.

As they made their way back to the surface they heard voices and commotion all around the grounds of Teachall. At least they had made it above ground, although they were still trapped in the ancestors' burial chamber.

The dim light inside came from the stained glass window. A distant security light shined to barely illuminate the space for the men to see. Lightning flashed. It was sporadic at first, but in no time it illuminated the sky like a disco strobe.

The vault needed to be closed. Open, it exposed the entire treasure repository system.

Nick said, "Okay Mordecai, you're so smart, any ideas on how to close her up?"

With one finger Mordecai pushed against the side of the Contessa's tomb. It closed and the sound of the latch clicked.

Nick said, "Ingenious—my next question: How are we going to get out of here? Men with dogs are all over this place."

Mordecai said, "I'm the cave expert. You're the brains."

"Gee thanks."

Someone rattled the door latch.

Mordecai said, "Follow me."

He led them to the end nearest the window. The sound of the attempts to open the door grew louder. Time was running out.

Opening the face of a crypt, he said, "Perhaps a bit crowded but get in."

"I ain't getting in there." Lil' Roost argued.

Nick and Mordecai pushed him in feet first.

"We won't close the door unless someone comes inside." Mordecai said.

The three climbed into the marble crypt. Nick almost closed the door but left it open enough for air. Cramped, they had enough room to lie on their sides.

In a moment the door of the mausoleum creaked open. Nick pulled the cell door even closer but it didn't latch. A sudden crash of thunder jarred the mausoleum to its foundation causing the door to close and lock. Nick's heart sank.

"Any more bright ideas?" Nick whispered.

Lil Roost sweated profusely. "Has I told you, I's closet-phobic?"

35

Bustin' Out

Suffocation threatened the men trapped inside the mausoleum's cloyingly confining crypt. The cool masonry and marble soon heated from the conniption fit Lil' Roost labored to birth.

"Just great." Nick whispered.

"Beats the alternative." Mordecai answered while he tried to wriggle into his space.

The footfall on the floor demanded silence. Almost impossible for Lil' Roost, his asthmatic breathing came shallow and fast, nearly loud enough to be heard in the mausoleum's hallway. Nick and Mordecai knew they must exit the cubicle soon or Lil' Roost's fears threatened to cause him to reach heart failure. Nick really expected the frightened man to have a stroke.

With few moments left they heard the front door of the mausoleum slam closed.

Mordecai said, "Good, let's get out."

Nick knew of no escape from inside. Lil' Roost had other ideas. Panting, he started wriggling. "I'm getting out'a here." With that he scooted into the depths of the crypt. He held his hands over his head just as a giant spider crawled from his shirt onto his face. The spider seemed to light the fuse for his surge's success.

Terrified, with one hard determined thrust and a piercing scream, he shoved with his feet against the end wall and drove his hands against the marble door, cleaving it into three pieces.

The crashing sound caused a stir outside. Detected. In haste Nick followed Lil' Roost out and picked up a slab of the broken stone.

Determined to save his hide, Nick ran behind the door and readied himself to clobber whoever entered. He had never killed anyone before, but he stood ready to bash this intruder's head without a second thought. He refused to allow them a chance to get away for help.

Mordecai saw Nick's action and grabbed a chunk and hid behind the Contessa's tomb. If Nick didn't succeed, Mordecai made up his mind to complete the deed. Lil' Roost bent at the waist, still in shock, braced against his knees and panted, holding his wrist with the other hand trying to regain his composure.

He said, "Don't y'all never sticks me in no box again."

Mordecai answered, "Lil' Roost, we owe you our lives."

Lil' Roost grimaced a smile through pain. Sweat poured from his pores.

Nick shushed them. Someone tried the door again. Nick's heart raced faster than a greyhound chasing a lure. Even his bare feet almost burst from throbbing blood surges.

The door sprang open fast enough to knock Nick off balance. He dropped the slab he held high. It missed his head but slightly clipped his nose. His reflexes allowed him to catch the stone somewhere around his waist. At least he was able to save his bare feet.

The deputy saw Lil' Roost who appeared harmless, but the commotion behind the door sounded threatening. Nick almost laughed as the deputy's head peered around, looking like a snapping turtle stretching from its shell.

With one powerful upward surge Nick slammed the deputy's chin from below. Stunned, he staggered back into the room. Mordecai bashed the thick marble chunk over the addled man's head. Shards scattered.

The sounds of crushing skull and marble rang. The deputy crumpled on the floor. This had turned into all out war and there was no turning back.

Mordecai asked, "Figured our next move? We're in

confounded danger."

Lil' Roost only thought the crypt scared him. The ramifications of robbing Blackbeard's treasure made every hair on his body bristle. His new occupation promised a gruesome death.

"Y'all, I-I-I think I b-broke my arm." Lil' Roost stammered, almost in tears.

Mordecai said, "Come here. All we can do is wrap it up for now. Have to get you to the doctor later."

Mordecai removed his belt and wrapped Lil' Roost's aching wrist. It seemed like his best shot at giving the man some relief.

Nick commanded, "Mordecai, get to the house. Luna Belle must open the safe. The books—I expect they're much more important than we realize. Can't leave without them. It's time to move on. Know what I mean?"

About the time Mordecai made it to the door the men heard waves of rain pummeling the roof. Mordecai despised exiting into the pouring water, but he had no choice. He understood more than Nick that running equaled futility. Safe places didn't exist. Once marked by these pirates, death followed without exception.

Nick said, "I have an idea."

Lil' Roost quipped, "Oh, now I'm confident. Your plan what landed us here, I can't wait to hear what's next. Can you, Mordecai?"

Mordecai shushed Lil' Roost. "We need a leader. You want to take over?" Lil' Roost shook his head.

Nick said, "We spread out. They don't know who we are. I'll head to the front of the house and hide. Mordecai, can you get inside?"

"I think so. Those men are preoccupied with digging Pink out. I know I can get to the folly. There's a tunnel from there. I'll get myself cleaned up and no one will know I've been out of the house."

Mordecai slipped out the mausoleum door into the inky threatening wet darkness.

"Lil' Roost, you head toward the creek. Didn't three brood mares escape to the bottoms this afternoon?" Nick gave Lil' Roost a big grin.

"That's right. They escaped didn't they?" Lil' Roost grinned back, comprehending the ruse.

"Did you bring your shoes with you?"

"They back in that box."

"I'll fetch them. I know you don't want any part of that place again."

"Thank you. Nick, if you 'round when I dies, have 'em burn me up or something. I don't wanna never lay in no box again."

"If we're caught we won't have to worry about that. Now get going, and for pity's sake, stay hid. Go around the other side of the house. All the activity's on this side. How's that arm?"

"It better. Not broke after all. I can tells that for sure." Lil' Roost ran out the door and also disappeared into the deep blackness of the dank night air with its sweeping surges of rain.

Nick changed his mind. After momentary thought he decided to sneak back to his house, shower, and wander out into the night to explore the commotion. Feigning ignorance might work. He didn't have a better idea. He followed Lil' Roost's path and left the mausoleum.

When he passed the front of the house his eyes landed on a sight that stunned him to his core. Luna Belle stood in front of an upstairs window drenched in blood. He forgot his plans and headed straight for the front door in a desperate attempt to get to her aid.

Locked. He had no tools and the front door was too secure to attack bare-handed. Without a better idea he headed around the veranda toward the kitchen. If he found Mordecai, that would be all the better. If not, he would have to try and get in the laundry room entrance. Nick knew where a key to that door was hidden.

He made it downstairs in no time and saw the sheriff's men frantically digging. Nick wanted to avoid being caught covered in tunnel filth.

He found the key and entered the room just as a sheriff's deputy turned the corner headed for the same door. Nick threw the deadbolt without a moment to lose. The deputy saw the door close and tested the lock. He threatened breaking the door's window. Nick readied himself with an iron—he felt confident in his new clobbering capabilities. The deputy saved himself a terrible headache because he left the door when someone in the garden called him away.

Torrents of rain turned the earlier fanning waves of almost splashing water into a full deluge. If his men failed Pink, he would soon drown when the hole filled with runoff.

Nick heard someone showering. He found the bathroom and called out, "Mordecai?"

"Nick?" Mordecai replied.

"It's me."

"I thought you went elsewhere."

"When I passed the front of the house I saw Luna Belle standing in an upstairs window, drenched in blood."

"Oh Lord, what next?" Mordecai said.

He turned off the shower and threw the curtain back. He barely dried himself before quickly dressing.

Nick started undressing. "I don't know what to do. I need to clean up. Any clothes that might fit? If I get caught with all this dirt—"

"I'm headed upstairs. Mose's clothes … laundry room. Grab some. I'll need help. There's a loaded gun in the kitchen drawer to the right of the refrigerator. Get it."

With that Mordecai ran out the door. Nick finished stripping then jumped in the shower. Washing the grime and spider webs off felt good, but he cut it short to rush to Luna Belle.

Black jeans and a black shirt stacked and folded in the laundry room worked perfectly. Mose's clothes fit Nick well enough. He spied a pair of black riding boots and shoved his feet into them. After he gave his head a quick once over with the towel he bounded to the kitchen. The drawer held the loaded gun exactly where Mordecai had said. A box of shells waited beside it. Nick filled his pockets.

He ran fast to the front hall. Before he hit the third step he heard someone talking from upstairs.

Rose said, "Mordecai, you come with us. Move."

Thunder crashed and obscured the voices. Nick recognized Rose's speech just before he headed up the stairs. Her tone exposed her malevolence.

"Luna Belle, we're going to open the vault. You know how, so don't even pretend otherwise. I refuse to accept 'no' for an answer."

Mordecai protested, "Missy Rose, you can see. She suffers from the trauma of standing awash in blood."

"Hush, before I blow your brains out. Luna Belle's fine. She's in good enough shape to open the vault. I know she knows how. She let that little tidbit of information slip before she whacked Sylvia. The gold lies buried under the Contessa's tomb. I've waited long enough for all this to happen. I want it. Now get a move on."

For the first time in his life Nick's heart threatened failure, but his fear emboldened him. He stepped aside into the nearest salon to hide behind a folding floor screen.

He could hear the conversation and might find an opportunity to pounce. From his hiding place he saw in a mirror that Rose held a gun to Luna Belle's back, making it too risky for him to try and rescue her. Mordecai complied, why? He walked a little in front of Luna Belle off to the side.

Women's fashion had never interested Nick; however, he did know when a woman was well dressed. His knowledge ended there. Why did Rose catch his eye?

She wore white stretchy pants and a tight sleeveless sweater that made her resemble a sack of country hams. A necklace of huge white plastic beads hung around her neck and accentuated her wattle. Matching huge white ear-bobs called attention to her too short hair. A string of huge black pearls marked a sharp contrast to the ensemble. Nick didn't know why, but that looked odd.

As the three continued their descent, he understood Mordecai's compliance. Rose had a bloody scimitar in the pit of the man's back. She had turned herself into a cold blooded fiend. Nick saw the fire in her eyes that held no intention of being delayed in her lust for the treasure.

Luna Belle appeared unharmed. Her dark sunken eyes stared off into oblivion. Her hands, arms, and nightgown were drenched in fresh blood and spoke of a desperate battle.

Once the trio passed, the coast looked clear. Nick almost jumped upstairs to discern what had happened. At the top of the stairs, Sylvia Black lay covered in blood, sliced up in a knife fight. Rose must have done this, but how did Luna Belle get soaked in blood?

Luna Belle wanted to bathe. She had never butchered
anything before. Her limited knowledge kept her from
an awareness of just how much blood might spew from a
struggling woman's body. Not meaning to kill Sylvia, she merely
successfully defended herself against the crazed woman's attack.

Sylvia made the terrible mistake of coming after Luna Belle
with a blade. What the young woman didn't know killed her.
Draped on the steps outside Luna Belle's bedroom door, Sylvia's
mangled body lay spread-eagle in her own blood and gore.

Luna Belle had often expressed her regret of being unable to
sing the great operatic role, Lucia di Lammermoor. It sounded
exciting—onstage, mad as a hatter, drenched in blood. If her
voice didn't curdle milk, it would have been one of her lifelong
ambitions.

Seeing her condition in a mirror instantaneously drove
her prima donna aspirations away. The horror of her situation
turned her formerly admired heroine's misfortune into an actual
personal tragedy with no promise of any good resolution.

Once the malicious intruder had fallen, Luna Belle dropped
her scimitar. Rose came from hiding and picked up the bloody
sword only to turn it on now defenseless Luna Belle. She'd been
there all along, mastermind of Sylvia's attack. Rose wanted the
will. In her mind, time had long since passed to settle this affair.

Rose's quarreling days ended at that moment. She demanded
obedience—not debate. She held her stubborn argument at full
tilt because the whole shebang fell to her through inheritance.

Now, her time had come. No one possessed any God-given
right to challenge her appointment as supreme commander. She
used Scooter as nothing more than a tool and now he stood in
her path no longer. She had accomplished her position all by
herself. She alone would find the treasure because she alone
held Luna Belle captive. Time for jubilation waited around the
nearest corner. Rose was growing more ecstatic by the moment.

Nick lost their trail but wanted no surprises from behind, so
he surveyed the other upstairs rooms for skulkers. Finding no
apparent danger, he darted off after the others.

In a moment he heard Mordecai's voice coming from Mose's

office. "Missy, see if you can open the safe for Rose."

"Open that damned safe or I'll blow your silly little head off. You hear me?" Rose screeched.

Luna Belle returned from her butchering stupor. "Listen to me you pluperfect fish-eyed fool. If you blow my brains out, how will you open the vault? You need me because I know the secret … but go ahead. I'm not so sure I want to live anyway."

Luna Belle's knowledge of opening the vault remained limited. Mose told her about the key and lock. She had gone to the mausoleum many times and scoured the Contessa's tomb. Luna Belle tried the ornate comb everywhere—anywhere near the Contessa's name carved into the side of the crypt. Nothing happened.

There were things complicating the trip to the tomb—more than knowing how to unlock the treasure chamber: a dead body and a crypt with the door broken. What else had Nick and Mordecai overlooked in their haste of escape? Pink might be too thick to figure two plus two, but not Rose.

Luna Belle stalled. "Rose, you must have known the safe's combination at one time. I'm sorry—I tremble too much to open it."

"You'd better open it. You know good 'n well I never knew the combination. Now get to it Missy, or I swear, I'll blow a hole in you that a man can crawl through. I mean business."

Luna Belle turned the tumblers, fumbled, then retried.

Mordecai caught a glimpse of Nick out in the hall.

A sudden loud clap of thunder and a crashing flower pot outside drew Rose's attention for a split second. Preoccupied, she never saw Nick spring into the room and within two leaps he overtook her. In no time Mordecai and Nick had the woman under control. They wrenched the gun and scimitar from her trembling hands.

Once the men disarmed Rose, Luna Belle shook her head. "Let her go. How dare you restrain my friend."

Nick didn't argue. He was too stunned. As soon as he released Rose's wrists the angry woman turned, slapped his face, and gave him a fierce scowl.

"Rose, these two men can serve as witnesses to my intentions. If you'll stay quiet long enough and listen, I'll tell you what I'm willing to do:

"First, I'm over this place. I want to leave and never return.

"Second, I don't want the cursed treasure. You can have it—lock, stock, and barrel.

"Third, I don't know how to open the vault, but if you'll help, me we can figure it out together. Rose, I've always considered you my friend. You've been led into this frenzy by Scooter and Pink. Stop and think back on our good times. I've loved you like my own sister all these years. I've never meant you one speck of harm. You know that. Don't let all this madness steal your soul. It's not worth it."

Rose protested, "If you really mean all that then why haven't you had Mose's will probated?"

36
Unbreakable

Rose held her hands up and shook them in crazed anticipation. "We need this all settled for good. Cow Bell Island threatens to explode because of all your outrageous shenanigans. I want Mose's will read."

"I'll tell you why I avoided a public reading. It's simple. I feared for my life. I have since decided my mental health is more important than what amounts to nothing other than *stuff*. I want off this devilish island, never to return."

"That can be arranged." Rose squinted with one eye.

"Mose wrote me a letter. He explained the dangers of my having the will read. Now I understand. He tried to protect me. At first I figured Mose's macabre humor had run amok, but it has become obvious to me that his wisdom far exceeded my own."

Rose chuckled with a threatening tone.

Luna Belle slammed her fists into the tops of her hips with defiant arms and grew more self-assured. "By waiting, my enemies exposed themselves. They haunted Mose before he died. I'm unfolding all this difficult situation in my mind. I see the instigator. Lardass? … Or … was it … you, Rose?" Luna Belle stared at Rose from the side of her eyes as her chest raised in pride.

"Astute summation. What tipped you to Scooter's involvement?" Rose asked in a cold voice.

"You remember the party in Savannah? The one where all

manner of bedlam broke loose?"

"Of course I do, but Scooter … I mean … what? What does that have to do with the price of rice in China?" Rose tried to seem nonchalant and picked her teeth with a fingernail.

"Mose disappeared from the house that night, no surprise there. He never missed a commotion."

"Go on."

"Scooter disappeared as well. Old Lardass never changed channels without a remote. Lulu looked for him without a clue of where he went. We both knew something terrible stirred outside. Then out of the clear blue, the media accused Scooter of robbing Irvin's warehouse. It was full of that Palo Cortado Lolly loves so much—all the property of that Gilder fellow we met at the club in Atlanta. Coincidence? I think not. *You* didn't even act concerned about any of it. In fact, you ignored us and switched on a late night movie. That's not like you … is it Rose?"

Rose's left eye twitched wildly.

Luna Belle raised an eyebrow and grinned over Rose's reaction. "Oh, but wait! You never met Gilder did you? That's right. Now I see. Scooter tried to frame Mose before Sylvia and Lars shot him. By the way Rose, where y'all keeping Rudine?"

Rose blushed crimson as the entire side of her face jerked and spasmed. "Rudine deserved to die, the meddlesome busybody." Pink had taken her to Tiddie Manor and in Rose's presence, put Rudine's head in a shop vice, sewed her lips shut, then shot her in the head. All that occurred just before Rose left for Teachall the morning Mose died.

Neither Rose nor her cohorts gave Luna Belle credit for her mental prowess. It amazed the sheriff's wife how much of the puzzle Luna Belle had pieced together in the short time since Sylvia's death.

Mordecai took a step toward Rose. "Miss Rose, you know good and well Missy means you no harm. She's one of your best friends"

"I told you once to shut up."

Luna Belle almost slapped Rose. "Mordecai always treats you with respect. Why are you acting like an uncivilized hick?"

"He never really respected me. He sided with Mother and Father. He helped Mose steal my rightful position. They started training me to inherit the pilot's position, then sweet little Mose came along and everything changed overnight."

"Why, Rose. No wonder you're upset. I don't blame you, but really? Mordecai influenced the Colonel? I didn't know your father long, but I doubt Mordecai—"

Rose turned her head to hide tears. Luna Belle caught Mordecai's eye and gave him a wink. His heart soared over so simple and kind a gesture.

Luna Belle's epiphany opened the doors to the whole nasty affair. Rose initiated this roiling predicament, even Mose's assassination. She held the keys of escape from death. Luna Belle's resolve strengthened. She wanted the memory of Cow Bell Island expunged from her life.

Mordecai said, "Rose, you yourself instigated the idea that I influenced the Colonel. Neither he nor I ever mentioned anything of the sort."

"Oh, come on. You held Mose and cooed all over him. Said he was the most beautiful baby you ever saw, never let him cry. My little brother … you took him away … acted like you owned him. I can still see it all as if it happened yesterday."

"You're being absurd, Rose. You and I shared our infancies; therefore, I lacked the ability to treat you the same as I did him. It was absolutely impossible."

"But you wanted Mose in charge. Why else dote on him the way you did?"

"Sure I played with little Mose. You did too. I didn't care to whom the position fell. I was too young to realize what it meant. To this day my understanding remains inadequate. I delight in being steward, no more, no less. I'm sorry for any offense I ever caused you."

Mordecai sounded sincere. Rose's heart faltered. She fought to maintain her contrived anger.

Luna Belle saw a chink in Rose's armor that perhaps revealed a way to cajole the beastly acting woman into civility. Another huge crash of lightening and thunder came together. In a moment a limb from a live oak tree crashed through a French door into the office, startling them.

Luna Belle gathered her wits and continued to attempt convincing Rose. "Grief owns me. You want to know why I refused to probate the will? Because Mose left everything to me. Get it?"

Rose protested, "Pish-tosh. Mose—treat his family like that? Preposterous. You're a lying whore."

Rose's heart spun back to flaming blood-lust. Luna Belle understood how the woman felt robbed after having been selected to be the next captain then turned away.

Luna Belle stammered, "I understand your reluctance to believe me but let me get myself settled. I'll open this cursed safe. You may read the will yourself. Good enough?"

"Open it. We'll see. Pink's somewhere outside. One call and quicker than you can say Blackbeard—the boys'll string y'all up."

"I'm pretty sure that's why Mose told me not to probate his will. He didn't want me strung up."

Luna Belle fidgeted with the safe's dial again. Still nervous, she fumbled and started over. "Why did he leave it all to me? I don't know. I never asked him to. Did I enjoy the ride while it lasted? Bet your bottom dollar—every minute of it."

At those words Rose's face again started to jerk ferociously. She took her fingertips to try and quieten the muscles.

Luna Belle laid her hand atop Rose's in an effort to calm the woman's neurological pulses. "You realize your mother and father bought me." Luna Belle witnessed the shock on Rose's face as more contractions surged. "That's right. They paid for me … two million dollars for me and two horses. Two horses mind you. Consider that if you will. I wonder how you'd feel if you were bartered with horse-flesh?"

Back when all that started on the day of Luna Belle's first visit to Teachall, Rose was a young lady, too tender to pay attention to such dealings. Several years later at Ashwood, if she had only listened, she would have heard the Colonel and Beulah when they purchased a mate for Mose and two stallions for two million dollars. Rose's insolent disregard for the transactions in Brunswick kept her from knowing exactly what happened between the families that fateful day.

Nobody paid for her husband, so she had endured a cretin for life. As she began to comprehend her parent's logic, the thoughts only served to develop her livid spirit's disconsolation.

Sure, let Rose pick her own mate. That saves money. Worthless
Rose. Revenge eked from the marrow of her bones and flamed
in her gut to burn her innards. Her blood's heat surged and
impelled her to further action.

A long flickering bolt of lightening cracked against the
broken window, shocking them. An electric fire-spur kindled
flames in the antique Tabriz carpet and quickly burned a hole.
The smell of singed wool permeated the office.

Rose jumped to her feet. "Fire! Fire! Y'all gonna stand and
watch Teachall burn?"

Nick stomped out the fire and looked at Rose with disgust.
If she discovered the treasure had been pilfered, hell's demons
forebode annihilation of them all.

Mordecai threw his shoulders back and spoke. "Rose, listen
to Missy, she's trying to explain. I believe her. Her happiness
fled with Mose. Allow her a shard of dignity because she means
you no harm. Trust her when she says she's willing to depart and
leave it all to you. I believe her."

Rose scrunched her eyes toward Mordecai. "Wait a minute.
Dare I trust you? Pink suspects strange occurrences around
here. He's been watching y'all's comings and goings. We'll deal
with all that later."

"That cuts me to the quick. I am a part of this family. We
share the same maternal grandfather yet you charge me with
mutiny? Really. I tried to help Nick get the equines and cattle
off Cow Bell Island. You despise them all. Is that what you're
upset about?"

Rose bit her lip in an attempt to stop her severe facial
spasms. Blood trickled down her chin from the wound inflicted
by her gnawing teeth. Agitated and unable to think, she came to
relish her condition of blood-lust and excited vengeance.

Mordecai continued, "Look at yourself standing there so
pretty. Aren't those the Contessa's pearls you sport? Aren't they
lovely draped around your neck?"

Rose rubbed the Tahitian beauties. "Yes. Luna Belle gave
them to me before she slaughtered Sylvia. Understand, she
murdered Sylvia to protect the treasure."

"It was absolutely self-defense. I knew you lurked outside the
door, Rose. You thought you were sneaky, attempting to make

me think you'd left the house. I knew better. Besides, you know good'n well, Sylvia drew first. I would have never fetched a sword otherwise."

Rose tucked her chin and placed a hand over her heart. "I stayed to protect you, Luna Belle."

"Bullshit. I heard you sic the bitch on me. It's not worth it. I'll walk away empty handed if you want it. I told you ... why can't you realize? It's over. I have nothing left here. I want out. Take your rotten treasure."

All pretension left Rose's face as she winced. "You know that's what I'm after, Luna Belle. Open the damned lock-box and let's get on with it."

Luna Belle once again turned to the safe behind Blackbeard's portrait. Seeing his image almost melted her. After her run in with the Contessa, this bozo stared hard, ready for his cut. Blackbeard and Juliana worked in cahoots. Luna Belle almost laughed as she wondered whether he might also wink at her. Her hand stopped short of hitting the buzzer. She feared it might bring possible reinforcements for Rose.

Luna Belle smiled because Rose wore the pearls and inherited the Contessa's jolly curse. Luna Belle grinned at Blackbeard while turning the tumblers, comforted by her traitor's impending calamity. She had always avoided looking at the horrid man's image until now. He appeared to smile down on her with some strange compassion. She looked into the portrait's eyes and took the opportunity to flutter her eyelids in thanks.

Another horrific bolt of lightening blew past the window, illuminating with the blinding brightness of a photographer's flash. In another moment the safe opened. Luna Belle reached inside, grabbed the Contessa's comb, and held it aloft. "The key. And here, dear Rose, Mose's last will and testament."

Mordecai gladdened at seeing spunk return to Luna Belle. She suffered as victim of the curse long enough. That was obviously why she gave the troublesome necklace to Rose. The woman claiming the treasure surely knew of her own ancestor's curse, yet she proudly wore the pearls.

Rose grabbed Mose's will and flung it open.

Luna Belle stood patiently. "Justice Elmozza has a copy. If you doubt the document's veracity ... call him."

Rose snapped the paper and read. It took only a moment because of the document's surprising brevity. Rose expected fussy lawyer-like jargon and verbose language. Instead Mose and Justice Elmozza wrote few words.

The two legal giants devised an impenetrable will. The simple document left almost everything to Luna Belle. Mose's foresight of his family's loyalty led him to bequeath one dollar each to every other family member and citizen of Cow Bell Island. Legal gobbledy-gook had been abandoned for simplicity and streamlined elegance.

Rose dropped her hands. Her countenance fell. "One measly dollar. Damnation!"

"Rose, I promise to sign over the entire thing. I don't want it. Can you live with that?"

Rose's brother's insensitivity throttled her heart. "I understand why you've hidden yourself and this horrid will, but offering to leave empty handed smells like a booby trap to me. What makes you so all fired anxious to abandon the riches your loving husband left you?"

"Because I found the Contessa's bill of sale. It made me miserable and started a disastrous ball rolling. The covert thing practically leapt on me from Mose's blanket chest. That's why I want to leave. Your dear Contessa Juliana became a slave to save her daddy's hide. I, to save my granddaddy's. Pity us both. You lived in freedom while I became enslaved. I can't improve my explanation. I dug my heels in and stayed here long enough to almost lose my mind, even beginning to see death's door lurking ahead."

"Why?" Rose demanded.

"Polly told me about some silly curse. I refused to believe in it, yet I subconsciously accepted the malevolence. A seemingly living organism took control of my mind and almost caused me to commit suicide."

"What curse?"

"Really, nothing. Some silliness Polly invented. I don't know why I ever listened to her. Believe it or not, she excused the funeral fiasco through the curse."

"I never knew you took to hocus-pocus. That amazes me."

Luna Belle refused to answer. The curse's transference

to Rose created hope. Who better to possess it? The cheated, abused little snot who pouted all her life because she received the boot from being Queen of the Castle—the Teachall Temptress.

Here, ignorant Luna Belle reigned in splendor while Rose's position as wife of an insipid dumb-ass sheriff left her hopeless. Rose abhorred Luna Belle. Rose had definitely come to deserve the Contessa's watchful eye.

Luna Belle saw no future for her life. Nick's silent presence in the room reminded her of his having offered her his love. Perhaps someone still cared for her.

She wondered if his love still lived. After the way she'd treated him, he seemed to have lost interest weeks earlier. She knew she deserved nothing more than desolation.

She would become a vagabond beggar and live on the streets of Savannah or Atlanta with a shopping cart, stinking to high heaven. She didn't care, anywhere but Teachall. Well—she preferred taking her custom made clothes. She at least deserved to ramble in style.

She would fly solo and become the South's most chic bag lady. The ramifications of hoboing evaded her mind, leaving her capable of cottoning to the idea. Nick could then remain free of her cloying pestilence. His skills with animals guaranteed his future without her to weigh him down.

It dawned on her that she had consented to the dispersal of her horses. The first pang of separation from Teachall washed over her. Also, winters in her beloved southern Spain would be cancelled. So many details that had not occurred to her earlier now haunted her mind.

Rose itched to take the comb to the mausoleum.

Luna Belle wanted this finished.

When Nick glanced at Mordecai, both men started sweating profusely over fears with no need for words. Nick inhaled deeply, quelling his trembling enough to speak when Rose demanded he and Mordecai accompany them.

The men refused to abandon Luna Belle, so without argument, the four went to the entrance of Teachall and opened the door onto the raging storm. Epic rain blew rubbish and debris straight across the horizon with hammering water that hampered visibility beyond ten feet.

Nick asked, "You sure about getting out in this kind of weather? Decapitation by flying debris don't sound like much fun to me."

Rose's greed spoke, "If you think I'm going to be put off by a little thunder storm, think again. I've waited too long. I want to go. Move!"

"Appears the hurricane's near." Nick insisted.

Luna Belle backed away from the door. "Rose, why don't we wait?"

"Nonsense, the storm's eye won't arrive for another six to eight hours. I checked the weather service advisory."

When Rose stepped onto Teachall's expansive veranda, she was almost swept away by a gust of wind. Nick grabbed her to hold her down. If her rotundity ever rolled she'd bowl her way to Alabama.

The four huddled and moved as a unit in a meager attempt to stay against the fearsome winds. A streak of lightening crossed the sky in front of their faces, yet Rose remained undaunted. On they pressed to the burial chamber.

After the harrowing trek, the belligerent bronze door balked.

"What's wrong, it's never locked." Rose shouted over the howling winds.

"I don't know. Want to try it yourself?" Mordecai bellowed back.

About the time Mordecai stepped away to give Rose a chance, the door opened. Nick almost bolted. He thought, *Play innocent.* He looked at Mordecai who gave him a wild look.

Mordecai had seen inside.

37

Where's the Loot?

Then all four saw inside. Everything appeared completely
intact. Nick and Mordecai looked at each other and could only
wonder.

Drenched from the flooding torrents, Luna Belle's filthy
nightgown now almost sparkled white. Losing most of the blood
and gore to the raging rain raised her spirits. The storm crashed
and slammed the sky, causing the room to flicker from a barrage
of fierce lightning. This leading edge promised one gigantic
storm to come.

Luna Belle said, "Turn on the lights."

"It's only visited in the daytime. There's no need for lights.
How absurd." Rose quipped.

Mordecai felt the wall. "Look, a switch."

With one flick, light washed the space. The two men looked
around in amazement. Chill bumps swept Mordecai's entire
body.

Nick muttered under his breath. "Where's that consarned
mess we left?" Too many peculiar things shot through his
brain. Rose wore the pearls. Nick refused to believe they held
the power to clean a grave site. On the other hand, Luna Belle
deserved a break. Maybe the Contessa forgave her and helped
them out.

It didn't take much to draw the men back to reality. Rose
wanted treasure. After waiting for decades, her present lust
drove her to ignore any obstacle.

Greed seethed within her. She revealed her anxiety by her voice's uncanny screeching. "Give me that comb."

Luna Belle immediately handed Rose the Contessa's tortoise shell comb.

"Tell me the clues. By the way, this gorgeous comb will be smashing in my hair at the grand mask. I'll look just like the Contessa."

Mordecai rolled his eyes. He wanted to chuckle. He knew baubles distracted Rose, the spangle-sucker.

Luna Belle shook her head. "Beautiful? Yes. Clues? Let me think, ... comb, key—name, lock, and voila."

"Where's Mose's damned letter?" Rose demanded. Her eyes squinted.

"Mose told me to burn it. I expect he knew his adversaries well enough to realize the importance of not having it floating around." She looked at Nick who stood with a sheepish grin. He had gladly set the parchment alight right there on his front porch.

Rose stepped toward Luna Belle and snarled her lips in a way that created the appearance of an enraged puffer fish. "Luna Belle, let me get something straight. As rightful heir to my Grandmother's fortune, I refuse to wear the name adversary. I was not the usurper. It was Mose. I, the eldest child, was bypassed because of my gender. Ring a bell with you, slave girl? Hello?"

Rose's mind sunk deeper into greedy oblivion. She unwittingly succumbed to the curse around her neck. The more Rose envisioned the gold, the more entertained Nick became.

Mordecai shook his head. Rose, raised at Teachall, self-appointed precious princess, oblivious to the curse? Polly knew. He knew. Mose knew. Poor birdbrained ignorant Rose didn't.

Mordecai understood why the Colonel bypassed Rose. She possessed neither the charisma to deal with the people nor the restraint to handle the money. The Colonel saw early on that a greedy spoiled brat lacked the discipline to accomplish the job.

This curse business now entertained Luna Belle tremendously. This malediction, this whammy that had turned Mose's last rites into a slap-stick boondoggle and drove her to the brink of insanity almost made her want to laugh. One way or another Rose stood to pay for her greed. The Contessa's rage rightly threatened greater retribution on Rose, the familial native, than on Luna Belle, the outsider.

Rose had snookered Luna Belle with charitably bogus friendship for decades. Now Rose, the patronizing phony, suffered the Contessa's rage. It refreshed, vindicated, and promised sport, even if a mangled body did sully the stair's custom-woven Persian runner back inside the house.

Luna Belle smiled in amusement at her adversaries' haste and stubbornness. "Rose, I have to tell you. I came here several times and stuck that blessed comb in every letter of the woman's name. It never worked."

Rose crawled around the base of the Contessa's tomb. She peered and pried into every nook and cranny of the deep carvings. Nick observed a pattern of holes and protrusions in a pendant carved on the Contessa's chest.

Uncertain whether he ought to call attention to it, his mind twisted into not much more than a confused bundle of nerves. Nick caught Mordecai's attention then pointed to the pendant. From previous experience both men recognized the lock. It appeared similar to the one on the leather books. In fact, the more they stared the more it became obvious that the tomb carving looked identical to the ornate bezel around the books' locks.

Eureka! The Contessa's tomb opening operated through this monogram. The women had made the same mistake he and Mordecai made initially with the key and fob.

The comb's teeth served as a decoy. The decorative end operated the lock. How clever of a pirate to hide things in clear view. Nick thought this pendant appeared as the reverse image of the comb's detail. If Rose laid the ornament in the carving, the tomb apparatus would engage. He knew for certain.

The monogram consisted of a composite of initials interwoven in a florid design common to eighteenth century royalty. Nick motioned, suggesting they tell the women. Mordecai shook his head no. Nick shrugged his shoulders, why?

Mordecai responded by saying, "I don't know, Rose. Why hide a lock so close to the floor? It seems rather indelicate to me. I mean … crawling around. I'm not certain the Contessa wanted folks moving about like animals. Why, look. This resembles a monogram."

Nick almost laughed. He understood Mordecai's motive to star in the limelight after Rose's earlier insults.

Mordecai mocked and taunted Rose at the same time. Mordecai, master mental technician, honed his skills for decades playing docile domicile majordomo.

"Suppose her name hides someplace else. I never liked this place. Now I hate it. What an inane place to stash treasure." Rose said.

Nick correctly thought, *Au contraire.* For three hundred years the obvious worked as perfect camouflage. The Contessa's wily cunning hid the entrance so well no one had discovered it and defied the system for three centuries.

The two women rose from their hands and knees. Nick slyly winked at Luna Belle. She managed a smile.

Slaughtering Sylvia Black had miraculously cleared her mind. Rose wore the pearls and proved Polly's thesis. A phenomenal awakening overtook Luna Belle, allowing her countenance to lift and glow. She looked back at Nick to return his wink.

The raging storm became irrelevant since Luna Belle had escaped bondage. The Contessa released Luna Belle from the vengeful clutches of a living perdition.

The dead woman obviously hated only one person at a time. Luna Belle's sudden inspiration overwhelmed her and washed her essence in a wave of joy.

She didn't care whether Rose found the treasure or not. Luna Belle wanted to leave—to be far away from this oyster shell prison. Her former resolution grew even more secure in her mind.

"Rose?"

"What?"

"I truly lost interest in all this. It belongs exclusively to you. I don't care who Mose named beneficiary. I'll sign anything."

Rose shook her head. The moment the vault opened and her ex-sister-in-law saw the expansive booty, she would recant.

Nick saw the blood in Rose's eyes. He still held that pistol in the waist of Mose's slacks from the laundry room. Once Rose opened the vault why didn't they knock her off, shove her down the steps, close the tomb, and leave her for spider fodder?

Multiple gunshots rang from outside, startling all except Rose. Luna Belle looked around at the solid walls and admired their thickness and strength. She felt somewhat safe being sequestered in the burial chamber away from stray projectiles. She had revived her soul and now wanted to live.

Rose fussed and fingered her besotted hair. "Never mind all that. It's just wind and thunder. Storms always create strange noises."

All the others knew better. Gunfire reports make specific sounds. Who fired the guns and why shoot at each other? Nick fathomed Pink shooting himself rather than drowning in the pit. Surely it wouldn't take that many shots to kill the goon.

How had Lil' Roost disappeared without a trace? Maybe he had already fallen to crossfire? Nick wanted out. If Lil' Roost still lived, he needed help taking on Pink's army.

Nick fidgeted. "Ladies, I can't stay in here and not know what's going on outside. I'm headed out."

Mordecai followed his friend without a word.

Rose screamed behind them. "Good riddance."

The men ran out the door.

"Wait, wait. Luna Belle, help me catch them. They know where the treasure is."

Nick heard the shrieking shrew, yet he totally ignored her. Both men hated leaving Luna Belle inside with the covetous thief, but Luna Belle's revived spirit assured them of her safety. The real Luna Belle Brigham Black had returned to her former glory.

Mordecai stopped. "Can you tell the point of emanation for the gunfire?" He searched the area.

"Not yet, but I'm pretty sure somebody's trying to hide on the veranda. See those outlines against the windows?"

"I believe you're right, Nick."

"I'm worried about Lil' Roost. Where do you think he is?"

"I don't know. You think he was the one who cleaned the mausoleum?"

"Him or the Contessa. We need to find him."

Mordecai said, "We require weaponry."

"I have this puny pistol but we'll need more'n that if we stand a chance in this battle. If we can make it to my place, we can arm ourselves to the teeth." Nick's face lit up. "Wait! Reckon we can get back in the laundry room?"

Mordecai didn't share his optimism. His expression fell flat. "I doubt it. This battle seems to occur on this side of the house. Wait. The folly. There's a complete armory off the tunnel."

Nick's sarcasm almost insulted Mordecai. "Really? That's just hunky-dory. I can't wait to get back underground."

"You'll be delighted to know that the armory is not underground. It's hidden in a secret chamber just inside the turret."

"Pardonnez moi, monsieur."

Mordecai grinned. "Let's go."

The two crept into the night's darkness and sporadic rain. It came in waves to almost drown a standing man. Then it would mercifully turn into a light sprinkle. In only a short time they reached the folly.

Nick seldom came here. During a rain slackened moment, he looked up at the parapet and admired its clever design. Pushing hard against the castle's water-sotted timber door, they burst inside. Mordecai opened the clever passage hidden in the stonework. Nick surveyed the masterpiece with wonder, though he didn't pause to follow Mordecai into the depths of the plentiful stash. Within moments they fully armed themselves with a vast assortment of high powered artillery.

They left the folly and headed back toward the house and the sound of continuing gunfire. Still, they remained confused about which direction to travel. The rain stopped completely in an eery quiet moment. All the lightening flashed distant enough to remain silent. Both men grew more antsy.

Nick looked up into the black shallow sky. "I don't like this one bit, Mordecai. I've never seen this kind of weather. Have you?"

"No. However, we have more important things to do right
now than dawdle over a few scattered clouds."

Nick wanted to laugh out loud but he feared giving away
their position in the thick hanging silence of the storm's tease.
Nick wanted to find Lil' Roost. Stealth remained essential.

He racked his brain. Where would Lil' Roost entrench
himself for a showdown? Maybe Lil' Roost defended the top of
the mausoleum. Surely he was the one who cleaned the debris
they left earlier. He couldn't have gone far.

"Mordecai?"

"What?"

"I think maybe Lil' Roost climbed on top of the mausoleum."

"Good place to look ... ideal cover."

The two trekked across the rain soaked ground only to
discover that Lil' Roost had vanished and was nowhere to be
found.

"Nick? ... Mordecai? ... Over here."

The men swung around. Lil' Roost sounded like he hid
somewhere behind them. Nick looked all around before he
figured out Lil' Roost sat high in a live oak.

Nick called, "Come down here. We've got guns."

"No. Y'all come up here. See the show."

Mordecai hated climbing. At least the old giant tree offered
low limbs and provided an easy assent. Lil' Roost perched
himself with a phenomenal view. When Nick and Mordecai
reached Lil' Roost's level they saw an unbelievable battle. The
combatants took full advantage in the storm's wave of quiet.
Before their eyes, a war of unbelievable scope raged.

"Look ... it's Pink Tiddie. It appears they did manage to dig
him out." Nick's eyes bulged.

"I figgered he be dead by now. Didn't you?" Lil' Roost
pointed toward the beer-gutted man. "But that is him, ain't it?
I can tells by the way his belly hang over his belt. How you
reckons he finds his gun under all that blubber? Don't look like
his tiny little ass and bird legs would hold him up, do it?"

Mordecai cocked his head and peered from under his raised
brow. "Lil' Roost, play nice now." He chuckled. "They dug the
old rascal out. I don't see Winston. He must have succumbed to
the cave-in's fury."

Nick almost laughed."Pink's drafted a whole army down there. Look at the entire east garden. He's totally covered it up with men. Pete Stagg ain't gonna like any of this. They're treating his landscape work like crap."

Mordecai pointed toward the house. "Who are those people firing upon the sheriff's men?"

"I not sure. It'uz raining hard when I climb up here. They'z several of em, though. I know that for sho." Lil Roost nodded.

Mordecai pointed toward the house. "Look on the upstairs veranda … Lardass."

Unbelievable. There in front of the giant window the Governor barricaded himself behind a pillar. He aimed a gun toward the garden. He shot and hit one of Pink's deputies.

Mordecai held his hand over his brows to block the rain. "What in the name of thunder?"

"Looks for all the world like a shootout." Nick punched Mordecai with his elbow.

Mordecai glared with disgust. "I can see that. Why are they shooting at each other? They enjoy a confederation. I'm confused."

Another hard wave of rain pelted the men out in the garden. It came hard enough to knock them out had they not held onto for dear life whatever they found near. It hadn't yet reached the tree where Nick, Mordecai, and Lil' Roost watched the melee.

Lil' Roost started toward the other side of the tree's bole. "If we moves around the trunk we stays dryer. It'll hit any second."

Nick's entire attitude took on a questioning appearance. "What's that?"

A man on the porch threw something far into the garden where Pink's men tried seeking cover. In a moment a huge explosion wiped out the east garden. The shooting stopped.

The three men sat speechless with widened eyes in disbelief. A crater reminded them of the truth. Pete Stagg now possessed a huge hole where a once sumptuous design of plantings and reflecting pools had existed.

From what Nick and his compatriots saw, Pink and his groupies had been annihilated. Who lobbed the bomb? This device of devastation appeared far too big to have been a grenade. This weapon's design allowed the removal of a large portion of an army.

The stained glass window of the mausoleum blew out with the blast. From their vantage point they saw the glass shattered into dust and left a gaping hole. Rain blew undeterred into the building.

Luna Belle came running out of the mausoleum's entrance, stunned. She stopped and looked around.

Nick called in a hoarse, low voice, "Luna Belle ... Luna Belle."

She heard her name.

"Luna Belle, up here ... in the tree. Look—in—the—tree."

She raced toward his voice. One of the figures saw her and opened fire. She barely made it behind the tree and climbed.

Mordecai took the opportunity to open fire on her assailant. The surprised man took Mordecai's shot in the chest and fell backwards as he crashed into the house in a spastic death throe.

Luna Belle climbed with ease to the men's level. Two others opened fire but they shot wild. The four in the tree remained so well hidden the only thing giving them away was the sound of their gunfire. The wind warped the reports too badly to reveal the quartet's true position.

It didn't take Nick, Mordecai, and Lil' Roost long to finish off all the adversaries on the veranda. Luna Belle wanted a gun, but Nick feared giving her one—she might shoot him.

After several minutes of silence the four decided to descend. They knew Scooter remained at large. They wanted to find and deal with him.

Nick turned to Luna Belle. "What happened to Rose?"

Luna Belle lowered her chin and placed a hand on Nick's shoulder. "Rose sleeps under the Contessa."

38

Shootout!

"You killed Rose? How?" Nick rubbed his chin.

"I'll gladly answer that, but first, can we get out of this tree?"

Climbing the tree seemed easy for Luna Belle. Descending turned into another matter because of her long flowing nightgown. It was hopeless without some kind of adjustment.

"Turn your heads. I'm stripping. And I mean it—if you perverts look, I'll gun you down before I die."

Nick grinned while he thought back on times past when they stripped and skinny-dipped freely in Ashwood's creek. Luna Belle showed no lack of temerity then. *Granted, it was long ago and we were children but Luna Belle certainly wasn't shy. Does she count me among the perverts?*

Luna Belle came out of her nightgown in one fell swoop, tied it around her neck, and was out of the tree within seconds. It took her about that long to get back into her garb.

"Okay boys. You may come down now."

"Thank you, your Majesty." Nick mocked.

Mordecai grinned. Even under fire the pair cavorted with each other's minds as if they romped like children in the woods.

All four filled their heads with questions for the others. A shot rang from Teachall telling them to wait and take cover.

As they ran to the back of the tree Nick said, "I thought we finished all that."

Mordecai pointed a finger. "I guess we're amateurs. We shouldn't have exposed ourselves to sighting."

"But who's there and why shoot at us?" Nick asked.

"Henry Swilley." Luna Belle declared.

"What is Henry doing here? Sure it's not Scooter Thadeu?" Nick quizzed.

Mordecai crossed his arms over his chest. "Missy, I find it hard to believe. Henry—here?"

"Rose told me in the mausoleum after you abandoned me. But what else can I expect? Long ago, I trusted you, Nick Polk. You too, Mordecai. Now I see that you've even managed to turn Lil' Roost against me."

Lil' Roost wanted to protest but decided he better stay quiet.

Nick argued, "Lil' Roost needed us to help him fight this battle out here. He'd been with us all night, helping in—" Nick stopped himself short of revealing their subterfuge. "I knew he couldn't take on Pink's army alone. Besides, he's the one who—" Nick again stopped short in his tracks. Mordecai stared at him and shook his head.

Luna Belle's voice became pensive as she glared at Nick and Mordecai. "He's the one who *what?* You're covering something up. I can sense it, and I don't like it one little bit."

Nick scratched his scalp. "He's the one that shot whoever threw that huge bomb. That's what Lil' Roost did." Nodding his head one time made him feel confident he'd covered his tracks. Luna Belle didn't need to know specifically what they'd been doing.

Before more questions could erupt, Mordecai devised a plan. "I think we should go to the house."

Luna Belle protested. "Are you crazy? We'd fall like spring grass in front of a billy-goat."

"We won't if we use our smarts." Mordecai replied.

Nick took Luna Belle's hand and gently rubbed it. "Luna Belle, listen to him. He knows little secrets you'd never believe. Go ahead, Mordecai, tell us your plan."

"We head for the folly. There's enough plantings to cover us. Take the tunnel to the house. It's not anywhere near the cave-in."

"Cave-in?" Luna Belle raised her hands.

"Action now—questions later." Nick snapped.

The four made their way to the folly with stealth. All the way she kept badgering about the cave-in—about Pink—what else they knew.

Nick stopped behind an enormous camellia and scolded her. "Luna Belle, I'm sorry. We need to know who's shooting at us. I promise, when we're safe I'll answer any question you can think up. Right now, let's get this thing over." She acquiesced and fell quiet.

Luna Belle had always avoided the cavernous tunnels. Nick knew her well enough—she would stoically persevere. Her bantering served her well in covering the overtaking nervousness about going underground.

When they made it to the folly Mordecai opened the entrance to the tunnel and went first. The armory near the tunnel's entrance held flashlights and all sorts of hand-to-hand combat gear.

Luna Belle and Lil' Roost also armed themselves. She chose a nickel pistol and a gleaming scimitar, having recently experienced the way one sliced so nicely.

She slid the sword out of its scabbard and tested its edge with her thumb. Approving its well honed perfection she sheathed it, strapped it over her night gown, and followed Mordecai's lead. Before they left the munitions room Mordecai handed each of them a powerful flashlight and showed them a concealed dagger in the handles.

Lil' Roost had lived at Teachall all his life. He'd been around the Lady of the Manor and watched her muck stalls and groom horses. Birthing foals or calves never bothered her in the least. Still—this? *This* impressed him.

She showed no qualms about the tunnel and stayed with the men, brushing spiders without missing a stride. Lil' Roost admired her fortitude, her stubborn determination to get to the house and end this all out war. Nick knew she'd prevail. She became a warrior as the farm girl reappeared, causing his heart to pump with pride.

When they came to a fork, Mordecai stopped and turned. "This tunnel goes to the office on the main floor. This one to the master's bedchamber, then on up to the chart room tower to the second, then third floors. This one comes out in the laundry room on the ground floor. Does anyone have a preference?"

Luna Belle spoke first. "I want upstairs. I'll take the chart room."

Nick asked, "Is there any reason for wanting to go upstairs?"

"Action first, questions later." Luna Belle snapped.

Nick nodded then said, "I'll take the office."

Mordecai said, "Lil' Roost and I will take the ground floor."

Nick said, "We need a plan."

Luna Belle answered, "Shoot first, questions later? Have a better one?"

Mordecai added, "I have one suggestion. Let's not shoot each other."

Luna Belle detested being alone in this spiders' burrow. Arriving at the stairs, she breathed a sigh of relief.

She grew more and more amazed with each step because she recognized where she was in the house. All these years at Teachall and she never knew a complete network was concealed between the walls.

Even between the floors, spaces tall enough to walk revealed themselves. No wonder the staircases were so long and elegant. The sixteen foot ceilings accounted for only a portion of the stairs length. Years earlier, Luna Belle noticed noises never transferred to spaces below. Now she knew why.

As she kept climbing, the stairs changed from tabby to wood. The creaking noises bothered her, but not enough to thwart her nearing the apex of her journey.

The back of Mose's fireplace came into view beside the stairs. She tried to open the passage to the side but couldn't find the sliding door's lock. Off to the side more stairs led on up to the chart room, just as Mordecai had said. Climbing higher, she opened a small door and found herself inside a chart room closet. A louvered door allowed her enough visibility to see that two men occupied the room.

It appeared they ransacked the place. In a moment, someone tried the closet's knob where she stood. Her heart almost leapt out her throat.

She jumped back to anticipated safety through the concealed door where she entered. Whoever assaulted the closet threatened beyond the thin partition.

Luna Belle's faith now rested in her hope that the panel

remained obscure. She heard things thrown around and
scratching on the wall. Cursing, someone yelled, "Not in here,
either. I'm telling you. He hid them in the library. Where else
would you hide books?"

She heard another voice from inside the room. She knew
Scooter's voice. "Listen to me, Mad Dog. He kept them here
close to where he slept. I can feel it in my bones. Besides, I knew
the man much better than you. The books are bound to be in
this room."

"You search here all you want. I'm going to the library." Mad
Dog gruffly barked.

Luna Belle didn't know what to do. In all her years at
Teachall she had never heard the name Mad Dog. Who could
this rogue be? Lulu would have never been able to keep a secret
like that.

Luna Belle's breathing became shallow and rapid. Her
fingers fumbled with the flashlight. "I wonder if I should go
back and try another way? Why was I always so insolent when
Mose wanted to teach me this stupid house's tricks?"

Too late, all those opportunities had long passed. She
decided to wait until Scooter left the chart room. In a moment
the room fell quiet. Luna Belle proceeded.

She again opened the panel in the back of the chart room
closet. Its strewn contents impeded her attempt by almost
barricading the door, but Luna Belle pushed with all her might.

Once the door moved, it gave way and Luna Belle almost
flew into the room from her own inertia. She had no more than
regained her balance when something crashed over her head.
She saw shards of a lamp pass her eyes as all went black.

Scooter had heard her trying to enter. He positioned himself
to take out whomever gained access to the room. When he saw
his victim was Luna Belle, he felt a moment of pity and didn't
shoot her. Instead he left the unconscious woman draped across
the floor's Nain carpet. Luna Belle retained her elegance even in
her unconscious state.

He scurried to rejoin Mad Dog, who had left the room for
the office. Nick beat them both to Mose's private space on the
main floor and locked and barricaded himself inside. It only
took him seconds to find the code books. To his disbelief the safe

still stood wide open and undisturbed. Quickly, he tucked the newfound valuables in his pocket.

Mordecai had predicted that the books existed exactly in that location. He searched further but saw nothing else that seemed important. He closed the safe, spun the lock, and headed back out of the office through the tunnel.

About to close the secret door, he heard an assault coming from the hall. Someone tried to open the office door. He decided to see who. In no time he recognized his brother-in-law's voice.

Why had Henry even come to Teachall? Nick figured Henry might go along with some of the other mutineers, but Nick would have bet all the tea in Ceylon that his brother-in-law hated Scooter Thadeu.

Nick heard Henry yelling. In a moment Scooter joined the angered man. Nick listened to their arguing protests.

"This door stood wide open when we came by here minutes ago. Someone's in there." Scooter bellowed.

Henry pounded on the door. No one answered. "The wind probably came through that broken window and slammed the door. I doubt anyone went in there."

Scooter tried the knob repeatedly. "We'd'a heard the door crash if the wind caused it."

After a few moments of quiet, Nick heard the sound of a battering ram against the heavy solid mahogany door. Whatever the men used as their weapon, it made a terrible noise. In three loud banging tries, the door splintered. Then a hand poked inside to release the lock.

The hand found the straight chair Nick had used to scotch the knob. With a flick of the wrist the chair flew and the door flung open. Nick pulled the panel closed leaving a small crack for hearing.

The two men made it inside as Mordecai and Lil' Roost arrived outside the office from the back stair hall. Mordecai knew how the hallway mirrors worked. He saw in but the men did not see him. An ingenious device he himself arranged for protection in case just such an occasion as this ever arose.

"Luna Belle broke in on me upstairs. She came into the room through a secret passage in the back of the closet." Scooter said.

Nick's stomach tightened.

"So how'd you leave her?" Henry asked.

"Oh, I took care of her." Scooter responded.

"You killed her?" Henry's fear escalated. This grew out of control. Scooter lost all rational thought.

Henry knew killing important people like Luna Belle Black brought dire consequences. Scooter kept quiet. Mordecai ran to check on Luna Belle, leaving Lil' Roost to listen. Nick's heart almost stopped beating. After all these years, to think his life-long love had been murdered by scum like Lardass.

Henry's voice grew shrill and pointed. "Did you kill her? Tell me. Now."

"I don't know. I clobbered her over the head with a lamp. Sunk like an anvil dropped overboard at sea. I saw blood and left."

"You're a miserable coward. If I live long enough, I'll see you pay for your deeds here tonight."

"What about you? You no good two-faced, lying, cheating—"

Scooter's tirade ended as Nick stepped into the room brandishing a double-barreled sawed off shotgun in one hand and a six-shooter in the other. He asked no questions. Instead, he took Luna Belle's suggestion and opened fire on Scooter's belly with both barrels. Lardass left for kingdom come in the form of a giant doughnut. Scooter's girth prevented the shot's spreading enough to hit Henry. Nick turned to his brother-in-law and pointed the pistol in his face.

"Now, brother dear. A few questions. I've listened all these years. You've been wanting me to leave. Why?"

Henry stammered while his face glazed with sweat. "I never meant you any harm. I swear to you I didn't. Sara wanted me to get you and Luna Belle out of here the moment she found out what went on around this place."

"I don't believe a word you're saying, Henry, not one word."

"Why?"

"Oh, I don't know. Maybe because you've known about something here from the outset. Henry, Henry, Henry, I don't guess you know how close my sister and I are. Sara told me about Venice. If working for a pirate didn't bother me, why the hell did it bother you?"

"Nick, you have no idea—"

"Oh. Really? How do you know what I know? You sure are short of answers, Mr. Big Shot Lawyer. Uh-huh, I know all about how you've made a living. Had that bird beak of yours so high in the air. All along you've been nothing more than a societal parasite. I know."

Henry's sweat poured over his face and stung his eye. It poured off his nose and chin.

Nick took another step toward Henry. "Being a divorce lawyer may have been a good front, but all this time you've been a virtual washing machine for mob money. Yep. Don't tell me what's in my own head."

"There's a lot more to it that that, Nick. If you'll allow me, I'll explain."

"Maybe some other time, perhaps over tea and crumpets." Nick sarcastically snarled his lips in disgust. "So now if you don't mind, tell me why you're here. Your companion oozes his last drops of blood on that fancy rug. Wanna join him?"

"Nick, it's a long story. If you'll lower that gun—"

"Not so fast. Strip."

"What?"

"If I'm gonna lower this gun, strip to your underwear. Now! You ain't pulling no concealed weapon on me, son."

Lil' Roost almost laughed. This was rich. He never realized what a fierce-some adversary gentle Nick could become under pressure.

While Henry undressed he talked nervously, "Nick, it's true. I've been laundering money. I won't lie to you any more, but you don't understand. Mose did offer me a job in Venice. Not even Sara knew—I took it."

By now he had his shirt and pants off. "Can I redress?"

"Spin around." Nick motioned for him to turn for inspection. Satisfied he nodded.

Henry started redressing and continued his apology. "That's right. I took the job and I've worked for him ever since, although it's not what you think. Mose experienced trouble even back then. Somebody pilfered from the till. He didn't know who. Wanted me as a double agent."

"Yeah, right. You expect me to believe that?"

"I'll go into detail later but listen first. Rose Black Tiddie stole the money. I've known for some time and tried my best to get Mose to accept it. He never believed me. He gave her everything she wanted. Pink didn't have to work. He just wanted to play at being a lawman. For some reason Rose resented Mose."

Nick nodded. "I know why. How did you find all this out?"

"Not that hard, Nick. Rose thought I worked against Mose. She recruited me years ago. What an adventure—I almost hate it's over. Rest of my life looks dull. I speak the truth. I know who shot Mose."

Nick raised his brows.

"Lars Haggley and Sylvia Black did it together."

"Where was Rudine that morning?" Nick asked.

"Right here. Came to see Luna Belle. Pink hauled her off later that day. I don't know where she is. If we can find her, you can ask her about Sylvia. I had coffee with Rudine one day at the drugstore and planted seeds of doubt."

"Why didn't you tell Mose about her? If he knew, this whole thing might have been different."

"I did tell him. After Rudine left that morning. Nick, you have to understand my communications with Mose remained limited. Otherwise, some of his closest adversaries might have figured out what I did for him."

Mordecai ran into the room. "Nick, Luna Belle lives. She's hurt. I'm pretty sure she suffers a serious concussion. We need to get her to a doctor."

39

Juliana Is Angry

"If you think she's got a concussion, it might be better for Jack to come here instead." Nick huffed as he ran at top speed.

The four men left the office and sprinted upstairs toward the chart room. Nick rushed with urgent need to get to Luna Belle. He saw concern in Henry's eyes which led Nick to believe maybe he had truly misjudged Henry all along.

Mordecai followed close behind. "Good thinking—I'll call. Wait. What about all the dead bodies? He's going to have too many questions."

They didn't have time for conversation. Luna Belle needed attention.

Nick started up the staircase. "You're right, but we can't move her. We'll have to cross our bridges one at a time when we get to them." Nick said.

Henry kept up with the others as best he could. He panted and chuffed but managed to speak. "Don't worry about Doc. He's on your side."

Nick left the other two in his dust. "What? I mean, he's never shown one bit—"

Henry stopped and yelled ahead. "Trust me, Nick."

Nick called over his shoulder. "You still have a whole lot of explaining to do."

Mordecai shook his head in disbelief. The more he heard the more he became confused. Why did Nick and Henry suddenly conspire? He had missed their entire conversation while tending

Luna Belle. Mordecai thought Henry Swilley was no friend.

When Nick found Luna Belle she was sprawled across the carpet. Blood oozed from a crack in her skull and dried in the fibers of the rare carpet under her. He tried to rouse her with no success. She breathed. He gladdened, however Luna Belle most definitely needed medical attention.

Mordecai wisely bypassed calling 911. All emergency personnel on Cow Bell Island stemmed from the sheriff's office. The man may have been grossly incompetent, but he managed buying faithful employees.

Besides, Mayhew and Gober ran the ambulance service. Mordecai speculated that those buzzards would kill her for the funeral business. Things hadn't gone well for them since Mose.

Mordecai trusted Jack mostly because the doctor had helped Luna Belle since Mose's death. He served her as a faithful friend, but Mordecai still didn't know about his reaction to strewn corpses.

Nick and Jack had enjoyed a sure friendship for years. They rode, fished, and camped together often. Nick never garnered one shred of evidence that Jack might betray anyone. Plus, the Blacks always treated Jack well. They bought him horses, stabled, and fed them. Mose had generously furnished him a place to ride—anything to keep him on Cow Bell Island.

Luna Belle's grave situation demanded action. Nick called Jack. Mordecai called Gloria. He wanted Polly to come with Jack.

Hanging up with Polly, Mordecai beamed as he interrupted Nick's conversation with Jack. "Tell Jack to swing by Gloria's. Polly will wait on the porch. It won't delay him five seconds."

Nick passed the message. Luna Belle needed Polly. Mordecai missed her. Their being apart had torn into his soul until he finally reconciled himself to its giving him more time to help Nick and Lil' Roost. Time arrived for Polly to come home.

Mordecai understood her recent departure. He wanted to go with her, but Polly insisted he stay because of her devotion to Luna Belle. When Luna Belle waked, she'd see the total absurdity of her past actions. Mordecai wanted things back to normal.

Nick moved beside Luna Belle. He called her name and saw

a little glimmer of hope. She groaned and tried to open her eyes. Luna Belle lived.

Within minutes Deamon, Polly, and Gloria headed toward Teachall's entrance. Polly saw through the rain, the house was torn apart at the seams. At first it appeared to be storm damage. The three climbed the steps to the veranda in disbelief. Rain soaked bodies carpeted the place.

Polly shook her head and looked from side to side. "Whoo-weee. I leave for a few days and just look what happens. If they thinks I'z gonna clean this mess up, they got another think a'coming."

Jack Deamon turned and scowled at her without stopping. Inside, Lil' Roost leaned over the banister beckoning them upstairs.

"We'z in de chart room." He called.

As Jack passed Sylvia's cold body he saw her sliced and diced condition. He passed without stopping to check because it was obvious. The woman lay stone-cold in death.

Jack knelt at Luna Belle's side and asked what happened.

Henry paced the floor. "Scooter Thadeu clobbered her with that broken lamp."

Jack examined her. In a moment he ascertained her wounds appeared minor. Her irises functioned in normal fashion. The gash on her scalp had clotted and stopped bleeding.

"She's fine … going to have a humongous headache, but she's not badly injured. I want a picture even though I'm sure her skull is undamaged. Luna Belle's a tough nut.

"From what I've seen, she's a lucky woman. What's been going on around here, anyway?"

Nick shrugged. "After all these years, it hit the fan."

Jack shook his head. He, Luna Belle, Nick—all outsiders—lived among the biggest group of clansmen imaginable. These people lived as an actual pirate crew. Now their mutiny had been strewn all over the Contessa's estate.

"It appears none of you've been watching TV. Correct?" Jack asked.

"We've been preoccupied. Why?" Nick said.

"Might interest you to know that a category five hurricane

has decided to head straight for Cow Bell Island. That's all.
In fact, you caught me by the skin of your teeth. I planned my
evacuation when you called. If you want my opinion, we need
to figure how we're going to get away from this place before it is
totally submerged."

"That bad?" Mordecai asked.

He'd ridden out many storms. What was so special about
this one?

"It's scheduled to hit at high tide … full moon … long
overdue."

"Can Luna Belle travel?" Nick asked.

"Travel or drown—choose." Jack answered.

Nick had things to do before he left. Three prized horses
were all the stock left on the island. They deserved to be
evacuated with the people.

Nick looked at Jack. "Get her ready to travel. I've got to get
a few things together before I pick y'all up at the front of the
house. Give me about thirty minutes."

"Perfect. It'll take me that long to get her secure."

Nick headed to the barn with Lil' Roost. The rain blew so
hard they found it difficult to keep from blowing away, so they
crossed their arms over each other's shoulders for stability.

After they loaded the last horses onto the eighteen wheel
horse trailer, they grabbed a few personal effects then headed
toward the front of Teachall. Nick had never taken the truck
across the grounds. He hoped it didn't sink in the saturated
sandy earth. Once, his heart stalled with the truck, but he kept
it moving. If he stopped he would become stuck.

Pulling to the front of the house he blew the horn. Jack
waited, ready. He had bandaged Luna Belle's head and bound
her to an ironing board Mordecai provided. She traveled in
safety even if her forsaken comfort eluded the men.

To pad the ironing board, Jack made do with the old quilt
Mordecai grabbed from inside Mose's blanket chest. The faithful
friend remembered its importance to Luna Belle's ancestry. He
folded it with care to fit the wood. It sufficed.

Jack wanted to stop along the way long enough to take her
to an emergency room for a couple of quick X-rays. Their main
concern centered on the storm bearing straight toward the

island. Medical treatment was shoved to the back burner.

Jack quickly protested the instant he saw the eighteen wheel rig. "We need speed, not this monstrosity."

"If we leave these beauties behind ... well ... I'd rather face the storm than Luna Belle. We can't use the bridge over Riggers Creek, so it's on to the ferry." Nick sounded confident.

"I don't like this one bit Nick. I want you to know that." Jack protested.

Nick said, "We'll find a place for Luna Belle in back with the horses. There's no room for her here in the cab on that board."

Jack's face grew into an incredulous expression. "Won't it ride rough?"

Lil' Roost said, "Not bad. I'll ride with her. There's a mattress we can lay on the floor and lay that ironing board on it."

Nick consoled the wearied doctor. "Jack, the trailer has shocks and springs. These horses are too valuable for jostling about. It actually rides pretty good. Besides, there's a video monitor in the trailer. If anything goes wrong, it's no trouble to signal the cab." Nick explained.

Henry climbed into the cab with Nick. Jack decided to ride with Lil' Roost and Luna Belle. The good doctor wanted to know any problem that developed. He grabbed his bag and jumped in.

"What about Mordecai, Polly, and Gloria?" Nick asked.

"They're coming behind us. Said not to worry about them." Henry snapped.

Nick still didn't trust Henry. He hoped the Swanns were okay. At this point he didn't know why, but he had a sick sensation that Henry may have disposed of them.

As they rode onto the abandoned ferry dock Nick and Henry's heart sank. They appeared trapped on Cow Bell Island.

Nick slammed the steering wheel with the heels of his hands. "We're trapped. There's no way that old rickety bridge over Axminster Creek will hold all this weight, and there's no other way off the island for us.

The weather abated its ferociousness for a moment which was even more disconcerting. The calm before the storm. Nick lived near the coast long enough to know the waves of intensity increased with the storm's approach.

Henry yelled back, but his voice lacked a solid sound of assurance. "I know how to operate the boat. I worked several summers on the ferry near Jacksonville. Let me out and I'll see if I can get it going."

Trapped. Nick saw no choice. Henry jumped to the ground and ran toward the moored boat.

In no time he came back huffing. "The thing's almost empty. I don't know if we should trust her to cross the sound."

"Got sixty gallons of diesel on the truck. Enough to make her work?"

"More'n enough. Where?" Henry said.

"Come on." Nick jumped down and headed to the back of the cab. A set of large fuel containers strapped there carried his reserve. He flipped a latch and one fifteen gallon container popped free. Henry watched and followed suit. Within a few moments the ferry guzzled diesel.

The tide plagued Nick's mind. It rose fast. He'd never seen the sound under such rapid development. No wonder the ferryman left his post.

Nick knew they needed to get underway or remain captives. The dock on the opposite shore threatened being under water if they didn't hurry. He didn't know whether to risk the voyage or seek higher ground on the island.

Teachall, the highest point, had never flooded since its construction, but this appeared to be a different scenario: Cow Bell Island's three hundred year storm. That's what Jack led him to believe.

Headed to the cab, Nick heard the giant engines of the ferry cranking out their noxious brew of smoke and soot. He risked all their lives but they had no other choice. Nick could either trust Henry or stay where they were. The sound itself indicated their need to move quickly before disaster struck its final blow.

He rolled the giant truck onto the boat with his heart in his throat. All he could do was trust Henry when he said he knew how to captain a ferry because it certainly never occurred to Nick how the thing worked.

A sleepy giant under normal conditions, the sound became a seething ravenous hungry monster. Her bulk grew while ferocious currents ripped and churned into a frenzied stew.

Eddies formed. The currents shifted and fought and made dangerous whirlpools inevitable. Henry wanted across the giant's treachery without delay.

Nick stopped the truck and jumped out to lash wheels to the boat to keep the rig from blowing off the ferry's deck by a sudden surge. While Nick searched for chain, Henry urged the ferry from the dock. Nick recognized that Henry obviously knew how to captain the vessel.

Both men feared the fast rising tumultuous water. Henry gunned the engines, putting heavy stress on the old boat. He dared not press them harder lest they explode.

The ferry fought the torrents. About half way across the sound, Henry unintentionally hit an eddy head on. It took about thirty seconds for the boat to spin one hundred-eighty degrees. Nick rushed to the wheel house to help Henry regain control.

Henry shouted over the roar. "I don't know if she'll take any more. I'm afraid to gun her harder, but we have no choice."

Nick yelled at the the top of his lungs. "Henry, muster gumption or we'll drown."

Henry shoved both throttles wide open and pushed the engines hard. They obeyed. She trembled with a roar resonating from the engines' power. This old girl pushed her strength against the treacheries swirling under her hull. Henry trembled. "Hope she holds together against the current."

He needed Nick to help steady the rudder. Valiant fighting against the jettisoned waters took all their strength. Great risk accompanied Henry's uncertain plan to land them at the opposite dock. He would have one shot at the goal. If his trajectory overshot the mark, no second chance remained.

Nick hoped the fuel lasted. "Do I need to take the other two canisters of diesel?"

"We're fine for right now. I need you here."

Nick almost swallowed his tongue. He saw the condition of the dock ahead. Because the boat turned midstream, the rig would disembark backwards. Nick didn't care. He'd get her off this contraption. He needed Henry to connect with land.

Both men almost lost hope when they saw the rising water overtaking the dock. Henry didn't know what to do. The ferry's construction demanded hooking to the shore's docking system. Without engaging, doom awaited.

Desperation engulfed them. Henry's sweat smelled of fear. He saw the dock overtaken by the chopping, lashing water. Nick felt their hard hit against the mooring. Henry kept pushing the engines to keep contact. "Go ahead—run! Looks like our only chance at getting the rig off the boat. Go!"

Nick rushed to the truck knowing full well the boat lacked being secured to the moorings. He must get off while a chance remained.

He removed the chains in lightening speed then jumped in the cab and pushed the trailer backwards. Henry kept using all his strength to hold her steady long enough to allow Nick's exit.

The trailer's rear made contact with the ground with a thud. It was a long way down but the wheels engaged earth. The water kept rising. The cab approached the jumping off place when the trailer jack-knifed. The ferry's ramp created a fulcrum causing a spastic fit.

He had to get the trailer going straight or be yanked apart, separating him from Luna Belle. He shifted the giant tractor into its lowest gear and pulled hard against the entanglement. The rebellion continued. After the second such try he straightened it, ready for another attempt. He pushed the behemoth hard while the cab jumped to the flooded ground beneath.

Henry remained trapped on the ferry. Nick heard a large explosion when an engine blew on the boat. While Nick watched in horror, Henry and the ferry swept into the sound's mighty waters. The boat spun out of control.

Nick knew he'd never see his brother-in-law again. Henry waved, striking Nick's heart with sorrow. If Nick had known of Mose's trust in Henry, things could have been so different between them.

Here at the end with the truth revealed—they bonded. Henry helped Nick save Luna Belle, now Henry swirled on his way to certain death. Nick had to focus on his current situation with no recourse to aid Henry. Strong intentions and heavy demands for the tractor urged Nick into a grinding attempt to get them away from rising water.

40

Stormy Weather

Leaving Henry behind tore at Nick's heart, although there was nothing he could do about it. Their separation after so short a bonding had become final with nothing more than a farewell wave. Nick wanted to cry, but he didn't have time.

Water already reached the rig's axles. If they didn't get to higher ground soon it would all be over. Nick sensed the storm's gaining intensity with each passing second.

Nick flinched at breakers reaching this far into the sound. The coast lay at least three miles to the East, yet these enormous waves brought the strength of the furious Atlantic inland. They came like clawing fists ready to ensnare them all.

The swells hitting the side of the rig rang in his ears over the howling winds' moaning causing Nick to proceed with slow caution. If he went too fast the water's momentum and the truck's own inertia could topple them.

Nick's heart raced. While catching a brief glimpse of the trailer monitor, he saw the panicked horses. Lil' Roost comforted them with his deft hands and soothing voice. Jack Deamon called Lil' Roost away from the animals to help keep Luna Belle alive. Nick could do nothing better than get them to safety.

The tractor pulled with all its might, yet they made slow progress. Another obstacle lay ahead—a swale in the road. If it had filled with sand from the churning water Nick realized a possibility of miring. If deep enough to stall the engine …

With no way around it, Nick determined to test their mettle against a storm drainage ditch. He could theorize its being nothing more than Satan's snare. Nick voided his mind as they approached the depression.

The rig's cab sank and instantly began filling with surging water. Nick held his tongue between his teeth, hoping not to bite it off while he felt water rising around his feet. The mighty tractor kept moving. He repeated thanksgivings over and over.

Not a religious man, he never saw a need. He quickly changed his mind, calling for divine intervention, literally begging God to intercede on their behalf.

The huge diesel motor backfired. Nick's heart sank. A giant wave crashed against the side of the vehicle, shaking it to its roots. Nick saw water in with the horses. He saw Lil' Roost and Jack struggling to keep Luna Belle above water.

A tear rolled down Nick's face. Henry rested on the bottom of the sound. Without a motor, he had washed away, engulfed in fury.

The tractor's engine sputtered and called Nick back. He tried feeding it more fuel. As if by miraculous auspices the thing again backfired and rekindled. Nick glanced up. "Thank you, Lord."

The truck pulled itself out of the swale and climbed the road. At least where Nick remembered the road used to be. He hoped it had not washed away leaving gaping wounds deep enough to swallow them.

The engine chugged and spit but kept pulling through the water. It receded with every inch they progressed. After they reached axle depth, Nick thanked God. They had been in deep enough jeopardy to sweep them away. There was no way around it, a higher power rescued them.

He pondered his recent escapades. Nick, a caring, giving person, didn't consider himself evil. He lived surrounded by evil. He benefited from evil, yet he never considered himself so. Still, he needed salvation.

The truck had not yet failed them. Almost two miles from the ferry docks, gales overtook them. None of the group ever experienced winds of this magnitude, especially in an eighteen wheel giant.

It only took a few seconds of being conscious for Luna Belle to start her protestations. "Untie me you fiend. How dare you bind me like a common criminal. Where am I?"

Jack explained things as quickly as possible then cut Luna Belle from the ironing board's confines. Managing her while strapped to a bunglesome board had become virtually impossible.

"That's some blow out there, Luna Belle." Jack cried. She heard his bold voice over the storm's rage but didn't respond.

Nick wanted the radio on so he garnered his nerve and pushed the switch just as a strong gust of wind mixed with salt water pummeled the side of the rig, almost knocking it over. Nick guided the goliath on its left wheels for several hundred yards. They all instinctively leaned in the opposite direction. Human nature told them to shift their weight. The truck dropped back amid cheers. Nick yelled, "Thank God for the gold, or we'd'a blown over!"

A mixture of static and broken reports filled the cab. Without enough continuity to hear, the pilgrim listened in anxiety for any tidbit about the storm. He heard an announcement that the barometric pressure was lower than any previous record. Then the radio signal vanished into white noise.

Luna Belle, Jack, and Lil' Roost held on for dear life. Even so her mind turned to Teachall. The ride she and Jack took not too many days prior played in her mind.

The passengers were suddenly thrown by a jolt of wind. Luna Belle grappled a stall divider to stay upright. "I'm glad to be leaving Cow Bell Island, and I'm not too sure I ever want to go back!"

Jack yelled over the howling storm. "I'm not too sure there will be anything left of the place after all this, anyway."

"Wonder how many of the islanders will try and ride this storm out? I don't wish them any harm or anything, but they are too stubborn to leave. Aren't they?"

"I expect a lot of them did stay."

Lil' Roost added, "I'z glad I got off that place with y'all. All the horses and cows is gone too."

Luna Belle said, "That's right. You know, I never asked where all the stock was taken." She shook her head. "What do you know about all that, Lil' Roost?"

Lil' Roost's eyelids spread wide apart. "I ... I ... Missy ... I don't know nothing about none of that."

Luna Belle looked around the interior of the trailer. "Where's Mordecai ... and Polly? Are they in the cab?"

When no answer came from either of the men, Luna Belle assumed the worst for the two faithful friends. Poor Polly and Mordecai stayed behind, and now they lacked an avenue of escape from Cow Bell Island. They perished. A cold knife pierced her breast. She abused them and never showed them the true depths of her love. Now, it was far too late for her to regain her lost chances.

Nick navigated his way using signs poking out of the water. Thankfully, the road again showed its drenched surface. He managed to see only a few feet ahead, but at least the road wasn't covered with water. If he hadn't traveled this route so many times in the recent past, he would have been lost because of the storm's ability to cut visibility.

About the time they all relaxed enough to smell a whiff of survival, a gust of wind hit the rear of the trailer and caused the whole rig to swing around. Nick panicked because they were now headed in the wrong direction, and he could think of no place other than an intersection at Midway to turn around.

If he made it there by backing the rig, he might have enough room to maneuver in the right direction. The problem being, Midway lay at least five miles ahead.

It would take too long to go that far in reverse. He sensed the hour glass sand quickly slinking its way to the lower chamber. The winds blew stronger causing Nick to fear tornadoes that were bound to be stalking the edges of these waves of wind and rain. The twisters promised unimaginable power coming from the excessively low barometric pressure.

Another gust surprised and sent them spinning again. Instead of heading them back in the right direction, this spin caused about the worst possible thing imaginable. The truck jack-knifed. Unlike when they dismounted the ferry, this time the cab jammed itself hard against the trailer. Nick jerked the transmission into the lowest gear and demanded power. Hoping against hope the monster could right itself again.

Nick needed reassurance that they were indeed headed inland. The truck's navigation system failed when the storm blacked out all satellite connections. Even the compass lost its sense of direction.

The digital instruments flashed nothing but nonsense. If he succeeded in getting the cab back in front of the trailer, he presumed he headed in the right direction, but he knew disorientation had overtaken him.

If he went the wrong way the water would consume them. They should be out of harm's way already, yet the water again rose almost axle deep and the storm's strong eye remained at least ten miles off shore.

Every time Luna Belle's mind drifted toward a reflection, a new event drew her back to the present. Not being able to see out, the three prisoners writhed on a volatile life raft without any chance of control over their safety.

Never before had circumstances so enshrouded Luna Belle in pure unadulterated fear and anxiety. She almost wanted to laugh while she yelled, "Bring it on, Possum Queen. Bring it on!"

Lil' Roost scrunched his eyes. Her sudden outburst startled him. He guessed her blow to the head made her lose all sense. She acted like a different woman than the lady who showed no fear of spiders and tunnels.

Nick needed to right the vehicle in the direction of safety. He rocked the cab back and forth enough to get the trailer behind before he proceeded.

With hope, he traveled at least another couple of miles before he came on the remnants of a billboard. His body slumped. For a second he relaxed enough to rejoice in being headed toward Midway.

He considered where to go from there. They needed to travel inland enough to escape the storm's strongest fury. Right now he assumed that someplace farther than Texas, but fuel limited their distance. Nick trudged onward.

No sign of life existed anywhere they went. During most storms, lawmen, TV crews, and stupid locals hung around. Not with this storm. It appeared everyone had battened their hatches and headed for the hills. The deserted roads offered Nick absolutely no consolation. Even after they went about twenty more miles, the road still flooded in low spots. Nick went on faith when they proceeded through ford after ford.

Out of the blackness and blasting rain, lightening illuminated the most horrible thing Nick had ever witnessed. An enormous tornado headed straight for them. When the lightning flashed, he saw its path wavered. Being blown about like a little whirlwind, the mother hurricane laughed at her marauding child.

Nick prayed, fearing a windswept trip into the sky. Who knew where they might land? Another crash of light showed the monster headed directly toward them. Within one hundred yards they would make contact.

The passengers in the back heard the roar and trembled. Each person braced. They all hoped the horrible roaring deceived them, but the entire trailer began to rumble as if it would implode at any second. In another moment a palm tree crashed onto the cab's roof, punching it flat. If Lil' Roost had been in the sleeper, he would have been crushed.

Another lightening flash and Nick shouted because the tornado was rising up off the ground. They rode under it's gaping maw, losing most of the trailer's top to the vortex.

Nick wanted to see how the passengers and horses fared, but the camera equipment had flown away with the roof. Left to continue toward his goal of safety, he still had no clue where.

They made it to Hinesville, Georgia. The storm still raged even this far inland, so Nick wanted to go farther. Such a strong system demanded utmost respect and caution.

At Hinesville, he had difficulty deciding whether to head southwest to Jessup or more westward. He chose the latter, not wanting to cross the Altamaha River any closer to the coast than necessary. Because the radio again worked in pulses, he became glad for his decision. Record rain flooded low lying areas along the Altamaha. Nick understood that river well enough to steer clear of its powerful unpredictability.

When they arrived in Glennville, Nick stopped. He knew Lil' Roost, Jack, and Luna Belle needed a break. Under the lights of a bellowing, flopping fuel station canopy, Lil Roost thought the struts of the trailer's roof appeared secure enough to open the rear doors.

Nick rushed back to check on the trailer's occupants, surprised and delighted to see all alive and well. Jack, Lil' Roost, and Luna Belle disembarked the now open box with glee.

Luna Belle laughed, "Well, Nick. When the water came up, I guess it woke me. Lil' Roost and Jack saved me from drowning. Right, boys? That's the second time in my life you've tried to bury me, Nick."

Nick grimaced. "You three move to the front with me."

"No argument there, Nick. None," she replied.

Lil' Roost liked the idea as well.

A small portion of the trailer's roof remained toward the front where the three had huddled and ridden earlier. Nick decided it best to give that area to the horses, providing them with at least a small amount of shelter.

With all this activity going on in the trailer, Nick refueled the rig. She had consumed an amazing drink of diesel in their flight. Nick estimated she had used up three times her regular amount from severe strain. Fighting winds and water had taken a heavy toll on the tractor but she still had enough life to face their upcoming perils. More tornadoes could come.

While the tractor's hungry tanks gulped their fill, Nick talked with a driver named Jonah who filled his rig at the adjacent pump. Jonah advised Nick to head toward Baxley. It made sense even though the Altamaha lay between them and that goal. He spoke with several other drivers who headed in the same direction They all agreed to ride along together. Nick liked the idea of having traveling companions on the road in case one of them fell into distress.

Jonah inspected Nick's damage. When the new acquaintance heard what they'd been through, he patted Nick's shoulder. "You was supposed to get out of there. I'd say the good Lord wanted it that way; otherwise, you'd'a been toast, my friend. Toast."

Nick only nodded his agreement and smiled at the true thankfulness in his heart.

Jonah continued, "Wife's in Atlanta. Been watching this monster all day. Said they're saying on TV they ain't never been one hit land this hard before. I believe she's right. I know I ain't never seen nothing to compare with it."

Nick propped against the cab and shook his head. "I've lived on the coast all my life. This is the strongest one I've ever been in."

Jonah leaned his hand on Nick's trailer. "I was headed from Daytona to Charleston. She called me and told me to get off that road quick as I could. I been sauntering my way around here on back roads for most part of half a day. I wound up here. Glad I listened to her. Otherwise I'd be nothing more'n a greasy spot somewhere in the ocean." The man laughed.

Nick wanted to water and feed the horses. They needed their strength amid all this excitement. These animals didn't deserve neglect. When he entered the trailer they neighed.

Nick's new friend told him the weathermen expected about twenty inches of rain out of this system far inland. The storm's path looked like it was bound to slowly blow all the way across Georgia. Its current estimated path took it all the way to Memphis before turning north. Truly, a three hundred year storm.

Nick did everything possible for the animals. He fed them oats from the protected feed bins at the front of the trailer. They had to suffice with wet hay. It was all Nick had. These horses never ceased to amaze him. With all this going on around them, when he came to them they calmed themselves and sensed their safety from his reassurances. Luna Belle stepped back into the trailer with Lil' Roost.

"They's glad to see you again, Missy."

"You too, Lil' Roost."

"I expect they're glad to see Nick more'n us."

"I think we all need to kiss Nick's feet." Luna Belle said.

"Yes'um."

"We still need to get farther inland. There's plenty of water left to be wrung out of those clouds." Nick admonished.

Luna Belle laughed. "I'm not sure we'd be safe from flooding on top of Brasstown Bald."

Nick scowled. "Knock it off. I'm nervous enough as it is."

When Lil' Roost climbed back into the cab with the others he shoved his body into one corner of the now cramped sleeper quarters without grumbling. He might have complained but he relished being alive and a little drier.

Nick decided to discuss their path. He explained his concern for the direction the convoy headed because of the unpredictable Altamaha, and instead recommended they go on to Vidalia. They all agreed once they heard his explanation.

They'd head to the onion capital. Luna Belle had no ultimate goal. She didn't care.

Jonah watched while Nick separated himself from the group of trucks and followed suit. The stranger trusted Nick's judgment more than the other drivers simply because Nick was a local.

They found shelter and beds in Vidalia. Luna Belle couldn't believe Nick's luck because the motel owner had a little stable out back where the three horses enjoyed shelter and more fresh feed for the time they stayed there.

After tending the animals the wearied travelers found the best rest they had experienced in several nights. Nick wanted to watch the storm reports on TV. Instead, a deep restful sleep overtook him.

He shared a room with Jack and Lil' Roost where they watched the news until after midnight. Nick managed to sleep through it all. Had he seen the reports, his heart might have failed.

The rain poured all night. Around three a.m. Lil' Roost was awakened and became curious at the beating against the motel's window. Inspecting the peculiar sound he called to Jack, "Come look—it's rainin fish."

Jack stood beside Lil' Roost in shock as fish of all sizes and shapes pummeled the area. "Water spout must have brought them. Strange they're this far inland."

Lil' Roost's shook his head. "It's a sign. That's what it is."

Jack and Lil' Roost sat shocked the first time Cow Bell Island's name blared on TV. The only identity they gave the island was that it had been the home of the late Governor Scooter Thadeu and Federal Judge Moses Black. The storm had stalled directly on top of their former home. At its height the island remained sunken under fifteen feet of tidal surge making survival impossible. Left on the island, their loved ones had vanished.

41

Onion Queen

Luna Belle found peace in Vidalia. "Nick, I'm so tired. I want to stay here for a few days and get some sleep."

Nick smiled, "My sentiments exactlåy. How's your head?"

"About to split wide open. I guess it's what I deserve after laughing at Rose's condition down in that pit."

"Jack predicted you'd have a doozy of a headache. Maybe once the barometric pressure changes, your head will return to normal. Well ... that's assuming your head ever was normal."

"Ha, ha! I'm in no mood for your levity."

Jonah left them the next day after the weather turned as beautiful as it had been ugly. The television revealed how lucky they had been to forego Baxley. Destruction overtook the entire convoy when they found themselves swept into the angry Altamaha River. Nick and Jonah rejoiced they hadn't followed the other truckers into their own demise. As Jonah drove away, he knew he would never forget the folks from Cow Bell Island.

Luna Belle walked from her room to join the three men beside the pool. "How long have I slept?"

Jack answered, "Better part of two days and nights. I don't know if you remember or not—we kept coming in and waking you to make you drink water. I didn't want you dehydrated."

"Yeah, right. I don't think I could have dried out after you guys tried to marinate me in salt water on an ironing board.

Why did you tie me to that thing in the first place?"

Jack grinned and turned his palms up. "You were unconscious with a head wound. I wasn't about to take a chance of transporting you without having you secured."

"How did I end up like that in the first place?"

Nick sat up and looked Luna Belle in the eyes. "Scooter Thadeu clobbered you over the head with a lamp."

"Wait, I was in the wall— How do you know it was Scooter?"

"Because I heard him tell Henry all about it."

"Henry? Henry Swilley?"

"Yep. That Henry. There's a lot you need to hear about your long-time enemy, Henry. Turns out, he was one of the good guys. Can you believe that?"

"Where is Henry?"

"That's a long story and we'll get to it. First we really need to be thankful to Scooter. Hitting you over the head actually saved all our lives."

"That's real cute, Nick."

"I'm dead serious. If Scooter hadn't whammed you over the head, we'd'a never called Jack. He's the one who told us to evacuate the island because of the hurricane. It's amazing how all of that worked out. You'll want to hear it, but let's do it in bits and pieces over time. I don't want to cause you to have a stroke."

"At least Scooter has struck his last blow."

She listened as Nick explained how he killed Scooter. "You blew a hole clean through him? But, you know what? Looking back, I can't believe he could even get close enough to hit me over the head. I'm proud of you. If anybody ever earned a ticket out'a here shaped like a doughnut, it had to be Lardass."

The lady who owned the motel where they rested took pity on Luna Belle. She scrounged around and found a little wardrobe. Not much, but at least she changed from the gore infested gown she wore while she butchered Sylvia.

Luna Belle had become a killer after she had been backed against a wall. She experienced an instance of pure self defense. Pride filled her chest for having the fortitude to accomplish the deed. Sylvia Black truly needed killing.

In their motel rooms, they watched the TV coverage of
Hurricane Juliana's aftermath. Luna Belle saw irony in the
Contessa Juliana. Cow Bell Island received the brunt of
the hurricane's fullest force. Rose took the full effects of the
Contessa Juliana's curse head on.

Helicopters flying over Cow Bell Island showed no remnants
of civilization. The remains of Teachall appeared as nothing
more than a huge vacuous outline on the island's scarred face.
Every structure, most of the trees, everything was gone. Except
for Nick's bravery, they too would have been swept into the
drink.

The news spoke of Governor Thadeu's being lost to the
storm. Even so, the media refused him a free ticket to glory.
They kept up their tirades about his impending impeachment.
He actually died a lucky man by pirate standards.

There loomed too many witnesses, too many photographs,
and voice recordings of him dealing with the warehouse
conspirators. He found no place as a hero of the state—his
epitaph replaced by an epithet.

Luna Belle's frustrated concern over Mordecai and Polly
grew. Nick fought against continual anger with himself for not
making them board the trailer. It never occurred to him they
would become trapped then washed away in the hurricane's
fury.

Nick explained with tears in his eyes how at the ferry he
wanted to turn back and retrieve them, but the water had risen
too high by that time. Leave or drown, those two choices faced
him headlong. He regretted his choice for their sakes. Since
leaving Teachall not one word came from the faithful couple.

As Luna Belle returned to normal a deeper contrition
overtook her toward Polly. Too late, Polly would never know
how much Luna Belle truly loved her.

Luna Belle's mind tumbled over accepting Henry's actions
on their behalf. He offered himself as a sacrifice to their
survival. The scoundrel of yore revoked his title and proved his
faithfulness.

Nick's mind continually saw hauntings of Henry's waving
goodbye and the resolve on the valiant man's face. The only
redeeming quality from his death grew from his noble actions.

Still, abandoning him on St. Catherine's Sound brought bitterness.

Nick's being helpless didn't abate his tormented guilt. He neglected his brotherly duty to Henry and never gave him a proper chance to prove his fidelity, until it was too late.

Nick dreaded seeing Sara again. How would he ever explain the depths of his sorrow to her? He had no options to save Henry, yet pangs of remorse still swept his heart often bringing bitter tears to his eyes.

Jack saved his stories for later. He sat with a glazed far away stare while rejoicing over his escape from Cow Bell Island. Before the storm hit, he determined to evacuate the place, never to return. The island's total devastation confirmed his choice. Having his old friends made things much easier.

Lil' Roost hoped he never again was stuck in the back of a horse trailer with an unconscious woman and a hysterical doctor. The three frightened Andalusian stallions stood with pride and demanded far less attention than his human companions. He wanted to live the rest of his life with horses as much as possible. He understood them more than he did his two-footed friends.

Luna Belle, Nick, and Jack talked while sitting by the motel pool one evening. She said, "The Contessa took care of us after all. I mean, think about it. What would have happened to all of us had she not acted like a clean up crew?"

Nick huffed on his nails then polished them on his chest, "Yep, she sure did. Swept all those worrisome corpses out to sea."

She punched his upper arm and rolled her eyes. "They would have haunted us for the rest of our lives."

Jack leaned onto one elbow. "It was war. I missed the fighting, but everything y'all accomplished deserves no consequence in my book. No reason for guilt or remorse exists."

Luna Belle added, "It may sound like a lousy attempt at an excuse but we really ended up with no choice but to defend ourselves."

Jack nodded. "I can gladly live anywhere other than that God forsaken place. I have no yearning to go back. The only attachment I might have ever felt was my dear Lola. She was entombed in that mausoleum, but even it was swept away leaving me absolutely no attachment to that little piece of earth. I miss nothing about it."

Luna Belle's smile vanished. "Thank you, Jack. What a poetic way of saying how I myself feel about that place. I know how much you still love Lola. I'm sorry she's not with us now."

Alone with Luna Belle later that evening, Nick chided, "So, when are we gettin' hitched? I figured we could start a little possum farm … go from there. Might not have much, but we'd sure have a boatload of memories, wouldn't we?"

"You think you're so clever. I don't have a thing to say to you right now." She turned toward him and smiled. "I guess you might be on the verge of cracking my shell … I'm not making any promises—just yet." All the terrors passed, she wanted to be with the man who truly possessed her heart.

The next morning Nick insisted they once again hit the road. Luna Belle had no idea where they headed. She didn't care. She even contemplated staying behind in Vidalia. She always liked onions, why not stay here? If it hadn't been for her new-found love for Nick, she might have seriously considered it an option.

When she quizzed him about their destination he smiled. "Action now, questions later."

Luna Belle nodded. His answer piqued her interest enough to abandon any aspirations of becoming an onion queen. In a flash she saw that Nick had no intention of telling her his complete plan. Nick, Luna Belle, and Jack sat in the truck's seat. Lil' Roost crawled in the cab's dinged up sleeper without hesitation.

A man at a local body-shop had beaten the cab's roof nearly back into position, providing a more comfortable space for Lil' Roost to nap. He dreamed about Dr. Deamon's terror in the trailer. Then Lil' Roost smiled while he dreamed of her—that Luna Belle Black was one amazing woman. He hoped one day to find himself a female with her backbone.

Luna Belle saw they headed back toward the coast. She began to realize Brunswick lay ahead. She didn't really care what Nick had in mind and he wasn't telling. When they finally arrived at Ashwood, Luna Belle's eyes danced in amazement.

The last time she saw her ancestral home it stood in terrible repair. Mose always kept the house dry but that was about all he had any interest in doing. Mose understood, Luna Belle never entertained an intention of coming here again to live. Why would she? Too many old memories flourished in her home-place for her to ever want to return. Miraculously, now it literally gleamed in bright summer sunlight.

As the battered yet encouraged entourage made their way toward the barn, Luna Belle became the happiest she'd been in years. All the farm buildings stood restored and painted with immaculate detail. When she saw a tire swing off toward the creek where one hung so many years ago, she wept.

"Nick Polk, I can't believe all this. I'm afraid to blink. I might reopen my eyes to nothingness. How did Mose—"

"Not Mose."

"Who? This took money ... a whole boat load."

Nick grinned. "Or two."

"I don't understand."

"Help get the horses unloaded for now. We'll discuss the details over a wonderful dinner. How does that sound?"

Luna Belle jumped from the cab only to hear cries from the barn. Running inside, all her prized horses greeted her with their nickering and snorting.

This whole situation seemed impossible. How had this happened? It dawned on her that Nick had done all of this. Who else? How? Nick didn't have this kind of money. Frugal, yes, but did he squirrel away enough for this?

Nick called her to the trailer. He and Lil' Roost lifted a mat from the floor. Luna Belle saw bar after bar of gold bullion glimmer in the sun before her eyes.

"What ... ? How ... ? Nick ... ? I'm confused."

"Didn't Mose leave it all to you?"

"Yes."

"Well ... there's more tucked away."

"How? I'm going to need pictures."

"How about detailed descriptions? You know I don't draw nothing but flies."

Later in the evening they all lounged on the front porch watching the sunset. Summertime, the evenings scorched. Luna Belle made lemonade all by herself.

Nick took a sip and puckered his lips. "After our wedding, I appoint myself chef."

She punched him in the arm. "Just shut up and drink. Anyway, I haven't said yes, yet."

"Ah … yet? Now, that's the first sign of encouragement you've given me. Jack, I do believe she's breaking."

Jack grinned. "Needs vodka," under his breath he finished his thought, "lots and lots of vodka."

Several days passed before a strange black car traveled Ashwood's long curvy drive. Luna Belle didn't recognize the large Mercedes-Benz and she showed no sign of eagerness to greet its occupants. It took a few moments for the driver's door to open before a svelte lady slowly stood. A large brimmed hat obscured her face from view.

Luna Belle dismissed the neighbor do-gooder, probably a member of the welcome wagon. The woman walked around the back of the car to the passenger side, opened the door, and started helping someone get out of the seat. Luna Belle screamed in delight as she almost jumped off Ashwood's high front porch.

A puff of wind blew the hat's brim back from the woman's face and Luna Belle saw Sara who had walked around to help Henry get out of the passenger seat. He was bandaged from head to toe. Luna Belle ran harder.

"Nick! It's Sara and Henry." She cried over her shoulder but didn't miss a step in her quest to reach the car.

Nick ran from inside the house and within an instant figured out what was going on. He followed close behind.

Luna Belle literally jumped for joy as she hugged Sara. "Oh my gracious Lord in Heaven! Thank you." Luna Belle wailed over Sara's shoulder. "However in this world did Henry survive?"

She wanted to attack Henry with a hug but realized his condition was far too delicate for being mauled, even if it did come from love and devotion. By forced willpower, she calmed herself enough to give him a firm embrace.

Nick took his turn at squeezing his sister, then his brother-in-law. Sara took the opportunity to wrap her arms around both men. It had been many years since Nick had embraced Sara with the devotion they now felt.

Nick said, "There's no way under the stars I'm going to ever let us be separated again."

Luna Belle added, "Henry … no … brother. I can't believe you're here. We never expected to see you again. I can never repay you for what you did for us all."

"You owe me nothing … any of you. It was the least I could do after all those years."

"How did you make it?" Nick demanded.

"Before we go into all that … I really need to get off my feet." Henry winced as he spoke.

By then everyone else had arrived at the car. Lil' Roost and Nick carried Henry up the front steps and laid him in the large double wicker chaise where he sighed in relief from being off his battered legs and feet. Nick sat on the side of the chaise's leg rest with Henry.

"Two can play at that game, mister." Luna Belle laughed as she gracefully took the other side. "We may crowd you a touch. Let us know if we make you uncomfortable. I'm not sure I'll get up but maybe Jack can give you something for the pain." Luna Belle laughed with enough gusto to shake the house.

After only a few moments everyone had chairs pulled around Henry before he started his story. "Nick, you won't believe it. The ferry landed on her side. I'm not sure how long I was unconscious … when I woke, I didn't get up enough steam to move far enough to be discovered until the next day. I was broken up pretty badly and dragging myself up out of that wheelhouse took all the strength I had."

Sara started tearing up. "I'm so lucky. I worried myself silly thinking Henry was dead."

Henry smiled, "I don't want to sound morbid, although buzzards did circle overhead. Funny thing, they looked for all the world like Mayhew and Gober." He twitched his eyebrows three times.

Luna Belle grinned then reached over and laid a compassionate hand on Sara's thigh. "Sara ... Sara ... I too had given up hope. All our lives we've been kept apart by our husbands' work. I've felt Henry was my sworn enemy while all this time he's been one of my staunchest allies. It's all hard for me to believe. I'm so grateful to have you both here."

Henry grimaced a smile. "I awaked to find myself larruped to a pulp inside that old beaten-up tub beside I-95. I realized it might be days or weeks before anyone found me unless I made my presence known. I somehow managed to get out of my shirt and scooted around enough to find a wad of black grease. I used the tar-like glop and wrote SOS on my shirt and hung it over the stern railing. Within minutes, with God's help, a helicopter pilot saw my struggle—"

Nick, with tears streaming, interrupted Henry's speech. "Henry, you're the answer to many prayers. You'll never know how watching you wave good-bye has haunted me."

"Nick, to tell you the truth, when the engine blew I figured I was a goner. In honesty, I didn't think any of us would get out alive."

Luna Belle placed a hand on Henry's knee. "Enough of all this morbid crap. Let's get happy and celebrate by building y'all a house anywhere on the farm you like. It'll be fun."

Sara sat upright. "I already know where I want to live."

Luna Belle asked, "Where?"

"Where our old house used to stand. I've been here so many times since we all left. I watched the old house finally cave in from neglect. The ground under that space is hallowed in my mind. It is filled with so many happy memories. I want to live there."

"We'll start on a house there tomorrow. Until it's complete you'll stay right here with all of us. I think you know everyone, don't you? Oh. I'll bet you've never met Lil' Roost."

"No, I don't think I have."

Nick interrupted, "Lil' Roost, this is my annoying little sister. She loves horses as much as Luna Belle and I. She'll be bothering you at the barn quite a bit."

Lil' Roost nodded.

In her suite, Luna Belle saw how desperately she wanted to share this space with Nick. He had turned Ashwood into something grander than ever before—more than she dreamed possible. He filled every inch of the house with his adoration and kindled her passion.

The haints and unpleasant memories had been swept away. Nick's love cleansed the house and turned it into their home.

42

Lemonade Anyone?

The next day a car almost tentatively turned onto Ashwood's driveway. Luna Belle knew the silver Rolls Royce Gurney Nutting Saloon limousine the moment she saw it. She ran toward her formerly lost hope.

Mordecai jumped from behind the steering wheel with a beaming smile on his face. Luna Belle hugged him and kissed his cheeks.

Pete Stagg sprang out of the passenger side to surprise Luna Belle. Glad to see Pete and Mordecai—her heart ached in disappointment because Polly wasn't in the car.

Luna Belle cried bittersweet tears. "Oh Mordecai, I've been awful. I know—" Luna Belle stopped in mid sentence. Her heart sank. Polly hadn't survived the hurricane. She would have never left Mordecai.

Tears flooded her eyes and blinded her vision to the other vehicle approaching the drive. A silver Panther De Ville roadster with black tooled leather upholstery. Polly and Gloria looked like an Amazon queen and her consort. Through her tears, Luna Belle recognized the pair and became ecstatic. She raced to Polly. After a long embrace, Luna Belle apologized over and over.

"Now don't you fret yoseff over none of that silliness. I'z just glad you's back to being Missy." Polly consoled. The two laughed and hugged, reveling in life.

Polly pushed away from their embrace and grabbed Luna

Belle's shoulders. "Help us unload these cars. You don't think we's gonna does all this by ourseffs."

"Unload what?"

Polly grinned from ear to ear.

Luna Belle screamed. "Kimono." She laughed at her fortune. "Polly Swann, I'm seriously thinking about strangling you right now."

"What?"

"You risked your life over these silly gowns. I've been in torment this whole time thinking I'd never see you again. It was all over a bunch of clothes."

"But we'z all okay now. We didn't know it at the time, I mean, that we'uz risking our lives and all, but really, ain't you glad we done it?"

Luna Belle asked, "Where have you been all this time? Why did it take you so long to find us here?"

Polly answered, "Mordecai couldn't remember where Ashweed were—"

Mordecai cleared his throat. "Honey, it's Ash-*wood*."

Luna Belle laughed. "Mordecai, I don't care what she calls it."

"Like not to'a been, though. We been driving all over the world down here. Course, ain't nobody down here ever heard of the place so we just had to keeps on driving for day after day 'til we finally run up on the place. Besides, you knows ain't no man gonna stop much and ax."

Luna Belle broke down in sobbing tears of joy as she embraced Polly. Polly's surprise overtook her and she too broke down. Life promised to be good for them.

Nick, Lil' Roost, and Jack came and took beautiful silk garments into the house. Nick walked over to the embracing women and put his strong arms around both of them. "I'm so happy. Luna Belle, I'm not going to have to eat your cooking."

Polly lifted her head and smiled toward Nick. "What make you think I'z come here to cook? You old rascal, you."

Nick winked. "Go pour yourself a glass of Missy's lemonade and then tell me who's gonna cook."

All three broke out in laughter. Mordecai walked up and joined the three in their embrace. He felt rested from the emotional labor of the last few months and looked forward to being able to live out his life in peace.

The group spent that evening on the porch. Polly had created a delightful chilled shrimp, coconut, and tangerine concoction out of thin air. Its freshness and coolness refreshed and spoke of the promise of sweetness ahead. The touch of cayenne pepper hinted of a little spice thrown in for good measure.

After dinner Polly and Mordecai wanted to hear about Rose and her demise. Being separated from the main party, they missed all the tales and adventure swaggering of derring do from the past few days.

Luna Belle started the story. "We figured out that the comb fit into the locket on the Contessa's tomb. I'm pretty sure you two already knew that. Didn't you Mordecai ... Nick?"

Mordecai steepled his fingers then pointed them toward Luna Belle. "That's another long story. Please continue." He didn't know how much Luna Belle already knew about the men's adventures moving treasure, and Nick deserved his chances at storytelling.

"Okay, but I want to hear yours, too."

"After you." Mordecai said.

Nick sat up and placed both his hands on the arms of the porch rocker. "Luna Belle, we've got enough yarn to knit a whole blanket with our exploits and your gold."

Luna Belle asked, "Who's we? And, may I remind everyone. It's *our* gold."

"*We* would be Mordecai, Lil' Roost, and myself." He thrust his chest out in pride. "Right now we're all waiting to hear about the way you killed Rose."

Luna Belle reared back in her rocker and with a look of satisfaction proceeded. "I didn't exactly kill Rose. Remember, y'all ran off and left me alone in the mausoleum with that bitch. Rose finally figured out how to open the Contessa's tomb. I couldn't believe how absolutely amazingly that thing worked."

Nick said, "That's true."

Luna Belle gave him a curious look. "As the thing swung off to the side we stood on the edge of a cavern. A set of spiral steps led toward a small pile of gold."

Nick cleared his throat. "A-hem."

Luna Belle knowingly smiled at Nick. "Rose became furious … livid … I didn't care."

Jack Deamon coughed. "Yeah, right."

Luna Belle argued, "In all seriousness, Jack. I didn't. Rose did. Land a Goshen—did she care. She'd been led to believe the treasure was unimaginable."

Nick said, "And she was right." He laughed. Mordecai joined him.

Luna Belle said, "Rose pitched a pure n'tee tantrum. I've never seen anybody carry on the way she did. Close as I ever want to get to somebody's hissy fit. I really wish you two fellows had stayed to witness her tirade. It frightened me. Boy howdy. Was I glad she didn't have a gun. She kept screaming at me, wanting to know what I'd done with her treasure."

Mordecai interrupted, "It's amazing how she twisted the whole thing to make everything hers."

Luna Belle nodded toward him. "Rose stood enraged on the cusp of her greedy imagination. Once she settled herself somewhat, she started screaming at me demanding I go first and ward off spiders."

Mordecai said, "Didn't I tell y'all that she was terrified of spiders?"

Luna Belle waved both hands. "And she certainly was. I told her in no uncertain terms that I wasn't about to go down those steps and clear the way ahead of her royal majesty. If she wanted her precious gold, she could combat the arachnids on her own. But you want to know what really cooked her goose?"

Nick grinned. "Can't wait."

"I told her I'd gladly go first for her part of the estate—one measly dollar."

It took a few moments for them all to regain enough composure for Luna Belle to continue. "About the time she calmed enough to explore the treasure chamber, that huge blast went off out in the garden and the window blew out. The commotion and force of the blast knocked her headlong into the hole. It was absolutely horrible. Her neck twisted and her head popped open into two separate pieces. She never knew what hit her … dead as Hector."

"So, she died with Pink. How about that?" Mordecai looked

up at the freshly painted aqua porch ceiling.

Luna Belle wrinkled her brows. "How's that?"

Nick said, "It was the blast that killed Pink."

Luna Belle contemplated Mordecai's words and sat still
for a moment before she continued her story. "Interesting ...
split wide open like a melon on the gold she coveted. That's one
powerful Contessa. I'm glad she took it out on Rose instead of
me. She treated me with much more compassion, didn't she?
I guess my being an outsider softened her. Rose grew up with
every opportunity to know such things. I wonder why she failed
to learn all the hocus-pocus that went with the place? Plus, the
pearls looked a heap sight better on me. Wish I'd kept them."
Luna Belle laughed.

Polly quickly sat up and scowled at Luna Belle. "Um-um! Is
I gonna has to wrings yo' neck?"

"Aw, come on, Polly. Loosen up a squint."

"No ma'am. Not that mess again ... anything but that. I'z
had my fill of that old dead woman and her curses. Nuh-uh.
Don't want to hear no more out a her."

Luna Belle rose from her seat, walked over to Polly's chair,
and helped her rise. Luna Belle wrapped her arms around Polly
and hugged her tightly. "You're worth more to me than all the
pearls in Tahiti. Besides, I teased you to see if you listened."

Polly gently brushed her away. "Go on now. Get out'a here.
Finishes your story and quits picking on me. I ain't in no shape
for to be abused like that."

Luna Belle returned to her seat and rocked. "Well, seeing
her like that scared the liver out of me. I ran out as fast as my
legs would carry me. That's when I found y'all up in the tree."

Lil' Roost said, "Missy, you one strong, determined woman.
I'z glad to know you."

Luna Belle turned to him and smiled. "Likewise, Lil' Roost.
We'd never made it without you. You're salt of the earth in my
book."

Nick said, "I wish I could have seen that conniption fit."

Laughing out loud, Luna Belle shook her head in disbelief.
"I'd love to show you but I can't. It's disrespectful to mock the
dead. I promise you one thing—it was a doozy. I want to know
how you found the treasure."

Nick tapped his foot. "A gentleman never reveals all his secrets."

She placed her foot over his. "Well, get over it."

"Okay, if you insist. Years ago—I got curious and followed Mose into the tunnel at the barn. I'd seen him and Mordecai disappear out of thin air and finally figured out there had to be secret passages all over that place. The more I watched, the more I understood."

Mordecai sipped his iced tea. "It's a good thing Mose didn't realize you'd followed him. The consequences would have been dire, had he seen you. However, had you not witnessed his going into the treasure chamber none of us would have known how to get in it ourselves, would we?"

Nick nodded toward Mordecai but he continued his story. "I've know for a long, long time how to get to the vault from underground. However, I'd never actually gone in there until Mose died." He looked over at Luna Belle. "After you went batty, I decided to discover the mystery behind that hidden door. Once my eyes saw the amazing amount of gold and treasure I knew time had come to get that loot to safety."

Luna Belle sat up. "Thank you men, all of you. I was ready to walk away empty-handed and leave the whole thing to Rose. Never in a million years did I sense the work you were carrying out on my ... excuse me ... *our* behalf. Just think—we're all rich beyond our wildest imaginations because y'all stole all my money." She began swaying in hula-like motions to the exotic music playing in her head.

"Watch it, sister." Nick tried to mock her movements and fell on the porch.

When she offered him her hand, he pulled her atop his chest. They laughed so hard it took Mordecai and Pete to get the tangled couple separated and back on their feet.

Luna Belle dusted herself off then sat back down. "Really, it's almost like you were supposed to follow Mose that day."

Nick kissed her hand. "Seemed logical. I mean, what else ... so I brought it to Ashwood. It was hard work. We kept hauling horses back and forth. I'd bring four here and cart three back. I didn't want to rouse suspicion. I knew that even counting all the mares and babies, we didn't have enough horses to get all the gold off the island. Don't you know those horses wondered what the hang I was doing?"

Luna Belle picked up her tumbler of Polly's tea punch and added a sprig of fresh spearmint from the garden. With her spoon she crushed the aromatic leaves against the side of her glass then deeply inhaled the herb's exquisite aroma.

Nick cleared his throat as he used his forehead to gesture at his compatriots. "Mordecai and Lil' Roost worked harder than me. We did it for you Luna Belle. Well, I did promise Lil' Roost a cut of the booty. I hope you don't mind that. It seemed fair at the time but I guess that's between the two of you."

"Whatever Lil' Roost wants, he can have." Luna Belle meant every word she spoke. Never before in her life had things meant so little to her.

A few days later, all the horse-lovers and Henry were in the barn helping Lil' Roost with the chores. He and Nick still needed to find a couple of stable hands to help out. Until then, everyone pitched in to get the job done.

It wasn't long before Nick and Sara picked up on their childhood antics and bickered with each other.

Luna Belle laughed. "Now listen you two. I don't want all that fussing and bickering here in the barn. You might upset the horses."

Sara poked Nick. "He started it."

"Did not."

"Did too."

Henry directed traffic from his seat. "Okay, you two. I think everyone here sees how much you love each other. Stop behaving like children and get me back to the house."

Before they could lift Henry from his seat, Sara screamed.

Luna Belle pursed her lips. "What's wrong with you?"

Sara started jumping. "Let me see your hand." Luna Belle coyly held up her right hand.

"Don't you be smug with me Luna Belle. The other hand."

Luna Belle had a wide grin on her face as she held up her left hand with pride.

"Well la-di-da. Look at that. Henry … this is my mama's ring. Dare I hope?"

Nick walked over and put his arm around Luna Belle's shoulder and kissed her on the cheek.

Sara's voice became high and excited. "So it's true? Y'all are getting married?"

Nick pecked Luna Belle again. "If she behaves. I've agreed to get tied up."

Luna Belle gave him a look to kill. "You scoundrel." Turning back to Sara, Luna Belle asked, "Do you still have your wedding gown?"

"Of course."

"Good. I want you to wear it and stand with us. Polly is wearing hers, too. It's symbolic to me. For the first time in my life I'm about to have two real sisters. When I wed Nick the ceremony is going to also bind us all together, if that's okay with everyone."

Sara asked, "Where?"

"Where do you think?"

"Christ's Church, Frederica."

"None other."

"Let me guess—reception following at the Cloister?"

Nick wickedly smiled. "Where else?"

Luna Belle regretted the distance she placed between Sara and herself. Now they had their pasts to recover and their futures to enjoy. Luna Belle decided to never again allow their parting.

Henry wanted to tell Luna Belle all the things that happened over the years. His tales left Luna Belle ambivalent about her relationship with Mose. She never recovered from having been sold, but neither she nor Mose were guilty of that transgression. Their families bore the shame for the unfortunate affair.

Not wanting to waste one moment, she determined to love. If Luna Belle Black had her way, not one of her dearest friends would ever again want for anything.

One evening while the friends rehashed their tales for the umpteenth time Luna Belle asked, "Has anyone here ever heard of a fellow named Mad Dog? He was with Scooter the night I got clobbered."

Henry dropped his chin and looked over the edge of his glasses. "I was Mad Dog."

Luna Belle straightened up in shock. "You. I thought I recognized that voice that night in the chart room. I can't believe it. I think you need to explain yourself."

"I was a double agent, hired by Mose in Venice on our honeymoon. To him I was known as Pegleg; to Scooter, Mad Dog. You see, I was initially hired because Mose knew someone was stealing money from the family and it was my job to track down the culprit."

Luna Belle asked in disbelief, "And you still were on the trail all those years later?"

"Well, the job evolved, but yes, I still hunted the last shred of evidence to convince Mose that his own sister, Rose, was the thief. He refused to believe I'd uncovered the entire scheme."

Luna Belle gasped. "So, Rose and Pink didn't get enough? They had to steal?"

"Mose gave them anything they wanted, yet they resorted to theft just because they possessed cold, wicked, covetous hearts. It was a bloody way to jab Mose the whole time he served after the Colonel's death."

Luna Belle's disgust rang in her voice. "Rose never was my true friend. She used me to stay near the house and Mose. Is that what you're telling me?"

Henry shrugged his shoulders. "Truthfully, I never did find out how she was stealing the money. It was coming out of some secret family accounts in Switzerland and the Caribbean."

Luna Belle shrugged her shoulders and held up a hand. "Secret accounts?"

"Well, yeah. That's how it all operated. It all was posted in some private ledgers that I help Mose keep balanced."

Nick started tapping his index fingers together. "Does this have anything to do with some little leather books?"

Henry lurched forward, momentarily forgetting his pain. "You know about the code books?" He inquired with a blazing fire in his eyes.

"I have them." Nick crowed.

Henry sank as fast as he had revived. "But they're worthless without the master ledgers. They're lost to posterity."

"What are they ... those master ledgers?" Mordecai inquired.

Henry dropped his chin toward his chest and spoke in a remorseful tone. "Three books that resembled the code books. But Mose kept them far away from the ones in his office. I never knew where. The code books he kept in the home office safe. That's what Scooter was trying to get his hands on the night of the storm. The other books contained the actual account numbers which were changed semi-annually. Those books were far too important and were obscured somewhere else. I fear they are far, far away."

"What did they look like?" Nick said.

"Like the others except locked in a bronze box. We used them twice a year in Savannah when I'd help him with the accounts." Henry talked himself into a little depression.

"What are they for?" Luna Belle asked.

Henry said, "They are the account books of all the foreign banks where the family stored the real wealth. The vast treasure you retrieved is just the tip of the iceberg. If we held those books—alas—they shall never be recovered."

Nick jumped up from his seat. "Wait a minute."

He left only to return in no time. He handed Henry six vegetable tanned plain leather books with hasp locks.

"How did you?" Henry grinned from ear to ear.

"That's another long story. Oh, by the way. Here's the key."

Luna Belle saw the key and its little comb shaped fob and smiled. It all jelled in her mind.

From this moment on life improved daily.

A grand celebration followed that afternoon's conversation. Nick helped Polly with a marvelous dinner of beef tenderloin kabobs and grilled lobster. For the first time in months Luna Belle felt like a champagne and caviar party-girl. After the fabulous dinner they all sat around trying to think up ways to use their new-found wealth to some positive effect.

Later that night in yet another of their ongoing postmortem discussions Luna Belle wanted to know how Mordecai, Polly, and Gloria escaped the fury of what she now called Hurricane

Contessa Juliana, Possum Queen, the Marsupial Menace. All agreed the name fit.

Mordecai sat back and crossed his legs. "Well, the old rickety bridge over Axminster Creek saved us. I knew y'all left too far ahead of us. We'd never get to the ferry in time because it took us quite a while to load all those kimono. The three of us hugged each other for what we figured might be our last time. We expressed our love in tears of expectancy and hope. Then Pete popped up. We were immediately delighted to have his company."

Pete said, "When I seen that hole in the east garden, I'uz out'a there. Glad of it, too. Much rather stay with you folks than be washed away by a mad Contessa." He laughed. "No. Truthfully, Missy, I figured we'd all go back there and turn that crater into a new pond on the east side of the house. I almost saw the wheels turning in that pretty head of yours, but I've poked around this place. They's a whole lot for us to do here, ain't they?"

Luna Belle smiled. "I can't wait to hear your ideas. That's exactly what this place needs—Pete Stagg's masterful touch. I know you'll turn it into an extraordinary showplace, but first I want to hear the rest of y'all's adventure getting off the island."

Mordecai said, "The radio came and went, but we heard enough to know if we stayed on the island we'd perish in the storm. That's the first time in my old life that I've run from weather. I'm glad I did. So ... we all voted and decided we preferred to die trying to cross the bridge than stay on the island.

"We persevered even though the water's rage scared us because it had almost completely inundated the bridge. The creek's meanderings had removed much of the swell's rage, so we held our breath while Polly and Gloria went first. I figured if any of us perished, it ought to be Pete and me. It seemed the most chivalrous thing at the moment."

Luna Belle looked toward Polly who returned her gaze with a big smile.

"Once the ladies' safely crossed, Pete and I began—"

Polly interrupted, "Can I finishes this?"

"Be my guest." Mordecai bowed and gestured toward his

wife.

"Mordecai and Pete nearly cross the stream, the front wheels made it to land. The bridge went with a big kaflooey. They'uz half on half off. Me and Gloria nearly wet ourselves and like to'a died right there, but we prayed hard."

Luna Belle gasped. "What happened?"

"Well, you tells me. We is all here—ain't we?"

⊗ɭ Epilogue ɭ⊗

As had become their habit while sitting on the porch of Ashwood, Luna Belle wanted Mordecai to tell her about the wax seals.

He began, "The rarely used Black Seal of the broken crown served as the ensign the Drummond family took when the Contessa changed their name to Black. It carried a double message: first, representing the failed attempt of the Contessa's father in his campaign leading to her being sold, eventually causing him to lose his title then head over his misadventures. Second, the black wax signified the victory of Blackbeard's having saved her from a life of bitterness. She chose the color as a sly reminder of the name's double entendre.

"The Contessa adopted the name Black to revere her dead husband's moniker and ambition, also to hide the family's true identity. Over the centuries, it proved to be a most successful ploy. Being a bright woman, she knew the names Teach and Drummond might lead to the family's being hounded by authorities. She chose the alias that, like the treasure, was hidden in plain sight. We enjoyed complete dissociation from the master pirate, Edward Teach Drummond, Blackbeard.

"The Red Seal, the seal of the fighting dragons, bears the weight of the heir of Teachall. Red wax signifies the blood of the ancestor Edward Teach Drummond, spilled without just cause by a vengeful governor. The dragons, fighting while intertwined, signify the Contessa and the pirate. Although in love, their relationship suffered many battles. The Contessa Juliana never recovered from her husband's murder. Though pardoned, a malicious political act of subterfuge turned against him and led to his death.

"Missy, I have the document from the blanket chest. I retrieved it when I fetched the quilt for the ironing board.

Perhaps you might examine it again. There remains a trace of purple wax under the black. In my humble opinion, the Contessa opened the document and became appalled at her father's intent to sell her. I remain almost certain, she felt the same as you, nothing more than chattel. Also, she once again sealed the document. That is my understanding; however, it remains complete speculation on my part. No one knows the actual truth."

Luna Belle responded, "You must know. I still find revulsion over the idea of slavery. Sold. The lady and I shared that plight."

Nick asked, "Does anyone know the real story of how the family came into all that money and treasure in the first place?"

Mordecai looked around. For the first time since leaving Cow Bell Island he realized, he and Pete were the true natives, but growing up away from Teachall, Pete would not know these stories.

Mordecai said, "It all began when the Contessa Juliana's father sold her to the Governor of Santa Domingo de Flores. Her father sided with the wrong folks during the war of Spanish Succession. In America, I believe we called it Queen Anne's War. He needed piles of gold to escape the axe.

"An enormous stash of conquistador gold had been hidden on Santa Domingo de Flores. At one time the property of the Spanish Crown, intrigue led to the gold's theft centuries earlier. Hidden on the island for almost two hundred years, it remained secreted there until its accidental discovery when the newly appointed Governor dug a well on the palace grounds.

"Back in Almería, Spain, as a young adult and an admirer of the Contessa's, the island's governor tried to rape her when she was a young girl. Later he proposed marriage. Because of his previous barbaric treatment, she hated him and refused his advances.

"He wrote from the Caribbean island to the Contessa's father in Spain, offering lucre for the lady's hand. Desperate, her father sent her, against her wishes, with an entire entourage: architects, artists, craftsmen ... all to help her build a home on the island. The old man would have his gold ... the Governor, his girl.

"The Governor loaded the tons of gold onto six ships and sent them on their way back to Spain as the bride price. Before getting too far out to sea from Santa Domingo de Flores, they encountered a terrible storm, in all probability a hurricane. They lost most of the crew from all six ships.

"Once the weather broke, Blackbeard found and rescued the tattered remnants of the vessels. Then he took the entire fleet to Cow Bell Island. He had discovered the place earlier, and saw it appeared an unrivaled hiding place for his treasure. It was perfect because this horde of gold made him one of the richest men in the world.

"The remnants of the beaten crew had grown fond of the Contessa on their voyage from Spain to Santa Domingo de Flores. They expressed their sorrow over leaving her with a man she loathed and despised in exchange for the gold.

"Once the salvaged men explained the whole story to the master pirate, he grew outraged at the indignities the Contessa suffered. His vow to save the damsel turned into living poetry. Edward Teach would have never bothered her if she had loved the Governor, but once he learned of her hatred for the man, he didn't rest until she found refuge from her adversary. After getting the ships to the island, he set out to rescue the Contessa.

"It didn't take much persuasion for her to go with Blackbeard, leaving with her entire entourage in the middle of the night. The Contessa thanked the pirate by accepting his hand in marriage. A Catholic priest in Saint Augustine, Florida joined the two.

"They emptied and buried the six ships' golden cargo on Cow Bell Island. Then they pulled the galleys back out to sea where Blackbeard scuttled them to the ocean's depths. No one other than Blackbeard, his crew, and the Contessa's people ever knew the whole truth. Her father thought the ships were lost at sea and never looked for them. After the report of the fleet's failure, her father was beheaded. It is my understanding that the Contessa never mourned his death.

"The Governor of Santa Domingo de Flores deployed several search parties to find his betrothed. He'd spent a fortune on her, six treasure ships laden with gold, and although his attempts lasted for years, he never found her.

"Part of the pirate's gift to his wife came in the form of a beautiful boy born to her after his death. For lo these many years, explorers and hunters have sought in vain to find and retrieve Blackbeard's vast treasure.

"The reason no one ever found Blackbeard's horde—it was never lost. Even to this day, the gold remains guarded, or at least, *so goes the legend of the trove.*"

TROVE

Thirteenth Colony Publications
kindly asks that you visit
Amazon.com
and leave a review
of this book.

Designer, Musician, David McGukin lives in Georgia with his wife and no pets.

Thank you for reading my first novel.
Look for more soon!